Once Upon A KISS

JAYNE FRESINA

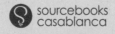
sourcebooks
casablanca

Published by Sourcebooks Casablanca, an imprint of Sourcebooks,
Inc.
P.O. Box 4410, Naperville, Illinois 60567-4410
(630) 961-3900
Fax: (630) 961-2168
www.sourcebooks.com

Printed and bound in Canada.
MBP 10 9 8 7 6 5 4 3 2 1

To Mrs. Jones

It is a truth universally acknowledged, that a single man in possession of a good fortune must be in want of a wife.

—*Pride and Prejudice*

One

"WELL, SOMEONE HAS TO GO FIRST, AND SINCE YOU'RE ALL a bunch of dainty blossoms, I daresay it will have to be me."

So declared Miss Justina Penny who, despite being one of the youngest in the group, saw herself as a fearless adventurer and hoped one day to see a statue erected in her honor on the village green.

"Without risk," she was fond of saying, "there is nothing gained."

The five young ladies of the Book Club Belles Society, rounding the bend together while involved in lively debate, had not seen the wide brown puddle lying in wait for them until it was at their feet. While the other ladies still pondered the best route around it, Justina made up her mind with the reckless aplomb for which she was notorious. Ignoring any words of caution uttered by her companions, she gathered up her skirts, reversed a good distance, and took a running leap.

Her walking boots left the earth, goose bumps fluttered across her skin, and she exhaled a joyful gust of triumphant laughter.

It turned out to be premature, which was also by no means unusual for her.

The first part of her journey proceeded well enough, even—it was admitted later by her sister—with a spectacular sort of style, if one could overlook the abundant display of leg and stocking. But where her flight failed most was at its end.

Justina felt herself descending far too quickly and several feet short of dry lane. In fact, she was headed directly for the deepest, brownest center of what now appeared to be a lake, rather than a puddle.

Compounding her misfortune, here came Mrs. Dockley, at that same moment, innocently opening her gate. The tidy, fragile old lady stepped out into the lane in her Sunday best, oblivious to the unstoppable airborne menace descending rapidly toward her with the speed and grace of a cannon ball.

◦⟳◦

August 29th, 1815 A.D.

Today I splashed Mrs. Dockley from head to toe, broke a china plate, and failed to heed Mama. Thrice. All these things, but for the last, were quite accidental. I was quarrelsome on four occasions and fibbed regarding the china plate, pieces of which will one day be found buried in the herb garden and not in the possession of a wild-eyed, knife-wielding gypsy with a wart and a wooden foot. Although I think my version of events is better.

Sometimes real life is very dull, or simply inconvenient, and things never turn out quite the way one expects or hopes. I have heard it said that challenges are sent to try us. I would like to know who is sending so many to me, for I believe they have been misaddressed. I am quite tried enough, and I suspect that someone, somewhere, is completely light since I have all their calamities as well as my own.

Speaking of which, today I thought of the Wrong Man again.

I know not why he continues to plague me, unless it is a developing, chronic case of Maiden's Palsy. It has been over a year.

All I can say is, the blasted town of Bath has a great deal to answer for and I would not go there again for ten thousand pounds and a life supply of hot chocolate.

Anyone coming upon Justina Penny's diary would be shocked, not only by the fullness of its pages, but by the fastidious attention to detail.

Her sister, Catherine, kept awake every evening in the bed beside her while she recorded these "trivial happenings and idle thoughts," proclaimed it to be a wicked form of self-indulgence.

"Your time would be better spent in somber internal reflection and prayer, Jussy," she said primly. "Why you bother committing all your terrible shortcomings to paper, I'll never know."

To which Justina replied, "Really, Cathy! How can I be sure of making proper recompense to those I wronged if I do not keep track of my daily malefactions?"

"If only it didn't take you quite so long to write them all down." Cathy tugged hard on her side of the coverlet.

"And if you did not keep breaking into gleeful snuffles, shaking the entire bed, I might get a few more hours of sleep. I begin to pass for a haggard scarecrow as it takes you longer each night to write in your diary."

"Impossible, sister. You could not look like a scarecrow under any circumstances." And Justina should know, having "trimmed" her sister's hair many years ago with scissors from their mama's sewing basket in an attempt to achieve something akin to that very look. "One cannot rush these things, Cathy. In order to feel the weight of my wrongdoing I must consider every word."

> *I cursed inventively when I caught my skirt in the kitchen door and again when I found a splinter in my finger.*
>
> *At approximately ten o'clock, when I saw Lucy in her new scarlet cloak, I was wracked with envy. But it lasted only until a quarter past, at which time she shared a jam tart with me and lamented the fact that her hair will never hold a curl so well as mine. Ah, vanity—one is hounded by it relentlessly when one has so little to be vain about.*
>
> *Yesterday we sat in the hayloft and watched Major Sherringham's hired harvest hands at work.*
>
> *Briefly I lusted.*
>
> *That is when I thought of the Wrong Man again. But even I do not suffer the Maiden's Palsy as often as Lucy, who will confess—when pressed—that she is seized by wicked desires at least twice daily, even with no militia encamped nearby. I suspect this may be due to the fact that she was once a sickly child. I shall advise her to eat nettle soup. And a quantity of it.*

Catherine peered over the edge of the coverlet. "If you feel the need to write your sins down, would it not be less time-consuming to behave properly in the first place?"

Ah, it was easy for *her* to say, thought Justina. Her sister was never tempted by the perfect target of a backside bent over, or a man needing his opinion adjusted. Catherine was angelic goodness itself, never lured into trouble by an unbound curiosity. Even laid flat in bed she managed to be upright.

"No other young lady in this village feels the need to leap over puddles, Jussy."

"That's their fault. It is a tremendous thrill to be flying through the air."

"Sadly one must always come down again, and in your case the landing has a propensity to be sudden, heavy, and lacking in ladylike elegance."

While Justina allowed this to be true, she still maintained it was not her fault that anyone else's petticoats were splashed in the descent. "How was I to know that Mrs. Dockley would come out of her gate at the exact moment I landed in the flooded lane?"

"Perhaps by considering the possible consequences before you indulge yourself in another of your *thrills*? No, I suppose that would be too much to ask. I wouldn't want to spoil the joyous spontaneity for you." Cathy burrowed again, mole-like, under the covers.

"Sarcasm is unbecoming, sister dear. It will give you wrinkles and dyspepsia. Possibly also gum boils."

The next words were muffled. "For which I shall blame you."

*The sky remains calm, although according to the
rusted weathercock on Dockley's barn, North is now
South. Some say it is a bad omen. I, for one, am glad.
It's time things around here were turned on their head.
Perhaps something interesting will happen.*

"Honestly," Justina muttered, pen scratching furiously
across the page, "it's no surprise to me that Nellie Pickles
ran away with some lusty sailors. There is no fun to be
had in this village."

The sheets churned beside her again and Cathy
reemerged. "Nellie didn't run away with any sailors.
Who told you such a terrible thing?"

"No one tells me anything," Justina replied gloomily.
"I have to imagine it for myself most of the time."

"Well, I wish you would not. You spend too much
time dwelling on these…unsavory ponderings."

"With entertainment so thin upon the ground, is it
any wonder?"

"But—"

"If people answered my questions, I wouldn't have to
make things up, would I? No one tells me what I want
to know."

"Because the things you want to know about usually
aren't suitable subjects for young, unmarried ladies. Lusty
sailors, indeed!"

Justina sighed in disgust as a large ink blot dripped
from her pen. "Do you not want to know either, Cathy?
Have you no curiosity about your wedding night, for
instance?" She didn't have to look at her sister to know
she blushed. "I'm sure you have questions about that,
just as I do."

"I do not think of it," Cathy replied. "It is not for me to know anything about."

"Why? Is the man supposed to do it all? What if he doesn't know either?"

"Of course he'll know. He's a man."

Justina laughed at that. "Saints preserve us! If everything were always left up to men, where would we be? If men can do it all without us, why are we here? I shall tell you, sister. Women exist to put right all the wrongs men do and to keep them from making a complete pig's ear of the world."

Cathy groaned. "Oh, do finish and put out the candle, Jussy. You've wasted an inch of wax tonight at least."

"Very well, but first you must admit Nellie Pickles left Hawcombe Prior to become the plaything of a shipload of sailors. 'Tis all there is to it."

"That is the fate *you* decided for her, is it?"

"I am resolved upon it."

Nellie Pickles was once a scullery maid up at Midwitch Manor, the grandest house in the village, until she disappeared one day, never to be seen again and with no explanation left behind. Three years later, folk still talked about the incident in hushed tones, everyone pretending they knew more about it, and more about Nellie, than they possibly could, considering she was a mute, unable even to write her own name.

"If she did not run off with the navy, there is one other option I will allow." Justina waited for her sister to ask, but upon hearing only a weary sigh, she continued, "Old Phineas Hawke did away with her. There, is that not better? Murder, I suppose, would be preferable to scandalous ruin at the hands of a half dozen sailors."

"Jussy!"

She snorted. "Phineas Hawke was a mean and miserly master to all his servants. I shouldn't be at all surprised if she's buried somewhere in the overgrown garden at Midwitch Manor. *If* he didn't eat her minced in a pie with his supper one evening."

"Did away with her, how?" her sister demanded. And then, much to Justina's amusement, she added a hasty, "For pity's sake." Cathy, of course, would never want to be caught encouraging her younger sister's wicked imagination.

"Strangled her, perhaps with her own stockings," Justina replied, perusing the ceiling and stroking her chin with the end of her quill. "Drowned her in the cider barrel, plucked out her eyeballs with a shoe horn, or threw her down the stairs in a fit of rage."

"That frail, grumpy tyrant? I don't believe he'd have the strength. He was wheeled about in a Bath chair for the past five years at least. May I remind you that Nellie Pickles was a stout, solid girl who could have pulled a plow?"

Justina shrugged. "Well, it is too late now to make old Hawke confess his wretched crime." Phineas had been found dead in his bed just a week before. Whatever became of the missing scullery maid, it seemed unlikely the truth would ever be uncovered. Suddenly a new idea came to her. "Perhaps the ghost of Nellie Pickles returned to settle the score with her rotten master."

"What nonsense you speak, Jussy. There are no such entities as ghosts. Now, do put out the candle."

"Believe there are no spirits of the undead then, sister, if that allows you to sleep comfortably." Justina got up to put her diary away in the writing box by the window.

Her feet were bare, the floor cold, so she raced back to bed and, in the time-honored tradition of evading robbers who might be hiding under it, launched into a flying leap, almost landing on her sister. While Catherine also took precautions every night against the possibility of strange men under the bed—an evil they'd come to envision as a likelihood when they were children—her more sedate method of precaution was to sweep a besom broom beneath it every night before climbing in. For Justina, however, wondering if a hand would flash out to catch her by the ankle as she leapt was part of the pleasure. In all honesty, she was disappointed when it did not.

But with that lurking, potential menace outsmarted once again, she snuffed the candle, leaving their chamber lit only by a silver harvest moon through the window.

"Papa said that old Hawke's corpse had such terror on its face that Mrs. Birch, who found him, had to be revived with several glasses of the trifle sherry," she muttered. "Now what, may I ask, would be the cause of that? When living, Phineas Hawke never had any expression on his face other than bitter resentment. In fact, as I told him once when he accused me—falsely—of trespassing in his neglected orchard, I did not think he had the required muscles in his sagging face to portray any other emotion." Justina tugged briskly on her side of the coverlet. "Mark me, Cathy, he was taken to his day of judgment by none other than his innocent victim, poor Nellie Pickles, and in extremis, the old bugger's countenance was finally moved to show something other than anger."

Her sister was quiet, staring into the shadows of their room, twisting the end of her braid around her fingers.

Justina gave a long, satisfied yawn and settled into her pillow. "Nellie Pickles might be dead and gone, but her spirit remains in that house, wandering the halls. I thought I saw her pale, pudding face peering forlornly from a window only yesterday when I passed the place. Yet the gates were locked, and no one was seen going in or out since they took the old man's shriveled carcass to the bone yard."

"Nellie is not dead at all. You made the entire thing up. Not five minutes ago you said she ran away with some sailors."

"Alas, you did not like that possibility," Justina replied gravely. "Murder is quite obviously the only other solution, or someone would have word of her by now." She wriggled her shoulders further under the covers. "The more I think of it, the more certain I am that Nellie was murdered at Midwitch Manor. It is unlikely she ran away. The poor, mute girl never got up much speed and had the wit of a gate post. But one must not speak ill of the dead."

"Ouch! Your toes are like ice blocks!"

"Not nearly as frozen cold as poor Nellie's feet. Wandering up and down the corridors of her murderer's lair."

"Stop it! That wretched imagination of yours, Jussy, is nothing but trouble."

But apparently it caused other folk far more trouble than it had ever caused her. Justina knew her elder sister was now wide awake, listening to every creak in the house, while she prepared to sink into her own deep, untroubled sleep. With her diary of wickedness complete for another day's entry, she could rest easily. It was always good to get things off one's chest. She urged

Catherine to do the same, but instead her sister bottled things up and kept more worries to herself than they had full pickling jars stored on the larder shelf. Then those anxieties and fears kept the silly girl awake all night.

Oh well, thought Justina, in her opinion, the less beauty sleep her elder sister got, the better. Catherine was already too pretty for her own good. It could only end in tragedy for a country doctor's daughter with very little dowry.

"It cannot be so dreadful, I think," said Cathy suddenly, her voice wavering a little, "to tolerate the physical needs of one's husband. It cannot be, or there would not be so many babes in the world."

Moved by her sister's faltering attempt to comfort them both, Justina patted her hand in the moonlight. Poor Cathy could have no idea, for she had not seen the thing Justina once, by terrible mischance, encountered in the Wrong Man's bed. Nor would she believe it. That too would be dismissed as an object conjured up out of Jussy's ragbag of lurid ideas.

But even *her* imagination, she thought with a sleepy sigh, was not wicked enough to invent him.

Wainwright.

And there, she had thought of him again. There was no escape, it seemed, from that particular misdeed, because it was the one event she had not dared confess to her diary.

Two

WITH A TIGHT SIGH, DARIUS CHECKED HIS FOB WATCH again. Ah, he knew it! One hour and twenty minutes into his Wednesday, and it was all arse about face.

Although he seldom allowed his day to vary from its well-regimented structure, already he faced a slight curve in his path. It was not a bump, or an obstacle, *per se*, but any deviation from the usual was unwelcome to a man who kept his busy life in order by maintaining clockwork efficiency. For example, dressing and his ablutions required no more than fifteen minutes— thanks, in part, to an unvarying taste in clothing that meant he never had to make a choice. Breakfast was then allotted thirty minutes, no more and no less. Therefore, at precisely forty-five minutes after rising from his bed, he expected to depart his house. Every day. Except Sundays.

But today, long after he should have digested the last few mouthfuls of a plump sausage and completed his perusal of *The Times*, he had not even opened the paper. It sat beside his plate, neatly folded and ironed to keep the ink from soiling his fingers. And there it would probably remain, because his mind was diverted by the contents of a letter just arrived from Buckinghamshire.

While it was by no means unusual to receive correspondence, this was an extraordinary letter because it contained a message that was neither connected to his business nor asking for money. In fact, on this occasion, he was to be the beneficiary. Someone actually meant to *give* him something rather than take.

It seemed so unlikely a circumstance that his naturally cautious and skeptical nature made him bring the letter to breakfast where it might be studied at greater length and mulled over with the assistance of coffee.

> *"...and so it is my duty to inform you, Mr. Darius Wainwright, that as the sole beneficiary of your great-uncle's will, Midwitch Manor—house, grounds, and contents—are now yours to dispose of as you wish..."*

He had not seen Great-uncle Phineas Hawke for thirteen years and quite expected to be forgotten by the old man, but, as the letter pointed out, Darius was the last surviving male with Hawke blood in his veins. Since his elder brother was missing and presumed dead, there was no one else to whom the old house might be left.

It was a surprise to hear the place still stood. As far as Darius recalled, it was somewhat shaky upon its foundations, just like old Phineas himself.

As his gaze reexamined the words upon the paper, his astonishment remained undiminished, but the lone footman in attendance could have no clue of the turmoil beneath that calm, stern surface. The Wainwright countenance, so Darius had been told, was one that rarely betrayed his thoughts.

"Contempt and hauteur you do very well, Wainwright," Miles Forester, his friend from their Oxford days, would say with a chuckle. "But anything else must demand too much effort from your stern features."

What did he care? Darius had far too many other things to do than worry about whether or not he might offend somebody with his face.

Damn it all! Once again his mind had wandered from its proper course. He set down the letter and reexamined his fob watch to confirm that he was now so far behind in his routine it was unprecedented.

May as well finish his sausages. Perhaps he should pretend it was Sunday. In which case he would allow himself an extra triangle of toast.

Darius picked up his knife and took a small, precise portion of butter, which he spread thinly over his toast. The rasp of his blade across the golden brown surface was the only noise in the room, apart from the solid, steady, comforting clunk of the longcase clock. Until his stepmother entered and peace was shattered.

"Gracious, you gave me a dreadful shock! What are you doing still here on a Wednesday?"

"If it helps, you may pretend I am not here," he muttered. "I'll gladly do the same."

"Where is Sarah?" she inquired, glancing at his niece's empty chair. "She rises late today."

He continued reading. "I believe she paints outdoors this morning."

"*Outdoors?* But it is the end of summer. She will catch a chill."

"Unfortunately, some people simply will not be advised against the risk." Attentive to the closing of windows and the exclusion of drafts, Darius had never suffered a cold in his life. But the trend for chancing one's health whilst in pursuit of nature's "delights" appeared to have gathered his niece up in its clutches.

Often he wondered what his elder brother would make of Sarah had he lived to see her grow up, for she had very little of her father's character. Lucius "Lucky" Wainwright had seldom risen from his bed before noon or gone back to it by midnight. It was safe to say he'd never opened his eyes to find himself in a sunlit garden on purpose. Far more likely he'd stumbled there the night before, passed out, and woke with a curious snail sitting on the back of his hand and his face planted in the grass. He would never have enjoyed a dawn chorus of birdsong without shortly thereafter throwing a boot at the tree from whence it came.

Perhaps Sarah's mother had partaken of outdoor rambles, although that seemed doubtful, knowing the sort of nocturnal creatures with whom Lucius once consorted. The less known about the poor girl's mother the better, for she had wanted nothing to do with the child and gladly turned her over to the Wainwrights, who could better provide for her.

But whatever drew Sarah outside, thought Darius, it kept her from under *his* feet and out of his stepmother's critical view, so perhaps it was a good thing at that hour of the morning. At least she had the capacity to entertain herself and was not all noise and giggling like most females of her age.

His stepmother, however, complained the girl was

withdrawn and peevish. "You're raising her to be as unsociable as yourself," she snapped.

"Sarah is fifteen. She is not 'out' and therefore not meant to be sociable."

"Whatever your future plans for the girl, she must learn how to hold a conversation and be gracious. She is too turned in on herself. Of course, she leads a solitary life in this house with no one her own age and no cousins, since you flatly refuse to marry and produce any."

But Darius saw nothing amiss in his raising of Sarah or in the way she turned out. He measured his success in the fact that he could sit quietly in her company for half an hour and feel neither the stressful need to fill an awkward silence, nor the beginnings of a tense headache. She seldom made any sign of disagreeing with his opinions and, in fact, had said very recently, "*I look at you, Uncle Darius, and know exactly what I want, and don't want, in a husband.*" He was pleased to think he had set her a fine example upon which to base future judgments.

"I do hope you have not forgot," his stepmother exclaimed, the moment she was seated with her coffee cup, "that my daughter arrives on Saturday with her little boys."

Ah, if only it was possible to forget. Darius could almost hear his stepsister Mary's strident voice already, echoing around the walls to find him wherever he hid, and the vibration of her heavy steps obscuring the comforting chime of his clocks. Her need for constant evening society never failed to cause discord in his quiet life.

"It will be splendid to have good company again to cheer me," his stepmother continued. "You are certainly no company at all."

He stabbed another wedge of sausage on his fork and pondered his letter.

"Darius! It is rude to read at the table when you have company."

"But the contents are of some urgency, madam. They require my immediate attention."

"What could possibly be more important than gracious manners? 'Tis no wonder you have no wife, with your grim disregard for etiquette."

"Yes. That must be what has held me back all these years." He read on. At the other end of his table, she fussed in her chair, making the legs creak so that he was obliged to read the same sentence of his letter thrice.

"Of course, Mary will beg us to return to Dorset with her for Christmas. How merry we shall all be there together."

"You can be merry in Dorset, certainly. I'll be merry in Town."

"Oh, but you'll never guess the news I just heard!" Apparently unable to get this gossip out quickly enough, she waved her hand and her knife, all her large round parts bouncing urgently. Darius calmly watched this performance over the top edge of his letter, wondering if she choked on a crust. "Cousin George is engaged again," she managed finally. "Let's hope this one sticks."

With a curt exhale, he returned to his letter.

She swallowed a hasty and audible mouthful of coffee and then, as the cup clinked in the saucer, resumed shrilly, "Only the daughter of a baronet, but one must make the best of it." She paused. "It's a pity you have such an aversion to marriage."

There it was, he mused. Hint number two. There

were usually, on average, five mentions of marriage and his lack of a wife made during any encounter with his stepmother. The desire to avoid these collisions with her, or at least to reduce their duration, was one of the reasons why he kept his day in such tight order.

Darius let her prattle on while his gaze wandered further over the letter in his hand.

> *"If you might apprise us of your intentions in regard to the property, we would be pleased, as Mr. Hawke's long-entrusted solicitors, to undertake the sale or lease, as required..."*

"You really ought to take a leaf out of my cousin George's book and stop avoiding your duty to the next generation."

When he glanced up, his stepmother was battling with a butter stain on her gown, tapping uselessly at it with a napkin. "I do not have the pleasure of understanding you, madam."

"Marriage, of course! You should have found a wife by now, but you make no effort. I've never seen such a grim face as the one you put on when you deign to attend a ball. And you won't even agree to come to Bath with us next year."

Bath. He shuddered inwardly at any mention of that place. The last time he was there, a strange young woman had conned her way into his lodgings one evening and leapt onto his bed, almost causing him a heart attack. She claimed a case of mistaken identity, but the very next day he encountered the same curious creature trying to burn down the Upper Rooms, a tragedy averted only by his quick thinking and brave actions. A perfectly good waistcoat was ruined. It was all far too much of a coincidence for Darius to believe these encounters accidental. Fortune hunters would go to any lengths, apparently.

In his opinion, this incident was an example of everything amiss with Bath and with the younger generation. No, he would not go there again, not for ten thousand pounds and a life supply of port and Stilton cheese. He preferred going to his bed at night without fearing an unguarded young hussy might leap out on him. In naught but her stockings and pink silk ribbon garters.

He thrust his fork at the last piece of sausage and missed, hitting the plate with empty prongs. The resulting scrape across china made his teeth hurt and apprised him of the fact that he'd been grinding his jaw rather tightly.

"Even *you* might have found a wife in Bath had you bothered to look while we were there last year." His stepmother boiled and bubbled away like a large, round, overheated witch's cauldron.

He put down his fork. "I rather think, madam, that I have enough females to manage as it is. The world is already gifted with you." A heavy sigh oozed out of him. "Surely one Mrs. Wainwright is enough."

"Nonsense. You must have a wife. I promised your father, on his deathbed, that I would make you marry. He was most distressed at the idea of your being left alone."

"I was unaware there might be any chance of that," Darius muttered.

"Mary will sort you out when she comes," she threatened sternly. "My daughter won't stand for your nonsense. She will get you a bride."

Odd, he mused, how *nonsense* meant different things

to different people. His friend Miles would say, "*But what a good thing it is that we are not all alike. Variety keeps life interesting, don't you think?*"

Darius could hardly agree less. He would much prefer it if everyone was like him, quiet and sensible.

His stepmother continued the restless creaking about in her chair, shouting at the footman, "You there! My coffee is cold. What am I supposed to do? Breathe on it?"

After carefully patting his lips with a napkin, Darius cleared his throat to announce, "I'm afraid you must tend single-handedly to the needs of your daughter and her delightfully unrestricted offspring when they arrive, madam. I leave at once for Buckinghamshire."

"Buckinghamshire?" she cried, as if it were John o' Groats or even farther away. "What on earth for?"

"I have come into some property there." Although he didn't like leaving his business for long periods, there were advantages in this instance. With any luck, by the time he returned, the ghastly Mary would have removed her gaggle of children and her mother safely off to Dorset for the Yuletide season.

"But my daughter brings a guest especially to entertain you!"

The contents of his stomach curdled. He might have known. Mary was forever pushing her friends at him as prospective wives. His neck began to itch.

Swiftly he folded his letter. "Alas, I am called away from Town. Pity, but there it is."

"I do not believe you for a moment! What am I to say to my daughter? She will be offended. I quite despair of you. Really, it is too bad, Darius, that you will not stay. Buckinghamshire, indeed! As if you ever go into the country if it can be avoided. Mary puts herself to all the trouble of bringing a young lady to amuse you and yet you cannot even stay to greet her."

"Madam, you may assure your daughter that since I have no time to be bored, I have no need of amusements. She may thus be relieved of putting herself to any future trouble on my behalf."

"You are the most obstructive, contrary man I ever knew." She enlarged upon her disappointment in Darius for another ten minutes, unabated, until he finally rose from the chair and made his exit. He left her with no one to shout at except the footman, who could smile benignly at the disgruntled lady, due to the foresight, Darius suspected, of having pressed two small lumps of cheese into his ears.

It was a method he and his brother had often employed for the same purpose.

Three

Hawcombe Prior, two days later

"I THINK WE SHOULD GO BACK, JUSSY. THIS WAS another of your very bad ideas, I fear." Seated in the bow, the young lady who uttered this caution kept one gloved hand gripping the side of the rowboat and one comforting a snorting pink snout laid in her lap.

At the stern end, heaving on the oars with all her might, Justina Penny, lifelong adventurer—but, alas, novice mariner—exhaled her words in a stream of gusty puffs, like an overworked chimney. "Do be silent, Lucy, before you wake the entire village!"

Moonlit ripples licked up over the rattling oar hooks as the small vessel pitched and yawed from the unsteady weight of its cargo and the violent struggles of its operator, who, despite the fact that plans very rarely succeeded for her, still refused to be anything other than indignant and surprised the moment they went awry.

"I believe the boat leaks," Lucy protested now, in a more hushed voice. "I am becoming very damp at the hem."

Although Justina also felt the slow gathering of water around her toes, seeping in through a worn hole in her nankeen boots, she was not about to let that little problem stop them. "You do want to save your pig, don't you?" she demanded.

"Of course. But sometimes I feel your methods are more theatrical than they are effective."

"Do you not think a little discomfort must be suffered for the cause? After all," she reminded her friend, "this was your idea."

"Not exactly," whimpered Lucy, gathering the hem of her fine new cloak out of the puddles slowly forming in the rowboat. "I said I wished Sir Mortimer Grubbins could be saved, since he was my favorite and I hand-reared him from a runt. I didn't suggest we appropriate papa's boat and row down the stream, in near darkness, to steal him back from Farmer Rooke before he goes to the…"—she lowered her voice even further and covered the pig's ears with her hands—"axe. This scheme was all yours. As usual."

Already annoyed with her friend for attending their secret, late-night mission in that bright red cloak—of all things—Justina's temperature rose another notch. The weed-laden oar splashed down again and she hauled it through the water, moving the boat onward with a shuddering lurch that was nothing like the smooth, speedy escape she'd envisioned. "I don't care for your tone, Lucy. You begin to sound like a wretched ingrate who cannot bear a trifle inconvenience even to save her beloved pet from slaughter."

"I am merely saying there must be other ways—" An owl hoot startled them both and they jumped several inches on their wooden seats.

Justina replied in a hasty whisper, "We must work at night to avoid being seen, and over water we cannot be tracked by hounds."

"But this does seem a rather extreme measure. Surely, when I get the pig home again, it's not likely I can hide him anywhere. This level of secrecy is perhaps excessive."

"Miss Lucy Bridges, your adventurous spirit is considerably lacking lately, ever since you turned eighteen, got that fancy new scarlet cloak for your birthday, and began showing more bosom at every opportunity."

Lucy's lips fell into a sulk, but it was a familiar expression these days. She was despondent ever since news came that there would be no soldiers encamped nearby this winter. No doubt the indignity of Sir Mortimer Grubbins' drool on her new cloak and wet boots on her feet were simply the straw that broke the camel's back.

Suddenly, a large winged shadow flew over the boat and skimmed the passengers' heads. Lucy let out a squeal that must have woken every light sleeper in the village. Justina finally lost her embattled grip upon the oars and, as they floated away from her, the stricken vessel drifted aimlessly into another band of weeds. Here they were apprehended, firmly stalled in the midst of the stream.

"Well, that's done it," Lucy somberly observed.

There was a warning creak, followed by a splintering crackle. More cold water pooled quickly into the bottom of the boat. Nestled in the tight space between his companions, Sir Mortimer Grubbins, the unsuspecting pig, let out a contented grunt.

"We shall be drowned," said Lucy, as if she'd always known such a thing would happen. In all likelihood the girl had already picked out a gown in which to be buried and an imaginary, weak-chinned suitor to lay flowers on her grave. But they both knew the water in that spot was merely two feet deep, and what worried Justina far more than drowning was the realization that they would have to carry Sir Mortimer between them to dry land. As the fate of the boat proved, he was no little weight.

The pig lifted his snout and grunted again, probably wondering when it might be dinner time. She patted his back.

"Worry not, Sir Mortimer, we'll find somewhere to keep you safe." She already had the very place in mind: Midwitch Manor, recently left empty upon the death of its cantankerous owner. There was a very pleasant orchard there with several small outbuildings, all currently abandoned to Mother Nature. What better place to hide a pig until other arrangements were found?

One thing was for sure, she thought crossly as cold water slowly wicked up her petticoats, no morsel of bacon or despicable sausage would ever pass her lips again after this.

A quarter of an hour later, using Lucy's cloak as a makeshift hammock to carry the noble Grubbins between them, the two young ladies finally struggled up the bank of the stream, through the bulrushes to dry land. They were both wet and exhausted, yet so busy arguing with one another—Lucy still protesting the use of her precious cloak in this manner—that neither heard the approach of hooves and wheels.

As they emerged from the tall reeds and into the narrow lane, the four horses charging along it at the same moment were startled and reared up. Although the coachman took swift evasive action, he was too late to prevent damage. The coach lurched and jolted. The lanterns swung in wide arcs across the lane, and with a tremendous creaking and groaning the vehicle finally came to rest in the opposite ditch.

She heard the coachman inquire whether his passenger was hurt and a man's voice confirmed that he was not. The door of the disabled coach opened and the apparent owner of the voice looked out. Immediately he must have seen the strange rescue party struggling with their burden. "What the devil..? You there!"

"Fine evening, is it not, my good fellow?" Justina shouted jauntily, shuffling along and straining under the weight of the lounging pig, attempting to ignore the first fat spots of rain dropping with quickening speed to the earth around them. If they let the bundle down now, she feared they would never pick it up again. Lucy had a trying habit of breaking into giggles when she had to lift anything, which invariably made Justina laugh too. They already fought to maintain their anger with one another while at the same time holding back their helpless laughter.

"Are you quite mad?" the stranger bellowed. "What do you think you're doing, woman?"

"Isn't it obvious?" she sputtered over her shoulder. "We're carrying a pig."

Lucy snorted and then made a small whimper of despair.

A determined, angry stride followed them a short way down the lane and she hissed at Lucy to pick up speed. If they put Sir Mortimer down to let him walk, he would meander along, snuffling at the ground, delaying the journey. They'd have to carry him at least until they were within sight of the manor house. Fortunately, the beast did not appear too distressed by his current leisurely repose.

"Someone could have been hurt," the man bellowed. "The horses might have trampled you both into the ground."

"Oh, dear, how dreadful. Sorry," shouted Justina. "Can't stop. I bid you a pleasant evening." There was no time for explanations. Rain spat down on her head now with more velocity and although they couldn't get much wetter, it would doubtless make their path much softer and more difficult. And really, what could be said about something dire that might have happened, but didn't? Couldn't he see she had enough immediate and actual troubles of her own?

Fortunately, by the time his carriage was forced into a ditch by the curious appearance of two drunken gypsy girls carrying a pig, Darius was close to the end of his laborious journey, and the lantern light of a public house led him through the rain to shelter. On foot.

"It's a rotten night out there, to be sure," the landlord exclaimed jovially, leading the way to a seat by the inglenook hearth and setting a tray of supper before him. "Whatever can have brought you out in it? On a night such as this, a man should stay by his fire with a pipe and a drop of port."

"I can assure you, I would happily comply with your vision had it not been for the inconvenience of a deceased relative."

"I'm sorry to hear it." The landlord hovered over him, clearly in no haste to go about his business. "A local man?"

"Phineas Hawke," he admitted reluctantly.

The landlord's lips parted in a gasp of surprise. "I never knew the man had any family still living."

"He preferred to think that way too." Darius removed his greatcoat, carefully hanging it before the fire to dry. "I am the surviving grandson of his sister, Arabella."

"Well, I'll be! Aye, there is a family resemblance now I think of it."

Darius cautiously surveyed the tray of cold supper he'd been brought. "His house is not far from here, as I remember, although it has been more than a decade since I last paid a visit."

"That's right, sir. Midwitch Manor lies up on the hill. Other side of the village."

He arranged and rearranged the knife and fork by his plate, checking the two prongs and the blade for any sign of poor cleanliness. "Good. If I can find a horse and saddle to hire, I can ride up there after supper."

The landlord had been about to turn away, but now he stopped and came back, his big, weathered face creased with concern. "But it's been shut up since ol' Hawke died and the servants all left. You'll find it a bleak place, damp, dark, and cold. I should wait until morn, sir. I've a room vacant above stairs. Nothing so grand as you're used to, I'm sure, but it does well enough. My daughter can slide a pan of coals under the linens to warm the bed for you." He looked over his shoulder, irritable suddenly. "If I can find the girl tonight. Don't know where she's dashed off to."

"Thank you, but I will make my way to the manor tonight."

"Aye, well...if you think that's best."

He cut savagely into his slice of ham, and the landlord eventually moved away to pester other customers.

But the heat of the fire began to warm his bones and the food was surprisingly good, calming and settling his stomach. As his general sense of irritation eased, Darius realized how tired he was after his journey, and the prospect of going out again that night held less and less appeal. Really, how urgent was it that he get there tonight? He was already a day later than planned due to the terrible state of the country roads, and now that it was dark, he would not be able to assess the place very well. The rain wasn't letting up; it still drummed hard at the windows. Thus the reasons for leaving that cozy fireside soon fell away completely. Tomorrow would be time enough.

A man seated nearby had glanced over at Darius several times. Suddenly, he scuffed his three-legged stool closer across the flagged floor. With a smile and a nod he announced his intention to speak, ignoring the social rules for proper introduction.

That was the trouble with country folk, thought Darius, they were always far too familiar and liked to intrude in a man's private business. They had a disturbing tendency to make up their own rules rather than abide by those laid down in refined societies.

In a small village like Hawcombe Prior there were no secrets and any stranger passing through was quickly relieved of his, in the same way a cutpurse would empty his pockets in London.

Well, they could try.

"Did I hear you say, sir, that you are related—were related—to Phineas Hawke?"

"He was my great-uncle."

"Fancy that! We always thought he were alone in the world."

"Being alone," he replied tersely, "has much in its favor."

The other man paid no heed to the hint. "Will you be moving in up at the manor?"

"No." His only purpose in visiting Hawcombe Prior and the house in which his great-uncle died was to see, first hand, the state of the property and for how much it might be sold or leased, but he felt no need to explain his motives.

"'Twas a beautiful old place once, that house," the fellow muttered, kicking a log back into the fire with his worn boot. "Shame how old Hawke let it go to wrack and ruin these past few years, but he couldn't get about much anymore. There used to be a gardener, but he moved to Manderson a few years back and the grounds are overgrown. There's a fine orchard too—or was at one time. All left untended now though."

Darius wondered why this stranger took it upon himself to open a conversation without the least encouragement. He had no doubt that even if he feigned sleep the fellow would continue his chatter.

"The village youngsters like to scrump apples over his orchard wall. But ol' Hawke were a mean old bugger—begging your pardon, since he were a relative of yourn."

Darius knew of his great-uncle's reputation. Phineas never replied to any letters from his family and seemed to prefer complete estrangement. Only when his sister died, thirteen years ago, did he send for Darius and his elder brother—her grandchildren—to see how they had "turned out."

Darius remembered meeting a bent, shriveled old man with shining, coal-black eyes sunken beneath bushy gray brows and cheeks crisscrossed with red veins like broken cobwebs.

"*There's treasure here on this property,*" Phineas had told them. "*Treasure hidden. What do you think of that, eh?*"

Lucius had exclaimed that he didn't believe a word of it. Darius, then a shy, lanky boy of seventeen, had not dared argue with his brother, but locked the idea away, keeping his thoughts to himself where they could not be mocked. His social awkwardness—a problem increased since he surpassed a height of six feet seemingly over-night and suffered ears of an equally excessive size—made him an easy enough target for his brother's scorn and amusement as it was.

"*Come on, Handles,*" Lucius had exclaimed as they left their great-uncle's house, "*let's get out of this mausoleum and find some good ale and jolly company.*"

After that visit Phineas did not send for them again, and Darius could only assume the old man was disap-pointed in what he'd seen of the brothers. Only two years later, Lucius went to India and never returned.

"Good ham, that, eh?" His nosy supper companion intruded once again in his thoughts. The fellow leaned back and poked his thumbs through two frayed holes in his corduroy waistcoat, as if they were pockets. "One o' my pigs, that was." He swayed forward again, winking. "You say the word, and I'll have some o' my best ham hocks took up to the manor for you. You look like a gent who's used to the finer things, and you won't find a better pork sausage in your life." Two small, round, button eyes gleamed in his pink face. "How do you like your bacon? Lean, streaky, or full o' lovely fat? You tell ol' Barnabas Rooke here and I'll send some up to the manor for you. On account, o' course."

Pigs? He'd had quite enough of pigs for one evening. "That won't be necessary. I leave on Sunday."

"But you only just arrived."

"I have a business in Town, and I cannot abandon it for long."

The other fellow squinted and back went his stubby thumbs into those holes in his waistcoat. "Surely you'll stay for the hunting season at least."

"I don't hunt," he replied. "I haven't the time, and I fail to see the appeal of blood sports." That, of course, along with his preference for quiet, solitary pastimes such as reading, was something else Lucius had teased him about.

"But I thought you was the idle rich. Begging your pardon, sir—a proper gent. No frayed edges and your buttons all sewn on with the same thread, like."

"Yes," Darius muttered drily. "I can see how it might be confusing."

Four

We had haddock for dinner last evening. It put me very out of sorts. The peas were soapy, and the potatoes over-salted. If Clara plans to poison us, she's going about it very effectively and speedily, but at the sacrifice of subtlety. I am still not yet recovered and could not eat breakfast, which is most unlike me. Everyone else appears as normal—a relative term for this family—so perhaps only my portion received the fatal dose. I should not be surprised, for she has never liked me and accuses me often of stealing from the pantry.

If anyone should read this after my demise, please apprise my good parents of the cause and let them know I did love them dearly, even if I sometimes tried their patience intolerably. Cathy may have all my bonnets and the amber cross, although the chain is broken.

Yesterday a pig was rescued from the axe, but my dearest friend's enthusiasm for adventure was finally lost to the crushing blade. It shall be mourned bitterly. Now I must take care that my own spirit does not meet with the same sorry end. Although I daresay Clara's egg custard will do away with me sooner than later in any case.

J.P. September 2nd, 1815 A.D.

If it wasn't for gluttony and a little bit of wrath thrown in, she would not have been late catching up with her sister that afternoon. But Justina had stopped to indulge in a spoonful of raspberry jam from the pantry and then, in the process of shouting through the window at the cat she saw digging in the herb garden, got sticky finger smudges on her bonnet ribbons. Another hat then had to be found, and by the time she'd discovered one that was not sat on or had the trimmings ripped off, Catherine was already halfway across the common.

As Justina ran out through the front door, she heard her mother calling for her, but since she was now late for the Book Society, and the only reason her mama could possibly want her was for another chastisement, she chose not to hear. Closing the door firmly, she looked for her sister. Catherine walked ahead in considerable haste, for the Book Society had recently acquired a new work of fiction which, according to their friend Diana Makepiece, was the most "delicious" story ever written. Her cousin had lent it to her, in three volumes, in return for her best taffeta ball gown. A frugal creature, Diana was not at all known for sharing her ball gowns, so it could only be concluded that this *Pride and Prejudice* was a highly sought after, life-changing tome. Several chapters had been eagerly consumed at previous meetings of the Book Society—where the ladies took turns reading aloud—and Catherine was on tenterhooks to continue the story.

"If only there were any headless corpse brides or poisoned chalices in this book," Justina had complained.

Although her preference for bloodthirsty horror stories was well-known, she was most often forced to comply with the desires of her fellow Society members and put up with another romance whenever one could be acquired. For vengeance she enjoyed proclaiming herself madly in love with the villain of the piece, while they were all cooing over the so-called hero, who was usually dull and palatable as stale bread crust.

"I've waited eighteen chapters for something interesting to happen," Justina had grumbled to her sister at luncheon that day. "The only character I like is Mr. Wickham. Everyone sits around talking and nobody *does* anything."

Catherine had ignored the comment. "Stop slouching, Jussy, or you will become terribly round-shouldered. Like Bessie Rooke. And we all know what happened to poor Bessie."

"Not much, by all accounts. I heard she went to Aylesbury once, but I don't believe it."

"No," Catherine replied sadly. "She never got married."

In Catherine's eyes that was a fate worse than death. Although not worse than running off with some lusty sailors.

"Pay mind to your sister," their mother had joined in from her end of the table. "No man wants a wife who sits like a pile of cold porridge, Justina. I should have set you in plaster to straighten your spine when you were younger. Too late now, and we must work with what we have."

"Worry not, Mama! At least when Cathy has gone off to be married, you will still have me to tend you in your dotage."

"Tend me into an early grave, more like. Never has a parent been more plagued by an ungrateful child."

Justina was all too well aware that the only reason her

family allowed her to walk about freely and unmanacled was in hopes of her unprepossessing face eventually catching some desperate fellow's eye. But healthy bachelors were in short supply. War had taken too many young men away from the village, and this led to some drastic husband-hunting schemes, including trips to places such as Bath. The Penny sisters had endured one trip to that infamous town and it was quite sufficient for both of them. Justina had marked the occasion by consuming too much punch and almost burning down the Upper Rooms, and Catherine developed a rash that made her so unsightly people crossed the street to avoid her—a circumstance she still wept over when in one of her mournful moods.

Bath was also the scene of Justina's most terrible mistake. Her failed, piteous attempt at traversing the bridge to womanhood under the capable tutelage of the dashing and witty Captain Sherringham, who, unbeknownst to her, had left Bath prematurely and given up his lodgings to another. To the Wrong Man. The subsequent ill-timed encounter with a complete stranger was a humiliation she would rather not remember. Therefore, whenever their mama threatened them with Bath, it had the same effect for either daughter as it would if she planned to send them to the workhouse.

Their father was just as eager as their mother to be rid of them. He had a vast collection of books, stuffed birds, and dead tropical insects, but not having enough space in his small library to display them all, he was constantly on the lookout for another space to annex. He'd recently begun turning a speculative eye to the bedchamber his daughters shared, remarking upon its suitability for other purposes.

As Justina followed her sister out of the house that afternoon, she glanced through the casement window to her father's library and saw him bent over his books, scratching his head. She smiled. Poor Papa, she often imagined he would like to stick a pin in her too, like his dead butterflies and beetles, to keep her still and safely displayed under glass.

When she waved at him through the window, he looked up—her shadow having fallen across his desk—and managed a hesitant wince, as he would if she asked for his opinion on a new bonnet. She mouthed at him through the small glass panes, "Book Society!"

Horror crumpled his face and another white hair drifted to his shoulder. His fingers inched across the desk, reaching for a magnifying glass.

"A romance, Papa," she shouted, grinning merrily.

He shuddered, clutched his chest with his free hand and returned hastily to his studies.

Justina spun around and hurried through the gate her sister had left open. She looked up the hill toward Midwitch Manor, a many-chimneyed, ivy-strewn building crouched like a fat cat and peering down on the village through a line of ancient oaks and younger chestnuts.

This weather would play havoc with the fruit trees in that orchard, she thought. The ground was probably already littered with wind-fallen, bruised fruit that would soon be wasted now there was no one there to gather it. She really ought to pay Sir Mortimer Grubbins a visit today, especially since Lucy was being punished and would not be able to go there. He had plenty of water and food, but he was a very pampered pig, accustomed to attention.

"Cathy!" she called. "Will you lend me your basket?"

Her sister stopped. "How many times must you be told not to run? It is not ladylike. And why do you need my basket?"

"I promised Mrs. Dockley to bring her some pears after accidentally knocking her bird feeder off its post with a cricket ball."

Her sister's lips fell delicately apart.

"I was demonstrating Mr. Newton's laws of motion for Lucy's little brothers," she explained with a shrug.

Catherine gave a deep groan. "We are on our way to the Book Society. There is no time for fruit picking."

"But the fruit will rot if it's left…" Justina let her gaze wander innocently off down the fork in the lane toward Midwitch Manor.

"Oh, no!"

"But Cathy! Such a waste. Those pears are the juiciest, sweetest in the whole village. Why should they be left to spoil?" She grabbed her sister's sleeve. "Think of the joy on dear old Mrs. Dockley's face. The gift of fruit will surely make her smile, and you know her tree has not produced any in years. Phineas Hawke is dead and buried. To whom does the fruit belong now?"

"Not to you."

"Well, goodness, if you find the proper owner, I shall repay him."

Catherine shook her head, her eyes weary, already drooping with an air of defeat. "Are you not afraid of spirits, sister?"

"Spirits?"

"Remember—the ghost of Nellie Pickles. You were quite certain she walks abroad at Midwitch Manor."

"Nonsense. How gullible you are." Dashing forward, she warmed her sister's cool cheek with a kiss. "I love you dearly, Cathy, but you are much too old to believe in ghosts."

"Well, I won't lend you my basket. I am having no part in this."

"Very well. Please yourself."

The intrepid fruit-picker hurried away on her mission, careful not to break into a run this time because she knew her sister watched and she didn't want to cause poor Cathy any further grief than was absolutely unavoidable.

Five

JUSTINA HAD ONCE BEEN TAUGHT HOW TO PICK A LOCK. There were many useful things, in fact, that Captain Sherringham—brother of fellow Book Society member, Rebecca—had shown her over the years. He would always claim innocence, of course, after the fact. When it was too late to be undone. "Knowledge, once given, Sherry," she often reminded him happily, "is a present that can never be taken away."

But on this evening, as she approached the gates of deserted Midwitch Manor, that particular piece of knowledge was of no use to her. The old lock previously in service had suddenly been replaced with a thick, tight chain, wound around the very top of the bars and secured by a heavy padlock that hung, curiously, on the inside. Out of her reach.

Annoyance traveled swiftly through her. It must be the work of Phineas Hawke's solicitor. She'd heard a rumor that he was seen moping about the place recently, a sniveling fellow with long feet, bony knees, and a turtle-like stoop. Well, that was most inconvenient. Now they'd have to find somewhere else to keep Sir Mortimer Grubbins.

Fortunately she was not averse to climbing, and since no one was with her to protest, she quickly gathered up her skirt and began searching for footholds in the rough stone wall. It had been a few years since she'd climbed it, but she found herself quite excited by the idea. Surely it was a skill she would not have forgotten once learned.

Ouch! She scraped her knee almost instantly and tore a hole in her stocking. Although not as tall as it had seemed to her in childhood, the orchard wall was still treacherous. A springy coating of moss had sprouted up over the years, taking possession of the crumbling stone, rendering the surface slick beneath her hands.

But she was not discouraged. Justina saw herself as a hapless heroine, mistreated, misunderstood, and much put-upon, despite her intent to perform good deeds. Therefore she expected hardships thrown in her path, could always appreciate the chance for added adventure, and did not even mind how the expected rain had turned into a cold mist that clung to her hair and her clothes. Indeed, a little froth of mist only added to the excitement of her adventure.

She might, however, have felt differently toward the mist had she realized how well it muffled any warning sounds of trouble proceeding in her direction as she dropped down over the wall. For when she finally saw those riding boots trampling the rough grass, marching toward her with a long, stern stride, it was too late to scramble back. She'd already lost her bonnet, ripped her skirt on some thorny climbing roses, and removed her pelisse to make a sack for the fruit. But by the time Justina realized Midwitch Manor was no longer unoccupied, the

state of her appearance was a minor problem in the grand
scheme of things.

Two large feet.

A pair of riding boots.

Knees. Hard thighs. Men's breeches. Two very large
gloved hands.

A riding crop tapping slowly and menacingly against
one aforementioned thigh.

Oh, crikey.

Midwitch Manor was supposed to be empty. Was he
a ghost, one of those grieved spirits still walking the earth
and not belonging anywhere?

Slowly she raised her face and with it her uncertain
gaze. Up and up. Far too tall to be old Hawke's solicitor,
he towered above her through the gathering mist, an
awe-inspiring monolith, a dark and stormy vision.

"What the devil are you doing in my orchard?"

Aha! He was a ghost with the power of speech. And
what a voice it was—deep, rich, and rumbling through
the ground under her knees and palms.

Her heart had almost stopped, and now it struggled
fitfully to resume its usual steady, confident trot. *Think,
think, you blithering fool.*

Excuses were not often so hard to lay her mind upon.

"Get up at once," he exclaimed, glaring down at her.
"I refuse to hold a conversation with someone rolling
about in this undignified manner at my feet. Where did
you come from, girl?"

Justina struggled upright with no assistance from him.
Still her brain sorted through various colorful excuses for
her presence there.

It was rare to find the likes of him in that village. He

must be six feet tall at least. Perhaps eight. Or it could just be the mist around his ears that made it seem as if he stood among the clouds.

But while he loomed over her like thunder and lightning in human form, Justina suddenly realized they'd met before.

At Bath.

Oh, no, it surely could not be. Not *him*!

The awfulness of that memory seized her in its cold grip and would not let go again.

Wainwright, the Wrong Man.

"I demand you tell me your name," he exclaimed.

The moment she told him, he would doubtless remember her. It must be marked in his memory as his name was in hers.

Had a girl ever been so mistreated by fate? she mused unhappily.

"Well?" he demanded. "Are you mute?"

Aha! That gave her an idea. She took a breath, clasped her bundled pelisse to her bosom and replied with what she considered to be a suitable amount of pathetic whimper, "I am the ghost of Nellie Pickles! Beware, sir. I take my daily constitutional in this orchard, and it is very bad luck to stop my path."

A frown plowed its way across his brow. Two dark eyes bore down upon her with all the belligerence of a warlike Norse god, but Justina, the intrepid adventurer, was not to be frightened. "Beware the ghost of Nellie Pickles, who was once stabbed through the heart with a toasting fork and left to perish under that..."—she looked around and pointed hastily—"that pear tree."

Tap, tap, tap went the riding crop against his breeches. "Is that the best you can do?"

"But, sir, take pity. I am a poor, wretched girl sent to my death by murderous hands. Alas, I wander here until I am avenged."

The furrows remained in his brow as his thin, hard lips snapped apart again. "Don't talk nonsense, creature. You are trespassing on my property."

"*Yours?*" She temporarily forgot her role as Nellie.

He squared his shoulders and shook his head, irritable as a nest full of wasps knocked with a stick. "Answer my question first."

"But I told you who I am."

"The ghost of Nellie Pickens? Of course. And I am King George."

"Pickles," she corrected sternly. "The lost scullery maid of Midwitch Manor. If this place was truly yours, you would know about me and why my spirit still wanders."

"I don't believe in ghosts." Making a sudden move, he reached for the sleeve of her gown, but Justina stepped out of his reach.

"Ah. See, sir? Your hand went right thought my cold dead bones, so it did." For some reason her accent had turned Irish, but she was too far in to stop. As was often the case. "Passed right through me, it did."

He arched an eyebrow. "No, it didn't."

Employing one of her customary spur of the moment decisions, Justina turned and made a run for it, but tumbled almost immediately over her torn hem and fell, with a piglet's squeal, to the grass.

In two steps his riding boots were beside her again. "For a ghost you're remarkably clumsy, Miss Pickles. Shouldn't you be able to pass through the wall, not have to climb over it?"

Even when caught in a lie, Justina had a tendency to argue her side of things to the point of breathlessness. This afternoon was no exception. "What would you know about it? You don't believe in spirits anyway. I daresay the arrogance of your skepticism has sapped my otherworldly powers."

"Yes. That must be the only feasible explanation for a ghost that falls like a lead sinker."

She tried to stand but twisted her ankle, thereby compounding her despair. Again she looked up at her pursuer, hoping she might have been mistaken. But no, it was him.

Wainwright.

The horrors of Bath returned full force, every detail of her shame as razor-sharp as it was when it first occurred.

Her family had traveled there last year so that Mrs. Penny could take the cures and Catherine could meet potential suitors. Justina, barely turned eighteen, was finally "out," but nothing much was expected of her. Although their parents still considered her behavior too unpredictable for society, Catherine had pressed for the company of her sister, and so Justina was finally permitted to make a great fool of herself before the general public at large, rather than limiting this joy to the honor of their close acquaintances.

Expecting few delights from the experience, Justina had been pleasantly surprised when they arrived in Bath to find that Captain Sherringham was also in town. Something of a hero to Justina and also a dear friend, the captain's presence had instantly improved her opinion of Bath. She'd decided it would be the perfect opportunity to finally confess her lusty yearnings for the handsome fellow. He was always so obliging and ready to teach her all manner of things that no one else would consider suitable for a young lady. In Justina's mind, the amiable, fun-loving Sherry was the ideal man for her awakening to womanhood.

She was constantly told that she must marry, and rather than parade herself about like a prize hog, why not take matters into her own hands and choose for herself immediately? He would marry her, she was sure of it. He must simply be made to realize she was no longer the little girl who made him laugh, but a grown woman who could be his companion in other ways.

A pair of new silk stockings and pink ribbon garters would help with his awakening, she'd reasoned, with all her vast experience in such matters.

But it was not Captain Sherringham upon whom she leapt in the semi-dark of a strange bedchamber. Later she would learn that Sherry had been called away at short notice to rejoin his regiment and another man had taken the room. It was the slumbering carcass of a complete stranger upon which she leapt.

They were in an orchard this time, instead of a bedchamber, but the Wrong Man's looming appearance had the same dreadful effect upon her pulse as it did on the first occasion.

Suddenly he swooped down and plucked her out of the grass with two strong arms. It was just like one of those horrid novels. But not in a good way. Very different in reality, with all her senses engaged.

"You are astonishingly solid for a ghost," he wheezed. "Not much of the frail and wraithlike about *you*, Miss Pickles." Thus he carried her toward the house with no further ado.

She belatedly found the strength to complain. "How dare you manhandle me? Put me down at once."

"Certainly not. You are now in my custody, apprehended in the act of theft."

"You have no right to lay hands upon me."

"How typical. Rights matter only when they are yours." Watching his lips, Justina thought she caught the twitch of a smile, but it was gone in the next breath. It might simply have been a wince of pain from the effort of carrying her. "We'll discuss the matter before the local magistrate, shall we, Miss Pickles? I doubt you're a stranger to him."

She stared at his determined profile. He wore no hat and his hair was dark, with the hint of natural curl. His nose—always an important thing to study in a man—was long, slender, and not too curved. In fact his features might be considered agreeably handsome. But his jaw had a very stubborn angle that suggested he ground his teeth a vast deal. Justina knew the signs, for teeth grinding seemed to happen a lot around her.

"It was just a few pears for old Mrs. Dockley," she muttered, sullen. "They will spoil if left on the ground." If Sir Mortimer Grubbins didn't eat them all first, she thought, glancing worriedly over his shoulder, searching for any sign of their rescued porker.

"All lawbreakers and degenerates begin somewhere, madam. The sooner the habit is nipped in the bed, the better."

"In the bed?" She grabbed his lapel as he stumbled and nearly dropped her. "You mean, in the bud."

"Yes," he muttered, his face coloring. "Precisely."

Her pulse was very rapid now. Had he recognized

her? She sincerely hoped not, or she would be in worse
trouble than she was already.

If she was any less sturdy a person she might have
fainted. Briefly she considered it, just in some hopes of
gaining his sympathy, but Lucy had once assured her she
was the least convincing "swooner" in the world, and
this man had already shown himself to be a skeptical soul.
Why waste the effort?

How typical of her luck that she should run into him
again. He had not been very understanding the last time
they met either.

"*For the love of all that's holy—and unholy—put some
blessed clothes on, woman,*" he'd bellowed at her, rolling
out of the bed and trying to hide his own nudity with
the quilt. The man didn't seem to realize that as he used
the bed covering to belatedly preserve his own modesty
he stripped her of anything to use for the same service.

So she'd done what any thwarted seductress found in
the nude would do.

She pretended to be French.

"Oh, where is the gallant Captain Sherringham?"
she'd demanded in what she thought was a very passable
accent. "What 'ave you done wif 'im?"

"Captain who? Madam, you have the wrong bed. I
suggest you leave at once."

He'd barely allowed her time to dress before hauling
her down the stairs of the house and putting her out. As
if she was the cat.

But that was not the end of it.

The next evening, she and her sister attended a public
ball at the Upper Rooms, chaperoned by their aunt
who introduced them to as many partners as possible.

Catherine was much in demand, naturally, but Justina was left like the last loaf on the baker's tray to stand at her aunt's side, trying not to look bored. Eventually she'd slipped away into the crowd and sought other entertainments. That was when she spied *him* again. A tall, pompous fellow who did not dance with anybody, he seemed to think himself above the event and superior to the other attendees.

She'd meant to avoid him and the evening might have passed without incident, had she not suddenly spied a mouse running about the ballroom floor.

Excessively bored and deciding—in her tipsy state—to rescue the creature before it was squashed, Justina had crawled on her hands and knees through the crowd. But before she could find her target, the haughty gentleman, known to her by then as the Wrong Man, stepped on her fingers and shortly thereafter all hell broke loose. Her indignant howls startled the gentleman so much that he spilled his drink and stepped back, knocking into another man, who subsequently lost his monocle and possibly also some spare coins, down the seldom-troubled cleavage of the exceedingly short and stout Dowager Countess of Somewhere Very Important. Justina supposed that, in the confusion of the moment, the fellow's immediate instinct had been to retrieve his property before it fell too far into the abyss to be recovered, but his efforts resulted in the indignant lady letting out an ear-piercing squeal that stopped the music. Pandemonium swept the ballroom. People fell like dominoes, not knowing if an escaped circus tiger had somehow appeared in their midst or the place was on fire. As it very nearly was when a candelabra tumbled and flames licked up the wafting pleats of a supper tablecloth. Fortunately someone had the instincts to stamp out the fire and smother it before much damage resulted.

When Justina was apprehended as the origin of all the commotion, Wainwright the Wrong looked down a yard of nose at her and exclaimed, "You? Again?"

Justina had advised him to seek the humorous side to it all, but he quite failed to find any.

"I'm sure mischief earns you a satisfying amount of attention," he'd muttered, wincing as he backed away from her. "With no beauty at her disposal a young lady must find other ways to be noticed."

Having insulted her before the entire room, he then left the place immediately, also taking his handsome friend who had been dancing with Catherine.

Now here they were again, and she doubted he would find anything remotely funny about this either. Perhaps it would be best not to mention they were already acquainted.

Six

FROM A DISTANCE HE'D MISTAKEN HER FOR A CHILD.
She was not very tall, and he certainly would never
expect to find a young lady climbing a wall to steal fruit.
But the moment he drew closer Darius realized she
was most definitely not a little girl. Whether she knew
or recognized this fact herself was another matter. The
large tear in her skirt—although exposing a portion of
undergarments—apparently caused her no embarrassment and was only inconvenient as it prevented her
escape. Evidently she was undisciplined, ill-mannered,
and a rotten fibber. Under no circumstances was she
leaving his property until he found out who she was.
Then he would return the woman to her lax guardians
and give them a stern lecture about her wild behavior.

He knew things were different in the country, but he
hadn't expected an encounter with a bonnetless savage in
his own orchard.

Darius had never carried a woman in his life, and
this one was a wriggling, noisy creature, causing him to
vow silently that such a circumstance would never occur
again. But there was something familiar about her.

Walking with his customary, determined stride through a thickening mist, he made the monumental mistake of turning his head to look at her again.

He slipped on a softened pear, lost his footing and balance, tripped over a mossy stump while trying to right himself, and finally fell backward, landing with his unwieldy burden sprawled across his torso.

There followed a shocked moment of silence while he tried to find his bearings again, and then, much to his further indignation, she began to laugh. Rolling off him and onto her knees, she laughed as if she was filled with the noise and had to let it out before it crushed her lungs.

He groaned, sitting up, clutching the small of his back. "Glad I am you find this amusing."

She exhaled another gust of rippling laughter. "Let me help you up."

Stubbornly refusing her hand, Darius made an attempt to get to his own feet, but the grass was wet and slippery. He went down again, causing yet more chuckles from the villainess.

"Oh dear!" She grabbed his sleeve. "We are quite an accident-prone pair, it seems."

A young woman like this, he thought crossly, was probably accustomed to getting away with all manner of travesty. One bat of her sinister lashes, one dimpled, artless smile, one merry, hearty laugh, and she must have all the men hereabouts at her mercy. Well, she wouldn't have Darius Wainwright falling at her feet.

Not in any way but the literal.

Reaching for a nearby tree trunk, he pulled himself upright. To his surprise, and more than slight horror, she did not relinquish his arm, but as they limped through the lowering mist toward the house, she hung onto his sleeve with her damp and muddy fingers. He moved his arm several times to shake her loose, but she clung on, apparently not noticing his attempts to get free.

A few struggling steps later, they passed through the side door into the kitchen of the house. She found a chair, sat him down, and then hurried off to locate the tinder box, complaining about the chill in the house. Her ankle did not seem to trouble her much now. She moved about that kitchen as if it was her own, with a great deal of bustle, but not much efficiency. Disrupting everything she touched.

Darius watched her shadowy shape exploring the kitchen. The strange weather that afternoon had brought dusk early and it felt much later than it must be. He fumbled for his fob watch to make certain of the time, needing to see it. The eerie mist had unsettled his day. So had she.

She must have caught him glancing at her muddy fingerprints on the sleeve of his superfine jacket, for she laughed yet again—this time with a hint of scorn. "A dandified town gent like you, all dressed up fine and pretty, oughtn't be left alone in the country. You could injure yourself permanently, sir." Another guffaw followed this statement, and then she resumed her uninvited exploration of the kitchen.

Darius struggled, thinking of what to say, whether to speak at all. As a boy he'd watched his elder brother consistently win over the pretty girls with his rakish charm. Lucius was like a gusty storm that blew through a room and left it transformed. He would tease Darius. "It takes you so long to say anything, Handles, we've all stopped listening by the time you're only halfway done!"

As a consequence, Darius developed a stammer and then finally stopped talking at all unless it was absolutely necessary. Better to say nothing than be ridiculed and mocked. Instead he remained in the background while Lucius made all the noise and frequently, with a careless, unrepentant glee, got himself into trouble. Whatever he did, Lucius always landed on his feet—or perhaps it seemed that way because he was never still enough to be caught, and managed to avoid consequences by disappearing when it was expedient. He did not earn the nickname "Lucky" for nothing. Darius, shy and withdrawn, often had the sense that no one would even guess they were related. Until, of course, someone was required to pay Lucky's debts and shoulder his burdens.

He rubbed his damp palms on his thighs and checked his watch again, as if the steadily clicking cog wheels inside the gold case might give a hint of how to manage this event.

Soon the would-be thief had a small fire crackling away in the hearth, and from that she lit a candle, placing it carefully in a lantern on the table beside him. The warm glow cast upward over her small face and gave him a clearer view of her features, particularly the slight dent in her chin and the uneven quirk of her lips that made them seem ever poised to smile.

He supposed he was still in shock. That must be why he sat without protest and allowed her to wipe a small cut on his forehead with a dampened handkerchief. Not that she asked his permission in any case.

"You'll live," she proclaimed. "It's just a scratch, after all, perhaps from the bark of a tree as you went down."

He took a breath of her scent—roses and honey. She

stood very close, almost stepping on his toe, requiring that he part his feet to let her between them. Although it was vastly improper to be alone with her and to let her touch him, it was too late now. When her torn gown brushed the inside of his knee he felt perspiration break through the skin under his shirt. Darius rested his knuckles on his thighs and squeezed his fingers tightly until they were almost numb.

Finally she moved away again, much to the relief of his shattered nerves.

Before he could ask any questions of his own, she had one for him. "What have you done with Sir Mortimer Grubbins?"

"I beg your pardon?"

"Sir Mortimer is our pig. I sincerely hope he's come to no harm at your hands, sir."

"A *pig*?"

"We have no home for him at present, and since this place was supposed to be empty, we put him in the orchard."

Darius could not make sense of anything: what she said, why she was there, or why he hadn't chased her off his property. But then he remembered the night before. Aha! A pig. Two figures rushing away in the rain carrying a pig between them after sending his carriage into the ditch. That must be why she looked familiar.

"He's quite harmless," she was saying, her behind propped on the edge of the table. "Sir Mortimer Grubbins, that is. The pig."

"Well, he cannot stay in my orchard, young woman." Darius looked her up and down, appalled by her casual manners, still unsure how best to deal with her.

"You'll like Sir Mortimer."

"No, I will not."

"He's very friendly."

"But I am not."

She frowned. "Yes, I had noticed you're not very civil."

"*Civil?*" He strongly objected to being lectured on civility by a thieving hussy. "If you mean I don't like being trifled with or taken advantage of, you are correct, madam."

"Don't you like animals?"

"I am not a swineherd."

Shaking her head again, she pushed herself off the table. "Of course not. I suppose your hands are lily-white and soft as a babe's backside under those riding gloves."

Darius angrily removed his gloves to prove her wrong, although why he bothered was a mystery to him. "I am no stranger to physical labor, madam." He had worked on the loading dock of his family's shipping business while he was still a boy, long before he took over on the death of his father.

"But you fell flat on your back when you tried to carry me."

"I merely underestimated your heft when I lifted you." That wiped the smug grin off her face. Good. Darius began to recover his balance and his bearings. "Now, you will tell me your father's name, young lady, and I will confront him tomorrow before I leave."

"Leaving already? Ha! Another weak-kneed dandy, afraid of a little country dirt on his clothes. I might have known."

"I am only here to dispose of my great-uncle's house." Oh, why was he giving her any explanations? Conversing with her had encouraged the forward girl to think she could stroll about his kitchen, touch his forehead, and generally take charge of things.

She'd touched his forehead. He could not get over it.

Had she touched something else of his? Odd, but somehow it felt as if she had.

He slapped his riding gloves furiously at the dirt on his knees, but since it was not yet dry, this was a disastrous effort and only succeeded in smearing it further. "The sooner I get away from this mud rut of a village, back to London and civilization, the better."

"Mud rut?"

Darius scowled. "The place is primitive, the people unsophisticated, mostly uneducated, and vastly annoying." When trying to find the village, he'd discovered that most folk in that district had a hard time distinguishing right from left, and they couldn't give any sort of meaningful direction, even if they appeared to be sober.

"Take the third turn before you come to the ford" was one of the most useful directions he'd received. Along with "Follow this 'ere road until it stops, and then take a left or right."

On his journey he'd been chased by swans, eyed by an angry bull through a flimsy gate, propositioned by a blacksmith's lusty wife, stung by a wasp, and harassed by a flock of wild children. And that was all in one morning.

She folded her arms. Another unladylike gesture. "I'll have you know, sir, that Hawcombe Prior is a very pleasant place to live. We may not have all the modern conveniences of Town, but we have plenty of what we need. We are just as content here as you and your fancy London friends are on any day of the week."

"Well then, I am happy to leave you to it."

"Splendid. The last thing we need is someone like you around."

She turned away, humming carelessly, looking through the window at the thickening mist. Finally, although he knew it would do him no service to ask, he did. He had to. *She'd touched his forehead.* "Do elaborate, madam."

"Someone who takes ownership of the manor, but has no interest in the place or the people here, spends most of his time in London, and never participates in village life." She looked at him again. "Nose in the air. Stick up the posterior."

He could hardly believe his ears. What place was this, where young ladies ran about unchaperoned, climbed walls to steal fruit, perched on tables, touched the foreheads of strange gentlemen, and used words of that nature without a solitary hint of blush?

"The case against you continues to mount, Miss Pickles," he muttered. "I begin to think you try my temper deliberately."

"Why, pray tell, would I do that?"

Darius studied her from the corner of his eye, almost afraid to look fully at the creature. Usually he avoided conversation with young ladies and would walk the long way around a room to avoid a noisy, impertinent one. Since he was generally accused of saying the wrong thing anyway, he found it easier simply to remain silent with females who were not part of his immediate acquaintance. A silent man could seldom be made a fool.

But he was soon leaving the place and need never see this one again. He decided, therefore, it was safe to answer. Just this once.

"Perhaps because your mind is unchallenged in this village. You haven't yet found a way to safely expend your energy. There is no one, it seems, to keep you out of trouble."

"Good luck to anyone who tries," she exclaimed in a terse rush.

"Certainly. He deserves a medal."

"And why should it be a *he*?"

Darius sniffed and brushed down his sleeves again. Her question was unworthy of an answer, and he'd already engaged her in enough conversation.

"I suppose you believe every woman needs a man to keep her in her place."

"How astute of you to know my mind."

"My father keeps dead butterflies under glass, sir, to examine them. Your mind is just as transparent to me." Her eyes were a dark, velvety blue, he noted, and now that her temper was up, little sparks spat and fizzled in their depths. He wondered why she hadn't run away yet.

"Am I an interesting study, madam?" Something must be keeping her there, arguing with him. Perhaps he was a novelty to her, as she—with her forward, easy manner—was to him.

But she denied it. "Certainly not. Good Lord, I can meet folk ten times more interesting than you in Hawcombe Prior any day of the week. I have been in your presence for one quarter of an hour and I might safely say it is the dullest fifteen minutes I ever spent."

This response was no more or less than he expected, even though he'd known her for such a short time. Her bold impertinence was palpable before she'd even opened her mouth. The moment he saw her tear that skirt rather than remain trapped by a tough, thorny climbing rose when she climbed over his wall, he knew she was reckless, determined. Possibly a very dangerous creature.

Suddenly he closed his eyes and saw a flash of stockings with pink silk garters. A woman, naked but for those items, flinging herself at him in the dark.

Dear God. It couldn't be. Not again.

He opened his eyes. She was watching him, hands on her waist.

It was her. The lunatic assailant of Bath.

"I'm sure you think, sir, that our entertainments in this village are few and unfashionable, but I can assure you they are not. We have a book society and an amateur players group. And a magician once came all the way from the Orient. Or Brighton."

Plainly she waited for a response. So he gave her the best he could manage. "I see."

Sometimes, when he was in danger of being overtaken by nerves in the presence of a troubling female, it was easiest to settle for those two small words. At least he was in no danger of faltering over them.

But this seemed to incense her further. She breathed harder now, ready to burst with indignation. Since she'd discarded her pelisse in his orchard, she wore only her ripped frock, made from thin material. Probably too thin for the time of year. Although it was sewn in a modest design, the mist-dampened cloth clung to her shape and drew his gaze to parts of her that he should not notice. Parts he'd seen before and haplessly admired, despite the impropriety and the sudden shock of having them land on his head just as he tried to get to sleep.

Darius struggled to halt the twitch at one corner of his mouth, and after a few moments it was successfully stilled, his countenance under control again. She was fascinating, really, if one had a morbid interest in forward young women of indeterminate age and with too much to say for themselves.

"What are you thinking now?" she demanded, pert.

"Can't you tell? I thought you knew everything."

"Your face has transformed to stone. Deliberately hiding your thoughts."

He paused, took a breath, and then said, "I am thinking that you are a young lady who doesn't want to face her future. Part of you would rather be a child forever and have no responsibilities, no adult concerns. That for you, life is always a game."

She stared.

He added, "And that I very nearly did not recognize you with your clothes on."

Finally, a rosy bloom darkened her cheeks.

"You did ask," he reminded her briskly.

She was silent at last.

Darius unfolded his arms and drummed his fingers slowly on the table. Just as he pondered, once again, her reasons for remaining there to quarrel with him, she slowly began a retreat, inching toward the open door.

Seven

"I BID YOU GOOD EVE, THEN," SHE CHIRPED, IGNORING his comment about recognizing her. "I'm late for the Book Society meeting." With a sharp, upward tip of the chin, she added, "They'll be expecting me."

His lip quirked. "You mean there are places where you are wanted and people who want you? I'm surprised you delay here with me then."

"Are you always such a pompous know-all?"

He sat looking at her with a strained countenance, his lips pressed tight.

The rarely experienced sense of having perhaps gone too far caused her to flinch, but she had become too comfortable while arguing with him. She had momentarily forgotten herself, Cathy would say. Or, at least, she had forgotten her manners. But he was not in the least polite to her, so why should she care? He'd already let it be known, when they met in Bath, what little he thought of her looks, and now he disparaged her character equally.

Although close to escape, Justina hesitated, her gaze drawn to his strong, square-tipped fingers tapping out a rhythm on the wooden table. She had been wrong about his hands. They were browned by sun and a little weathered, just rough enough to catch her attention. Despite his haughty manners, they were not the hands of a dandy. Suddenly she blurted, "May I have the fruit, then, for Mrs. Dockley? She grows none of her own anymore."

She couldn't think why she chanced her luck, but the need to do so was too much for her to manage. There was no one there to stop her, of course; no gentle word from Catherine to correct her.

"I thought you wouldn't mind me taking some, since you're leaving tomorrow anyway." How could she leave without fruit after all this? "You don't want it," she reminded him. "Sir Mortimer Grubbins can't eat it all or he'll get a bellyache. So it'll be left to waste, won't it? If no one claims it."

"I see," he muttered. If she was not mistaken, he was looking at her gown as if he could see directly through it. Then he lowered his lashes, hiding behind them. His jaw hardened as he tightened his lips, apparently resolved to say nothing more. A little drop of moisture hovered from a lock of hair on the left side of his brow, and she watched until it gathered enough weight to drop to his cheek.

Justina swallowed. "If you don't mind, then…"

He pushed back his chair, scraping its narrow legs across the stone floor, and then he stood, leaning his broad knuckles on the table by the lantern. He looked at her for what felt like a million years. Or ten minutes at least.

Finally he conceded, "You may take what you can carry." In haste to be rid of her, it seemed, he gave in. She could barely believe that victory was hers.

Justina bobbed a curtsy, aware it was too late and not in the least elegant. Poor Catherine would despair. "Thank you, sir."

He simply shook his head and looked away, deep in thoughts. Dark ones, too, by the look of it.

A shiver lapped over her as if a window had blown open and let in a cold draft. She hadn't realized, until then, that his eyes held a peculiar kind of heat that, despite her damp clothes, kept her warm when he looked at her.

How strange that they should meet again after the first horror. Fate, it seemed, had given her a chance to apologize for what happened in Bath. If she didn't do something, would she regret it forever? He seemed lonely suddenly, standing in that quiet kitchen, half his face in shadow.

He didn't smile and his words came out begrudgingly, as if rationed, just like old Phineas Hawke. No doubt this fellow would end his days the same way, unloved and alone. She knew there was no woman in his life. How could there be? A woman would have tied his cravat in a more fashionable bow. A woman would make him grow his curl out a little to soften his profile and give her something in which to tangle her fingers. A woman's love would surely have caused a few laughter lines in his stern face.

Making another hasty decision, Justina walked to where he stood, rose up on tiptoe, and kissed him. "God speed," she whispered with her usual flare for the dramatic. Her lips skimmed the bristles of his cheek just above his high collar.

He turned to look at her. His eyes, dark and angry, tore into her face.

Oh, why had she done that? This man was a stranger, fierce, stern, and disapproving. He had done naught but insult her, yet she'd kissed him. As if, somewhere inside, she thought she might improve his opinion of her. Impulsive fool! What on earth induced her to do it?

Mischief, of course. She never could calm those impulses. There was always a temptation to see how much she might get away with.

Suddenly his hands were on her waist. He lifted her off her feet for the second time. In that dreadful moment she thought he would toss her across the room; he seemed furious enough. But instead he lowered her again until her lips met his.

For balance, she placed her hands on his wide shoulders. Her breasts were tight against his upper chest, her head bent and tilted, her toes dangling in the air. The beat of her heart became so hard and fast that it turned into one long, loud flutter in her ears.

His lips, cold and hard, pressed hers apart in a kiss that left Justina breathless, her wits powerless. When she felt his tongue move shockingly over hers, searching inside her, she wondered if he sought there for more of her crimes. The heat of his body invaded the pores of her skin and then her bones, melting them until she was an appalling mess of a woman and only his hands around her waist kept her from seeping out of her stays like cider from a leaky barrel. She heard a low sound from deep inside him and it seemed to express everything she too felt at that moment—the surprise, wonder, delight, confusion. And desire. White hot, those flames consumed her body, devoured her, and then brought her back to life again in a new way.

Slowly, inch by inch, breath by breath, he lowered her down the length of his frame, until her toes touched stone again. There were parts of him that were just as hard as that flagged floor under her feet, and Justina suffered a burst of yearning that she feared would cause her to spend even longer writing her confessional tales that night.

His large hands spread against her spine and swept upward, pressing her even closer, her breasts crushed against him, aching suddenly. A warm heaviness took control of her body. An intense throbbing had begun between her thighs. This was far, far worse than Maiden's Palsy.

He swept his tongue around hers and then finally withdrew the kiss. But his hands kept her tightly imprisoned against him.

Now on her own two feet again, she looked up at him. "Why...?" Further words got stuck halfway out of her throat and lodged there painfully.

"Payment for the fruit, of course," he replied gruffly, his fingertips moving down her back, briefly tracing the curve of her bottom. He cleared his throat. "Fetch your pears. I'll unlock the gate."

But as she moved to leave, he suddenly tightened his hands on her again and pulled her back. Justina grabbed his upper sleeves, her fingers not nearly long enough to encompass even one third of the hard muscle beneath, and this time when he bent his head, she lifted slightly on her toes. Enough to meet him partway.

Oh, she wanted more. Much more. It was terrible. It was delightful. It was every forbidden thing, wrapped up in temptation, topped with a bow of opportunity.

A wicked inner voice whispered, *He's leaving the village. No one need ever know.*

Again she felt the hard ridge inside his breeches, pushing against her belly through their clothing. His fingers spread over the cheeks of her bottom, cupping the flesh and holding her indecently, greedily. His lips feasted upon hers, his tongue thrusting like a sword to claim her mouth once more. As if he had not done so to his own satisfaction the first time.

He smelled of spice and sweat and earth. The heat of his muscles surrounded her, seemed to enclose her on all sides, and she was, for those breathless few moments, entirely his prisoner, a weak woman of the sort she'd always heartily disdained. But she did not mind it. Heaven help her, but she did not mind being his prisoner then.

His hand came up and closed over her left breast, the palm so hot she feared it would melt the material of her gown. That touch, firm and possessive, made Justina suddenly very conscious of her breathing, of her heart thumping away beneath her chemise and his hand. Her nipple tightened, responding instantly to that caress. Every pore of her skin was awakened to the strangeness of a man's intimate touch.

The wet tip of his tongue brushed the side of her neck and she caught her breath in a shuddering gasp.

Abruptly his lips left her again. His hands followed. The fingers that had touched her breast now swept up and back through his hair. He looked down at her, his eyes dazed.

Neither spoke.

For once she was at a loss for words. It took all she had just to keep breathing.

Finally Justina forced her feet to move away from him and back out into the orchard. The mist still hung heavy between the trees, deadening sound, so that all she heard was the reckless thump of her heart. The moisture in the air surrounded her, but that was no longer the only warm dampness she experienced. He had melted parts of her.

Once she had filled the sack made out of her pelisse, she found her way to the gate where he waited.

Fingers tightly gripping her hard-won prize, she looked up and prepared to say her thanks again. She even intended to wish him a safe journey back to London.

But then he grumbled down at her, "Now be gone, woman. I have things to do here, and you've kept me from them long enough."

Justina was relieved to find her frown again, for it came much easier than a smile while her lips were still afire and throbbing. "Such arrogance."

"Such insolence."

She hurried through the gate before he might try any further ravishment of her person. Before she might let him.

❦

Darius barely had time to recover his wits before another figure appeared at the gate through which she'd vanished. This one was slower on its feet, but no quieter.

"Well, here's a fine how d'you do!" she exclaimed when she saw him standing there holding the bars. "If I'd known you were coming, young sir, I would have been here to air out the linens and light a fire." Materializing fully through the mist, she pushed her way by and hobbled toward the house, leaving him to follow. "I just heard you were here by chance, from the landlord at the Pig in a Poke. You should have sent word, Master

Hawke!" Waddling through the open kitchen door, she tossed a large sack of potatoes onto the table, followed by two dead rabbits. "*Why*, says I, when Mr. Bridges tells me you came up here, *that young man can't stay up in that cold, empty house all alone. With no food put by!*"

Everyone seemed to think he shouldn't want to be alone. When it was the one and only thing he wanted. Was every soul in this rotten village out to annoy the spit out of him?

"I am not Master Hawke," he exclaimed crossly. "The name is Wainwright. Darius Wainwright. I am Mr. Hawke's great-nephew. And you are?"

"Mrs. Birch, o' course!" She pulled an apron over her brown frock. "Cook and housekeeper to old Hawke. The only one that stayed. The others couldn't put up with his temper."

Darius scratched his head, still deeply absorbed in pondering the curious woman who had just left his presence. "I can manage perfectly well without household staff. I am only staying until tomorrow."

But the newcomer didn't seem to listen to him any more than his last unwanted visitor had. "I'll have my niece Martha come up and tend your laundry on Monday." She carried a large pot to the water pump in the scullery. "You should keep that door closed, young sir, or the fog will come right into the house. I'll make a nice rabbit stew for your supper. Then you'll feel better."

He wasn't aware of being ill, but perhaps he was. Could be the reason he'd acted in such an unusual way just now. Fortunately that kiss hadn't been observed.

The housekeeper carried the pot of water back out to the fire. "What was Justina Penny doing in here?"

"Penny?"

"Dr. Penny's youngest daughter, from down in the village. I'd steer well clear of that troublesome miss, if I were you."

Dr. Penny's daughter. Yes, that was the name.

He groaned, briefly closing his eyes again.

It was her. Not that he'd needed the proof of her name. But now he could not even pretend he didn't remember her. Dr. Penny, the miscreant's father, had sent a written apology to Darius after the incident in the Upper Rooms and also sealed with it some shilling coins for a new waistcoat to replace the one she ruined.

"She said she was on her way to a Book Society meeting," he snapped. *Could one believe anything from her lips?*

"Aye. The Book Club Belles, so they've been called. I don't know what the world is coming to these days, with young girls reading stories instead of good, honest sermons. I don't hold with it and never did. I'd rather have a coven o' witches in the village than a book society to addle the minds of our young girls. And I hear they've got their hands on a romance! Of all things! Five impressionable young girls, left to indulge in wicked exercise of that nature for their minds. No good can come of it, to be sure."

Darius slowly shook his head.

"They need to be married. That'll knock the romance out of them quick enough," Mrs. Birch added. "It's the only way to keep some out of trouble. A husband is a sure way to rid a girl of romantic inclinations."

He straightened his shoulders. That young woman had better not come over his wall again. Although he would not be around to worry about it, would he?

Raising unsteady fingers to the knot of his cravat he was relieved, but slightly surprised, to find it still neatly tied.

"Perhaps you can enlighten me, Mrs....Birch, to the supposed existence of a ghost by the name of Nellie Pickles."

"Nellie? Why, that girl took off three years ago at least and no one's seen her since. But that's nothing new. I've worked at Midwitch since I were a young housemaid, back when Phineas Hawke still had two good legs, and no other servant has ever stayed longer than six months. Except me. I just put my head down and got on with it. Aye, and I think old Hawke respected me for it. Knew I was a hard nut." She rapped her knuckles to her brow. "Like him."

Again Darius thought of the fruit thief touching his forehead. Her hands were soft and quite comforting, he must begrudgingly admit. But he had never seen a pair of eyes so insolent, a face so impertinent, a mouth so ready to insult. Neither had he tasted lips that must be spiced with a dangerous herbal elixir because of the speed with which he became intoxicated by their merest caress upon the bristles of his cheek.

That same forward young woman had once leapt naked onto his bed, expecting a night of wicked sport. With pink ribbons around her thighs and her hair tumbling loose over her shoulders. Who was it she claimed to be looking for that fateful night in Bath? Captain Something-or-Other.

How would a girl of decent family get herself into such a predicament? Whatever would she do next?

He sincerely hoped fate would not put her in his way again, because he was a busy fellow and had far more important things and many other responsibilities with which to concern himself. Not that he could remember what any of them were at that moment. Her antics had shamefully muddled the neat order of his thoughts.

This must be a temporary fever that would soon pass; he was sure of it.

Frivolous pink ribbons. Tied up like bows on a present.

Whatever could he...Darius loosed his neckcloth with one rough tug and finally took a breath...whatever would she do next?

Eight

SHE DASHED INTO DIANA MAKEPIECE'S PARLOR AND slumped gracelessly onto the small sofa beside her sister.

Since Diana was in the midst of reading a chapter, no one spoke to Justina. Instead she received a worried frown from Catherine and several inquisitive glances from Rebecca Sherringham, during which she kept as steady and composed a countenance as she could manage under the circumstances. Fortunately Lucy was not there. Confined to her room at home after returning so late last night following the misadventure with Sir Mortimer Grubbins, the poor girl was not even allowed to send a note out. But Justina was relieved not to face her friend at that moment, for with her sly talent for ascertaining Maiden's Palsy in others, Lucy would instantly see something amiss.

> *"I remember hearing you once say, Mr. Darcy, that you hardly ever forgave, that your resentment once created was unappeasable. You are very cautious, I suppose, as to its being created."*
>
> *"I am," said he, with a firm voice.*

"And never allow yourself to be blinded by prejudice?"

"I hope not."

"It is particularly incumbent on those who never change their opinion, to be secure of judging properly at first."

"May I ask to what these questions tend?"

"Merely to the illustration of your character," said she, endeavoring to shake off her gravity. "I am trying to make it out."

"And what is your success?"

She shook her head. "I do not get on at all. I hear such different accounts of you as puzzle me exceedingly."

It was difficult to remain silent during Diana's slow reading. Justina, having absolutely no interest in the character of Mr. Darcy, wished Elizabeth Bennet would simply crack the fellow over his fat head with a chamber pot and be done with it.

She was bursting to tell them all about the forbidden kiss and the dark, beastly stranger lurking at Midwitch Manor. They would probably never believe her; she could scarce believe it herself. Touching her lips, she was astonished to find them cold now, for they felt very warm inside.

When Diana finally finished the chapter, all three pairs of eyes then fixed upon Justina. And suddenly, just when the chance to shock them all was in her feverish grasp, she found herself unwilling to relay the story. It was as if she'd been enjoying a large, juicy plum, until she choked on the pit that lodged in her throat.

"Well?" her sister demanded. "What happened to you?"

"Naught, sister. I got the pears and took them to Mrs. Dockley."

Catherine's gaze meandered slowly downward. "Your frock is in ruins."

"How you do exaggerate, sister. It is no more than a small rip. I'll sew it tomorrow."

"You're very flushed, Jussy," observed Rebecca, who had a habit of pointing out the obvious, especially when other people meant not to notice it. "Also quite out of breath."

"I ran all the way here. Did not want to miss anything the wondrous Mr. Darcy might have to say."

There was a short silence and then Diana said, "But you missed a whole chapter and now you'll have no idea what's happening in the story."

"On the contrary. I wager I can tell you the entire thing already, including how it ends. Lizzie and Mr. Wickham will have several misunderstandings perpetrated by the evil menace Mr. Darcy, but finally love will win the day. There will be much uncertainty and heartache. The despicable Mr. Darcy will lock her in a cupboard at some point, intent on starving her to death. She will uncover a dark mystery about his family, but Mr. Wickham will ride to her rescue and all will end happily ever after, with him never even kissing her."

Diana looked appalled and then grieved by this brusque assessment of a book she'd acquired by sacrificing her best taffeta. She raised a slender hand to pat her ebony ringlets and remarked tightly, "Always so sharp, Jussy. Always so clever. I wonder why you bother to read at all, since you know everything and can learn nothing new from the pages."

"But I wish I *could* learn from these pages! For once I'd like to read a story where it doesn't all happen behind closed doors and off the page. How are we supposed to be prepared for men and life when we're kept in the dark. *It's not fair!*" In light of her most recent misadventure, Justina felt the inequality more than ever, and her unsettled emotion gave her speech extra passion.

Rebecca readily agreed, adding that she'd heard of a woman who was in such shock after her wedding night that handfuls of her hair fell out. Diana, newly engaged herself and keen to mention the fact as often as possible, scoffed at the likelihood of this claim. While the two other women proceeded to argue, Justina felt her sister's eyes observing her closely.

"You didn't meet anyone at Midwitch Manor, did you?"

"Not a soul." Another fib destined for her diary tonight.

It was fortunate indeed that he didn't mean to stay after tomorrow, she thought. A man like that was the last thing they needed in Hawcombe Prior. A single man, darkly handsome, well-dressed, and arrogant. Thought he knew all about her and how she should be managed. Ha!

With no beauty at her disposal a young lady must find other ways to be noticed.

For some reason that had wounded her far more than it should. Justina knew she was no diamond, but hearing it fall casually from his lips last year in a crowded ballroom was almost like hearing it for the very first time.

As if that was not enough, he now proceeded to mock *her* village! How dare he? She might say that Hawcombe Prior was a very dull place and nothing ever happened there, but having lived in the place her entire life she was entitled to say it. He was not.

Then, despite all that, he'd kissed her.

He'd kissed her the way a man might if he thought he had some claim upon her.

One thing was certain: The puzzling stranger and his hot hands would definitely have caused a vast deal of trouble for her had he stayed.

Darius carried the lantern into Phineas Hawke's library and found the solicitor waiting with papers at the ready for his signature.

"I believe we can arrange tenants for the place by the end of the year. Just sign here, Mr. Wainwright, and we'll take care of matters for you."

He took the quill in hand and placed the nib to the paper.

Something caught his eye. He glanced over at the window. A wood pigeon had settled on the ledge outside, carrying in its beak a ribbon, from which dangled a lady's bonnet.

Hers, it must be.

There was a small bunch of faux cherries attached to the ribbon and the confused bird began to peck at them.

Darius looked at the pen again, then at the bird.

He knew that what happened between himself and the owner of the bonnet could have put them both in a compromising position. Just because the encounter passed without witnesses did not make it any better. If he ever caught a man behaving in such a manner with his niece, Sarah, he'd knock the fellow out.

Despite flinging herself naked onto his bed once before, the way Miss Justina Penny had kissed him suggested innocence. Was that merely another performance or was it genuine? In the same way as the bird tapped his beak at those wax cherries, Wainwright's mind picked tentatively at the very few things he knew about her.

"Sir? Is something amiss?"

He looked down at the paper and found that he'd still made no mark upon it. The quill would not move. "Do you know what happened to a scullery maid who once worked here? Nellie Pickles?"

"Pickles, sir?" The solicitor thought for a moment and then smiled. "Ah, the sturdy young woman who never spoke a word. She left to marry the gardener. Your great-uncle did not allow romance between the staff, so they had no choice but to leave his employ."

"*Married?*"

"Indeed. Mr. Hawke sent me to Beaconsfield with a present of money for their wedding. Anonymous, of course. I rather think he liked his miserly reputation. Relished it, in fact."

"So she was not murdered and buried in the orchard."

"Good gracious, no. She's alive and well and living in Beaconsfield with three children."

"It seems certain people hereabouts have overworked imaginations of a lurid bent."

"Ah yes," the solicitor replied grimly. "There is much of that about these days, particularly among the young ladies of the local Book Society. I understand they plagued your great-uncle quite frequently while he was still living."

"I can believe it. I met one of them."

"Oh, dear. I'm sorry, sir."

"So am I." He sighed and looked at the paper again. The quill almost slipped from his fingers when, for just a moment, he thought the words he read there had changed into an accusatory scrawl.

Darius Wainwright, you are a cad. A rotten scoundrel. What were you thinking to act that way with a young girl, innocent or not?

He blinked rapidly and the words on the paper changed back to what they should be. But a shy voice repeated them inside his head. It was a tiny sound, but insistent. And it clung to him, just as her small, impertinent hands had gripped his jacket sleeve.

Nine

"I CAN'T SEE WHAT ALL THE FUSS IS ABOUT." JUSTINA blew out her words with such angry force that she misted the glass window pane before her. "It will be the same harvest dance we've attended every year, with the same faces, the same conversation, and the same music." After a pause, she added grandly, "I've a good mind not to go."

Her sister fluttered about in the corner of her eye like a distressed butterfly. "Of course you'll go. You always enjoy yourself, Jussy."

But this year she did not view the forthcoming annual village dance with the usual anticipation. There was a time when any excuse to misbehave while the adults drank too much cider and forgot themselves was something she looked forward to for weeks beforehand. Now nineteen, however, Justina began to see the futility of it all. She felt the dreadful weight of maturity pulling the corners of her lips down as Father Time marched her inexorably toward old age and decrepitude.

"What ails you lately?" her sister exclaimed. "You're like a pillow with all the goose down knocked out of it."

What ails me? Oh, you wouldn't want to know, sister dear.

She hardly knew herself, although she had done her best to diagnose the problem and found a handy scapegoat.

"I have an intestinal colic brought about by Clara's cooking. I am wasting away with it. I daresay I shall not last much longer. If only I had more than my collection of pressed flowers and that ugly sampler to leave behind." She jerked a thumb over her shoulder at the framed handiwork hanging on their wall—*Children Shewed Be Seen And Not Heered*—sewn haphazardly across calico a dozen years ago when she was set the task by her annoyed mama.

Catherine laughed. "Before you take your last breath, do look at this gown and help me decide how I can trim it. Somehow I must make it look new again."

Laid across the window seat on her belly, feet in the air, chin in her upturned palm, Justina was more interested in the view of the rain-washed lane below than she was in assessing her sister's old frock. "There goes Martha Mawby looking dreadfully pleased with herself." She watched the stout figure leave their front gate and waddle up the lane with much more than her usual amount of purpose. The sight of that broad, jostling backside made Justina yearn for her trusty old catapult, confiscated five years ago at least, yet still sadly missed and remembered with fondness. "She must have had scandalous news to impart. That always makes her vastly contented and silly. Here comes Barnabas Rooke. Today he has two...no, three pieces of frayed string holding his breeches up. He must have gained in girth. I am quite sure he has more holes than patches. 'Tis a wonder how the seams of his coat hold together. His breeches too for that matter, although we must be exceedingly grateful for whatever magic keeps them up."

"While I appreciate the commentary of events in our lane, Jussy, I would much rather you look at my gown, the shortcomings of which are of more import to me, at present, than the sartorial failings of Farmer Rooke. Should I purchase some dye?"

Justina finally turned her head away from the window and assessed her sister's appearance. "Looks well enough to me. Save the four shillings. Remember what happened last time we dyed one of your gowns? The stitches all fell apart and the color was more mottled than a jester's suit."

Cathy sighed. "Yes, but—"

"As I said already, this is only the village harvest dance, the same as it is every year." But she was obliged to admit that even on that grim day, in gray and dismal light, her sister was a graceful figure standing at the long mirror in her blue muslin. "How you do worry about naught, Cathy," she added in a gentler tone. "You could wear a grain sack and still be the most beautiful girl in Hawcombe Prior." As their mother had reminded them all that morning at breakfast, Catherine was wasted in that village.

"True," Justina had replied drily. "We might have got a far better price for her carcass in a big place like Manderson."

This comment was ignored, as were most things Justina exhaled at breakfast when her family was too preoccupied with their own thoughts about the day ahead. As the least significant person in the room, she was seldom paid any attention, but, since this often had its advantages too, she did not complain.

"Perhaps some new lace over the frayed cuffs and a fresh trim for the bodice might make it look less tired," Catherine murmured, head on one side as she assessed her image in the mirror, holding up various silk and satin ribbons.

Justina glanced over at the bed where her own best frock lay in a crumpled knot. It needed letting out at the bosom and the hem, but sewing was one thing she always put off as long as she might. There were far more interesting things to do, and who cared what she looked like when all eyes would turn to her sister anyway?

At that moment the door to their bedchamber burst open and their mother dashed in, her breath in shreds and her face crimson. "Oh my goodness, girls, you will never guess what has happened."

"Someone left a newborn baby on the parson's doorstep and claimed him to be the father?" Justina volunteered hopefully. "Captain Sherringham has married a scarlet hussy, an adulteress twice his age with an eye patch, a gin habit, and six bastard children?"

Their mother had her mouth open to speak, but paused, flustered by the interruption. "What?" She looked askance at her youngest daughter. "Heavens no! Such a shocking imagination you have. I cannot think where you came by it."

"I must be a changeling."

"I shouldn't be at all surprised. No, no...*this* is my news." Their mother clasped her hands together and turned her full attention to the elder daughter. "Martha Mawby says there is a new resident at Midwitch Manor. A handsome gentleman of means." Then came the master flourish, the cherry atop the trifle, "*A bachelor.*"

While their mama went into giddy fits of delight following her announcement, Justina hastily resumed her perusal of the lane through their window. Her heart felt like a fist pounding in her breast and her former lethargy melted away, but she forced herself to remain in her careless pose. Only her fingertips—one set rapidly drumming away on the seat cushion and the other upon her cheek—might have betrayed her altered state. If the other two women present paid her any attention, that is. This was another of those occasions when she was glad to be the matter of least consequence in the room.

"Apparently," their mother continued, "he inherited the place from old Phineas Hawke, and although he had planned to sell it, he arrived a few days ago and quite suddenly decided to stay!"

While they could not see her face, Justina stared at her panicked reflection in the window and watched it slowly vanish behind another cloud of breath. Her mother's words had rendered her suddenly full of more holes than Farmer Rooke had in his garments. And things might slip out of those holes if she was not careful. For two and a half days she'd managed to keep her encounter with the Beast of Midwitch Manor a secret.

Her fingertips tapped ever faster upon the seat cushion.

"Martha has been there to tend the laundry," her mother continued. "Her aunt recommended her for the post, and I daresay we would have known of it sooner if Harriet Birch were not such a despicable deceiver and always looking to out-do everybody. She kept the news from me deliberately, of course."

Harriet Birch and their mama had been at odds for ten years or more since they fought over the trophy for best marmalade at the county fair and each accused the other of sabotage. It was a bitter feud that no one else but the two of them had ever cared about.

"Martha says his name is Wainwright. He came up from London last Friday evening and was seen to eat his supper with only a meager appetite at the Pig in a Poke. His clothes are very well made and costly, but Martha says he has ten shirts all identical and the same in waistcoats. He rises early each day and spends long hours shut up in his great-uncle's library. He keeps the windows sealed, and if he enters a room where one is open he closes it immediately. However, he does not like a large fire. He insists upon polishing his own boots every day and has already set about mending all the clocks in the house, for none of them, it seemed, were working with enough accuracy to please him. He reads a vast deal but does not yet require spectacles. His hair is very dark without a sprig of gray yet to be seen. So although he has no female attachments at present, it seems likely he is young enough still to want some."

Justina rolled her eyes at the window. "He sounds a precious ninny. We might have a shortage of bachelors in this village, but we're not that desperate, surely."

"Of course, there is not much to be done with Jussy," their mother continued merrily, "but you, Catherine, must have a new gown for the harvest dance. I have just come from your father's library, and he agrees we may have a little extra this month for the haberdasher."

"But Mama, is there time to sew a new gown? 'Tis barely a fortnight away."

"We'll make time for one, my dear. I knew a chance would come your way soon. I knew it!"

As she listened to the excitement in the room behind her, Justina quietly pitied the addled, naïve creatures. They could not know, of course, that the new subject of their romantic fantasies was an arrogant gentleman who looked down on that village and everyone in it. This Wainwright person was, in her opinion, a man best avoided. But there would be no telling Mama. To Mrs. Penny, any single man of wealth was a candidate for marriage, and where her eldest daughter was concerned, what man in his right mind would not fall in love?

For Justina, on the other hand, no one had very high hopes, herself included. The only fellow she'd ever considered as husband material was Captain Sherringham, but that idea was nipped in the bud after the embarrassment of Bath and her reckless, failed scheme to seduce him. She now said a silent prayer of thanks, ironically grateful after all that she landed on the Wrong Man last year. Knowing Sherry, he would have ruffled her hair and laughed at her attempt to play the temptress.

After that near miss, Justina decided a husband would only get in the way and be a terrible drain on her patience, so she stepped into the role of future spinster. Without expectations heaped upon her, she had an easier life and a liberty her sister would never know.

Not that Cathy seemed to mind her role as the one upon whom all hope now rested. She bore the burden of her good looks with a solemn sense of responsibility, almost like a religious calling. Nothing Justina told her could dissuade her from the idea of marriage.

"When you marry," she had warned Cathy, "a husband will dole out the pin money and tut-tut over ink-stained fingers."

"Our father does that now," her sister replied complacently.

"But a husband will expect you to manage his house,

no matter how little you care about dust on the shelves or weeds in the garden. And be polite to his guests, even if you are not in a mood to make pointless chat and sip tea. He will lose things incessantly and expect you to find them for him."

"Goodness, how dreadful!" Cathy had laughed. "Worry not, Jussy. You may yet find the perfect gentleman for you. One who would not mind a wife occasionally drifting off into daydreams of a somewhat bloodthirsty bent. A wife who would prefer tutoring her daughters in sword play with garden canes than teaching them at the pianoforte."

Quite certain such a man did not exist, Justina let it be known, at every opportunity, that she would be a great nuisance in anybody's life.

Now along came the Wrong Man again, with his dark eyes and stormy frown. The new owner of Midwitch Manor had fixed her in the stern rays of his perusal until she felt as if he'd tipped her upside down and emptied her out. He'd dared suggest she was a troublemaker who caused mischief because she was bored, had nothing more worthwhile to do with her time, and no one to punish her. Insufferable, conceited man!

"...*You are a young lady who doesn't want to face her future. Part of you would rather be a child forever and have no responsibilities, no adult concerns...for you, life is always a game.*"

Remembering the heated way he'd looked at her while tapping a riding crop against his boots, Justina felt certain his sudden change of mind, his extended stay in the village, did not bode well for her.

Like a fool, she had felt the need to kiss his cheek and

thank him for the fruit. She gave him an inch; he took a yard.

Teasing prickles breezed across her skin as she recalled the way he'd kissed her in return. How his tongue had tasted of cloves. How his firm lips took possession, stripped her of any chance to protest. The know-it-all had ravished her mouth, fondled her breast.

Justina squirmed on the window seat, wriggling on her belly as she felt that tightening begin again, the low, thudding pulse seizing her body in its heavy rhythm. Once the Maiden's Palsy started, she had great difficulty making it stop.

As for the cheeks of her posterior, she was afraid to look in the mirror, but she was quite certain his fingers had left her bruised. She could not watch Clara knead bread dough these days without blushing and fanning herself with whatever came to hand.

She propped her trembling chin on her knuckles, still staring angrily through that window, her back turned to the other women in the room.

If the sly blackguard knew what was good for him, he would keep his arrogant lips shut in regard to their encounters. She certainly would never speak a word to anyone about it, or her mother would be ordering wedding clothes before she could run off with the gypsies. Usually every argument and every set-down Justina enjoyed giving was proudly and faithfully scribbled in her very full diary. Every shocking encounter with Mr. Wainwright, his stiff appendages and his firm hands, however, were markedly absent from the dog-eared pages.

She prided herself on being a lifelong citizen of

Hawcombe Prior, one of its most outspoken residents and a tireless recorder of events, but Justina had learned there were certain happenings better kept to oneself. Not even worth risking to pen and ink in her diary. As a young lady who generally found news burning to be let out—especially if it was scandalous and might be embellished a little with her own imagination—the value of discretion was a new discovery for her. At nineteen, she realized with chagrin, it was probably an overdue one.

Ten

DARIUS BLOTTED THE LAST LETTER AND REACHED FOR
the wax to seal it. When news of his decision to remain
a little longer in the wilderness reached his friends and
business associates in London, they would immediately
wonder at his sanity. But there, it was done. Heaven
help him.

In answer to his bell, the study door eventually
opened to admit the housekeeper he'd inherited along
with the property.

"Mrs. Birch, will you see to it that these letters are
taken with the post at the first opportunity?"

She advanced with the wide, plodding, uneven gait
of a bulldog. "Shall you be ready for a slice of game pie,
young man? I noticed you haven't eaten all day. That
won't do you any good, will it?" She glanced at the fireplace. "And you need some more coal on the fire before
it goes out. You'll catch your death o' cold in this drafty
old place. I'll bring up some coal from the cellar and then
a nice slice of pie. Can't have you fading away, can we?"

Darius could not remember a time when anyone
concerned themselves with what and when *he* ate, or

how warmly *he* dressed. Perhaps this was "motherly." He would not know, having grown up without one—only a busy, stern, no-nonsense father whose first concern was always work, and a rakish brother whose first concern was always getting out of it. His stepmother had come along when he was already a young man and his character formed, which was a very good thing, since she seemed to view Darius and his brother as mere inconveniences that must be suffered if she wanted the comforts of being married to their father.

Most women he knew were concerned only for the well-being of his bank account, not for his health or his stomach. Mrs. Birch's attempts to fuss over him, therefore, were puzzling for Darius. He did his best to discourage her, but the housekeeper treated these attempts as if they were no more than a fractious child's tantrum. He got the distinct impression she might squeeze his cheek between her thumb and forefinger one day while urging him to eat all his crusts. Perhaps that same curious deafness and thickened skin with which she handled *him* had helped her deal with crotchety old Phineas Hawke when the other staff gave up and left.

"Any news on my carriage, Mrs. Birch?"

"Oh aye, Sam Hardacre says he's nearly done putting the pieces back together."

"He has been *nearly done* for two days. Does that phrase mean something different here in the country?"

"But he says he'd never seen such a wreck as you made."

"Me?" He scowled. "I certainly didn't—"

"Racing along recklessly, no doubt. You young men! I don't know. Shouldn't be on the roads, if you ask me. There's enough death and danger about without you lot careening up and down the countryside, galloping yourselves into ditches."

Irritable and not having the patience to argue further with her, he glanced at his fob watch. "Perhaps I'll ride down into the village now and see these letters to the post. Then call upon Mr. Hardacre myself."

Although he generally avoided too much fresh air, he wanted his letters to go with the next post, not in a day or two. After observing the housekeeper's somewhat eccentric temper for several days, he knew she did things in her own time, when she thought they were necessary, not always when she was asked. It was, he supposed, a country thing. Another one.

"Be sure to wear a warm coat, and don't dally. It's a brisk, windy day out there, and I shouldn't be at all surprised to see rain this afternoon." She gave him a crooked-toothed smile. "You mind how you go, now. The lane into the village is little better than a mire since the ditches overflowed in that recent spell o' rain. You'd do well to go the long way by Rooke's farm. Take a right out of the gate and follow the elm trees until you get to the crossroads and you'll see the church spire."

"Yes, Mrs. Birch, I did come by that road when I arrived." He was hardly likely to get lost anywhere in the three lanes that made up Hawcombe Prior, was he?

"If it were drier out, you might cut across the fallow field by Dockley's old barn, but with the ground so soft, you should stick to the road. Wouldn't want you to get mud all over your fancy breeches and coat."

Letters in hand, he edged around his desk, keeping a careful distance from the housekeeper. "Quite."

"And what do you mean to do about that pig you found in the orchard?"

Ah, yes. The pig. Sir Mortimer Grubbins, as a certain irritating, undisciplined creature had referred to it when she climbed over his wall to steal fruit last Saturday.

How she ever got the pig through a locked gate he had no idea.

Looking out on the orchard through his study window, Darius shook his head. She'd had the sheer unmitigated gall to suggest he become guardian of an animal that had no more right to be there than she did.

He knew country folk were different, but he'd not expected to be ambushed in his own orchard by a hoyden. With full, rebellious lips, dangerous curves, and wide eyes full of curiosity.

A woman in need of guidance, before she got herself in worse trouble. If she had not already.

Of course it was none of his business. He should count his good fortune that no one saw him kiss her.

He squeezed his fingers tighter around those letters.

"I will make inquiries in the village, Mrs. Birch," he replied finally to the housekeeper, "and see if I can find someone to take the pig away."

"Oh, I thought you were growing fond of it." She chortled.

Turning swiftly from the window, he used his frown upon her, but she shooed him toward the door with her apron.

"Off you go then, young lad. When you get back I'll have your supper laid out and a fire in the dining room."

It *did* sound rather comforting on such a bleak day, he must admit.

"Now you be wary of the young ladies down in the village. If I were you, lad, I'd take care not to make eye contact. They're a troublesome lot and some worse than others." She sniffed, folding her arms. "They get up to more than they should. What with the reading of romance novels and the like. I ask you, what good can come of it?"

She made it sound as if they were headhunters and cannibals, but since he had met one of them already, this warning was not required either. "Rest assured, Mrs. Birch, I am quite safe from their villainy."

In fact, *they*, he thought, should be wary of him. One of them should, in particular.

❧

After hearing Martha Mawby's news, the Penny sisters walked arm in arm down the main street of Hawcombe Prior that afternoon, with Catherine valiantly pretending that the arrival of a strange bachelor in their village made no ripple upon her placid waters.

"Gossip is so dreadfully unladylike," she said.

"Quite so, sister." Justina nodded with more fervency than was required. Sadly, while she still battled the demon temptation, all her gestures had a tendency to be stronger and less controlled. It was a failing she'd noticed before, but the more she tried to rein in her body parts, the more they misbehaved.

"Even if there is a strange gentleman taking possession of Midwitch Manor, even if he is single and has a large fortune, that is no one's business but his own," said Catherine.

Justina knew her sister was not so much upset by this

item of gossip—which was undeniably interesting in a village of so few unattached males—as she was by the fact that it was the slovenly laundress, Martha Mawby, who bore the news. In claiming to be one of the very few souls, so far, to meet Mr. Wainwright, Martha had transformed into a person of importance. Anyone might think she was his intimate friend and privy to every move he made. But Catherine was widely acknowledged to be the loveliest girl in this village, and therefore Mr. Wainwright, in the minds of many, was already her property—should she find him agreeable. With this state of expectation in the air, it must have been galling for Cathy that she had not yet caught a glimpse of her man, while Martha Mawby had already handled his unmentionables. Justina could see that her dear sister was very nearly forced to say something unpleasant about it.

Fortunately she didn't need to, because she had Justina to say it for her.

"Martha is an ungainly slab of mutton with no manners, sister, and no couth. Nor does she have the presence of mind to keep rumors to herself." She slid her arm out from under Catherine's so they could skirt a large puddle in their path. Only a week ago she would have been tempted to take another of her running leaps over that puddle; today she struggled to hold her natural instincts at bay.

A child with no responsibilities and no adult concerns, indeed! She'd show *him*.

"I know I shall ignore everything Martha says about the man," Justina exclaimed. "We all should. That is the surest way to stem her gossiping."

"Very true, Jussy. But I would have imagined you

to be most curious about the stranger and to have scandalous stories collected about him already. Mostly made up."

She blinked rapidly. "Me? Good gracious no. I have too many other things to do with my time." Keeping her gaze sternly on the road ahead, she struggled to think of anything that might keep her face from changing color. "Why would I care sixpence about him?"

"Because he is something new. You constantly lament that nothing significant happens here, and we are all so dull." Catherine halted abruptly. "You went to Midwitch Manor on Saturday to steal pears. Did you see him there?"

"Certainly not! I told you, sister, I met no one at Midwitch when I went there. Neither was I *stealing*! The fruit was left to rot there since old Phineas Hawke died. No one wanted it. Why should we not have it?"

Catherine digested this reply with evident skepticism. Nineteen years of her younger sister's company must have taught caution, yet surely, Justina reasoned, poor Cathy would not wish to know what really happened. In a sense, she was saving her virtuous sister from no little anguish by denying the entire incident.

Obliged to be mute and dignified, she must let the lumpish Martha Mawby bask alone in glory this time.

Clearly in need of something more with which to admonish her, Catherine pointed out that her coat was unbuttoned. "You'll catch cold," she exclaimed.

Too busy maintaining an innocent face to bother with a little thing like buttons, Justina tucked her arm under Catherine's again and gave her a wide smile. "Let's make haste or we shall be late for the post."

The mail coach was due to pass through the village that afternoon, and Justina awaited a reply to a parcel she'd sent to a publisher in London several weeks ago. Her sister didn't know why she'd taken to waiting for the post so diligently, for it was a venture about which she'd told no one.

They walked on a few more steps. "I cannot make you out, Jussy," her sister muttered. "I know I shouldn't believe you, and yet if you *had* met that man, I'm quite certain you could never keep silent. It would have burst out of you at once. Unless," her eyes narrowed, "something happened there that you do not want anyone to know."

Looking about with some desperation, Justina was exceedingly thankful to spy a familiar shape hurrying toward them, skirt billowing in the wind, bouncy wheaten ringlets visible under the hood of a scarlet cloak. "Ah, look, there's Lucy!"

Catherine turned to observe the approaching breeze-buffeted figure. "I thought she was still punished and not allowed out."

"No, no, that is all over with. Her father has relented and given her permission to join us for the Book Society meetings." Justina was glad to have Lucy back again after the unfortunate demise of her father's rowboat.

His *former* rowboat, strictly speaking. Really it wasn't a safe vessel in which to be out, as Justina had assured Mr. Bridges when they returned the pieces. "In fact, sir," she'd earnestly explained, "we have probably saved someone else from a certain drowning by disposing of the boat for you."

Lucy's father did not reach the same conclusion. Then he discovered they'd also lost his pig.

"I'm afraid poor Sir Mortimer Grubbins took such fright, sir, that he ran away into the woods," Justina had told him.

"He *ran*?"

"And speedily indeed for such a plump creature. I believe he was betaken by a sudden *joie de vivre* that gave lift to his trotters. Certainly he did not look back, and given that he owed us a debt of gratitude, I think he might have made an effort to show his appreciation in some way. But no, there was not even the slightest grunt of thanks."

Lucy's punishment would probably have been extended a full month if not for the approaching harvest dance, but her father could hardly ban his only daughter from the most important social event of the year, especially with a strange, wealthy bachelor at large. In the end, since Justina took the blame firmly upon her own shoulders, he forgave his daughter and let her out of the house again.

Although Justina was also punished over the same incident, her time was served not by confinement—even her own parents didn't want her under their feet all day in their small cottage—but by making her perform at least one helpful deed to every household in the village. Only when she could show her father the list of worthy acts completed would he give her the necessary coin to repay Mr. Bridges for the loss of his boat.

She should have found a way to blame the Wainwright person, she thought suddenly. Surely he was at fault for something.

When she touched her lips with two gloved fingers, they felt different these days. Perhaps, she thought sadly, because they were forced to spend more time shut tight rather than joyfully spinning a tale of her undoing at the hands of a merciless ogre.

Stop it! Stop thinking about it, you ridiculous little fool!

Thrusting aside the hovering image of imperious Mr. Wainwright the Wrong, she greeted Lucy with more warmth than ever before, as if that excessive gesture would block him from her thoughts.

All three young ladies stopped outside the haberdasher, the one and only village shop—which also happened to be the established stop for the mail coach—and there they admired some new printed muslin on display. With the harvest dance only two weeks away, their conversation turned to dresses and decoration for the hair.

"I am to have a new gown," Lucy told them. "Mama is most anxious I should look my best this year. She is lending me her good pearls."

"Yes," replied Justina morosely, "we too are being trussed up like pork loins." Aware of her sister's frown, she hastily amended the comment. "Not Cathy, of course. She will look beautiful as ever and does not need the frills and embellishments a sad, drooping creature such as I must suffer to be noticed."

"Poor Diana," said Lucy, "to have given her best taffeta silk away and just as a new man comes to the village. Although she is engaged now and has no need to catch anyone's eye. Still it must smart to know she has only her old green muslin to wear. I would never barter my ball gown for a book." As they all stood looking in at the shop window, she added, "I suppose Mr. Wainthrop *will* attend?"

Before she could think better of it, Justina had muttered a surly, "It's *Wainwright*. And I hope not."

The faces on either side turned to look at her. "Why should he not?" The sharp tone in Cathy's voice suggested her sister might have done something terrible to prevent the fellow ever leaving his house.

Justina began to wish she had.

"I merely meant it would be best if he did not." Finally tending to the open buttons of her coat, she threaded them hastily through the braided frogs. "I wish he would go back to London where he belongs. Strangers never fit in here."

What if he felt obliged to tell someone what had happened between them? Not just in his kitchen, but in Bath? In his bed? Just because she liked to see how much she might get away with didn't mean he was the same. Her mother and father would demand a wedding at once, as soon as they were recovered enough from the shock. She'd really outdone herself this time.

Suddenly she had a stitch in her side, as if she'd just run down the length of the street without stopping.

"Have you seen him yet, Lucy?" Cathy was asking casually. "We heard he dined at your father's tavern on Friday and stayed in the guest room."

"No, I have not," came the sullen reply. "I was so late home Friday"—here Lucy shot a quick scowl in Justina's direction—"that I was sent directly to bed. I didn't even get a glimpse. But Martha Mawby says he is exceedingly handsome."

"I'm sure he is also wretchedly proud," Justina snapped, adding quickly, "Gentlemen from London always are."

"He is a very rich man, so they say. As such he is allowed to be proud. I could overlook pride and any number of shortcomings in a man that rich."

"Lucy Bridges," Catherine gently admonished the younger girl, "it is indelicate to speak of money in such a fashion. It makes you sound mercenary. I'm sure it should not matter how much wealth he has, as long as he is of good character and sensible."

Justina looked at her sister. "I suppose you are already thinking of him as *your* Mr. Darcy, Cathy." It amused her to see how the other young ladies fell into palpitations over that obnoxiously proud, meddling, smug character in *Pride and Prejudice*. In real life, if they had any wits about them, they would give a cold, judgmental man like Darcy a wide berth, no matter how much money he had.

Her sister's cheeks flamed a brilliant cherry wine. "I have not given any such consideration to Mr. Wainwright," she protested, clutching her muff tightly to her bosom.

Oh, poor, innocent Cathy, she thought, feeling so much older and wiser. With a head already turned by the fantasy of Mr. Darcy, her sister was ready to fall, moon-eyed, over the first man who bore a slight resemblance to the character.

Romantic novels had much to answer for.

While she pondered her sister's naïveté, they were joined on the path by Rebecca Sherringham, who was in a merry mood. "I have had a letter from my brother at last, and he hopes to return in time for the harvest dance!"

All spirits were lifted by this information. With spare young men in such short supply, the arrival of another in time for the dance was manna from heaven. Captain Sherringham, handsome, witty, and an energetic dancer, was generous with his charm. For Justina especially this was wonderful news, and she began to feel there was something to which she might look forward. The sky was now far less gray. Had the captain ever known about her foolish escapade in Bath, of course, she would never be able to look him in the eye again, but now they had nothing to complicate the friendship and again she quietly celebrated the twist of fate that landed her on the Wrong Man's bed.

"Aren't we all late?" Rebecca exclaimed suddenly. "Diana will scold us, as she so loves to do. Oh"—her eyes narrowed upon sight of the window display— "new muslins!"

Suddenly Lucy pinched Justina's arm, and she looked up to find the Wainwright person's critical gaze once again assessing her, this time from horseback and across the distance of that narrow, muddy street.

Lucy gasped, "That must be *him*."

Quickly Justina looked away. "Get a hold of yourself," she snapped, her pulse beating an even faster rhythm. "He's not the Duke of Bloody Wellington."

She prayed—with far more fervor than she ever did in church—that he would be struck with sudden, enduring memory loss and never tell another soul about her leaping upon him in his bed.

How she wished she could walk away, but the mail coach horn was heard already, and this might be the day she had her answer from the publisher. Justina could be on her way to becoming a woman of independent means. Therefore she had no choice but to stand and wait.

Eleven

THE RULES OF ETIQUETTE DICTATED THAT HE COULD not approach the cluster of young ladies on the other side of the street, for he had not been formally introduced, so Darius merely slowed his horse. Although there were four women in the group, his eyes were drawn to one in particular, as they would be to any stain or thing out of place. Anything bothersome and in need of correction. She was scowling, visibly agitated by her dawdling friends.

Nellie Pickles, indeed.

Someone, as Mrs. Birch had said, ought to put a stop to her.

Darius had negotiated with some of the most uncompromising traders in the world; he'd sailed for weeks on ships that were barely seaworthy; he'd managed a team of mercenary, work-shy, and bone-idle step-relatives without so far murdering any; and he'd served dutifully as his niece's guardian since he was nineteen and she only four. He should long since have left that socially awkward boyhood behind.

But for Darius, women remained a terrifying entity.

They so seldom made sense, rarely thought in practical terms, and often seemed to prefer a quarrel to a reasoned debate.

He hesitated, poised to urge the horse forward.

She might be impertinent to him again. Although he had dealt with her before and answered her with a tongue that surprised him by not stumbling much at all, Darius balked at the sight of so many other ladies in her company. A murder of crows hovering in the stark branches of wintering trees would have less sinister appearance. The beat of his heart was distressingly uneven and his stomach felt hollow. He wondered if he should have eaten some of Mrs. Birch's game pie before he left the house, after all.

Just then he caught the Penny woman glancing his way. Her lips were set in a very obstinate moue, her eyes narrowed in a fierce glare, attempting to warn him off. Unbeknownst to her, it had the opposite effect. This reckless creature, accustomed to getting away with her antics, thought she could kiss a gentleman and cause him a vast deal of trouble without suffering any consequence. He would be extremely surprised if there was any such man as that Captain Whatshisname—the gentleman she claimed to be expecting when she leapt onto his bed last year. Darius was inclined to believe her sights were set upon him and his fortune. When her first attempt failed, she tried the slightly more subtle approach of setting light to the Upper Rooms to get his attention.

Well, now she had it.

The coat she wore today was too small for her, the hooks straining to embrace the pleasing fullness of her figure, the sleeves ending too far before the wrist, and the hem, although showing a darker stripe where it must have been let down recently, finishing several inches above her muddied walking boots. Clearly she needed a new coat, but the expense, or perhaps her stubborn nature, meant that she could not part with the one she'd outgrown.

His shoulders relaxed. On this occasion, he decided, the rules of introduction could be bent for once. After all, he did have some acquaintance with her already, however unfortunate and unwelcome it might be.

But before he could steer his horse across the street, the mail coach clattered around the corner, a bulky, creaking, swaying vessel with boxes, packages, and people clinging to the outside with the bouncing resilience of fleas on a dog's back.

It came to a halt between him and the group of young ladies. There was a general ruckus while a man with a large sack alighted. Darius handed over his letters, as did several others gathered there in wait. Then the coach prepared to depart and the villagers dispersed. He watched curiously as Miss Penny darted around the snorting horses, demanding to know whether the sack had anything else in it to be delivered there. When informed there was nothing, she accused the poor fellow of not checking his mail bag sufficiently and even offered to do it for him.

"Nothing else for Hawcombe Prior, madam," he replied again, clutching his bag out of her reach and leaping up onto the back of the coach.

A few seconds later they were off again, horse hooves and wheels splattering mud at her coat as she stood forlornly watching it pass. The cold wind kicked up its pace, and she gripped her bonnet with one hand to keep it from flying after the coach.

As she rejoined her friends, shoulders drooping, head bowed, Darius steered his hired horse across the street toward them and placed himself directly in their view. When the troublesome young lady finally looked up, he tipped his hat. "Good afternoon, Miss *Penny*." One of the ladies in the rear of the group blushed prettily as her friends turned to look at her. He belatedly realized there must be more than one Penny in the bunch.

"Miss *Justina* Penny," he corrected, looking hard at the scowler in their midst. "We meet again. Alas."

Now the other three faces turned to her in surprise. Wind tugged on their hems and bonnet ribbons. She seemed resolved not to speak, but the auburn-haired woman standing directly behind her must have poked her in the back, for she jumped as if woken from a trance and reluctantly replied, "Mr. Wainwright." The way she exhaled his last name was like two iron doorstops dropping with a thud at his feet.

Today she was aloof and haughty, but the higher she raised her pert chin, the more Darius was reminded of his tongue traveling swiftly over the pulse at the side of her neck, and thus he recalled the sweet taste of her skin.

Before she could move her friends around his horse, he said, "I hope my pears were put to good use."

In the rear of the group, the young lady who had blushed when he first approached now gazed at the miscreant with wide, saddened eyes.

"Should you desire additional fruit, or anything more from my grounds and store cupboards, I trust you will ring the bell at the front gate next time," he added. "Save yourself the trouble of scaling the wall."

Miss Justina Penny replied with the insolence already familiar to him. "I shan't bother you again, sir. Your fruit is quite safe from me. I'm sure it is rotten and maggoty anyway."

"You'll require a key to the store cupboards if you want the silver and gold plate too, as it is locked away for safekeeping."

"Thank you for the warning. Good day."

"By the by…you left an item in my orchard."

Now the small, fair-headed girl on her right looked fearfully at her, almost losing the hood of her red cloak when the wind gusted.

The villainess stared up at him, her eyes heavy and dark.

"I thought you would want it back by now," he added.

"No, we haven't anywhere to put—"

Her little friend nudged her arm.

"—whatever it might be," she finished hastily.

"Your bonnet, Miss Justina Penny. That is what you left behind. I found a confused pigeon pecking at its cherry embellishment."

She blinked. "Oh. Yes. I forgot that old thing." Her gloved fingers fumbled over the braided frogs that barely closed the front of her coat. "It is of little consequence to me."

"So it seems." He cleared his throat as he watched the progress of her hands and remembered the arousing sensation of her bosom against his chest when he held her and kissed her. After she put her lips upon him first, devilish temptress! "Like good manners," he added huskily, "and ladylike behavior."

When he finally looked at her face, hot spots of color tinted her cheeks, but he doubted they were the result of embarrassment. Her eyes were the color of deep ocean, and today there was apparently a storm at sea. When he gazed into her eyes, he felt unsteady, as if he stood upon the rocking deck of a ship and struggled to keep his footing.

She made no move to introduce her companions, but Darius did not wish to make their acquaintance in any case. She was the only one of interest, damn her.

The storm in her eyes was clearing and darts of light became visible, like schools of fish through that blue shaded water. Suddenly gathering together they burst to the surface, catching on a patch of new sunlight. It was a shining color absent from the real sky above them today, but she—this lively creature—somehow had it at her disposal. He gripped his reins tighter.

"We were just talking of the harvest dance, Mr. Wainwright," she said coyly. "Will you attend?"

The very idea caused Darius a chill of terror. "No. I have...anything else to do."

The other three faces now looked up at him, their lips moving as one, drawing in a quick rush of indignant breath.

"Oh, but you really must come, Mr. Wainwright. We need all the dancing partners we can get," she exclaimed, blinking, tilting her head to one side. "Times are hard for single ladies."

"I'm sure you'll manage," he muttered. "You seem... resourceful."

Justina gave a broad, triumphant smile. "I thought you were going back to London. You promised you weren't staying." These words, brusque and accusatory, shot out of her, it seemed, while she was still celebrating whatever victory she thought she'd just enjoyed at his expense.

Her companions reacted to this impolite outburst in three different ways. The small one in the hooded cloak stared at the ground; the tall redhead looked at Miss Justina Penny with bemusement and curiosity; and the apparent elder sister glared with somber disapproval at some distant trees. Meanwhile, the culprit herself raised a fidgeting hand from her coat buttons to her lips, and Darius—much to his distress—relived the sensation of sinking into their softness and warmth. He vividly recalled the sweetness of their taste as they parted, surprised, uncertain, and yet curious under the demanding force of his returning kiss. He was still trying to understand why he'd allowed that to happen. It was most troubling to find there existed a pair of lips he would allow to insult him and yet still want to kiss immediately afterward.

The horse under Darius became restless, as if it sensed his unease. "I changed my mind, Miss Penny. A matter came up that dictates I remain a while longer at Midwitch Manor."

"Something unexpected?"

"Very." She had no idea how unexpected.

"Such a pity your plans must be changed. You were so eager to leave. I believe you said there was nothing here to entertain you."

He could not tear his eyes from her lips. They were pouty this afternoon and very pink. Bee-stung might be an eloquent description, he mused with an unusually poetic drift of thought. "I stay for a kiss…ness matter"—a hot flush swept over his face—"*business* matter. Not for entertainment."

Now she overflowed with politeness. "Let's hope your *business* does not keep you long here in this mud rut of a village."

He paused, studying her self-satisfied countenance and then the tattered ends of her bonnet ribbons as they fluttered in the wind. "Yes, Miss Justina Penny. It is a pity indeed, but it seems you must tolerate me a while yet. Good day." Turning his horse, he rode away, anxious to remove himself from the temptation of looking at her too long. He was suddenly painfully conscious of one side effect of paying her too much attention in public. It was an uncomfortable development, especially when astride a saddle.

Twelve

ON THE THIRD PULL OF THE BELL CORD, THE DOOR opened and a petite woman wedged herself in the gap, peering up at him in quick annoyance and slight confusion, as if her body was one place, her mind in another.

"Dr. Penny will not see patients today, sir. Come back tomorrow unless it is a matter of urgency." But as her blue eyes focused finally, her mouth softened. "Oh, goodness! You must be the new—"

"Wainwright, madam. I came to introduce myself and to discuss a matter of private business with the doctor."

"Private business?" Her lashes lowered demurely. "Of course, do come in, Mr. Wainwright."

"If it is not convenient, I can return another day."

"No, no. You must come in. We are delighted to make your acquaintance, to be sure." She seemed uncertain whether to curtsy or not, but settled for a lurching, backward series of bobs as he walked into the house after her. She circled him in the same awkward manner to close the front door and shut out the cold wind. "Such a pity my daughters are not in, Mr. Wainwright. They will be disappointed to miss your visit."

He hesitated and then muttered, "Will they?" He couldn't imagine ever being missed. He'd been assured his absence was often more celebrated than his grim presence.

"Dr. Penny and I have two daughters. Perhaps you have seen them about?" She beamed up at him, rather like a panting King Charles Spaniel might look at its master while waiting for a treat. Aha, so this was the doctor's wife. He had not realized at first, for he expected a maid or housekeeper to answer the doorbell. Now he studied her features more closely and found traces of the daughters he'd briefly met. Her face maintained a frayed prettiness under soft brown ringlets and a lace cap. "You must have seen my daughters in the village," she pressed eagerly.

He stepped back, afraid she might put her hand on his arm, for she had raised it to wave her fingers in an odd gesture.

"I do not know," he replied when it became apparent that she was waiting for some response.

"Surely you must have. They are always about." She smiled brightly.

"I have not been in the village long." That was the safest answer, he decided, ever cautious.

"I am told my eldest girl is the beauty of Hawcombe Prior—indeed, of the entire county—but she is not vain with it. She's the sweetest of young ladies with a very gentle temperament. Every man who meets her quickly falls in love with Catherine, but she has not yet been struck by Cupid's arrow."

"How fortunate for her. It sounds a grisly business."

Her smile wilted a little. "Here I am rattling on!

What must you think of me? I know my husband will be vastly pleased to meet you. Do come this way." Turning swiftly, she led him down a narrow passage. "I hope you are finding your way around the village, Mr. Wainwright. If there is anything you require, don't hesitate to ask my husband. And now we have made the acquaintance, you must dine with us soon."

He merely looked at her. Or rather, at the edge of her lace cap. The last thing he intended was to become part of the Hawcombe Prior social circuit. Such as it was. Darius already felt stifled by the woman's hints about her eldest daughter, subtle as a butcher's cleaver.

A soft sigh exhaled from his lips, but she didn't appear to notice. Fortunately she did not seem to expect any reply, either. Not that he would have given her any if she did.

He was shown into a warm study that overlooked the lane, and she introduced him to her husband, a sturdy fellow with surprisingly youthful blue eyes, made all the more startling in proximity to a full cloud of white hair. He leapt up from his chair as if he'd been caught doing something he shouldn't and then tried to shake hands while still holding a magnifying glass.

"Good Lord," he muttered. "Well, I was not expecting...oh, dear. What has she...what could be...?" His words petered out on a heavy sigh. He turned wary eyes to his wife who, apparently thinking Darius would not see, gave her husband an anxious, wobbling grimace and a shrug. When she caught their guest's eye she turned her expression into a hasty, rather silly smile and hurried out. Darius concluded that if the doctor and his wife were at all accustomed to social visitors, they must be of an unwelcome variety. It was not difficult to guess the reason.

"Dr. Penny, please forgive the intrusion." He glanced at the man's desk which was covered with dead, giant beetles. "I thought I should become acquainted with the principle residents of the village, since I've decided to remain at Midwitch Manor while I sort through my great-uncle's papers and belongings. Perhaps I should have sent you a note first."

The doctor's face relaxed a little. "I feared you had come on some other matter…but I am pleased to hear it is nothing of that sort for once." He laughed uneasily and glanced at the door through which his wife had departed.

Darius was about to speak of that "other matter," when the doctor hurriedly continued. "We don't often have visitors to the village, Mr. Wainwright. We must appear rusty, no doubt, in our manners." He set down his magnifying glass and put on his spectacles, peering at Darius through them with an intense curiosity. "So you are staying at Midwitch, eh? The manor must be in a state of some disrepair. On the last occasions when I called upon Mr. Phineas Hawke, I noticed the rapidity with which the house crumbled just as he did. A carved acorn atop the newel post came clean away in my hand as I left the place. Very sad to see it fall into such disrepair. I hear the place was very grand at one time."

"Yes. There is much work to be done, inside and out."

"Do sit down, sir. A glass of port?"

"No. Thank you." Darius lowered his seat to the edge of a chair. Feeling watched suddenly, he swiveled around and encountered a large stuffed owl observing him sternly from its perch atop a tall bookcase.

"It is pleasant indeed to see a new face about the village. Do you plan to stay long?"

"No," he replied sharply, turning again to face the doctor. "I do not care much for the country."

The other man looked hard at him for a moment, unblinking, just like his stuffed owl. "You are a man of business, I understand, and a bachelor."

"I am."

"It is unfortunate you do not mean to remain with us for long." Dr. Penny managed a cautious smile. "All the single young ladies of the village will be disappointed."

"No doubt they will recover. I can hardly be their first disappointment, and I doubt I'll be their last."

The doctor squinted, coughed, and cleared his throat loudly. "Yes. Well. If there is anything I might be able to do for you…although I don't suppose a gentleman such as yourself is ever in need of—"

"I believe you might be of some assistance to me, sir, in the disposal of an item I seem to have inherited with the property."

At this news the doctor sat up, eyes agleam. "Certainly. Phineas Hawke must have kept some books I could—"

"Is it possible, Dr. Penny, that you recently misplaced a pig?"

Surprise ruched and lifted the doctor's brow. "A pig?"

"I seem to have acquired one in my orchard, and I am informed his name is Sir Mortimer Grubbins. If he does belong to you, sir, I would happily return the fellow."

"But I have never kept pigs, Mr. Wainwright." His thick eyebrows ruffled gently together into one center knot.

"*Not* yours?" Apparently her thievery extended beyond fruit.

"May I ask why you thought the animal might belong to…me?" Even as he finished his sentence, the doctor's voice grew quieter and then his eyelids drifted downward in disheartened acceptance of the inevitable, like a man ascending the steps of the gallows. "Ah. Sir Mortimer, of course." His head moved slowly from side to side and a lengthy, tremulous exhale blew out over his plump lower lip. "I daresay I can find someone to take the fellow off your hands. I'm sorry you were inconvenienced."

"I should not like to put the burden upon you, Doctor. Since the pig is not yours, it is not your responsibility to dispose of it."

"Worry not, Mr. Wainwright." The man's gaze drifted to the window and out into the lane. "I am accustomed to burdens of this nature. You may safely leave the matter to me and concern yourself no more about it. I see you are a busy man and must have plenty to fret over."

Darius had not planned for such a hasty resolution. He'd expected her father to require more proof of her mischief and a full account of her crimes, for there was more to it than the hiding of a pig, of course. There was the matter of her climbing his wall to trespass in his orchard and steal fruit. But the doctor disposed of his daughter's misbehavior swiftly. No wonder she thought she could get away with so much.

Well, that was that, then. He could politely take his leave of her father and turn his back upon the entire incident. No one would ever know about that kiss or anything preceding it. Miss Justina Penny made it plain she had no intention of telling anyone. Her warning looks to him that afternoon were proof enough of her wishes regarding the unfortunate matter.

He could safely leave the place and never think of it again.

If not for the nagging whispers of his conscience.

Others might not know what he had done, but *he* would.

As for Justina Penny, if what he heard of her behavior was true—and he had witnessed regrettable samples of it with his own eyes now on several separate occasions—she required a stronger hand on her reins. A less preoccupied and, apparently, indulgent hand than her father's.

Darius tapped his fingers on his knee. "It is no trouble, sir. I'm sure I can manage the creature myself."

Dr. Penny looked askance. "*You?*"

The sound that followed that word out of the doctor's mouth was very nearly a guffaw. Or would have been, had the man not hastily raised a handkerchief to his face. "You foresee a difficulty, Doctor?"

"But surely, sir"—behind the round spectacles those bright blue eyes gleamed with wily amusement, just like his daughter's—"a fine gentleman like yourself has no time for—"

"I'm quite sure the keeping of a pig is not beyond me."

The doctor looked doubtful, a strand of ivory hair drifting to the shoulder of his coat. "I admire your gumption, sir. I have never known much success with beasts of the live variety." He gestured at the moths and butterflies displayed on his walls. "My preference is to study them when they are dead and cannot study *me* in return."

A curious admission from a man of medicine, Darius mused, making a hasty note not to fall ill while he remained in the wilderness.

"Wainwright," the doctor muttered. "*Wainwright.* Why is that name familiar to me? Have we met before, sir?"

"Not that we met, sir. But there was an incident once. In Bath."

"Bath?"

"When you were there, Dr. Penny. Last year. With your daughters."

The creases slowly unfolded from the other man's face. "Ah. Of course." He shook his head. "The waist-coat. Oh, dear."

"Yes. Quite." There was a great deal more than a stained waistcoat he might have brought to Dr. Penny's attention, but he made the swift and irreversible decision to handle those "other matters" himself.

❦

The young ladies of the Book Society had temporarily lost interest in the fate of the Miss Bennets of Longbourn, setting their reading choice aside to question instead a certain Miss Justina Penny of Hawcombe Prior and its surrounding environs.

"It was nothing. Entirely nothing," she exclaimed with another grand sigh as she retrieved her crumpet from the prongs of a toasting fork and quickly slathered it with butter. "You are all making far too much out of it. You especially, Cathy! You are usually so sensible, and I am the one generally accused of making mountains out of molehills."

"I knew you were keeping something to yourself. I knew it!" Catherine turned to the other girls for sup-port. "She's been so very odd of late. Secretive and unnaturally quiet."

"Well, what is he like?" demanded Diana Makepiece, now the only one of the five who had not yet seen the stranger.

"He has enormous ears," Justina assured her, knowing that Diana was very particular about ears and thinking this the best way to discourage her curiosity. The sooner he was dismissed from their conversation the better.

There followed an immediate chorus of protest from the others, however. "Oh Jussy, what a fib!"

"I did not think his ears very out of proportion," said Lucy. "But he *is* quite tall, and I'm sure a lot of him is on the…"—she faltered, her blue eyes growing misty—"larger side."

"He was on horseback, so how could you tell the man's height?"

"I can estimate! He must be close to seven feet."

Rebecca, less prone to exaggeration, allowed that he was "reasonably handsome." As a young lady known for a frequently blunt, critical tongue when it came to the opposite gender, this was a generous concession for her.

Only Catherine refused to give any opinion of his appearance. "I'm sure I didn't dare raise my eyes to the fellow," she said. "He was very forward in approaching us without a proper introduction, but I did not know what to look at when my sister spoke to him in that manner. What must he think of you, Jussy!"

She snorted. "It cannot be any worse than what he thought of me *before* I spoke. The man has such a great opinion of himself, and such a low one of other folk, that nothing I might have said could please him. I'm certain he must live in a constant state of discontent with the world around him. I wonder why he bothers to get out of bed at all. You all heard him admit he is too grand for the harvest dance and will not descend from his lofty heights just to please a few ladies."

Rebecca replied thoughtfully, "It is unfortunate that he did not smile. He might look less fearsome then and much more handsome."

"He never smiles, because he has very bad teeth," Justina blithely assured the others. "Many are misplaced. The spaces between the pegs that yet remain are so wide they could pick raisins from a Christmas Pudding through fence railings."

Perhaps this statement was a little extreme and not *necessarily* founded in fact, but really the man was insufferable and the sooner her friends realized it the better. There was no point encouraging any romantic daydreams about Mr. Wainwright, so she would save them the trouble and heartache, by putting them off as best she could.

"How you do fib, Jussy." Rebecca laughed. "There is nothing amiss with the man's teeth. You simply took an instant dislike to the fellow, as you so often do."

"Me? That is an amusing statement, Becky, coming from the girl who has been known to chase unwanted gentlemen off her doorstep with a loaded blunderbuss."

"That happened only once," Rebecca protested as the others laughed. "And it was a man who tried to sell me a miracle cure for freckles. I," she raised her chin grandly, "took offense."

Justina chuckled along with the others, glad to divert the discussion away from her and Wainwright. Besides, her dislike of that man was not instant, but she could hardly let her sister be reminded of Bath—a place that held no happy memories for either of them. Catherine had failed in her mission to find a husband there and, making matters worse, had suffered that dreadful rash. Even now, any time she felt a slight itch, Cathy worried the mysterious affliction was about to descend upon her again. It must be hard, thought Justina, to possess such beauty, for with it came not only great expectations, but the terrible responsibility of maintaining it.

How glad she was that such a burden would never be hers.

Looking around at her friends, she considered herself the least pretty of all. Diana was elegant and stunning with her juxtaposition of ivory skin, raven hair, and green eyes. Lucy had her baby-soft, wheat-gold hair and a face of doll-like innocence—even if it was deceptive, she mused. Then there was Rebecca with her lush, thick, wavy hair, all the shades of autumn, and that warm laughter which, even when her lips were silent, was ever-present in her wide hazel eyes. But Justina did not pity herself. As she told them all, many times, she would be content in the background, observing their romantic trials and tribulations from a safe distance.

"I rather think," said Rebecca, "that you are afraid, Jussy."

"Afraid of what?"

"That one day a gentleman might come along, sweep you out of your old boots, and make you fall in love with him. Then you might have to make an effort to be more ladylike and admit that you do believe in love and romance."

She glared at her crumpet. "A man to suit me does not exist." How could she tell them that her ideal of the perfect man was Captain Sherringham? Her friends—especially Rebecca, his sister—would tease her without mercy.

"But if you never marry you will die an old maid," said Lucy. "That is a terrible way to go."

"Nonsense. A terrible way to go would be dragged under carriage wheels or burned to a crisp by lightning or fallen on by a moonstruck cow or being poisoned by deadly nightshade in one's hot chocolate. *Old maid* is simply a title, Lucy. It is not a cause of death."

"But you will be alone and even more curmudgeonly than you are now."

She stared at Lucy, who had never before dared suggest she was in any way *curmudgeonly*. For a moment the sheer injustice stole her capacity for speech. But it soon returned. Head high, she declared, "I can think of nothing better. I shall grow warty and wizened, wear thick worsted stockings, and frighten all your children on All Hallow's Eve."

Diana exclaimed solemnly, "But it is every young lady's desire and duty to be well married. Otherwise you will remain a burden on your father and when he is gone, what will you do? Even a lady of only modest accomplishments and little beauty should try to find a husband."

"Indeed, I shan't be a burden on anyone," Justina exclaimed. "I'll live with the gypsies if I have to. Don't fret about plain, unaccomplished, curmudgeonly little me."

"Perhaps, one day, you will meet someone like Mr. Wickham," Lucy suggested, "and he will charm you."

"Out of her petticoats and her coin," added Rebecca with a wry grin.

"I have no coin," she snapped.

"It would be typical, of course, for Jussy to lose her heart to a villain," Diana stated. "She must always be contrary!"

And Catherine offered gently, "Those so determined never to fall in love are always those who fall hardest."

If Justina was not still chewing her crumpet she would have stuck out her tongue at all four ladies. But she contented herself with a weary flutter of eyelashes. Let them all think what they would.

There was one way to win out over the other ladies' teasing, of course. "I would much rather be a rich man's mistress than a wife," she exclaimed, sighing extravagantly.

"Jussy!"

She looked at her sister. "What's the matter now? A mistress has all the fun and none of the responsibility."

"That is a wicked thing to say. And Becky, stop laughing! You're only encouraging her."

"Oh, I forgot," Justina rolled her eyes, "I'm not supposed to know anything about it. But you all know I speak the truth. A wife is the dutiful acquisition, the one who bears babies, manages the house, frets over the accounts and woodworm in the rafters. What does a mistress do? Puts up with the man for a few hours here and there, and has no need really to ever get out of bed. If it were me, I would lounge about all day in a bath filled with asses' milk and have hot chocolate brought to me on a silver tray."

While the other young ladies were deeply engaged in dissecting the horror of her terrible suggestion, Justina victoriously swiped the last of the crumpets and speared it on her toasting fork.

Thirteen

WHEN THE GIRLS RETURNED HOME, THEIR MOTHER WAS waiting to regale them with the story of Mr. Wainwright's visit. Although there was not much to tell, she managed to stretch the facts by repetition, peppered with a lot of her own suppositions regarding the event, and by the time they sat down to dinner it was still the subject that dominated any other.

"I could have been knocked down by the tickle of a feather duster when I saw him standing there on our doorstep. So very handsome." She reached over to pat her eldest daughter's hand, apprehending it in the motion of reaching for the tureen of potatoes. "So elegant and refined. With shoulders surely the width of our door-frame and enough height to necessitate bending his head just to enter the house. What a delight for us all to have his company."

Their father looked up from carving the beef. "I doubt we shall enjoy much of that delight, my dear. Or the sight of his remarkably wide shoulders. Except from behind and at some rapidly expanding distance."

"Why, pray tell?" she demanded.

Justina, aware of Catherine glaring at her across the table, fixed her attention to her own plate.

"He must be accustomed to much grander company than ours, my dear, and yet I sense he is not the sort to enjoy society in general."

"How can you conclude that much already? He was barely a quarter of an hour in your library."

"His words may be few, but they are succinct."

"Well," their mother muttered crossly, banging her glass down as if it were a judge's gavel, "we do have *two* parlors and you set the broken arm of Lady Brockhampton's nephew in Manderson. And he once had his eye on our Catherine."

"Mama, she was fifteen," Justina interrupted. "And he was fifty if he was a day."

"So? Many a time has an older gentleman married much younger, particularly when he is a widower without children. Such admiration from a distinguished gentleman of mature years is most gratifying. That he should have noticed our Catherine was nothing to sniff at, and you, my girl," she pointed with her fork, "would be lucky indeed to win similar notice. But, of course, you have not that same sweet temperament a man requires in his wife and the mother of his children."

Justina looked at her sister. "How nice for you, Cathy, to be bought as mild-mannered breeding stock, but at least he wouldn't have troubled you long since he had one foot in the grave already. Feed him some of Clara's bread pudding and you could finish the job nicely."

Their mother addressed her husband again in a louder tone, increased agitation visible in vibrations of the lace around her cap. "I hope you told Mr. Wainwright that you have served the medical needs of every owner and leaseholder of Lark Hollow estate for two and twenty years, including Admiral Vyne, a war hero. I'm sure we are good enough company for a man who made his fortune in trade."

"You might think so, my dear," said their father, "but as you are entitled to your opinion, Mr. Wainwright is entitled to his. He, like our youngest daughter, seems to have plenty of them. A slice of beef, Jussy?"

She lifted her plate.

"It is not ham, of course," he added. "I know you have no liking for ham these days."

Justina caught his eye and then he quickly looked down again, maneuvering the slice of roast beef carefully onto her plate.

"It seems Mr. Wainwright has no liking for ham either," he muttered. "Another thing the two of you have in common, Jussy. Pork."

"Goodness gracious. Is that all you could find to talk to him about?" their mother exclaimed. "*Pork?*"

"I see nothing amiss with that for conversation. One must talk of something, and it was Mr. Wainwright who raised the subject in the first place. Porcine flesh appears to have been much on his mind." He returned to his carving, and Justina felt panic prick like pins and needles in her veins.

"Why on earth would you talk to him of pork?" their mother cried, excessively upset, as she often was, by her husband's eccentricities and lack of social graces.

Sadly for his wife, he took delight in all the same things that so distressed her. "'Tis another of life's mysteries, my dear. Since he is such a fine gentleman from

Town I thought it might be the fashionable subject and so I let him talk of it. Heaven knows he did not have much else to say."

"Pork indeed!"

"Quite. I would suggest you read up on the matter, my dear, in case he returns."

But Mrs. Penny preferred to speculate on a topic far more pleasing to her than pork. "He must have seen Catherine about the village, determined who she was, and came here to begin the acquaintance. It is not unexpected. I asked him if he had seen her about, and he was very reluctant to say so, as only a gentleman smitten would be."

"Are three days of distant sightings enough to produce such an effect, my dear? I did detect Mr. Wainwright to be struggling in something quite deep, but I did not take it to be a state of smit."

"He is a man with a determined aura, and I daresay he makes up his mind with alacrity. Besides, many a courtship has begun thus with love at first sight." She looked proudly at her eldest daughter. "I suppose he wanted to be sure your father would introduce you at the harvest dance, Catherine, and that's why he came."

It was on the tip of Justina's tongue to exclaim that the man did not plan to attend the dance, but she remembered, in the knick of time, that she had nothing to say on the matter and knew naught about the man. So she contented herself by stabbing a fork into her potato.

As it turned out, her interruption was not required in any case. Dr. Penny poured a moat of gravy on his plate while somberly assuring his wife, "I asked the man myself, and he has no plans to attend the harvest dance."

"Of course he will attend. He must. It will be very strange if he does not."

"I rather think, madam, that Mr. Wainwright would prefer to be thought *strange* than to put himself in the way of dancing and general merriment. He is a man of business, as he took great pains to remind me, not a gentleman of leisure."

Although she said no more on the subject then, their mother had a quietly satisfied look on her face for the remainder of dinner. Justina suspected she was already plotting a spring wedding for Catherine and Mr. Wainwright.

For her part, Cathy did nothing to discourage their mother. If anything, her silent blushes seemed only to reinforce the likelihood of a soon-to-be blooming romance. Justina observed her sister worriedly, fearing that Catherine would lose her heart quickly and rashly to a marble-hearted man unworthy of her affections. A man who went around insulting and then kissing other women without so much as a "by your leave."

Justina thrust her fork into the boiled potato again with great energy as she thought of how the Wainwright person had stared at Cathy in the street that day and although his face hardly moved, he must have felt admiration. Why would he not? The man had two functioning eyes in his head. He could hardly fail to compare Cathy's beauty to *her* looks—which he had already disparaged.

As for Cathy—she pondered her shortage of beaus as if it was entirely her own fault, lying awake at night in their bed, twisting her braid around her fingers, and sighing heavily like a set of well-primed organ bellows. Now here came a man at last, and she would think it her duty to seize him.

Having stabbed her boiled potato into submission, Justina could not summon her appetite at all now.

"Pass the horseradish, Jussy," said her father softly, breaking into her thoughts. As she reached for the little china dish, he added, "I see you are not hungry."

"You should not have eaten so many crumpets at Diana's house," said her sister.

"Jussy's eyes are always bigger than her belly, as they say." Their father chuckled. "One day she will take too much onto her plate and that will be the end of her adventures." He gave her a sly wink. "Perhaps that day is already upon us, eh, Jussy?"

Later he called her into his library, and although she prepared herself for yet another punishment, Justina was shocked to discover that her father thought the matter settled.

"Mr. Wainwright has taken upon himself the burden of keeping Sir Mortimer Grubbins," he explained calmly.

"What did he tell you, Papa?" She folded her arms. "It was all lies, to be sure."

"Really? He did not strike me as the sort to employ falsehoods. Indeed he was brutally honest and to the point, Jussy. A refreshing change in a young man, I thought." Her father smiled benignly.

"Why would he keep a pig? He knows nothing about pigs!"

"That is a question only Mr. Wainwright can answer. Why do you not go and ask him yourself?"

"Me? Go there alone? It would not be proper."

He jerked back in his chair. "I am glad to hear you know the proprieties. I thought you did not care for them, as we seldom see examples to prove that you do."

Justina paced before her father's hob grate, but it was not a very large space and so the dramatic effect of her protest was severely curbed.

"And when you go there, Jussy, if I were you I'd find a way to apologize to the gentleman for putting him out. You may not care for his approbation, but it will not soften your mama's mood with any of us should she discover you've put him in a sour temper. After all," he sighed, "Mr. Wainwright will never look at your sister with a favorable eye if his impression of the family is not improved. But it seems we must all hope he marries Cathy. Your mama clearly has her heart set upon it."

His life, of course, was very much easier when their mama was happy and not in one of her fretful moods. It was so for all of them.

❧

The creature eyed Darius as he approached cautiously, holding the bucket of scraps. It greeted him with a deep grunt, spiraled tail twitching happily. Although he had, with Farmer Rooke's assistance, provided a makeshift pen in one corner of the orchard, the pig found its own way in and out of the enclosure with very little trouble. Now it stood proudly on the outside of the fencing, watching Darius and his bucket with the benevolent amusement of an indulgent uncle.

"Here…pig." He tipped the bucket over the fence and the contents cascaded into a small trough. "Food. Eat…pig." He refused to call the creature by its name. Why people thought it necessary to anthropomorphize he had no earthly idea. It was a pig. A pig, therefore, he would call it.

But the animal looked at him expectantly and grunted. Again Darius pointed at the trough within the enclosure. "Eat, pig."

Four muddy trotters carried the beast toward Darius with an almost menacing stride, backing him to the fence. Man and pig eyed each other. That large, dewy snout lifted and twitched.

He felt as if he were back in school and the Latin master stood over him, tapping a cane to his palm and waiting for the recital of a conjugated verb.

Finally, since there was no one present to witness the concession, Darius cleared his throat and muttered, "Sir Mortimer, please do eat."

With another grunt, Sir Mortimer Grubbins trotted amiably back inside his pen through the hole he'd made, and inspected the offering with another grunt. Snouting through the trough, he selected the tastiest morsel—a cabbage leaf—and proceeded to chew greedily, still watching his new caretaker with those cleverly complacent eyes.

"Bon appetit," Darius added, bemused and gaining considerable respect for his charge.

The sudden clanging of the bell at the gate drew his attention away from the pig, and he made his way around the trees to find two figures peering through the bars, one of them in a scarlet hooded cloak. Despite that bright flare of color, his gaze went immediately to the second figure in her drab gray coat with the frog clasps across the bosom and the wilted-looking bonnet that someone had possibly retrieved recently from a well, a cider press, or the jaws of a goat. Perhaps all three. He'd never seen a woman quite so dilapidated, and he could only assume that was the reason why his eyes sought her out. He immediately thought of going quickly inside for his coat. Visitors this early were unexpected, and he was not dressed to receive them. It was too late, however. They'd seen him.

Besides, she had scornfully referred to him as a dandified gent before. She could not do so today. Not that he cared what she thought, of course.

With the empty bucket dangling from one hand, he lifted the gate latch. "Miss Penny, do come in. I wondered when you would grace Midwitch with your presence again."

Scowling, she walked through the open gate. Her gaze traversed the length of his exposed forearm for he had rolled up his shirtsleeves rather than risk getting them dirty while dealing with the pig. "This is Miss Lucy Bridges," she muttered sullenly. "Sir Mortimer Grubbins is really her pet."

The girl in the scarlet cloak couldn't seem to raise her eyelashes, but she bobbed a curtsy and moved her lips. He thought she might have whispered something, but he couldn't be sure. The gate clanged shut, and he gestured for them to follow him through the orchard.

The chatterbox began at once. "We will take the pig off your hands, sir, as soon as—"

"That is not necessary, Miss Penny."

They both stopped and looked at him, the little one in the red stumbling into her friend, behind whom she seemed intent on hiding herself.

"I have decided to maintain the animal myself. I paid Farmer Rooke this morning, so he is made whole again. Sir Mortimer now belongs to me."

"Oh," said Miss Lucy Bridges.

"You may visit him, madam. Whenever you wish."

"Oh," the girl whimpered again, her eyes concentrating on the ground between them. He wondered if she had breathing problems, for there was a noticeable amount of inflating and deflating going on beneath her cloak.

"And when you sell the house, what then?"

Darius turned to the impertinent questioner. "I'll worry about that when the time comes, Miss Penny. Since he is now *my* pig. My property."

Her glare, had it formed a physical blade, could have cleaved him in two. So he ignored her and returned his attention to Lucy Bridges, whose shyness made his own reserve seem like the height of outgoing affability. He led her through the trees to where Sir Mortimer was busy with his trough. "As you see, I am tending to the animal. He is quite safe in my hands."

"Oh...oh, yes," Lucy mumbled, reaching over the fence to pet the pig. "Thank you, Mr. Wainwright, sir. It is...it is very good of you, indeed."

He nodded sharply, pleased to find that not everyone in Hawcombe Prior lacked basic manners.

The other woman pushed her way around him to examine the pig for herself. Finally satisfied the animal was cared for, she swung around to face him again.

"Sir Mortimer Grubbins," she said firmly, "is not to be slaughtered."

"Since he now belongs to me, I believe that decision is mine to make."

She pursed her lips, and Darius was betaken by the sudden distressing thought of kissing them again, even with her friend present. He took a step back, placing his free hand on the fence. "Now that I have assumed the burden of caring for the pig, you can do something in return for me."

When her lashes flickered uncertainly, he imagined their soft caress fluttering against his cheek.

"My great-uncle left a vast number of papers and ledgers in disarray," he continued, keeping his voice stern. "I need an extra pair of eyes and hands to help sort through them or I'll be here for months."

She grimaced. "Goodness, we can't have that, can we? The sooner you're gone the better."

He chose to ignore the rude remark. He knew, of course, why she wanted him gone from Hawcombe Prior. As long as he stayed she would be reminded of certain misadventures she evidently tried now to forget.

"It seems my great-uncle seldom disposed of any-thing. Even the most insignificant scrap"—he let his gaze wander down to her feet and then back up to her bonnet—"was kept. I must put everything in order before I leave."

She peered up at him, her large eyes doubtful.

"I have already sought your father's permission to employ you for the task. It is quite proper."

He could almost see his face reflected there in her pupils as they widened. Was she surprised or annoyed? Or simply curious? Was she drawn to looking at him, as he was to looking at her? He had never felt so confused in his life as he was by Miss Justina Penny. At his age it was a remarkable development and not at all cheering. He'd survived eleven years without complications of this sort, and he'd really expected to continue in the same way. Sensibly. Decently. Calmly. Animal husbandry and wayward women had not been part of his plan.

Now, here he was taking ownership of a pig. And seeking methods to keep Miss Justina in his view.

"Your father agreed that, since you have little else to occupy your time, this might keep you out of trouble," he added.

Before she could say anything her little friend chirped, "I would be happy to help too, sir." She thrust back the hood of her cap and let her yellow hair shimmer in the dappled shade. "It is the least I can do now that you are taking such good care of Sir Mortimer."

Her shyness had quickly been set aside, and in its place was a heavy-breathing, saucer-eyed, rosy-cheeked miss. Even Justina looked at her quizzically.

Darius had not planned to invite both young ladies inside his house, but there seemed nothing he could do now to prevent it. They came together apparently and could not be separated.

On second thought, perhaps it was just as well. He wouldn't want Miss Penny to try taking advantage of him again.

Fourteen

She realized this was her punishment for trespassing and leaving Sir Mortimer Grubbins in his
orchard. Together her father and Mr. Wainwright had
cooked up this scheme. But she was not unwilling to
enter that old house and pry around inside it. Justina was
certain Midwitch Manor held many dark secrets, and she
was not afraid of ghosts. In fact she felt her excitement
mounting when she considered all those mysterious
rolled up scrolls she was likely to find hidden among the
old miser's things. Really, it was hardly a punishment at
all, but Mr. Wainwright could not know that.

He led them into a large study overlooking the
orchard. It was a gloomy chamber, all dark wood and
stagnant air. Piles of books and stacks of yellowed paper
covered almost every surface, in some places slithering to
the worn carpet or taller than Justina and leaning precariously as if the slightest draft would be their undoing.

"Where on earth does one start?" muttered Lucy.

He walked around his desk, and Justina tried not to
look at his exposed forearms. It was very improper of
him to wear rolled up shirtsleeves in their presence. She

feared not for herself, of course. Good Lord, no. After all, she'd seen him without a stitch of clothing and somehow came out of it unscathed. But the sight of those surprisingly brawny limbs might be the cause of Lucy's sudden eagerness to enter a house she had previously believed was haunted. Certainly something must account for her friend's tremulous smiles and breathy sighs.

Poor child, thought Justina dourly. Lucy still had much to learn about men and life.

"These papers can be sorted into three categories," he explained. "Items of business, household matters, and then personal documents."

"Is there something in particular that you look for among your great-uncle's papers?" Justina asked.

His eyes danced over her with a tentative amusement. "Perhaps."

Was that a twinkle trying to hide from her? "But you are not inclined to tell us what it is," she pressed, her curiosity captured.

"No. I am not. At present."

"Then how will we know when we find it?"

"We'll know it."

This punishment began to sound more interesting.

Justina strode up to his desk, and he immediately backed around it, putting more distance between them and in the process stumbling against the corner. When he winced in pain and his eyelids lowered to half-mast, her attention was caught by the surprising length of his eyelashes. It was not the first time she'd noticed their peculiar elegance, but today she was more at liberty to study them.

"Is it another will?" she demanded. "A diary full of

all his wicked confessions? Is it a pile of love letters from a sweetheart who abandoned him to his lonely, miserly life? Or is it a map to buried gold?"

"Perhaps," he muttered. "Better get looking, had you not?"

Aha! A game of sorts.

"It should not take too long to go through all these if you come every day for an hour," he added, stern again. "One pile will be for those items that can be burned. One will be for those of more importance. If you are uncertain, please ask me first."

"Will there be refreshments provided for our labors?" People seldom wanted her company and looked for other ways of punishment for her transgressions—methods that generally put her as far away from them as possible. She would have expected the same from him.

He scratched his dark head. "I'm sure Mrs. Birch can provide some tea."

She followed his gaze to Lucy, who stared at Mr. Wainwright with dewy-eyed admiration. Her scarlet cloak had somehow, within the last few moments, become unhooked, and since she wore no chemisette under her bodice today, Lucy's very full bosom overflowed with every deep inhale. Clearly the Wainwright person noted it too, for he fumbled with a pile of books on his desk, dropping one to the dusty carpet.

When Lucy sneezed she almost came completely out of her dress.

"What if we can't come every day?" Justina snapped.

His eyes flashed back to her face. "You will make the time, Miss Penny. If you want to save Sir Mortimer Grubbins."

Grimly, she nodded. "Blackmail. What else might I expect?"

He merely looked at her, his lips pressed tight, grinding his jaw again. The brief hint of playfulness was gone.

Justina ran a gloved fingertip along the edge of his desk and made a trail through the dust. "Old Phineas Hawke once told me there was treasure in this house," she said. "Do you think it's true?"

His eyes narrowed sharply. "When did he tell you that?"

"As a little girl I used to come over his wall to climb the orchard trees and sit among the blossoms. I liked to pretend I was an angel in the clouds."

"An angel?" His lips twitched in a skeptical smirk.

"An angel of vengeance," she replied proudly. "I wrought lightning down upon those who required punishment."

Lucy chirped up suddenly. "She means, sir, that she used her catapult to fire Brussels sprouts at people from the trees. Jussy could see the lane over the wall, but those who passed by couldn't see her for she was hidden in all the blossoms."

Justina glared at her friend. Trust Lucy to lose that shyness in time to squeal about her old childhood crimes.

"In any case," she continued, "old Hawke caught me there once in the blossoms. Before he had me chased out, he told me there was treasure in his house. Of course, he was senile. He might as well have said there was an elephant in his attic and mice in his drawers."

Wainwright was looking at her in an odd way again. If he wore a wig, she would think it must be too tight.

"You should search every corner of the house," she added, "just to be sure. There must be many nooks and crannies, perfect for hiding treasure."

140   JAYNE FRESINA

"Yes, well...you may start with those." He thrust a finger at the leaning pile close to her elbow. "The sooner you begin, the sooner you'll be done, won't you?"

She might have known he didn't believe in treasure, she thought glumly. The man clearly had no imagination.

❧

It did not take her long to settle into the task. She was soon seated and sorting through a large stack of papers. He had hoped the job at hand would keep her from chattering while he concentrated on mending one of the household clocks. He was mistaken.

"I do hope your business is going well," she said suddenly.

Darius was still trying to grow accustomed to her proximity on the other side of the desk, but even her breathing pattern was distracting and her soft scent— possibly lavender soap—was such a new addition to the usual mustiness of the room that he found it almost spell-like in its power. "My business?"

"The one that keeps you here, when you would much rather be anywhere else."

"Yes, Miss Penny. It...is developing"—he glanced over at Miss Lucy Bridges, who sat in the light of the tall window and continually threw him shy little smiles, when she wasn't engulfed in a storm of sneezes—"well enough."

When he looked again at Justina, he caught her eyeing the little brass cogwheels spread over his blotter. "Wouldn't it be quicker if you helped us with the papers, Mr. Wainwright?"

He hesitated, unable to find an immediate reply.

"Or is the keeping of perfect time more important to you than how it is spent?"

He sniffed. "One task is just as important as the other. I doubt you know anything about clockwork mechanisms, however."

"No." She smirked down at the papers in her hand. "I'm never on time for anything. The worst person in the world when it comes to being punctual."

"You sound proud of the fact, Miss Penny."

"One has to be proud of something, and there is so little about me that might ever come to any good. I may as well boast of my inabilities since they are plentiful."

Darius scowled, shifted in his chair, and rubbed his chamois cloth with increased velocity over one of the cogs. He could never be sure whether she spoke in jest or whether she truly meant what she said. It was most troubling that the woman not only operated in an unpredictable manner, but seemed to thrive upon it.

"Will no family be joining you here, Mr. Wainwright?" she asked.

"No."

"They are all in London?"

"Yes."

"Do you have a large family?"

"No." He didn't care to explain all that.

She exhaled another sigh, as if she was out of breath pushing a heavy wheelbarrow uphill. He tried to look away, but found his eyes drawn to her repeatedly, quite unable to stop their thorough and inquisitive examination of her face. Not knowing what she might do next was a dreadful state to be in. Also strangely alluring. He thought he might quite like to peer inside her mind and study its curious workings. See how all her intriguingly unusual parts fitted together. Yet he could not ask her questions. He did not know where to begin.

Miss Penny, on the other hand, had no such qualm when it came to her own curiosity. "What is your business? Do you travel a great deal? Why did you never come to visit old Hawke?" The questions tumbled out of her, fired speedily by the trebuchet of her tongue and yet without any particular aim, as far as he could tell. Darius was certain she merely asked to fill the silence. Something that, in his opinion, never needed filling.

But he did his best to provide answers.

"My shipping business exports certain items made here, and we also import various provisions…rugs, fabrics, tea, coffee, rum—"

"And chocolate?" Her eyes widened with a new burst of interest.

"Yes." He paused. "You like hot chocolate, Miss Penny?"

"Is grass green?" She shook her head, huffing. "For pity's sake, who doesn't like hot chocolate?"

Relieved to find he'd had a hand in something for which she might be grateful, Darius took a breath and forged ahead. "So yes, I have traveled extensively."

She stared for a moment and then looked down at the papers again.

"As to your other question, I visited my great-uncle when I was seventeen. Apparently he saw enough of me then, and I was not invited back."

"But now he has left you his house."

"Yes."

"Why?"

"I….suppose I was the only male relative left."

"That's a very dull reason." She sighed.

"You would prefer another?"

"It could be something mysterious and ghoulish."

He was amused. "As in one of those novels that Mrs. Birch tells me the young ladies of the Book Society devour, to their detriment."

Up went her prim nose. "I would not expect you to understand, since you have no imagination and are the most boring man that ever breathed."

After a pause while they both got on with their work and Darius sought some way to prove he was interesting, he finally managed, "Perhaps you would like a tour of the gallery. There are some fine land-scapes and portraits—"

"Oh, I've seen them already," she interrupted, punctuating her remark with a small, ungracious yawn.

"I haven't," her friend meekly piped up from the window seat.

Darius frowned at the woman across his desk. "You've seen them? When?"

"A few years ago. We had a scavenger hunt." She chuckled, her gaze skimming the paper in her hand. "One of the items to be retrieved was Phineas Hawke's pipe. I was the only member of the Book Society that returned with all the items on the list, including the pipe, so I won." She beamed proudly. "No one else dared come here. They all think the house is haunted, but I was not afraid. There's nothing wrong with this house that a little cleaning and painting wouldn't cure. And a little love, of course." She looked around the dark walls of the room. "This house has been neglected, left unloved for too long. It needs cherishing. It needs a family in it. Children running up and down the corridors and laughing."

He sniffed. "There are few things I can think of that would be more annoying than ill-behaved children scuffing and nicking these floors and the walls with their careless games."

She shook her head just enough to disturb a curl by her cheek. "Of course. How foolish of me. Children should be seen and not heard. Probably not even seen, as far as you're concerned."

"Badly behaved children, certainly."

Exhaling a small snort of amusement, she replied, "I cannot imagine you as a child. Were you born an old man?"

Darius polished his cog wheel even harder. "May I ask how you gained admittance to the house when you stole my great-uncle's pipe?" He paused. "It seems you have a knack, Miss Penny, for entering places where you are not invited."

"I told Mrs. Birch that my father had sent me to deliver a bottle of elixir for old Hawke."

"So you took your time exploring his house while you were here under false pretenses."

"When one is bound to be in trouble anyway, one may as well make the most of it, don't you think?"

Abruptly he thought of her flying through the air and landing on him as he lay in bed trying to sleep. It was more than a year ago, but he still vividly recalled the sensation of her naked, nubile body tackling his with only a quilt between them. His fingertips accidentally brushing her silk garters as he tried to save himself from the assault.

"Mr. Wainwright?"

"Hmm?" He grabbed the clock face to adjust the hands. His tongue felt very thick suddenly, and he feared it would stumble if he forced a reply.

"When one is bound to be in trouble anyway, one may as well make the most of it, don't you think?" she repeated.

"No."

Her eyes flashed upward. "Have you never done anything wicked and forbidden, Mr. Wainwright?"

"No."

"Are you sure?" She licked her lips and fluttered her lashes as artfully as a society miss would wield her fan. He could not be sure it was deliberate, but a flaming arrow of desire shot through him nevertheless. "There must be at least *one* thing."

Darius felt the minute hand slip from his fingers to the carpet. When he bent out of his chair to recover it, he banged his head on the edge of the desk. The resulting cacophony of seemingly uncontainable guffaws proved that Miss Penny found this hilarious.

❧

When they left the house that day, Lucy's step was decidedly jaunty, and she could not stop talking of Darius Wainwright. How he looked, how he spoke, how he walked. Even how he breathed and paused between words—a habit she concluded meant that he considered every word with great care and wisdom. She plainly saw him now as her pet pig's savior, despite the fact that Sir Mortimer really owed his survival to Justina's resourcefulness.

At the Book Society meeting that afternoon, Lucy still had not changed her choice of subject.

"I thought we were here to discuss *Pride and Prejudice*," Justina remarked at one point, having heard Lucy's description of Wainwright's very plain waistcoat for what felt like the fifty-first time. "Might I remind you, Lucy, that you were violently in love with Mr. Darcy this time last week," she drawled acerbically. "How quickly he is thrown aside, poor fellow."

"But this gentleman is not fictional, and he is right here in our midst," Lucy replied with a lusty sigh. "He is…" she said, lowering her voice to a whisper, "the embodiment of Mr. Darcy."

Clearly Lucy was about to fall victim to another bout of Maiden's Palsy, if she had not already. Someone ought to give that girl an ice bath.

"Mr. Wainwright is certainly proud and haughty," said Rebecca. "Very like Mr. Darcy."

"But Mr. Darcy only appears haughty because he is reserved," Catherine offered timidly. "Elizabeth Bennet is quick to judge him after his insult at the dance in the beginning of the book. Now she is in Kent with the Collinses, she has begun to see him in a different light. I am quite sure we will soon learn that she has been misled, not only by her own impressions but by Mr. Wickham's tale of mistreatment at Darcy's hands."

"I still prefer Mr. Wickham," snapped Justina. "He is ten times more fun than that old windbag Darcy." With a grieved sigh she glanced out of the parlor window and watched speckles of new rain dash against the small panes. So what if he imported the marvelous treat that was chocolate. It was no reason to change her first impression, and she certainly would not tell the others for fear it might weigh too heavily in his favor.

The conversation did not linger long on the book today. With the harvest dance looming ever closer, this was the topic that distracted the ladies most often, and Mr. Darius Wainwright came a close second.

"Although he did appear at first to be an arrogant gentleman, I'm sure he has finer qualities," said Cathy.

"Yes," Rebecca laughed, "and they're all in the bank."

But Cathy continued to defend the man in her quiet, steady voice, seeking to find good in him, as she did in anyone. Now she had Lucy on her side too and Rebecca merely found his quirks entertaining. Diana did not feel as if she could speculate on the fellow since she was an engaged woman, a fact of which she reminded them, in case they might have forgotten.

Since Justina took no pleasure in discussing Wainwright or Diana's wretchedly uninteresting fiancé, no one heard another word out of her. She would take a leaf out of Elizabeth Bennet's book, she decided, and save her breath to cool her porridge.

Fifteen

It was surprisingly sunny this morning, as if the summer suddenly returned for an encore. The Book Society has been out collecting donations for a new roof on Dockley's Barn, so the Priory Players can perform at Christmas without fear of being rained, hailed, and snowed upon.

Lucy insisted we ask Mr. W for a donation. I told everyone he was a lost cause, but as usual my warnings were rebuffed. We caught him at his gate as he returned from a ride. Although Becky boldly promised him a front row seat at the next performance, he was his usual amiable self and said he could imagine "nothing more heinous to sit through than a performance of amateur dramatics." And it took him forever and a day to get that sentence out. I really think he begrudges the air it takes to form words in our presence. I'm sure he has far more important people with whom to share his wisdom.

I made some attempt today to mend my best frock. I was also lured by Lucy into trying burnt cork for darkening my eyebrows. I cannot imagine why, but I suppose I was at loose ends. When one is reduced to fussing with one's eyebrows, it must signal the very end of all hope.

I feel as if we are all changing and everything is adrift. Like *the weathercock on Dockley's barn, things are pointing the wrong way…*

J.P. September 8th, 1815 A.D.

She came every day and stayed for the full hour. The housekeeper warned him that he welcomed trouble by letting them inside the house.

"I can assure you, Mrs. Birch, I am well capable of handling two young women at once." When she looked skeptical, her broad face clenched like a fist, he continued hastily, "They are here to do a job for me, and that should keep them occupied."

"Well, they'd better not get under my feet."

He might have hired a clerk or two from the solicitor's office in Manderson to help sort through his great-uncle's things, but Miss Justina Penny was a more interesting companion for that hour every day. Her father had vowed she was a fast reader with a smart mind, if she applied herself to a project and did not let her imagination take over. Darius decided he would see for himself how clever she was. Many an eager father had sought to recommend their daughters to him in the past and he had long since ceased to believe a word he was promised.

He saw her in the village several times, waiting impatiently for the post's arrival, and he wondered what had her on tenterhooks. The latest edition of a lady's magazine perhaps, he mused. But no. It seemed doubtful. She didn't appear very troubled by fashion. He'd seen his young niece poring over cut-out scraps with illustrations of new gowns and hairstyles to try out—although she always hastily shut them inside her copy of Fordyce's

Sermons whenever he drew near. He'd witnessed his stepsister's peevish discontent if she caught another woman wearing a similar bonnet and looking better in it. Fashion, he'd concluded, was tremendously important to the females he knew.

Justina Penny, however, often looked as if she'd dressed in the dark and at the last minute before exiting her house. He would have thought this was simply a protest for his benefit, but she dressed that way even when she was not coming to Midwitch.

Soon her conversation—that insistence on chattering away to him across his desk, however hard he scowled to discourage her—kept Darius too busy to criticize her attire.

In the back of his mind he heard his great-uncle promising, *"There's treasure on this property. Treasure hidden. What do you think of that, eh?"* It could be some-where amongst all these documents. The house held an eerie, watchful essence that hinted at secrets. The dark, paneled walls might almost be whispering at night when he lay in Phineas's old four-poster bed and tried to find sleep. When the sun went down, the creaks and groans multiplied, as if the house was also restless, waiting, impatient, unable to close its eyes and fall into pleasant dreams because of business unfinished.

There remained the curious fact that Phineas had told Justina Penny the same thing about hidden treasure. Whatever the old man's reasons for telling her, Darius guessed this could be why she came there so often to trespass over the years. She might pretend not to believe in it, but she couldn't help herself from wondering.

So they did have something in common, after all.

Whenever he set before her a new box of papers to delve into, she could not hide her excitement.

"If there is treasure and I find it," she said to him once, her eyes gleaming with little stars, "I shall expect a fair share of the bounty."

"We'll see, Miss Penny."

"Don't think to cheat me out of it, after I've been here every day, put to work like your personal slave."

"I sincerely doubt a slave would be tolerated if she talked to her master they way you talk to me," he muttered, bemused.

"People shouldn't be allowed to keep slaves anyway. It's wrong."

"I agree."

She looked up in surprise, pausing her search through a bundle of papers. "You do?"

"I do. Human beings are not commodities." There, take that, Miss Quarrelsome, he thought, satisfied by her expression—the way her lips hung open, thwarted before they could begin another argument.

He realized he was hitching forward in his chair, as if he prepared to reach across the width of his desk and touch that dark curl that bounced by her cheek. A seal stamp fell to the carpet.

She returned her gaze to the contents of the box and resumed her rummaging. Having destroyed any chance he had of concentrating on his own work, she then began to hum, tapping her feet merrily to the rhythm.

As he pieced his great-uncle's clocks back together, Darius found his mind wandering over Miss Justina Penny's wayward cogs and considering the boisterous clatter of her little hammers as they chimed out various impertinent remarks. It was disconcerting, to say the least, that he spent so much of his time considering her playful mechanism and how it ticked.

There had not been many interesting women in his life, and only one had ever found her way into his heart. At nineteen Darius had enjoyed the company of a pretty, lively, amorous young woman, to whom he formed a deep and tender attachment. A mistake, of course. When she ran off with another—and the less said about *him* the better— the wound torn out of him was considerable and slow to heal. Perhaps had Darius not been such an introverted, insecure young man, it might not have had the dire effect it did, but after that he turned in upon himself even more than before, deciding it was safest to avoid entanglements of that nature. Time passed and he became consumed with work, having no time for pleasure in any case.

Over the last decade, a few brief encounters with women of easy virtue had kept his parts in working order. That, he thought, was sufficient. Occasionally his stepsister organized uncomfortable social events in an attempt to thrust her various friends at him as marriage material, but he did his best to avoid them.

Now he had met a woman he felt no urge to avoid. Not only that, but he went to some lengths to keep her in his company.

One day Justina brought him a small lavender pouch she claimed to have sewn with her own fingers. Later inspection of the large, clumsy stitches would suggest she told the truth.

"Keep this under your bed pillow," she said, pushing it into his hands. "The scent of the dried buds inside will help you sleep. You'll feel much improved."

For a moment he was quite at a loss for anything to reply. The little pillow was warm from her hand and some of the sweet scent was released as she passed it to him.

"It does work," she assured him, wide-eyed and earnest, as if she thought his silence was skepticism.

"I'm sure it does," he replied finally, following the two girls up the steps and into his house. "Might I ask how you knew deep sleep eluded me, Miss Penny?"

While her friend walked into the study, she spun around to face him. "Because you look tired and fretful and agitated. Like a babe that has missed his nap."

He tried to frown, but could not make the necessary muscles work. Ten minutes ago it would have been easy, but now she was there again—the irritating woman—and he did not even mind the gray skies.

"Except for one noticeable difference, of course," she added, stepping closer. "A very important difference between a babe and a grown man."

Darius waited, the little pillow crushed tight in his hand.

She whispered, "You have more hair, Mr. Wainwright." Her saucy arrow having pierced its mark, she turned away, but he caught her wrist in his free hand and stopped her from entering the study.

Justina did not pull away. Slowly he lifted her wrist to his mouth. Her leather gloves were discolored and worn. Darius succeeded in sneakily moving that barrier aside with his lips, intent on touching some portion of her directly, however slight, to inhale more of her. "Thank you, Miss Penny," he muttered against her pulse, his lips lightly tracing the soft skin. "For the gift."

Darius held her fingers longer than he should. She made no effort to retrieve her hand until Lucy's footsteps were heard returning across the creaking floorboards to find what kept the two of them.

He knew then he was in danger. Very real danger. No woman had ever given him a gift or spoken to him as she did. Or tied him in these breathless knots. Or left him so aroused just by standing close and letting him hold her hand.

Quickly he put up his fences again. "Have you not delayed enough, Miss Penny? You are already late today as it is and now you try to distract me from your lack of p...punctuality."

"Well, of all the blasted cheek! Give it back to me then!"

"Give what back?" He had slipped the lavender pillow quickly inside his jacket.

Her eyes narrowed and she stepped closer. "I give them to everybody," she exclaimed, sounding short of breath. "It is nothing special."

Perhaps not to her.

Darius blinked and kept his countenance unmoved. "That's all right then, isn't it? I would not want you to do anything *special* for me. People might talk."

"About us?" She gave one of those peculiar snorting laughs. "I'd sooner be linked romantically to Sir Mortimer Grubbins."

He smirked. "Did you make him a lavender pillow too?"

"Yes," came the pert reply. "But he ate his."

"How do you know I won't do the same?"

Her lips popped open and shaped a small sound, very like a rusty gate hinge. But it seemed he had silenced the mischievous creature. It was a temporary victory, but satisfying nonetheless.

〜✠〜

"Well, Jussy, I trust your excursions to Midwitch Manor are of use to Mr. Wainwright," said her father one morning.

"Yes, Papa."

"You have not told us much about the time you spend there."

"There is not much to tell."

She felt her father's gaze quizzing her above his newspaper. "Not much? Goodness, I expected you to be full of tales by now. Mr. Wainwright has not mentioned anything to you of his future plans yet with the manor house?"

"Why would he share anything like that with me? He barely finds the will to speak at all, let alone say anything interesting."

Before he could reply, her mother chimed in. "I hope you are not rude to the gentleman. Such a pity it was that he did not ask Catherine to sort through his papers. I wonder why he did not."

"Because Cathy does not need an occupation to keep her out of trouble," Justina exclaimed hotly, fumbling with her needle and pricking her finger.

Yet she'd begun to anticipate her hour each day in his company with some unexpected pleasure. It was the newness of it, she supposed. Wainwright was something rare in that village. He had seen a great deal of the world, experienced things she'd only read about. Perhaps that was part of his allure. He could, no doubt, answer all her endless questions. If his patience held out long enough.

She rather liked watching him puzzle over those old clocks. His long fingers were very precise, very clever.

Apart from the occasional bout of dropping things, which seemed to happen more and more lately. Perhaps he needed spectacles. Might explain why he spent so much time squinting at her, as if it hurt him to look at her ungainly person and unfashionable attire.

When she made him the lavender pillow she pretended it was a common thing for her to do, but that was a lie. She had no explanation for it. An anxious search of her father's books had not enlightened her to any strange illness she might have contracted. There was no diagnosis for this. No reason why her pulse should quicken to a hideously uncontrolled pace when he pressed his damp lips to it.

"I shall be vastly annoyed if he dines with the Sherringhams first," said Mrs. Penny. "I'm sure the major is eager to get him through their door, and Rebecca won't waste her time once they do. She's always been a forward, brazen creature. And the Lord knows she needs to catch herself a stranger because anyone intimate with that family knows what she is. Yes, indeed, she needs to find herself a man who knows nothing about her. He will be duped. Quite thoroughly taken in."

Dr. Penny lowered his newspaper again midway to his knees. "I always thought Miss Sherringham to be a charming, witty girl, my dear. What has she done to set you so against her?"

For a moment, Mrs. Penny did not answer, too busy fussing over her sewing basket. Finally she grumbled, "One only has to look at the brother. A rakehell of the very worst order."

"But what has that to do with Becky, Mama?" Catherine gently protested, not looking up from her neat embroidery. "She is not at fault for her brother's misadventures."

Mrs. Penny sniffed resentfully. "That girl *is* her brother, but in skirts. Since her mother died when she was so young, she's been raised up like a boy alongside that reckless brother of hers. They both think that all in life is a jape. For a man it is bad enough, but in a woman it is unseemly. Her father drinks too much port and has no earthly idea how to raise a young lady." After a pause while she examined her sewing, their mother added, "She has spent too much time around military camps and it shows. Maidenly modesty is absent in that girl. Quite absent."

Their father peered over his paper again. "You mean to suggest, my dear, that Rebecca Sherringham is a strumpet?"

Justina smothered a snort of laughter, and Catherine shook her head at her sewing.

"I did not say that," Mrs. Penny protested thinly to her husband. "But if her manner leads others to assume it is so, Major Sherringham has nothing to blame for it but his own laxity."

Catherine kept silent from then on, holding her thoughts to herself as usual, but Justina would not sit quietly and tolerate this condemnation of their friend or of the lively brother who had always been a great favorite of hers. "Captain Sherringham is a very jolly soul, whatever people say about him. And Becky is one of the most generous and selfless people I know. Excepting Cathy, of course."

Mrs. Penny was appalled by the suggestion of anyone else's unmarried daughter having admirable qualities to rival those of her jewel. "Generous, indeed! I'd like to see where that gets her in life. For all her bold ways, she is nowhere near your sister in beauty. Nowhere near! Not with all those freckles."

As it happened, their mama soon had her opportunity to pounce on Mr. Wainwright and save him from the wicked intentions of that flame-haired hussy otherwise known as Miss Rebecca Sherringham.

On Sunday he finally showed his face in church and was, naturally, a dreadful distraction in the front pew. Justina, who had barely given a thought to the new vicar's sermons before now—except to be glad they were shorter than those given by his predecessor—felt great sympathy for poor Mr. Kenton, who struggled manfully and in vain to keep the attention of his flock from straying.

After the service the Penny family was almost at the lych-gate when a deep voice brought them to a stumbling halt on the path.

"Miss Penny, I believe you dropped this."

They all turned to observe the great tall cloud looming over their small group. It was Mr. Wainwright, with his large claw outstretched and a lady's glove laid over it. He must have recovered it from the aisle, read the initials sewn inside the cuff, and chased them down to return the item.

Justina felt her pulse quicken, as it always did when he was near. Her gaze went at once to his hands, remembering the way it felt to have them holding her improperly.

At her side Catherine was startled. "But I did not lose a glove, sir." She lifted her hands to prove she had both gloves where they should be.

Their mother bounced forward, elbowing a route between her daughters and almost catching Justina in the eye with the lively feather in her bonnet. "Why, that is mine, sir. How good of you to return it."

Justina smothered a groan.

"I too am a Catherine," Mrs. Penny explained, quickly taking the glove from his hand, "but you were not to know that. I daresay your thoughts are filled only with one by that name." Following this extraordinarily presumptuous remark, she laughed lightly, throwing her head back to do so and this time successfully poking Justina in the eye with her bonnet feather.

Wainwright winced and leaned away, perhaps fearing her millinery handiwork might attack him next.

The path under the lych-gate was very narrow and people already piled up behind them, anxious to get by. Mrs. Penny had him where she wanted him at last, for he was thrust into her clutches. He had no choice but to walk with her through the gate.

"Mr. Wainwright, on your very first visit to my husband you promised to dine with us. Do say you will join us tomorrow evening. You simply must!"

Justina fully expected to hear one of his rude refusals. Instead, the giant inconvenience bowed his head with stiff politeness and replied, "I would be honored, madam."

It must be for Cathy, she realized. He'd practically raced after them to return the glove he thought was hers and now he accepted their mother's invitation. There could be no other reason but Cathy.

She glanced at her sister and saw the soft blush covering her cheeks like a spread of watercolor on canvas. But even as a smile lifted her sister's lips, something sank inside Justina. Sadly she knew Cathy must marry sooner or later and then the bed they had shared all these years would suddenly seem very large and empty. Cathy was a quiet soul, but her presence would be much missed in the house, her absence likely to destroy the balance. It would be a parting inevitable and heartrending. Until that moment Justina had been able to keep the thought in the back of her mind, swathed in shadows, but here before them was the object that could very well bring that moment to pass. He had all the qualifications.

Now their party, joined by Mr. Wainwright, moved onward down the lane. Justina hung back, looking for Lucy, an action which gave her cause to turn away and ignore the intruder in their midst. The sun had gone in, and she felt a brisk chill under her clothes.

❧

When Darius realized that the younger Miss Penny was no longer with the group, he looked back, hesitating, but her mother gripped his arm and dragged him forward, chattering with the same breathless speed as her daughter often employed. Before too long the path rushed away beneath his feet.

"I do hope Justina has not caused you too many pains, sir. I have been told the story of the pig and I must apologize. I'm afraid Dr. Penny is overindulgent of our youngest." The lady lowered her voice as she rushed him along, the tall, full feather in her bonnet sweeping against his arm. "She was a very small baby—came out kicking. Feet first, of course. Contrary from the moment she was born. I had hoped for a boy with my second child, but what a disappointment. Alas, the delivery quite put a stop to my poor body bearing any more children. And the midwife did not get to me in time, so Dr. Penny was obliged to tend me himself. He never quite got over it and has spoiled her ever since, despite the fact that she soon flourished and never looked back after those first few difficult weeks. He fussed over that child as if she was made of glass and would barely let me near her. All she had to do was look up at him with those big eyes of hers, grip his finger with all her might, and he was a lost man." She shook her head, making a clicking sound with her teeth. "Now my husband says she has high spirits, but I call it an attraction to mischief that she should have outgrown by now. Perhaps"—she put her head on one side, looking coyly up at him—"when her elder sister is settled in a home of her own, Justina will put such childishness aside."

Shocked that this woman—a stranger still—felt it necessary to regale him with such a story, Darius did not know where to look or what to say. Childbirth was something he preferred to know nothing about, and since he was a man he didn't expect ever to hear it talked of in detail. It was enough to raise the hairs on a man's neck, for heaven's sake.

"I see," he managed finally, his voice taut.

Again he looked back to see where the errant daughter had gone, but she was nowhere in sight. The villagers streamed out through the church door like inmates released from prison, almost trampling the vicar in their haste.

Miss Catherine Penny, walking on her mother's left side, quietly asked how he liked the village.

"I am finding my way about," he replied.

"You must allow our Catherine to show you the sights, Mr. Wainwright."

He sighed. "I believe I've seen them."

If the lady heard him, she did not appear to absorb his words. "You must view the village through the eyes of a local. Catherine can tell you all the secrets, show you all the beauty spots."

At this, Catherine laughed lightly. "Although I do not know so many secrets as Jussy. She is really the one who can tell you where the skeletons are buried, Mr. Wainwright. And she can do so with great bravado."

Her mother shot her a quick frown. "Well, I'm sure he would not want Justina's company longer than he has had it already. No one ever does. Skeletons indeed!"

Darius heard the younger sister laughing and chattering with her friend as she followed along the path behind them. Good. He breathed another relieved sigh. At least he knew now where she was and that she couldn't leap out on him from the yew trees.

He liked the sound of her laughter. When it was not directed at him.

Sixteen

THE NEXT DAY, WHEN SHE ARRIVED FOR HER DUTIFUL visit, he was waiting at the gate.

"Miss Justina Penny"—he showed her his fob watch—"you are late. Again."

Her eyes glittered with annoyance. "I do have other chores, Mr. Wainwright."

"But none more important than me, surely." Oh, he knew he pushed his luck. For some reason that day he could not help himself. She marched ahead of him through the orchard and he followed, realizing that he had grown addicted to having her fiery, sparking gaze turned upon him. Whenever it was turned elsewhere he felt…bereft.

She did not respond directly to his last remark, but having arrived at the pig sty she leaned over the fence to pet Sir Mortimer and exclaimed breezily, as if she could be talking to either man or beast, "Lucy had to stay and help her father this morning. So you'll have to make do with me alone."

Darius instantly put his watch away, for the time no longer mattered.

They walked into the house together. Mrs. Birch could be heard banging pots about in the kitchen. Since it was Monday he knew her niece would arrive soon for the weekly laundry. He didn't want them knowing he was alone with Miss Penny. Although her slightly eccentric father was aware that she came to his house to help him, he wouldn't want the village gossips to suggest there was anything untoward going on, so he led her rather hastily into his study and shut the door.

Immediately he realized the duplicity in his actions, for if he did not want to chance scandalous rumor he should have sent Miss Penny home; instead he brought her inside with him, alone, behind a closed door. These were not the actions of an upstanding gentleman, and he was surprised at himself. He should have left the door open for they had nothing to hide. Nothing at all.

"Is there anything amiss, Mr. Wainwright?" she asked, frowning.

He finally left the door, having decided not to reopen it, and helped her out of her coat. "Should there be?"

She chewed on her lip for a moment. "You don't mind that I'm here alone?"

He considered her carefully. "*Should* I mind?"

"You look as if you're afraid of what I might do to you."

Darius banked a sudden chuckle, swallowing it down hard. "If I am, you must admit I have some reason to be."

She squinted.

"There is a certain precedence set," he added drily.

With a huff she began to turn away, but then stopped and faced him again. "I'm not sorry it happened."

He waited, unsure of which transgression she meant. They were, after all, plentiful.

"Without risk there is nothing gained," she added. "I learned a lesson that night when I leaped upon you."

Ah, that one. "I sincerely hope you did, madam. I would not want you leaping on any other gentleman."

Her nose wrinkled. She removed her gloves with an extravagant gesture, as if acting in a play, and dropped them to the chair where he'd set her coat. "Rest assured, once was enough to cure me of the urge."

"Glad I am to hear it." He took a step toward her. "And I am not sorry it happened either."

Her lashes flicked down and up. She had begun to breathe hard, he noted. Her dark curls shook slightly, little tremors he might not have seen if he wasn't standing improperly close.

Suddenly he imagined his brother's mocking voice, *"Handles, what on earth are you doing? You enormous great drip. Kiss her, for pity's sake. What are you waiting for?"*

Lucius would kiss her without qualm.

But that was "Lucky" Lucius—he of so little conscience.

This girl was utterly unsuitable, naught but trouble for any man. Darius knew it was madness to let her into his house, especially today when she was unescorted. Her scent invaded his thoughts again, and he saw her as she was once before, in his bedchamber, her soft skin warmed by candlelight. Those damned stockings and pink ribbon garters...

"As long as it taught you a lesson," he muttered. Was that his hand raised and sliding slowly under her hair? Yes, of course it was his. And no, he didn't want her leaping on any other man.

She tipped her head back a little. "If you're going to kiss me again, hurry up and do it."

"Why would I want to kiss you?"

"Because we're alone in this room at last. Who knows when these circumstances will be repeated? We might as well make the most of the opportunity. We both know we're not going to tell anyone. You'll be gone soon, back to London, and I have my own plans."

She was an unscrupulous young woman, he mused. Perhaps she was after him for his money, just like all the other scheming fortune hunters. But there was something different about this one. She tempted him as the others had not. She drew him in not just with her looks, but with the things she said and the extraordinary workings of her mind.

"Your own plans?"

"Yes. And I'm not going to tell you, so don't ask. The less we know about one another the better."

With that he could not agree. Darius wanted to know all about her. He wanted to drink her down. Every last bittersweet drop. "I suppose when you find yourself alone with gentlemen you always act this way?"

"I'm never alone with other gentlemen."

"How fortunate for me then that the honor falls to my lot."

"But if I kiss you now, you must promise not to come to dinner. My sister is too eager to fall in love, and you are the wrong man for her. She would accept your attentions out of a sense of duty, but you would never make my sister happy. She must marry for love, not out of duty or because it's what our parents want, or because you are stinking rich." Just like her mama she rattled away, all her words tumbling out in haste. Typical of a crook's guilty confession, he mused. Or their hastily fired excuses when caught in the act.

"Your sister?" He had forgotten, in those last few seconds, that she even had a sister.

"Yes. She already thinks of you as Mr. Darcy, but she needs someone kind and civil."

"Mr. Whocy?"

"Oh, never mind!" She hitched up on tiptoe and placed her hands upon his shoulders. He felt her soft, warm breath skip over his lips. "Just kiss me and get it over with."

Darius had never followed a woman's command in his life. Until now. There was no point in pretending he didn't want to kiss her.

So he obliged the temptress with a long, deep kiss, his fingers cupping the back of her head, tangled in her curls, his other hand on her hip, caressing the soft muslin and the curve beneath.

In the back of his mind a voice protested. She was too young, too wayward. Nothing good could come of this.

He was not Lucius. He had always promised himself that he would never act this way.

What sort of young woman tried to bribe a man with kisses? The same sort who accosted strange gentlemen in bed, naked.

Thus, with that image leaping back into his mind, the gentlemanly voice of caution was silenced.

Greed and desire surged within. Hungrily he devoured her mouth, moving her back until she stumbled against the Grecian couch and fell onto it. Darius thrust aside a pile of papers and followed her down. There was no protest, only a gasp of surprise. And then her arms came up around his shoulders and an excited chuckle blew against his cheek.

Had she come there alone that day with this in mind—the idea of bribing him to stay away from her sister? An intriguing method of bartering, certainly, but she was a novice. Luckily for him.

❧

She couldn't breathe, couldn't think with any sort of clarity. His kiss drained her of the will to do either. The weight of his body laid over hers on the couch was something she'd never experienced, of course, and she might have expected to feel stifled, but she did not. As he moved against her, his lips now pressed to her throat and then lower, to her bosom, the hard ridge in his breeches became too prominent, too intriguing to ignore.

Justina ran a hand over it slowly, and he lifted his head to grumble, "Don't do that."

Naturally, she did it again.

"When one is in trouble anyway," she whispered, "one may as well make the most of it."

In retaliation his lips closed over her nipple as it poked through her chemise and rose eagerly against her muslin bodice. He sucked upon it gently at first and then with more hunger until she felt the warmth of his greedy mouth dampening the material, even wetting the sensitive skin beneath.

Justina arched against him, gripping the hard length inside his breeches even tighter, amazed to feel it throbbing and growing. Heated ripples of forbidden pleasure overtook her too quickly, but she did not feel inclined to stop them or him. She wanted to learn. She longed to know the truth and have her eyes opened, to know all the secrets that were kept from her.

Suddenly Wainwright stopped. He pushed away from the couch and stood, turning away and cursing under his breath.

Disorientated, she lay there a moment longer, very much aware of the strange feelings still holding her in their grip. Her nipples ached. The tightness in her belly was unrelenting.

Why had he stopped?

"You had better leave," he growled, still turned away from her, shoulders hunched as he leaned over his desk.

Slowly she sat up. "Don't come to dinner." She tried to keep her voice even. "You promised."

He half turned his head, but did not quite look over his broad shoulder. She heard something like a husky laugh of derision. "I promised nothing, woman."

"Villain!" she cried. "I said you could have one kiss if you promised not to come."

"And did you hear anything from me in return?"

There was nothing else to say, and she could not trust her voice anyway.

"Let that be a lesson to you," he said, his voice low. "Never fulfill your side of a business transaction while negotiations are still underway. Wait until the ink is dry."

She grabbed her coat and gloves and ran out. Justina knew she should be furious. He had made her act like a hussy. He had got more from her than a kiss.

But as she ran out of his gate and let it swing shut behind her, she felt no real anger, only disappointment that he stopped when he did. After all, she had urged him to kiss her. It wasn't truly all his fault, and even she could not pretend it was this time.

❧

In a pointless effort to seem less desperate, their mother had also invited Mr. Kenton to help "round out" the numbers at dinner. A harmless fellow, but dull and overly solicitous with his advice, the rector was often put to use at social events as the only single man available. Justina might have felt sorry for him, since he must know the invitation was extended only for want of any better company, but her sympathy was tried whenever he felt obliged to advise her. And his concerns were not all of a moral tone. Mr. Kenton believed in guiding his parishioners through every aspect of life, from the shoes on their feet to the food they digested. He had once spent fifteen minutes in Justina's presence vilifying rhubarb tart—which happened to be one of her favorite dishes and one she would not abandon under any circumstances.

"My dear Mr. Kenton," she'd assured him, "I am no stranger to risk, and I would thank you for letting me take my own."

As a consequence he thought her a very stubborn, opinionated young woman and directed most of his sermons at her on Sundays.

Tonight the silverware was polished and the best plate got out, minus the one broken by Jussy, as their mother reminded her tersely.

"I did not break it, Mama."

"Oh, and I am supposed to believe a mad gypsy dashed in and stole it from the drying rack. My very best serving platter, handed down to me by my own grandmother who received it as a wedding gift from Lady Blundeson of Stoke, who—"

"Who always condescended to take much care and interest in your grandmother's family. Yes, I know. As does the entire village. I daresay the thief knew the value of that plate, Mama. Since you are forever telling people about it, 'tis no wonder your china has become the target for robbers. Perhaps greater discretion and humility would behoove us in future."

Her mother's mouth flapped open. "Behoove? *Behoove?* I'll give you behoove, young madam!"

But since that was the very moment the doorbell echoed throughout the house, she was saved from being given anything other than a very dark look and a hasty warning to hold her tongue if she had nothing pleasant to say in the presence of their guests.

Wainwright arrived promptly for dinner, of course. The man was a slave to his clocks and watches.

"Are you not afraid, Mama," Justina remarked as Clara was sent off to open the front door, "that in addition to poisoning us on a daily basis, our alleged cook will now have access to the unsuspecting stomachs of strangers? A gentleman of consequence, no less, from London? We could all be hanged."

Her mother waved a hand dismissively. "Clara is a perfectly adequate cook. For a child who once refused to eat anything but bread and jam for two years, you are remarkably hard to please these days. Now do go and wash your hands, and for goodness' sake, do something with that hair."

She had not realized there was anything amiss with her hair today, but as usual her mother's disgust was vague, never helpful, and thrown out in irritation. It was far more important that Cathy, the family's great hope, be tended to. Justina fully understood that. But just once she would like to know exactly what it was about her own appearance that was so very lacking and how she might even attempt to put it right.

Surely "beauty," while there were certain standards of it upon which everyone would agree, could also be found in the eye of the beholder. Was there nothing about her that had the slightest promise, she wondered gloomily, staring at her face in the bedchamber mirror. Would she ever emerge from her unsightly chrysalis? Would she ever learn not to leap first and think later? Apparently not.

Tonight Mr. Wainwright, handsome bachelor and dark menace, had been invited there for Cathy. And he came there for Cathy. He made it clear to Justina that he would do as he pleased, regardless of her wishes. Her hopes and feelings were inconsequential.

The longer Justina sat staring at herself in the mirror, the less symmetrical her features appeared, and the angrier and darker her mood became.

So he had kissed her, but she had practically cornered him into it, she thought, chagrined. There was absolutely nothing subtle or elegant about her or her methods. As Lucy had complained to her recently, her solutions to imminent problems were often more theatrical than effective. Wainwright probably feared for his life if he *didn't* kiss her that day. Or he wanted rid of her and therefore kissed her to chase her out of his study.

Justina decided a protest of sorts was necessary. Waiting until she heard everyone assembled below in the parlor, she came down late from dressing and when she opened the door, everyone looked over.

"There you are, Jussy," her father exclaimed and then immediately looked confused. Her mother, who had been in the process of offering a tray with a sherry glass to the rector, was frowning, frozen in place.

The Wainwright person, seated on the couch beside her sister, winced in her direction and kept his lips very tight.

"Good evening, everyone," she said politely. "Oh, good! Sherry. I'm fair parched."

As she advanced with arm outstretched, her mother swiftly moved the tray out of her reach and set it on the pianoforte, forgetting the rector, who was left clutching at the air. "What on earth have you got on your head, Justina?" she hissed under her breath.

"Why, they are butterflies, Mama, can't you see?"

"I can see, young lady, that they are from your father's collection. What are those wretched insects doing in your hair?"

Justina blinked. "*You* told me to do something with it." Then with a wide smile, she moved away from her furious mother. "Mr. Kenton, how lovely it is to have *your* company this evening."

The rector stared at the precariously tilting arrangement of curls and colorful dead butterflies careening around her head. "Yes, quite."

Across the room Wainwright jerked upright, belatedly remembering his manners. "Miss Justina Penny. Good evening."

"Mr. Wainwright." She kept her smile pasted to her face and returned her attention to the rector. In her peripheral vision she saw Wainwright finally lower his seat again to the couch. Surprisingly enough he hadn't brought his own chair in which to place his superior buttocks.

But Cathy appeared pleased with his dour company. Poor, unsuspecting creature.

Seventeen

WHAT HE WAS DOING THERE DARIUS COULD ONLY explain as morbid fascination. He might have claimed that Mrs. Penny forced him to accept her offer of dinner, but that would be false. There were plenty of occasions when he had no qualm about turning down an invitation. He spent a great deal of his time doing that.

Yet tonight he stepped into her small house and forced himself to be sociable, for several hours, with near strangers.

His palms were damp, his head hot and aching. There was some considerable guilt he felt in regard to his continuing encounters with Justina. He had never acted that way before, and it was even more worrying that he knew it would happen again. Anxious to gain some grip upon himself and the situation, he focused his thoughts upon the eldest Miss Penny.

She was not a demanding conversationalist by any means, but neither was she terribly inventive when it came to subjects. Since Darius was no better at falling into an easy swing of conversation, they were quickly stalled. She did not have her younger sister's sharpness, or that outrageous, reckless courage. He suspected Miss

Catherine Penny's attempts to continually restart the discussion were prompted by the anxious glances of her mother and not by any true desire to become better acquainted with him.

Thinking back to Bath and that evening of chaos in the Upper Rooms, he recalled his friend Miles dancing with this young lady and being immediately in love. As was Miles Forester's usual habit with a pretty girl. At the time Darius had not thought her much more than that—a pretty girl, rather shy—but Miss Penny's appearance had improved over the past year. Her skin was clearer, certainly, or else she had been wearing too much powder of some sort when they were in Bath. Her eyes were a paler blue than her sister's and did not hold the same challenging impertinence.

When they were shepherded through to the dining room, Darius was seated between Miss Penny and her mother, with Justina diagonally opposite. By then the strange creation on the troublemaker's head had begun to deflate, a few of the butterflies suspended upside down, seemingly about to take flight into the soup.

"I do hope our Jussy hasn't been too much in the way at Midwitch," her mother said suddenly. "She usually is."

He forced his gaze away from the general disarray of the woman across the table.

"If you desire the assistance of another pair of hands, I recommend Catherine. She will sort your papers most efficiently, Mr. Wainwright. You'll never find a faster worker than our Catherine. Ever since she was a tiny thing she's been a most obliging workmate and nothing is ever too much trouble. She's been reading and writing since she was five and has a very quick mind for sums.

Lord, that girl can add three or four numbers together while I'm still getting my fingers out to count, Mr. Wainwright." She laughed giddily. "Catherine will soon have you and your great-uncle's papers squared away!"

"It is almost done, Mama," Justina replied. "He won't need anyone there in a day or two."

Darius squinted at her. "On the contrary, it is far from done."

"But there are—"

"Many more chests and drawers to empty," he snapped. She needn't think she was getting away with a slipshod, half-finished job. Suddenly the thought of not having her there each day was causing him a headache. That manor house would be very dull and dark without her chattering presence.

"Then you haven't found what you're looking for?"

"I have not. Yet." *Damn you.* He knew he had to stop looking at her. It was impolite and surely obvious to everyone else at the table.

When her father asked what it was he sought among his great-uncle's things, Darius managed to reply in a voice that was almost calm, "A document of value, Dr. Penny."

"It's a map to a buried treasure chest," the girl across the table exclaimed, eyes shining. "Full of gold doubloons. From old Hawke's misspent youth as a pirate and a smuggler."

Short silence followed this, everyone looking expectantly in his direction. She reached for her wine and smiled smugly, leaving him to continue the story and probably expecting him to drop the ball she'd tossed.

"Not pirate gold," Darius replied. "That would be mundane in comparison to the truth."

She shrugged, her sparkling gaze turned away from him.

Darius did not care to be dismissed by this girl with an insolent face and dead insects in her hair. "As a matter of fact you were closer to the truth with one of your earlier guesses, Miss Justina."

Aha. That got her attention!

She set her glass down. "I was?"

"I seek a parcel of letters written to a lady." He dabbed his lips on a napkin. Still with the weight of every eye upon him, he continued in a low voice. "Phineas Hawke apparently had a secret love, and he left her a provision in his will."

"Goodness gracious!" Mrs. Penny almost dropped her spoon in her soup.

"Who was she?" her eldest daughter enquired in similar amazement. "A local lady?"

Darius thought for a moment and then replied, "I know not. Unfortunately, my great-uncle referred to her in his will only by a...pet name he had for her."

"A pet name? Fancy! And all this time we all thought he was such a miserable old fellow." Mrs. Penny laid a hand to her cheek. "Oh, I did not mean he was so very bad, Mr. Wainwright."

"He was a mean old devil," her youngest daughter exclaimed with great energy. "I will not pretend he was anything else, even if Mr. Wainwright *is* his great-nephew."

Darius watched her splashing her spoon around in her soup, but he knew he'd caught her interest when she added, "Well, go on then. Tell us the rest of it. Did he throttle her because she did not return his love? Did he stab her through the heart with a hat pin? Now he means to make amends and absolve himself of the crime by leaving money to her heirs, no doubt."

He quickly hid the hapless tremors of a smile in his napkin.

"Justina!" her mother protested. "The stories she tells, Mr. Wainwright, would curl your toes. Please forgive my youngest, sir. She is dreadfully outspoken and nothing we can do seems to curb her. I shall never forget the time—"

"Mama, there is no need to talk about me as if I'm not present." She twitched irritably and a butterfly dropped on the end of a springy curl to hover by her cheek. One more bounce and it would be in her soup.

"Rest assured, Miss Justina," Darius muttered, "your presence could never go unnoticed." He spoke with feeling, since he suffered the effects of it whenever she was near. All sensible thoughts careened out of his head when he looked at her lips, her eyes, her bosom. Even when she mocked him, he was drawn in, forced to relive the moment on his Grecian couch. Her hand exploring, her nipple blossoming and swelling between his lips. How he'd longed to tear that muslin aside. He'd had to push away and turn his back before he embarrassed himself and spent like a green youth against her hand.

She glowered at him across the table and then turned her head to speak with the rector.

Darius loudly cleared his throat, making her look his way again. "The solicitor believes my great-uncle kept all the letters she returned to him—some still unopened—at the end of the love affair. It seems likely, as he seldom burned any papers. If I can locate the letters, I can discover the lady's identity and see to it that she receives the bequest left to her." He brought the spoon to his lips, tasted over-salted soup, and quickly lowered it again.

At the far end of the table Dr. Penny spoke up quietly. "As I observed during my visits to the manor house, Phineas Hawke kept himself surrounded by so many things from his past. It will be an adventure to go through it all, eh, Jussy? There must be rooms in that house which have not seen daylight in fifty years and drawers unopened just as long."

"But what if the lady does not wish to be found?" Miss Catherine Penny muttered softly. "She may not care to be reminded of an old love affair. By now she will be aged, as he was, and her life went on without him, for better or worse. It is not pleasant to revisit old wounds, and some things are best left in the past. "

"Well, good Lord, silly girl," her mother exclaimed with a snort, "I should say she'd still want the coin if some has been left to her. It's surprising how quickly money can mend a few wounds." And she briskly rang the little bell beside her dish for the next course.

Darius watched Justina's expression. She seemed nonchalant, but he knew her enough already to guess this was an act. The story would have sparked her eager curiosity.

She suddenly looked up from her soup and their eyes met. Or rather, they collided. He watched the candle flames reflected in those large, dark blue, satin pools. Again she raised her glass and touched the crystal rim to her lips. The tip of her tongue, just a tiny kiss of pink, caressed the glass before she took a sip, and then he observed her swallow.

Darius felt the ache in his loins at once. The heat

and heaviness returned. Perspiration formed under his clothes. He swept his gaze lower, down her slender neck, to the simple amber cross she wore on a thin gold chain. And then lower to her beautifully rounded, firm, pert bubbies.

Bubbies? He groaned inwardly, where only he heard it, for that was a word Miles or Lucius would use. Apparently he was on a fast descent to debauchery thanks to that small, messy, butterfly-strewn woman across the candles.

Anxious to halt his fascination with her, Darius ran through the list of her many and varied faults in his mind. She was too young, foolish, and unguarded. She insulted him even when offering a kiss. She laughed at him when he was being deadly serious. She had not the slightest compunction about her behavior and yet she had the audacity to call him uncivil. And the most boring man that ever lived.

He watched her breathing quicken, the little amber cross winking in the candlelight as it rose and fell with the high swell of those two pretty parcels of warm, sweet, intoxicating delight. His tongue curled inside his mouth, imagining the taste of her nipples without that damn gown in his way. Briefly he closed his eyes and saw an image of her in his bed, nude, breathless, damp from his kisses. Thank God no one could read his thoughts, he mused, shifting in his chair. He was not usually such a fidget, but his breeches were uncomfortably tight this evening.

It seemed as if reminding himself of her utter unsuitability had a disastrous effect, the complete opposite to that which he'd expected and sought to achieve.

Reaching for his wineglass, he misjudged and knocked the stem with the backs of his fingers. Fortunately it did not tumble, but rocked dangerously, spilled a little on the cloth, and woke him from his reverie. Darius grabbed it quickly, splayed his fingers over the base to steady it, and drew his attention back to Justina's face. When she blinked and then continued to stare at him, it was as if she'd leaned over and whispered an improper suggestion.

Accepting another refill of wine—something else he never usually did—Darius drank it down swiftly to wash away the awfulness of the over-seasoned soup. He was soon feeling quite pleasantly warm and wishing he had a very large butterfly net.

One more glass, he thought with a strange burst of mischievousness, and he might not feel the need to rely upon a net at all.

෴

Throughout the dinner, Justina felt his dark, sinister gaze settled on her too often and with deepening intensity. Did he watch the butterflies, expecting them to take flight from her head? Although she'd meant it as a form of protest, the spectacular arrangement of her hair had also won her his attention and now she realized he must think that was the reason why she did it. He had accused her before of misbehaving to be noticed.

Perhaps he was right, she thought, and her "protest" had been another terrible error of misjudgment, or else it was an unconscious ploy to capture his attention.

She must be going mad. A woman accustomed to attacking problems and obstacles head-on, she was quite at a loss with this particular crisis.

"Mr. Kenton," the menace across the table said suddenly to the rector, "do you serve other parishes as well as this one?"

This was his fifth abrupt question shot out at the man beside her. Apparently Wainwright had stored these arrows up to fire at the rector whenever there was a pause in the conversation. But his victim handled the interrogation quite happily. Mr. Kenton was not often the object of anyone's interest beyond a few polite words, so he must be enjoying the rare chance to explain himself and actually be heard.

"I have only the one living, sir," the rector replied solemnly. "I did not wish for a plurality, as I prefer to be resident among my dear parishioners, to provide proper guidance at every opportunity."

"And we are very grateful for it," Justina assured the rector with a wide smile. "Mr. Kenton has made quite a difference here since he came," she added. "His guidance has been invaluable."

"Really?" Wainwright choked and quickly wiped his mouth on a napkin. "I cannot imagine how ill-behaved you were before his *guidance*."

Biting down on her anger, she watched him swallow another glass of wine. It must be at least his third, she thought. Clearly it loosened his tongue and his wit.

"Mr. Kenton always has the very best counsel," she said primly. "And it is dispensed with kindness and generosity." She felt the rector's astonished gaze, but continued with determination, "He recently advised me against rhubarb, and I have not touched it since."

"I see." Wainwright's lips twitched. "Rhubarb."

She studied his fingers around the stem of her

mother's best crystal wineglass and remembered their
touch upon her breast and then her waist. She refused to
think of them anywhere else. That was far enough. Her
throat was dry and tight, little sparks of a bonfire spitting
about inside her.

Poor Mr. Kenton was awash with blushes. "Well, I...I
must say, I do try, of course, to help wherever I can."

Their mother merrily jumped in with her common
refrain. "Oh, there is nothing to be done with Jussy. We
quite despair of *her*. If we did not have Catherine, I do
not know what we would do."

"I understand the owner of Lark Hollow estate has
the living of this parish," Wainwright exclaimed in the
unnecessary volume of someone unpracticed in speaking aloud in company. Someone, perhaps, for whom
conversation was useful mostly as a conduit to business,
seldom pleasure.

"Yes, indeed," replied Mr. Kenton. "Admiral Vyne
currently owns the property, and he granted me the
living when it became vacant on the death of the
previous vicar. Admiral Vyne is a distant cousin on my
mother's side. I was most fortunate to—"

"Do you know the admiral, Mr. Wainwright?" their
mother interrupted. "He is a very fine, very particular
gentleman, despite being a naval man. Dr. Penny is often
called up to Lark Hollow to tend his health. Admiral
Vyne has great respect for my husband's skill and won't
have any other man of medicine in his house."

Justina and Catherine exchanged glances, both
cringing at their mother's unsubtle attempts to portray
the family as one of consequence in the neighborhood.
Any moment now, thought Justina, she will mention

her grandmama's tenuous connection to the Blundesons of Stoke.

"No, I am not acquainted with the admiral," Wainwright replied as soon as he could get a word in.

"Well, you must pay him a visit. Lark Hollow is not five miles and in dry weather it is an easy journey. He does not go out much himself, but is always glad to entertain visitors and is a lavish host. We had one of the best dinners there, did we not, my husband?"

"Indeed we did, my dear."

"Ice sculptures! Imported fruit! The largest salmon I ever laid eyes upon. We were honored to be invited there, you know, Mr. Wainwright, as he plays host only to a few local families deemed worthy." She laughed with excruciating gaiety. "If he had any sons, I suppose he would try to get our Catherine for one of them. He has said several times how pretty she is. A man of exquisite tastes."

"Yes," their father remarked, "Admiral Vyne does have an eye for the elegant and costly. One cannot help but wonder how he affords to live as he does on a navy pension."

"My dear, you do speak nonsense at times! The admiral made a fortune in the war. Everyone knows it to be so."

"Ah, then, if everyone knows it to be so, it must be true. I stand corrected. But since Mr. Wainwright knows nothing of the admiral, I'm sure we can find some other subject of conversation in which he might have a share."

Their mother considered alternatives for a moment and Justina cringed in expectation of the worst.

"Pork!" was the word that shot forth. "You must talk to us of pork, Mr. Wainwright."

There was silence while the gentleman froze with his spoon halfway to his lips.

She turned to Mr. Kenton and explained, "Mr. Wainwright is an expert on the subject."

"Is that so?" The rector smiled and looked expectantly at Wainwright, whose expression was a priceless combination of horror and confusion.

Justina feared she might explode with laughter and have wine come out of her nose. But fortunately, having paused a sufficient time and found her guest unprepared to discuss pork, Mrs. Penny, who never liked silence at her dinner parties, forged in a new direction.

"Perhaps you know of the Blundesons of Stoke, Mr. Wainwright?"

For the remainder of dinner, Justina devoted herself to Mr. Kenton, who continued to be visibly surprised by the attention she heaped upon him so suddenly.

At the end of the evening, her father sent her into his library for a book he had promised to lend Mr. Wainwright. He told her it was sitting on the desk and would be easy to find, but to her annoyance it was nowhere in sight. She spent several minutes searching until she found the book upon his shelf, and as she left the room, Justina almost collided with the borrower himself.

"Your father sent me to find you and tell you he was mistaken," he muttered dourly. "The book is on the shelf, it seems, and not where he told you."

Undoubtedly, he thought this was a deliberate ploy by her father. Anxious that Mr. Wainwright should know any mischief afoot was not of her own doing for once, she thrust the book at him, almost taking a button off his waistcoat in the process, leaving it hanging by a loose thread.

They were in a narrow corridor leading from the wing of the house that held her father's study and his surgery. A mere twelve feet away the end of the passage opened into the foyer where the rest of her family were saying their good-byes to Mr. Kenton. But in that slender, dimly lit space, for those few moments, they were unobserved by any other soul. And he was not allowing her to pass. Nor did he take the book she held out to him.

"I must commend you, Miss Penny, on the arrangement of your hair this evening. It is most...remarkable."

"Thank you. Excuse me, sir."

Still he did not move.

"Do you want the book or not?" she demanded in a terse whisper.

Slowly he raised his hand and took it, his fingertips brushing hers in the process. A frisson of heat darted through her from head to toe.

"You had better not tell a soul what happened between us." It rushed out of her in a panic.

With the same slumberous pace as he employed in accepting the book from her hand, he arched an eyebrow. "What happened between us."

"Yes, you know very well what I mean."

"Do I?" He swayed slightly toward her.

She frowned up at him, trying to ascertain whether he was really confused or if he inferred that he would pretend not to remember. "The incident in Bath. And more recently...I'm certain you don't want to suffer the repercussions either, should anyone find out."

"I see. Repercussions." The second eyebrow now joined the first like the wings of a hawk caught on a swell of cool air.

"Precisely."

"I see."

"I hope you do," she replied firmly.

"Your kisses were supposed to frighten me off, is that it?"

Justina could hardly admit that she didn't know why she'd kissed him, that it had seemed necessary at the time, and she only sought for reasons after the fact. Leap first, think later. "I hope you will be discreet, sir," she muttered.

"So says the woman who willingly leapt into the bed of a stranger. Where was her desire for discretion then?"

She stared at him in the dim light of the narrow passage. "It was an unhappy mishap. The wrong bed. You weren't supposed to be a stranger. You weren't the man I expected—the man I wanted." The excuses flowed hurriedly from her. "I was a mere child then."

"Only last year?"

"Fourteen months ago."

"Ah. I see."

"Stop saying *I see* like that," she whispered frantically.

The candle flame stretching up from the single wall sconce suddenly ducked and danced. She knew the front door had swung open and the rector was leaving.

Wainwright lifted his thumb to her mouth and ran the broad, square tip of it along her lower lip. She felt powerless to react, but she was not, of course. The sad truth was she didn't mind him touching her and looking at her as if she was the only soul he could see. It was an indescribably wicked sensation.

He bent his head down to her. She should have seen it coming, but it startled her that he would take the risk there and then.

His lips touched hers, pressed them apart and claimed her shocked gasp as if it were an after-dinner cordial. Tonight his cheek was warm and smooth, with a faint scent of spice. She took a startled breath of it and then, as the kiss lingered, he dropped the book. His hands went to her back, lifting and securing her body firmly against his until her toes left the ground and she could feel his heart pulsing hard against her bosom. How strong he was, she thought in some alarm. And what did he mean to do with her? It briefly occurred to Justina that she ought to shout for help, but with her mouth otherwise engaged the idea was soon lost.

He did indeed consider her part of his meal, for his tongue swept over her warm cheek, tasting her with unmistakable relish. Savoring her. The wandering tongue slipped into the little dip beneath her ear, where his breath tickled and his teeth gently nibbled. A butterfly drifted from her hair and was temporarily carried on a draft. In that moment, as she watched it from the corner of her eye, it seemed as if the lovely creature was flying again as it once had. Her heart soared with it for those few seconds and then spun wildly, before both butterfly and heart came back to earth.

Slowly her toes touched the floor again, but as she slid down his hard length, she felt every muscle, every bump.

Wainwright the Wrong looked at her with a fiery, lusty regard that made the skin of her arms prickle and every hair on her head felt as if it had just curled itself tighter.

It was confirmed, then; this man thought she was a light skirt. What else would he assume after the way she acted in his kitchen and his study? And after her performance in Bath last—fourteen months ago? Did he think to use her in this manner whenever he chose? Another light shiver skipped along the surface of her skin. Wicked excitement, but of a different sort to that which she usually experienced when she misbehaved. It was not in her control this time.

Alarmed, she stumbled back and pressed her shoulder blades to the wall. "How dare you?"

He looked surprised by her question. "I am Darius Wainwright. I dare as I please." Then he stooped to retrieve the borrowed book, tucked it under his arm, and bowed stiffly. "Good evening, Miss Justina. Thank you for the entertainment. It surpassed my expectations."

She stared at his back as he strode confidently away from her. Despicable man! Her mother was right, though—he did have extremely wide shoulders. And Lucy was correct in that all his parts were on the larger side and in proportion to his height.

For the first time in her nineteen years, Justina felt in danger of a swoon. A real one.

But as he turned the corner at the end of the passage, his shoulder knocked into the wall. He straightened quickly, his tall form tipping upright again. It suggested that pompous Mr. Wainwright had drunk a little too much wine that evening. Justina smiled. At least she was not the only one who felt control slipping through her hands.

Eighteen

This morning, when I went to my duty at Midwitch Manor, Mr. W appeared to be in a worse mood than ever before. He could barely open his lips to speak, looked gray and disheveled. He left Lucy and me alone in his study for most of our visit. Very rude and unmannerly.

Cathy's new gown for the harvest dance is all but finished. We are to wear ribbon roses on our slippers, which seems patently ridiculous for an event to take place in a leaky barn.

I would not bother about the state of my own gown, but Becky assures me her brother will be home in time to attend the dance tomorrow, so I shall make the effort. I would much rather dance with the captain than anyone else, and I daresay he is the only one who will ask me in any case. Not that I care a shilling about dancing.

I'm sure I should turn anyone else down, even if they did ask. Even if they did venture down from their exalted heights to attend.

J.P. September 15th, 1815 A.D.

❦

She started on the new pile of papers with a sigh so heavy that she blew a cloud of dust into the air above his desk and sent Wainwright into a sneezing fit. While he was still grappling for a handkerchief, her eyes alighted on a penned note sticking out, part way down the towering pile. It had been signed with a line of smudged crosses. Clearly not a business letter.

Justina's heart quickly shook off that sluggish beat.

Could it be that here she had found one of those love letters he'd mentioned at dinner the other evening? A billet-doux between his miserable great-uncle and a secret sweetheart?

Darius buried his face in a large handkerchief as his sneezes continued, one after the other. She glanced over at Lucy who was daydreaming by the window. No one else would know what she'd found.

Very slyly and carefully she removed it from the pile and slid it onto her lap beneath the desk. From there it was transferred into her small reticule.

She soothed her conscience by promising herself that she would indeed inform Mr. Wainwright of her findings. At a later date. As soon as she'd had a chance to read the contents herself and, perhaps, had discovered the identity of that mysterious lady. There would be time enough to hand it over to him then, surely.

That evening, while pretending to write in her diary and with Cathy asleep beside her, Justina read the note.

> *I wonder if I'll ever find*
> *A way inside your dexterous mind.*
> *But if I did, I must confide*
> *I might not make it back outside.*
> *I am already trapped and bound*
> *Lured in too far to keep my ground.*

And I, 'tis true, would be remiss
to claim I did not like that kiss
I hope for more, I fear it too
Perhaps this is unfair to you.
But still I am a selfish man
and keep you near how 'ere I can

How strange that Phineas should imagine himself a poet, she mused. And yet the attempt was touching too in its fumbling naïveté. The paper was tinted pale brown with old age and crumpled as if once discarded. Perhaps he had written many drafts of the same sentiment and never given it to his lady in the end.

There was no clue to the identity of his fancy, but Justina was eager to uncover more. Where there was one letter, there must be others.

She folded the note and slipped it away inside her diary for safekeeping.

The next day when she arrived at Midwitch, Wainwright wanted to know whether she'd found anything of interest yet among his great-uncle's papers.

"No," she replied primly. "It is all endlessly dull."

"Goodness," he muttered. "We'll have to remedy that, won't we?" He dropped another tall pile atop the one she had barely begun to sort. "That will keep idle hands away from the devil's work," he added, turning away to peruse his shelves, dismissing her with the nonchalance at which he excelled.

That day she found two more of Phineas Hawke's messages to his secret love—bad, sentimental poetry, just what one might expect from an old man with little practice. But if they were very ancient letters, as they appeared to be, the man who wrote them would not have been the same decrepit old curmudgeon who chased her from his house and grounds, would he? She tried to imagine Phineas as a young man. There were no portraits in the house for he was not the sort to enjoy looking at himself.

She took to studying Darius Wainwright more closely during her visits. Perhaps, in his youth, Phineas might have borne a resemblance to his great nephew. The shape of the nose was very similar, from what she remembered, and there was something the two men shared about the jaw. Something more than the grinding that happened in her presence.

"What are you staring at?" Wainwright demanded one day, looking up from the entrails of yet another disemboweled mantel clock. One she was quite sure he'd already mended.

"I was comparing your grumpy face to your great-uncle's and finding it much the same."

Lips pressed together, he shook his head as if mildly irritated and then got on with his work.

"If you would like more things to mend, Mr. Wainwright," she suggested coyly, "I would be happy to break some for you."

Under his breath he muttered something about her having done enough damage already, which she thought was most unjust and yet quite typical.

❧

"So here I find you, old chap! *This* is where you hide away."

Miles Forester swept in on a brisk whirl of cold air, his greatcoat billowing around him, that familiar, booming laugh bouncing against the wall paneling.

The noise shook Darius out of his daydreams, and he hastily set down his pen, turning over the sheet of paper upon which he'd been writing moments before. "Forester? Good God, what are you doing here?" His first thought was how lucky that Miss Penny and her friend had left, for he was not prepared to answer questions about them, and Miles would, doubtless, have plenty.

The tall, smiling man lurched across the study like a young, amiable Labrador. "I hope you don't mind. I thought it would be jolly fun to surprise you, Wainwright. I decided to come and see what you're up to all the way out here."

Mrs. Birch followed close behind, complaining about the mud he'd brought in on his heels and why didn't he wait to be announced properly.

"But I didn't want to give my friend here any warning and have him dash away to hide, as he surely would! Please accept my apologies, madam." Miles beamed warmly at the housekeeper. "I shall scrub that dratted mud from the hall tiles with my own hands!"

Mrs. Birch, however, was perhaps the one woman Miles and his charming grin would never impress. "In future use the boot scraper by the door, if you please."

"I am duly chastened." He held his hat to his chest and looked extremely sorry.

She glanced over at Darius. "That tea must be cold by now, young sir." She gestured at the large cup on his blotter. "Why, you have not drunk any of it, but you spilled it all over your letter again! I've never known a young fellow so clumsy. I shall bring you another cup."

"That is not necessary, Mrs. Birch, thank you." He quickly

moved the tea-stained papers, slipping them inside a drawer.

With a shrug and another glare at the new arrival, she waddled back out again, slamming the study door in her wake.

Miles laughed abruptly. "She's quite a tartar. Wouldn't like to run into her down a dark alley."

Darius carefully closed and locked his drawer, then got up and walked around the desk. "What on earth possessed you to come here?"

"I did think you might be pleased to see me, old chap."

"Hmm." In truth, he wasn't exactly sure how he felt about this unexpected guest. On the one hand he always enjoyed Miles's company. It was hard not to, despite the fact that they were two complete opposites. On the other hand, there were certain complicated matters afoot, and Miles would relish interfering and giving his "advice."

"I won't stay long," his friend added, assuming a quick and unconvincing sulk, "if I'm in the way."

Darius sighed. "You're not in the way."

"I could always stay in that charming little tavern down in the village. The landlord—delightful chap by the name of Bridges—tells me he has a spare room above."

So he'd already been to the Pig in a Poke; that would account for the strong odor of cider emitted with the first gales of laughter. Miles never wasted any time and quickly made himself at home wherever he went. He had a knack for fitting in, whereas Darius was the eternal square peg in the round hole.

"Apparently he also has a spare daughter," his friend added. "Took the opportunity of mentioning her several times."

"Yes. There is a lot of that around here."

"And I met a robust fellow who eagerly gave me a lecture on bacon and tried to sell me some there and then. An excellent salesman, I might add. I was tempted to take him up on it, until I remembered I don't care for bacon."

"There is a lot of that here too."

Miles scratched his chin, his gaze hastily and somewhat slyly taking in the contents of the study. "Well, I'd be content to stay at the tavern, if you haven't the room. I don't want to put you out."

"Don't be ridiculous. Of course you can stay here."

Miles beamed anew, the veneer of a huff speedily forgotten. "Splendid. I noticed the woods and parkland behind the house. There must be excellent shooting this time of year."

"So I understand."

The unexpected guest nodded his sun-gilded head, dropped backward into a chair, and put his heels up on the desk. "Now what's this I hear about a harvest dance tomorrow?"

"Bridges told you about that too, did he?"

"Sounds like merry fun. We must attend."

"Certainly we must not."

"But I insist. I must get to know all the lovely young ladies. Can't have you keeping them all to yourself, Wainwright. It is my duty—yours too, as a gentleman—to see they don't go without partners."

"I'll leave that task to your capable hands. You can dance with them all."

"Even the one that has kept you away from Town these last two weeks?"

Darius strode to the sash window and wrenched it open

for some air. As much as he distrusted fresh air, sometimes large gulps of it were the only cure for a feverish headache like the one he suddenly suffered. "Well," Miles demanded, "it is a woman, isn't it? I knew it must be."

He took a few deep breaths and then turned to face his friend again. "Ever the optimist and the romantic. I can assure you the reason for my extended stay has nothing to do with a female." Perhaps it was a good thing Miles had come, he thought suddenly. His friend's presence was a timely reminder of real life and matters about which he *should* be thinking.

Miles waited, brow quirked, his palms pressed together as if in prayer, their fingertips propping up his chin.

"My great-uncle left his affairs in some disarray. I stayed to put them in order."

Still Miles was silent, but his pale blue eyes gleamed slyly. Darius spun around to the window again and tugged harder. The warped frame was stuck fast and as he sweated over it, he hissed out a terse question to his friend over his shoulder. "Have you ever known me distracted by a woman, Forester?"

After a short pause his friend replied softly, "Only once. More than ten years ago."

Darius finally left the window, resolved to tackle the problem later. Turning, he rested against the ledge and glowered at Miles.

"I began to despair of seeing you ever so pleasantly distracted again, Wainwright. That's why I had to come and witness the event with my own eyes."

Shaking his head, Darius looked away at the wall, his hands curled around the window ledge behind him.

"I only hope this young lady has more wits about her

than the first," added Miles.

"I hate to disappoint you, but if that's why you came, you made a wasted journey into the country. There is no young lady, and I cannot imagine why you think there is. Can't a man come and go around the country without his friends assuming he's lost his mind?"

"Whatever you say."

"If you came here to tease me, you'll just have to find other diversions, won't you?"

"You know me, Wainwright—I'll find my entertainment while I'm here."

"Good. Just don't expect me to make any for you."

The Book Club Belles had reached a very dramatic chapter in *Pride and Prejudice*, and today was Justina's turn to read aloud.

> *"I have never desired your good opinion, and you have certainly bestowed it most unwillingly…"*

Her friends were hushed, listening in awe as Elizabeth Bennet berated Mr. Darcy with every gusty word and rejected his marriage proposal.

> *"With so evident a desire of offending and insulting me, you chose to tell me that you liked me against your will, against your reason, and even against your character?"*

As soon as the scene was complete, Catherine exclaimed, "Poor Mr. Darcy. I cannot help feeling he has been wronged. Elizabeth Bennet is too ready to believe all the bad she hears of him."

Justina gazed at her sister in disbelief. "*Poor Mr. Darcy?* The man is a terrible prig and deserves every severe word."

"I cannot help feeling he has been wronged," Cathy insisted gently. "Elizabeth Bennet is very sure of herself. While confidence is an admirable quality, an excess of it can be unbecoming in a young lady."

"The clue is in the title," said Rebecca, reaching over to pour tea, "*Pride and Prejudice.* But which is the victim of which?" She handed the first cup and saucer to Lucy, who had to be called away from the window where she'd been standing for some time.

With the arrival of Mr. Wainwright in the village, Lucy had lost much of her previous interest in the fiction, just as she grew tired of adventures and mischief. Justina suspected she only came to the Book Society meetings now to keep up with the gossip and show off whatever new trinket she had lately acquired.

"The mail coach is late again," Lucy exclaimed impatiently, taking the tea cup she was offered without turning away from the view outside.

"You are usually the one on tenterhooks for the post," Rebecca said to Justina with a smile. "Have you given up waiting for your mysterious letter?"

She shrugged. "A watched pot never boils, as they say. Perhaps if I do not expect it, the wretched thing will come at last."

"And you will not tell us what it is?"

"No!" She had decided not to inform her friends of the manuscript she'd sent away to a publisher. Even Catherine knew nothing about her ambitions and would probably think her vain. Changing the subject to direct their attention away from her, she added hastily, "Lucy hopes for sight of your brother, Becky. That is the reason she waits for the coach."

Of all the Book Society ladies, only Diana Makepiece showed no excitement at the prospect of seeing Captain Sherringham again.

"I suppose you told your brother of my engagement in your letters," she said as she stirred her tea, sitting very prim and straight in her chair.

Rebecca replied breezily, "Of course. Such important news must be shared. Nate insists upon knowing all that happens in his absence."

Justina looked at Diana, waiting for more, but nothing came. Her spring green eyes were downcast, her black lashes leaving a shadow on her ivory cheeks. Diana was a classic beauty, but her countenance did not have the natural warmth and kindness of Cathy's—as Mrs. Penny would be quick to point out.

Diana and her widowed mother lived carefully on a slender budget, but they did so with their heads high and never let anyone show pity. Always aware that she would be expected to marry well and shrewdly, Diana must have experienced great relief when she received a proposal from William Shaw, but although she spoke of her coup repeatedly, almost as if to reassure herself of her success, there was never a vast deal of emotion apparent in her face. This much-needed betrothal had not melted her icy exterior.

When Diana finally took her spoon out, the tea in her cup spun in a deep vortex. Cathy asked her if William Shaw was coming from Manderson to accompany her to the harvest dance. Diana replied that he would try, but his grandmama was sick and he may not be able to leave her side.

"Mustn't risk his inheritance," Justina remarked dourly. "I would tell him to remain with Old Moneybags rather than come to the dance."

Her sister gave her a quick frown.

"What now? I am only being practical. Who cares about the silly dance anyway?"

Behind them all Lucy suddenly jumped, cup clattering in her saucer. "Oh, there is Mr. Wainwright riding by. With *another* handsome gentleman."

At once Rebecca joined her by the window and beckoned to Cathy. Justina, restraining her curiosity with difficulty, kept to her chair. Diana, who seemed lost in thought while staring into her teacup, did the same.

"I wonder who it can be?" Rebecca muttered. "He certainly has a sunny smile."

"Oh, he looks familiar," said Cathy, her voice soft and puzzled. "Do come and look, Jussy. I believe we have seen that gentleman before."

Now Justina had an excuse to look. Sighing heftily, she put her cup aside and went to the window. Her gaze instantly, and against her wishes or intentions, caressed Wainwright from head to toe. Spotless and devilishly handsome as ever.

The fair-haired gentleman riding beside him had an open, friendly smile.

"Never seen him before in my life." Justina returned to her chair. She knew it was the gentleman who had danced with her sister in Bath—the one who was obliged to abandon Cathy, most humiliatingly, in the midst of a set because his friend would not stay with a stained waistcoat. It was a surprise to her that Cathy had not recognized Wainwright before now, but her sister had understandably paid more attention to her pleasant partner than to his disagreeable friend. Now she saw them together and it must have nudged her memory.

But Justina was not about to help her sister remember an incident, and a stained waistcoat, that she was doing all in her power to forget.

Nineteen

THE EVENING OF THE HARVEST DANCE WAS UPON THEM
at last. Weeks of frenzied preparation came to this. The
ladies of the Book Society gathered together, admiring
one another's gowns and hair. Lucy, as promised, sported
her mother's pearls, and this caused her to walk about with
her head lifted and to utilize a rather foolish, high-pitched,
exaggerated laugh that shook her head and made her ear-
rings jostle to catch the light. All this, however, could be
overlooked when she greeted Justina with giddy flattery,
so surprised and unrehearsed that it had to be genuine.

"How lovely you look, Jussy. I almost didn't recognize you!"

"It is nothing," she replied with a nonchalant wave
of her hand.

"But your hair looks so pretty tonight, and there is
a glow about your face. Oh, I do wish my hair curled
naturally like yours, but mine will hang like wet willow
branches by the end of the first dance."

Lucy had a knack for saying these things. It was artless and usually left the recipient feeling guilty for being
irritated with the girl only moments before.

The harvest ball was held in Dockley's barn, the largest covered dancing space in the village. As long as the rain held off, the old building served as an adequate function room. As the name inferred, it had once belonged to the property of old Farmer Dockley, but when he died without sons to tend his farm, his widow sold the land to Major Sherringham. The major was a merry fellow who declared there was nothing he liked to see more than young people enjoying themselves, so he had donated the broken down barn for the general use of the villagers. Of course, his benevolent gesture also absolved him of any responsibility or expense when it came to repairing the place.

Despite a leaky roof and leaning walls, the village ladies made the best of it, always gathering together to decorate the barn for annual dances and festivals, as well as the occasional wedding party.

Tonight, bowers of willow and autumn leaves cascaded from the rafters and benches were set around the walls for seating, but Justina always preferred the hay bales. It was not a harvest dance, in her opinion, without a hay bale to sit upon, and those who chose the benches were missing out, not truly getting into the spirit of things.

Diana arrived with her mother, but no William Shaw. His grandmama's health, it seemed, had taken yet another turn for the worse when she learned of his plans to leave her for the evening.

"It is no matter," said Diana, reminding Justina of herself a few moments earlier when she'd hurriedly dismissed Lucy's admiration. "I would not have come this evening myself, if Mama did not want to go out. She insisted."

Despite the fact that she was not wearing her best gown, Diana still looked elegant, her fine features and naturally graceful, well-balanced figure not requiring any artifice. She wore a simple green ribbon in her hair and it matched her eyes almost perfectly. Looking around the barn, she fidgeted with her long white gloves, which—like the roses on Justina's slippers—were really too grand for the harvest dance, and asked whether Rebecca had yet arrived.

"No," Justina replied, "nor has Captain Sherringham."

Diana shrugged. "Oh…" She caught her breath and looked down at her gloved fingers. "I do not expect he will come."

"But he promised his sister he would be here in time," said Lucy.

"That rake is forever making promises and forgetting them." Gloves adjusted finally to her satisfaction, Diana looked around at the other villagers, letting her gaze skim the barn with casual carelessness. "I do not hold my breath to see *him* again."

"Well, of course," said Justina, carefully keeping a solemn face. "After all, you are an engaged woman."

"Precisely."

The musicians seated at the end of the barn had just begun to play. Justina looked over at the benches and saw her mother poking and prodding at poor Cathy's hair and dress. Her sister tolerated it with remarkable patience, as always. "One of these days I wouldn't be at all surprised if Cathy doesn't simply snap and take a wood axe to the pickle jars in the pantry," she muttered. "No one could possibly hold all that inside and not suffer for it."

Diana replied, "It is surprising how much a person *can* keep inside. Especially when they are bound by duty."

Before anyone might react to that statement, a whispered exclamation swept the barn, gathering volume as it traveled. Every face turned. There in the open doorway stood the tall, breathtaking figure of Darius Wainwright.

Justina's heart forgot to beat. Now, quite suddenly, she was torn between wishing she'd stayed home and being glad for the silly roses on her slippers.

◡◠

"What a jolly scene this is," Miles exclaimed, beaming, rubbing his hands together. "And so many lovely ladies. I hardly know where to begin."

Darius had been forced out of the house by his friend's enthusiasm to dance. Miles Forester, when determined, was like a strong storm at sea. It buffeted him about until he relented, weary and clinging to his mast. He took in his own sails and let the blustery gale lead his ship until it had worn itself out.

"If you don't care to attend, I'll go by myself," Miles had threatened. "I suppose the good innkeeper Bridges will introduce me to the ladies of the village, if you cannot."

Well, Darius could not let his friend go alone into the fray, could he?

As soon as they entered the place, every eye turned to observe them standing there. Like two stupid bookends, thought Darius, the tips of his ears feeling cold and exposed.

"What splendid fun," Miles burbled away at his side. "I've never been to a dance in a barn before."

"Really? I *am* surprised."

"Oh, do take that dour expression off your face for once, man, and enjoy yourself."

"*Enjoy* myself?"

"Yes, you know, stop worrying. Forget business for a few hours."

"I hope the weather remains dry this evening as I understand the roof leaks."

"All the better." Miles chuckled. "I shall see the ladies running about in wet clothes, in need of me to shelter them."

Dr. Penny and his wife had spotted the two gentlemen and were already urging their eldest daughter forward, but several other couples did the same with their single daughters too. They were about to be converged upon from all sides.

"Welcome to hell," Darius muttered.

Miles quickly focused his sights on Miss Penny as her mother dragged her through the crowd of rowdy dancers. "Aha! Here comes a very pretty girl, indeed. There in the blue. Fancy you keeping her all to yourself, Wainwright! Introduce me at once, you blackguard!"

"I doubt you'll need my help with an introduction. They don't stand on ceremony around here."

Darius left his eager friend to it. Moving away from the dancers, he collected a glass of punch and found a seat on a corner bench, away from the general commotion, where he might observe from a safe distance.

Justina watched her sister dancing and felt the usual forlorn mixture of pride and envy. Two more sins to note in her diary tonight, alas. There would, she had no doubt, be more by the end of the evening. As much as she knew Cathy was a most deserving object of that beauty—for she

was just as sweet on the inside—it was very hard sometimes that all the good looks should have gone to one
daughter, when they might have been shared in smaller
measures between two. But perhaps *she* was destined for
other things in life. Justina liked to think that was God's
reason. If He had one, other than a capricious delight in
giving out challenges and setbacks to good people.

At the sight of a bright scarlet coat coming through
the open barn doors, her mood lifted. Captain Nathaniel
Sherringham, escorting his sister, made his way through
the mob of villagers far too slowly for Justina's patience.
Usually she would set her punch aside and run through
the dancers to greet him, but tonight, too aware of a certain pair of dark, disapproving eyes observing her from a
shadowy corner, she must be more mature and that most
terrible of all things—ladylike.

At last, after an interminable wait, the Sherringhams
arrived at their small group and all the usual polite saluta-
tions were quickly dispensed with in favor of the friendly
jocularity more familiar to all those present.

"You look—dare I say it—quite grown up tonight,
Miss Jussy and Miss Lucy," the captain exclaimed. "Have
I been gone so long?"

"Indeed you have! So much has happened here,"
Lucy replied excitedly. "There are new folk in the
village, including a youngish rector and a very grand
inhabitant at Midwitch Manor. And Diana is engaged."

"So I heard." He swiveled briskly on his heel to
address Diana, who had not yet said a word. "William
Shaw is a lucky fellow."

Unsmiling, she opened her fan and fluttered it wildly
before her face. "Thank you, Captain Sherringham."

"He is a shopkeeper in Manderson, I understand."

Her eyes narrowed and her slender neck lengthened. "Mr. Shaw is a landlord and businessman with two shops and potential to expand with a third."

"And...not here tonight?"

"He was unable to attend due to family obligations."

The captain stared at Diana while she kept her expression composed. Her fan was the most demonstrative thing about her. "I am disappointed," he said softly. "I should like to meet the fellow who won your heart *and* your mama's approval."

"Excuse me." Diana swept away, still fanning herself with extreme force. Her mother had been waving to her from across the barn for several minutes, but from Diana's manner anyone would think she had not seen her immediately.

Mrs. Makepiece was a handsome woman who, twenty years ago, having found herself widowed suddenly, left with nothing but a baby and her deceased husband's gambling debts, moved to Hawcombe Prior to keep house for her brother, the previous vicar. Now that he too had tipped up his boots, she and Diana did the best they could living on what little he'd left them. Justina had heard that Mrs. Makepiece came from an upper-class background, but she left her family behind when she entered a misalliance with a man beneath her—a man who was handsome and witty, but faithless and untrustworthy. It was a bitter lesson, plainly read in the hard lines that sometimes appeared across her brow, spoiling the features of her face.

Her brother, for many years the only family member who would acknowledge her after the scandal of her elopement, had sheltered the widow and her child out of charity. And he never let her forget it. Indeed the people of Hawcombe Prior might never have known she was his sister, for he always referred to her as his housekeeper and treated her thus.

Over the years, as Diana grew into an intelligent, attractive girl with good manners, she was apparently deemed "acceptable" by some members of her mother's estranged family, for she had been invited to visit cousins near Oxford on occasion. But Mrs. Makepiece kept a tight rein on her only daughter, and Justina suspected Diana would not be allowed to make the same mistakes with her life.

The captain watched her go and then turned back to the other ladies. "Well, I must say, Miss Makepiece has become quite tired and sour-looking. I might not have recognized her. She has lost her bloom."

"I am sorry for her," said his sister.

"Why?" he demanded, hands behind his back, a curt, hard laugh sputtering out of him. "It is her choice. Through bias and persuasion one might be prevented from marrying a person, but no sensible woman is forced to wed against her will in this day and age."

"It is all so simple for you, Nate." Rebecca scowled at her brother.

He shrugged. "I cannot see that there is anything to pity her about."

His sister explained in a low voice, "I am sorry for Diana because she has bartered her best gown all for a little fictional romance, in hope it will replace the lack of real love in her life. She yearns for what she doesn't have and thinks she cannot have." She looked over to where their friend now stood with her mama. "But I suspect she would thank no one for pointing that out to her. She is doing her duty, making her sacrifice for the mother who struggled all these years to raise her alone."

Justina followed Rebecca's gaze and realized it was true. She had been so busy mocking the romance in *Pride and Prejudice* that she failed to see how it fulfilled certain needs in the heart of the young woman who went to such trouble to acquire it. "Well, it makes me angry that Diana would marry a tedious fellow like Shaw if she doesn't love him. I would not marry for anything other than the most passionate and devoted love."

"I did not think you believed in love, Jussy," Rebecca retorted with a wry smile.

"I never said that," she replied, feeling very warm suddenly. "I merely believe it does not happen often. And I think it very sad when the presence or lack of money blinds people to the things they really need to be happy."

"I do not blame Diana for getting William Shaw while she could," said Lucy. "Even if he does tell the most uninteresting stories ever and has hairy nostrils. A girl can overlook a few faults for that sort of pin money."

Justina once again wondered at the things that went on inside that fair head lately. "Lucy Bridges, you have become quite a mercenary hussy."

The others laughed and Lucy pouted.

"You would not marry for money then, Miss Jussy?" the captain inquired with a playful smile.

"Indeed I would not."

"I am glad to hear it. Very sensible of you."

"I don't plan to marry. I may not be a woman of independent means, but I shall always be of independent spirit!"

"But she *would* be a rich man's mistress. She said so. It is preferable, she thinks, to being a wife." Lucy's high-pitched voice won out over the music and several faces turned their way, including—to Justina's horror—that of Wainwright and his friend.

Fortunately Captain Sherringham was a gallant fellow, who knew what to do in a crisis. He offered Justina his hand and bowed smartly.

"Perhaps you'll honor me with a dance, Miss Jussy?"

"Certainly, Captain," she replied, head high despite her over-heated cheeks. "Delighted to oblige."

Twenty

I<small>T WAS VERY WARM IN THAT CROWDED BARN</small>. D<small>ARIUS SAT</small> with his hands on his knees, feeling out of place in his fine evening clothes, watching the villagers become slowly more inebriated. His head spun with the unremitting noise of giddy, raucous laughter. So much dust was kicked up by the dancing, stomping feet that he could taste it on his tongue.

Watching Miss Justina Penny dance with a very smug fellow in a scarlet coat, his discomfort rapidly multiplied. The couple laughed and chattered easily in a familiar way, teasing one another when they forgot the steps or moved in the wrong direction.

Darius, who always worried too much about getting his steps exactly right, could not imagine being able to laugh at a mistake.

Fingers digging into his knees, he watched the two of them making sizeable fools of themselves. When the dance was over, they stood close together, talking. Then they walked, arm in arm, to where her friends waited.

Miles returned to his side. "Have you not danced yet, Wainwright? Surely you cannot say there is no one to dance with. There are far more ladies present than gentlemen."

Darius felt his tight, reluctant lips crack like a fissure in marble. "I'm sure the ladies prefer your company." Without moving his head he searched the crowd and saw that Miss Justina and her friends had dispersed. Lucy Bridges was now dancing with Sam Hardacre, who spun her around like the sails of a windmill, and the tall, auburn-haired girl danced with the rector. There was her quieter friend—the one with the somber expression and pretty green eyes, talking to the elder Miss Penny. But no sign of Justina in that virginal white muslin gown with the little yellow sprigs.

He raised a finger to his cravat and loosened it. His gaze picked over the scene with increasing irritation.

Where could she have gone? It was never wise to let a lively young woman out of sight. Her parents were there by the punch bowl, and they did not seem at all concerned about their missing daughter. Darius shook his head. This was how bad things happened. Crowded, noisy parties like this, wild young girls left unguarded. Too much punch consumed and smug fellows in uniform, hanging about to take advantage of a stolen moment.

Was this buffoon, this "wag," who seemed to find everything an amusing jape, the captain she'd planned to meet for an illicit bedchamber romp in Bath?

Ice slivers formed in his veins.

"I need a rest, old chap," Miles was saying. "I give you leave to take my place with the ladies. Try not to bore them too much."

"Thank you. I prefer to sit here and wait for you to be done making an exhibit of yourself."

"But look, Wainwright. Over there is the very lovely

Miss Penny. Imagine my surprise when I realized she and I had danced together once before in Bath! And she is currently without a partner. I would dance with her again if it was not unseemly to monopolize the same young lady all evening. You must dance with her now, before she is snapped up by another."

"I appreciate your concern to find me a partner, Forester, but rest assured I am content to observe the festivities." Darius still could not see that red coat or Justina. He tugged again on his cravat and then the cuffs of his evening coat. Something about his attire was extremely uncomfortable. He had never perspired so much simply from sitting in one place, and yet inside he was cold to the bone.

In a deeply disgruntled tone, he added, "I have seen enough folk making dancing fools of themselves tonight, acting without decorum or dignity. I've no intention of doing the same."

"But Wainwright—"

"I see a great deal of misbehavior that can only lead to trouble and if you ask me, those Penny girls are left unguarded far too often. The younger one in particular. Her manners leave much to be desired. I've never known a young woman so brazen. Every encounter I've suffered with her has left me wounded or stained in one way or another." And then, afraid he'd said too much about her and was in danger of rousing his friend's suspicion, he added, "Whatever her name is. I have forgotten it."

❧

Justina had approached the benches with the intention of saying a polite good evening to Wainwright. He may not be the dancing sort, but she could at least show her maturity and notice his presence. There was also a slight satisfaction to be had in forcing him to acknowledge that he'd seen her. She was, after all, wearing her mended best gown and Cathy had helped dress her hair in a new style. She'd been told she looked quite passable for once.

Then she heard his comments.

Quickly she changed her mind about approaching the miserable fellow. Just before she turned away, Miles coughed and got Wainwright's attention. He glanced over his shoulder and saw her standing there, half in shadow. She had no doubt her face was glowing. His, however, was suddenly drained of color.

There was nothing to say to him, she decided, and he could not possibly have anything to say to her. The girl whose name he did not even know.

Returning to the brighter side of the barn, she sought out her sister, who was full of excitement at having recognized her dancing partner from Bath.

"Jussy, do you not recall that he was dancing with me when you caused that riot and he had to leave with his friend? I knew he seemed familiar, but I could not place it!"

"I did not cause a riot. It was not my fault."

"Yes, but Mr. Forester was the gentleman dancing with me when it happened. I was terribly sorry to see him leave."

"He left you in the midst of a dance, Cathy. It was very rude."

"But he had no choice. He had to leave with his friend for they came in the same coach."

Justina sneered. "I daresay everyone does what Mr. Wainwright says." She straightened her spine in a manner that would have made her mama proud. "He must be accustomed to having folk at his beck and call."

"Here he comes now, moving very purposefully toward you."

Justina's pulse was as uneven as a line of her own hasty stitches.

"I do believe he will ask you to dance," said Cathy.

"Me? I very much doubt it." He had better not dare, she thought angrily. Just let him say one word to her and she would—

"Miss Penny." He was there before them, bowing. "And Miss Justina. No butterflies this evening?"

She looked up in time to see his lip curl disdainfully. While she was still composing a suitable reply, struggling to calm her temper and move her stiffened tongue, Cathy politely replied to his greeting and asked how he enjoyed the dance.

Justina's mind raced. If she had a cup of punch in her hand she might have thrown it all down his dull, spotless, very expensive waistcoat. Let that one be stained too, just like the one in Bath.

He'd fondled her and kissed her when no one was there to see. He treated her like a plaything. Would no doubt take advantage of her innocence if she had stayed in his clutches. But he was still sneering at her and her family. Still looking down his long nose at her, as he did in Bath.

And she, swept up in a generous mood after perusing his great-uncle's love letters, had imagined he too might have a gentler side, and that she might befriend him.

Befriend him? Ha! He would not want her friendship.

The blasted man could not be helped. He would never get out of the way of his own arrogance and conceit.

"May I have the honor of the next dance, Miss Justina?"

Oh, the sheer bold-faced gall of the man! "Did your friend remind you of my name, sir?"

"Of course not. I do not need reminding of it."

Perhaps he did not realize what she'd heard. She swallowed, stared at his broad shoulder, tried to catch a breath.

He stood before her, waiting, expecting her to feel honored, no doubt, that he singled her out. That he lowered himself to dance with her.

Justina licked her lips, heaved a deep breath and demanded, "Why?"

Wainwright's eyes narrowed like arrow slits in his stony fortress face. "*Why?*"

"You don't actually *want* to dance, do you?"

He paused, apparently confused for a moment. "I am assured by my friend that it is the established mode of movement on such occasions."

Justina bit the inside of her mouth and it smarted. "I hope you do not assume I stood here waiting for a partner. I don't feel the need to dance just because everyone else does."

"Neither do I, madam. It seems we can agree on that much, at least."

Cathy pinched her arm.

She ignored it. "I am quite exhausted from dancing already, sir."

"I am not surprised, madam. I am exhausted from watching you."

He did not move away, but remained before her like

a great obstacle in her path, his face grimly forbidding, eyes unblinking, lips firm. Apparently he would not allow her to dance with anyone else until she danced with him. In her peripheral vision she spied their mama heading toward them and knew the mortification was only about to get worse, so she finally accepted the hand he offered and let herself be dragged into the dance. All around them, she knew people were watching and must be marveling at his strange choice of partner.

The band struck up a new tune—a rowdy country jig. Usually it was a dance that Justina enjoyed more than any other, since it gave her an excuse to bounce about vigorously, but this time there was none of that joyous freedom she felt when dancing with Captain Sherringham. It was an ordeal, painful and dolorous. She went through the motions, her heart simply not in it. This man danced with her because he felt obliged, or else he wanted to correct her manner of dancing. Either way there could be no delight in it. There was too much anger bubbling away inside her and, try as she might, she could not be like Cathy and bottle it away in a pickling jar.

"If you meant to dance only so late in the evening, you should have danced with one of the other ladies, Mr. Wainwright. Any one of them would make a more obliging, more elegant partner. I have a tendency to forget the steps." She pressed her toe hard upon his. "Oops."

He wheezed, "I have observed your peculiar manner of making up your own steps."

"I cannot help it. I always feel mine are more suited to the music." She turned the wrong way and clapped a beat before everyone else. Let the wicked old bugger try to keep up with her, she thought smugly.

He gripped her fingers a little too tightly and she stifled a yelp. "Do you like to paint, Miss Justina?"

"Oh, Lord, are we going to have blasted conversation?" she groaned. "Is it not bad enough already? I doubt either one of us really wants to *talk* to the other, and I ought to concentrate or I might embarrass you with my ineptitude. As well as my brazen manners."

Wainwright squeezed her hand again. "It is a civil question, madam. It deserves a civil answer. I have always endeavored to answer your many and varied questions."

"Yes," she snapped. "I paint. What else do you want to know? I paint with all the wrong colors stirred up together," she added smugly, "and I always paint outside the lines."

"If I might make an observation then, it is a very good thing that some people stay within them."

She scowled. "I despise the lines. I never follow any." She tugged her hand free of his and clapped so vigorously her fingers throbbed and her palms stung. But no worse than her heart after she'd overheard him deny that he even knew her name.

"And yet if there were no lines at all," he replied, "you would have nothing to rebel against, would you?"

He recaptured her hand and thus her best efforts to turn the wrong way again were stymied. At the edge of the dancers, she saw her sister seated on a hay bale with Captain Sherringham, talking amiably. Rebecca was now enjoying a dance with Wainwright's friend and laughing heartily at something the man just told her. They both looked over at Justina and her partner, making the subject of their hilarity quite obvious. Justina's insides turned over in a sideways flip. She knew the story of her debut in the Upper Rooms at Bath last year would soon be the talk of the village. Wainwright's friend was evidently a jolly sort and saw the joke in it. Unfortunately for Justina, while not so long ago she too would have laughed and made sport of herself, she was less inclined to see the humor in it now.

"Do you play, Miss Justina?" her partner demanded, making no apparent attempt to soften his pitch from its usual air of self-righteous interrogation. "Do you sing? I know you like to use your voice loudly."

"This attempt at polite chit chat is not required, Mr. Wainwright. I wish you would not speak at all."

"But you like to talk."

She glared at him. Was he mocking her? "From now on I shall be silent, sir."

"We must have conversation. It is expected when two people stand up together for a set."

At once she forgot her promise not to speak. "You always do what is expected?"

"Of course."

"Did you think you were expected to dance with me?"

"I did."

"Then, if *I* might make an observation, you must see that always doing what is expected of you can have severe drawbacks." Again she stomped hard on his foot.

Twenty-one

DARIUS OBSERVED HOW ALL THE LEAPING, JUMPING, and clapping increased the glow in her cheeks and the vivacious sparkle in her eyes. The husky, breathless tenor of her voice forced him to listen closer, watch her lips, made him forget his bruised toes.

Tonight Justina Penny had emerged from her cocoon of dowdy, deliberately unkempt eccentricity and shaken off the rumpled girl in muddy petticoats. Now he had her closer, he recognized that the tiny yellow sprigs on her white gown were, in fact, daisies. It was a reminder of summer and of her youthfulness. Not that he needed reminding of the latter.

He was, he realized glumly, entranced by her and no longer capable of denying it to himself. His Wainwright countenance had begun to crack under the pressure. He felt it. He was also suffering a wretched sensation he could not identify, but it had come upon him when he saw her standing near and realized she might have overheard his comments to Miles. Surely he had nothing to feel remorse about, nothing for which he need apologize. Everything he'd said was quite true. This young woman was left unguarded too often, and it could only end badly. She was recklessly curious, temptation personified, and rather wicked.

After all, he ought to know, since he'd taken advantage of her several times.

And there it was. Guilt.

He knew she'd heard him pretending not to know her name, but since she insulted him readily enough at every opportunity, he did not think that could be so great a sin. But apparently she thought differently, if the stomping of her feet upon his was anything to go by.

Fortunately for the sake of his toes, the second dance of the set was a more sedate minuet.

Just when he enjoyed a sense of calm comfort, thinking he had done his duty as far as the requisite conversation and could now simply enjoying looking at her, she said suddenly, "Your friend seems very amiable. From watching him dance, I would say *he* does so for pleasure."

Darius did not reply.

"Is there anything that you do for pleasure, Mr. Wainwright?"

"Not very often."

"And when you do, it would be....?"

He sought for something. What *did* he like to do? Obligations were many in his life, pleasures rare. Images passed through his mind: of himself at his desk, writing correspondence, checking ledgers of figures, addressing his employees, or striding briskly across a loading dock. He pictured the slender slices of private life spent at home in London: visiting Sarah in her quiet wing to check on her progress with the governess, trying to avoid his stepmother by taking servants' doors and passages around the house. Then came the half hour a month he spent checking the accuracy of all the timepieces he owned, large and small.

"I mend clocks," he said finally. "It is a fascinating task and satisfying."

"Of course," she murmured, looking away from him. "Clocks."

"I hear a tone of scorn, Miss Justina." Because he did not leap about like a fool, capable of making her laugh?

"Not at all. You are entitled to find pleasure wherever and whenever you choose."

"Thank you, madam. I shall. And I hope, in the future, we shall find activities of a mutual enjoyment. In fact," he curled his fingers tighter around hers, "I have no doubt of it."

She frowned at him briefly, but then looked a second time for longer and with surprise upon her face, as if she'd never seen him smile before. It was, in actual fact, just as startling to him when he felt it there, moving his lips. He should have been concentrating on the steps.

"Are you quite all right?" she demanded.

He gave a solemn nod, straightening his lips again, quickly terminating their foray into geniality. "Perfectly."

"I would advise you not to drink too much punch, Mr. Wainwright. I'm afraid Mrs. Dockley makes it from an ancient family recipe and rumor has it that she strains it through her old, unwashed stockings. Many a strong gentleman has been felled by the strangely intoxicating brew, including her dearly departed husband who drank far too much of it."

"I am duly warned, madam. I shall proceed with caution."

The dance ended, and she walked away from him at

once, barely sparing the time to rise from her begrudging
curtsy. Within moments she was dancing again with her
favored partner, the jolly soldier with grinning teeth,
floppy, uncombed hair, and gleaming brass buttons.
Darius was not the friendliest of men, but even he had
never disliked a person so intensely on sight.

Even if it might be considered improper to dance too
many times with the same partner, Captain Sherringham
wouldn't care and neither did she. Between them there
was none of that dreadful, heavy tension she felt when
in Wainwright's presence. In dear Sherry's company,
all was easy and uncomplicated. With Wainwright
everything was difficult and vexing, pulling her in too
many directions.

But the captain's mind was on Diana Makepiece. He
began talking immediately about the mistake she was
making with William Shaw. Justina found the twinkle in
her old friend's eye—usually to be depended on in any
circumstance—muted for once.

"Diana has certainly become very tedious," she agreed.
"I expect she will bore you too with the subject of her
engagement. It is her only conversation these days."

"Fool woman! Why on earth would she fix herself on
him? I thought she had more…more…" He shrugged,
unable to finish apparently, exasperation clear in the set
of his jaw as they moved down the dance together.

Justina remembered what Diana had said to her
earlier, and she repeated it now for the captain. "It is
surprising how much a person can keep inside. Especially
when they are bound by duty."

"A marriage should not be for duty's sake. That is the sure way to misery."

"I could not agree more." As always, she was glad to have her own opinions vindicated by a man who was older and ergo, supposedly wiser.

"Who is that dreadfully grim fellow I saw you dancing with? I thought he must have some constipated disorder of the bowel with that look on his face. Is he one of your father's patients?"

Both she and the captain glanced through the crowd to where Darius Wainwright stood talking to his friend again. Just at that moment he looked back at them and his face bore more than passing resemblance to that of a bull newly cognizant of trespassers in his field. Or his orchard, she mused.

"That is a very fine and fancy gentleman from London, by the name of Wainwright," she explained. "He has been here little more than a fortnight and is not liked by anybody."

They were parted for a few beats of the music and then joined hands again. "He seems to keep a very keen eye on you, Jussy."

"He looks at me only because to him I am a clock that is out of order. He would like to fix me, make me chime at his bidding and in unison with everyone else." She wrinkled her nose. "But he's nothing more than a cockatrice trying to kill me with his stare and I"—she put her nose in the air—"shall ignore him completely."

"Quite right, too!" The captain feigned a schoolmasterly expression and shook his finger in her face. "You make certain to keep him wanting—lure him in, sigh by sigh, wink by wink, petticoat by petticoat, before you capitulate, and he might offer you plenty to be his mistress. *If,* as Lucy tells me, that is your plan."

She snorted with laughter, quickly forgetting to maintain her imperious expression. "You must tutor me in the ways of a Cyprian, Sherry."

Now a little of that old gleam returned to his eyes, and her pulse skipped to see it there again. She much preferred him in a happy, carefree mood than a contemplative one. "Capital idea, Jussy. I was afraid all my friends here in Hawcombe Prior had grown too old and serious, but I see at least one of you may be relied upon to amuse me." He looked over his shoulder, pretending to be sure they were not overheard, although with all the shouting and laughing from the dancers around them they had to stand closer just to hear one another. "I shall take you under my wing and teach you the arts of the fan, how to pour and warm brandy, how to light his cigar—"

"Cigar?"

"I have some from France. I'll show you one day. A mistress must also know how to serve her lover with grapes and sweetmeats. How to tantalize"—he lowered his voice and shot a sly glance sideways at the distant, hovering figure of Mr. Wainwright—"her haughty lover."

They both laughed. It was just like old times, she thought happily. Captain Sherringham was not afraid of mischief and for as long as he encouraged her, as long as he was amused by her, what harm could there be in the friendship? She felt her mother's eyes scorching into her back from across the barn, but this only urged her on. It was easier to win her mother's disapproval than to struggle for her approval. Besides, to have the dashing captain sharing a jape with her was almost as good as a kiss.

Yes, indeed, she was glad of dear Sherry's company tonight. It chased away the menacing dark cloud of Darius Wainwright and helped her forget that she was at least partly at fault for catching the Wrong Man's attention in the first place.

Under the influence of *Pride and Prejudice* she'd been ready to forgive his stiff manners and look beyond them. But she was misled into thinking she might find any tenderness of feeling beneath his grim surface. Thank goodness she was reminded now that life was no romantic novel. It might not have been the first time her imagination and optimism ran away with her, but she swore it would be the last.

The two gentlemen stayed up late that evening, discussing the dance. Or, at least, Miles spoke of how much enjoyment he'd had. Sprawled in a chair by the hearth, a glass of brandy resting on his chest, he rambled at length about Miss Catherine Penny's sweetness and grace, which survived despite her mother's unconscious ability to undo both with one thoughtless comment. Then, obviously keen not to be heard picking a favorite already, he talked also about the aloof beauty of Miss Makepiece, the delightfully freckled Miss Sherringham's witty and rather daring banter, and Miss Bridges' amusing naïveté.

Darius said very little but stared into the drawing room fire and pondered his predicament. Of course, by dancing with only one woman that evening, he had singled Justina out publicly. It was a declaration of sorts. He had not really thought about what it meant when he felt the overpowering urge to make her dance with him. It was simply instinct, the need to have her in his company, make her look at him and talk to him. An excuse to hold her hand. Truth was, he couldn't bear it when he watched her dance with others. Any of them, but particularly that laughing fool in the red coat. The captain reminded Darius of his elder brother, and he knew the sort of trouble Lucius used to get himself into. And women into.

He rubbed his brow with two fingers and then ran the hand down over his face. All this time he had assumed that when she claimed to find herself in the wrong bed it was merely a fib, an attempt to save face because he spurned her. But now he remembered the name "Captain Sherringham." So she had not been a fortune hunter setting her nets for him; she truly did find herself in his bed by mistake.

Glancing up at the mantel clock he noted the hands were stuck again on the figure one. He sighed fretfully and scraped his fingertips over the curved chair arm, feeling the rough, worn threads of velvet upholstery where Phineas must once have sat, just as he did, and contemplated that clock in frustration.

Miles laughed. "It's no good, old chap. You can't wipe that scowl off your face. You'll just have to do something about her."

He glowered across the hearth to where his friend's face was lit by trembling amber slivers of firelight. "Her?"

"The Penny girl. The one with all the pretty brown curls and the spirited eyes. I found her a delightful partner, but I think she preferred you. And you, so I saw, could not take your eyes off her."

Darius pushed himself to sit up and stop lounging. "Me? Don't talk nonsense."

"The entire two dances I shared with her, she questioned me about you! Most disheartening for a fellow who prefers to be the center of attention." He laughed good-naturedly. "But when I realized she is the very same little miss who caused all the alarums and excursions last year at Bath, I knew why she looked familiar. I suppose she's the reason for your extended stay in Buckinghamshire. Yes, I am certain of it now. Not know her name, indeed! She is quite intriguingly naughty, I suspect. A young woman does not have bright eyes like those without having a wickedly wayward mind illuminating them from behind."

"Forester, I told you why I stayed. It was certainly not to get another waistcoat ruined."

"Aha, but the delightful little Miss Bridges told me all about dear Sir Morty and how she and her friend have been invited here to help you with your great-uncle's possessions." He paused, grinning. "Do stop drumming a tattoo on the arm of that chair. You'll wear the fabric away and get shouted at by your formidable housekeeper."

Darius stilled his fingers, resting them in a claw over the end of the chair arm.

"If I were you," Miles added, stifling a yawn, "I'd take that lively creature off the market before someone beats you to it. Take my advice, Wainwright. If you want her, act now."

"She is not a shipload of Persian carpets."

"Aha, but see!" Miles lurched forward, almost tipping out of the chair, brandy sloshing up the sides of the glass. "This is where you go wrong. You should think of her precisely as that, because trade is where you are expert. That is where you are at ease. The conventional courtship is not for you, Wainwright, you're far too... well, just *you*. You are to romance what a bull would be to a roomful of Wedgwood plates and china cabinets. But think of her as a commodity to be bartered over and won." He fell back in his chair, shaking his golden head. "For a man who is so firm, decisive, and ruthless in business, you're a complete ass when it comes to women."

Darius hardly ever paid heed to his friend's warblings. They were well-meaning, certainly, but not often well-thought out. Miles gamboled through life chasing pretty birds under rainbows and a pleasant summer sky. As the third son of an earl he'd known a life of privilege without the responsibility of property or a title. He had never worked a day in his life, but at least had the grace to appreciate that other folk weren't so fortunate. He had a generous spirit and a good heart. He was also much valued by Darius because he knew exactly how to handle women, including the dreaded stepmother and stepsister. Miles didn't mind keeping them distracted, entertained, and out of the way when Darius was at the edge of his patience.

So if his friend could be trusted on any subject, it was that of women.

"You know what they say about the early bird," Miles added drowsily.

"Yes. He's damned annoying."

"Well, don't say I didn't warn you, old chap. At the sluggish pace you move with females, someone else will snap her up before you get a foot in the door."

It was many hours before Darius could get to sleep

that night. Even the little lavender pillow did not help. If anything, it made him more awake to those strange emotions careening about inside him with as much clumsiness as she—the cause of those feelings—had stepped upon his toes earlier.

Twenty-two

Mr. F is a charming fellow and really very sweet. It is quite inexplicable to me that he should have befriended W, for two more different men could scarce be found. Mr. F is already a favorite in the village, full of smiles for all he meets. He has promised to dine with us soon, much to Mama's delight, but I hear he has made the same promise to almost every family in the village. For the same night. Clearly he needs someone to keep his calendar in order.

He attempts to paint his dour friend W as a generous gentleman with many burdens and no faults. But I suspect the amiable Mr. F has a very rosy view of the world and would not recognize the bad in others since he has none within himself. In that respect he is very like Cathy. I hope the two of them do not fall in love as they would be quite insufferable together. I may yet be required to shave dear Cathy's head if I hear one more word from her about "poor Mr. W" and how he is misunderstood.

Or perhaps I will shave my own head instead. It cannot make things any worse.

J.P. September 22nd, 1815 A.D.

The day after the harvest dance, Justina was alone in the house, arguing with Clara. Her intention was to make a cake, but while she fought the cook for space on the kitchen table, the doorbell rang. Clara, her hands full of feathers from plucking a chicken, marched off to answer it, having received a terse command to send whomever it was away. Justina was in no mood, and certainly in no state, to sit with visitors. But as soon as Clara left the kitchen, she had a second thought.

What if it was Sherry? He'd said he might call on her and here she was in this state, cake batter in her hair and on her face.

Her parents had gone to the next village to help a woman in labor, and Cathy had left for the market in Manderson, traveling in Captain Sherringham's stylish new curricle with Rebecca and Diana. It was a plan decided on while they all talked at the dance, and although the curricle was really only big enough for two, the joy of crowding three into the vehicle had caused much excitement. The captain had offered to ride a horse alongside the ladies, to ensure they had a safe journey, but his sister had mocked him.

"You only want to keep an eye on your precious curricle, Nate, and don't trust me with it!"

Then, upon discovering that the main purpose of the trip was helping Diana shop for wedding accoutrements, he went off the idea in any case and said he would stay home. It would, therefore, be the perfect time for the captain to call upon Justina. Not that she held out any romantic dreams in that regard, of course, she reminded herself churlishly, but just to have his company for half an hour without interruption would be pleasant indeed. She longed to hear of his latest daring adventures. He might bring those cigars he told her about.

Edging close to the kitchen door, she heard the low tenor of a man's voice in their hall and her excitement mounted. A few moments later, Clara's flat, heavy feet came back down the passage, her large soles flapping against the wood planks. Justina dived back to the table and her bowl of lumpy batter.

"Gentleman's in't front parlor," Clara announced in her dull voice.

"Well, for pity's sake, I told you I can't see anyone. You should have said I am not at home."

Clara gave a loud, careless, gelatinous sniff, wiped her nose on her sleeve, picked up a cleaver, and swung it hard to sever the head of the dead, bald bird.

Sometimes Justina considered giving up her haberdashery allowance if it might mean they could afford a better cook. But then she would remember that Clara had come to them from the Charity School; she had no family and had been all alone in the world since childhood. Someone had to give Clara a purpose, a bed, and a fire beside which to sit and soak her chilblains in warm water and bran.

"There are people in the world far worse off than us, Jussy," her sister would say. And then Justina would feel guilty for ever complaining. However eccentric and irritating her family could be, at least she had one.

She wiped her hands on her pinafore and slipped it off over her head, but she forgot to remove the head scarf until she was already opening the parlor door, and by then it was too late.

To her vast disappointment, which made itself known

at once in the rapidity with which she lost her smile, the visitor was not the much anticipated captain. Justina had swung the door open with such alacrity and excitement that her visitor jumped nervously and dropped a small bunch of golden yellow chrysanthemums to the carpet. As he stooped to retrieve them, she had a mad moment to imagine it was someone else entirely, but once the visitor had straightened up his tall length again, her misfortune was confirmed.

Before her stood Darius Wainwright—hat, gloves, and wilted flowers in hand—a strained look upon his face. He had brought a rush of cold air in with him, and it filled the small room, made her shiver as if someone just walked over her grave.

Oh, why was he here? What had she done now?

She tried to put her thoughts in order. "My father is out, sir, and my mother with him," she blurted. "Clara should have told you, but she is, as I'm sure you noted, sparing with her words."

He bowed his head. "It is you I came to see, Miss Justina."

Had he come there to complain because she'd missed the visit to Midwitch that day? Justina decided not to ask. Let him explain himself, she thought angrily.

And what on earth were the flowers for? They looked extremely out of place in his hands and most of them appeared to be crushed flat.

Abruptly the man began to pace, making the room seem even smaller, a shower of petals falling to the carpet. She wondered about the proper etiquette under these unexpected circumstances. Cathy would no doubt be composed and calm. So she folded her hands before her, like the vicar poised to greet his parishioners outside church on a Sunday.

Wainwright continued pacing.

She was surprised he hadn't made any pithy comment about her appearance, as it must surely be a sight to behold at that moment. But when one had a cook like Clara, it was necessary occasionally to enter the kitchen and take matters in hand, she thought sadly. Of course, he would not understand. He probably kept three or four French chefs at his grand house in London. There would never be batter in *his* hair. Unless someone had the presence of mind to throw it at him.

Finally he stopped. He looked at the ground, at the hob grate, and then swiveled on his heels and stared at her hands.

Justina sincerely hoped he would hurry up and get it out, whatever it was, because knowing her luck dear Sherry would arrive at any moment, and she would not even have time to make herself presentable.

❧

"I must…"—he shook his flowers in her general direction and several more petals drifted loose, falling slowly through the air—"apologize, Miss Justina, for the remarks you overheard yesterday evening."

She looked at the flowers, but seemed confused and did not take them.

Rather than stand awkwardly with his arm outstretched and a bunch of tattered flowers dangling in the air between them, he placed them gingerly on the table. He'd dropped them twice in the mud on the way to the Pennys' house and accidently stepped upon them once, because he had not slept much last night and was dreadfully clumsy today. It was a nervous state that had become ten times worse whenever he passed anyone in the lane who made a comment—however innocuous— about the flowers.

When he finally allowed his gaze to reach her face, he found it looking bored. Her eyes were glazed over, and if he was not mistaken, she had just taken two sneaky glances through the parlor window, as if hoping for someone else to appear in the lane. Was he even in the room? he wondered acidly. There was a thumbprint of flour on her cheek and a smaller dot of the same on her chin. Something else marked the tip of her nose. Around her head she wore a scarf of ragged material, tied as a sort of half-turban, probably meant to keep her hair out of the way, but several stubborn curls had escaped, bouncing like broken springs each time she moved her head.

"Miss Penny," he added, louder this time, making her look at him. "I would like to apologize."

"So you said once already." She blinked and the stray sprigs of curl twitched again, exhibiting possible signs of irritation. "Is it really worth it, Mr. Wainwright?"

He swallowed, set down his hat and gloves, and drew his hand quickly over his brow. Hidden in his palm he kept a tightly folded handkerchief to swab the first beads of perspiration. "Yes. It is worth it. I must get this out."

The dark blue velvet of her gaze seemed even more startling today in the cool light through the parlor window. He had missed seeing her face that morning, and her unexplained absence had driven him here to confront her with a hasty proposal. It was madness, but there was nothing else to be done about the situation. She had him utterly at sixes and sevens.

"I should not have spoken as I did yesterday...at the dance," he mumbled awkwardly. "I did not know you were behind me."

Her eyes narrowed, simmered. "Oh, I've already forgotten it, sir. Wiped it clean from my mind."

There followed what was possibly the longest silence he'd yet known in her company. Darius swabbed the hidden handkerchief across his brow again.

Finally she said, "Is that all, sir? I am rather busy in the kitchen this morning."

His heart stumbled over its usually steady rhythm. "Miss Penny, I am aware that our recent encounters have not been conducted with propriety."

"If you're going to lecture me again about my behavior, you needn't put yourself out. I can promise you, sir, that I will not be under your feet any longer. You won't see hide or hair of me from now on. I'm sure it will save us both a considerable number of headaches." The words tumbled out swiftly, like rambunctious children released into the fresh air after a Sunday visit with strict relatives.

So much for wiping her mind clean, he mused.

"Miss Justina, I fear we are at cross p...purposes. I did not mean to say that you are to bl—"

"Please don't give it another thought," she replied sharply, eyes flaring. "As I said to you before, I know my faults. If only other people always knew theirs!"

"I never said I was without f...fault. I'm sure I have made p...plentiful errors." He stopped, aware of his tongue beginning to stumble as it had not done since he was a boy.

"If I might say so, sir, I think it was a rather foolhardy decision you made to come here this morning, considering every encounter with me has caused you wounds and stains of one sort or another. I wonder what you can mean by it." Again she glanced at his savaged flowers and frowned.

"Foolhardy? Madam, I have never made a foolhardy decision in my life."

"Apparently you've never had a tender feeling or a modest thought, either," she scoffed. "But I shall stay silent and let you chastise again, as you like to do, and then perhaps we can be done with it. I suppose I ought to be grateful that you take on the trouble of setting me straight, as no one else bothers and I am an unguarded little trollop."

Well, he was quite certain he'd never said *that*, but before he could protest, she continued.

"How charitable of you! First Sir Mortimer Grubbins and now my training! So many burdens you are willing to take on."

Darius squared his shoulders, wishing he had something other than his handkerchief to keep his hands occupied while she stood this close, looking so angry and at the same time as wildly beautiful, dangerous, and breathtaking as a thunderstorm at sea. A face to sink a thousand ships, he mused, shocking himself with the ability to feel a lighthearted tremor at such a moment. Whatever spell she'd cast over him, it was powerful and warm. It refused to let him lose his temper with her, even while she railed at him and seemed intent on a quarrel.

"Do tell me something, sir, I am genuinely curious." She put her hands on her waist. "Is there any woman, anywhere, who ever met with your approval? I should like to meet her. Or, on second thought, perhaps not. I might be completely overwhelmed in the presence of a living saint."

"There are some—"

"Have you no appreciation for the spontaneous, Mr. Wainwright? Life is not always neat and tidy and all in its place. I feel sorry for you that you cannot simply enjoy life and dance without worrying about the right steps or what you look like while doing it. There is no romance in your life, no pleasure for the sake of it, no emotions. I pity you, indeed I do."

Pity was the last thing he wanted from her. "Mrs. Birch was right," he muttered. "All those novels have gone to your head."

"Pardon me for *reading*."

"It's not the reading, madam, that matters. It is the choice of material which clearly does more harm than good."

"Explain!"

"You expect life to mimic fiction and when it does not you are disappointed. You wait for a man like one of those you read about. One who spouts poetry and makes an ass of himself on bended knee."

"Why not? You ably make an ass of yourself upright." She snorted. "I only hope, for your sake, you find a woman one day who does not mind risking her happiness on a man who can barely put himself out to be gracious." Stopping abruptly, she flushed pink. "Still, that is no business of mine and does not concern me at all."

Words suddenly would not come to him. He felt as if only spare letters fell over themselves in a meaningless jumble on his tongue, forming stupid sounds that made no sense.

"You pride yourself on being a gentleman of sophistication, education, and manners," she added. "Good Lord, you are so quick to fault mine. If your arrogant behavior is the fashionable idea of manners, I'm glad I have none."

It was unbelievable that this little person in her rumpled attire, with custard on her nose, should make him feel small and insignificant. This woman who jumped, reckless and naked, onto strange men's beds. He knew far more about life than she did. Yet he let her preach to him. Suddenly he could do nothing else but listen.

His silence apparently troubled her as much as anything he'd said.

Her brows arched even higher. "What now?" she demanded. "Why do you look at me that way?"

"You have custard on your face, madam."

She screwed her lips tight in an angry moue and then exploded. "*It's batter!*"

Unmoved by the gust of furious air blown out with those two words, Darius raised his folded handkerchief and wiped the mark from the end of her nose. "I don't suppose that happens to the heroines in your books."

It would, apparently, cost her too much to thank him, but her lips softened very slightly and her dark lashes fanned downward in a slow blink. "Shall I show you out, sir?"

"Perhaps you'd prefer throwing me through the window? I hear you like drama."

"I may be a common, provincial girl with terrible, brazen manners," she stepped closer, "but I am perfectly capable of civilly showing you the door."

"And I may be a fancified London toff," Darius advanced a half step until they were almost touching, "but I know a door when I see one."

"I meant I could open it for you."

"So that you might have the pleasure of slamming it after me?"

"That, sir, would be childish."

"Exactly."

She exhaled a small, exasperated huff. "Are you still here?"

He held out his arms. "Apparently. I must not have had enough insults from you yet today."

Her eyes widened as if she'd just swallowed a walnut whole and was about to choke.

"Insults from *me*?" she sputtered. "Of all the blasted cheek!"

For a long moment his gaze held hers.

The doorbell rang. They had both been too caught up in their argument to hear anyone pass through the gate.

Only seconds later the parlor door burst open and there was Captain Sherringham, grinning as he invited himself in, not even waiting for the maid to announce his presence.

"Jussy, here I am as promised, to—"

When he saw the two of them standing so close his smile drooped, but only for a moment.

"Sherry!" she cried, hastily moving away from Darius. "Have you met Mr. Wainwright?"

"We were introduced yesterday evening. Didn't interrupt anything, did I?"

"Of course not." She laughed, her color deepening.

Darius knew she waited for him to leave. So did the

merry, bloody captain. "*Sherry*" indeed! His jaw hurt. His head ached.

He should leave them to it, he thought furiously.

Instead he stayed. He took a chair at the small table, lowering his weight so suddenly to the worn seat that its fragile legs creaked in surprise and alarm.

The captain had ruined his visit and now he would repay the favor. He muttered a gruff "Good morning" to the other man and then stared at the embroidered screen by the fire.

It was, quite possibly, the most uncomfortable fifteen minutes she'd ever spent in that parlor. Justina had never enjoyed the company of two men there to visit her at the same time, and she was quite certain there must be proper etiquette for such a circumstance, but sadly she was a poor student of any rules. She'd never had cause to consider this predicament a likely one for her.

The captain had a box of cigars under his arm, and he placed them on the table beside the shattered bouquet of chrysanthemums before taking a seat by the fire, quickly making himself at home and launching into one of his amusing stories. It was a tale Justina could attend to with only half her mind, for she was still in a state of confusion in regard to Mr. Wainwright's very strange visit. She turned to face the captain, but all her senses were distracted, most of them focused on her other visitor.

Although he remained silent, every slight move and sigh he made seemed heavy with portent. She expected him, at any moment, to leap up from that chair and storm out. Sherry would rib her about Wainwright and his flowers, no doubt.

Their unfinished debate hung in the air like the augury of a thunderstorm. At last, to her relief, Mr. Wainwright stood abruptly and took his leave.

When she prepared to walk with him into the hall, he snapped, "I'll see myself out."

Perhaps it was just as well. Perhaps they'd both said quite enough.

She heard the front door close so firmly it even shook the little silhouettes above the fireplace.

"What on earth was he here for?" Sherry asked at once. "He looked as if he'd sat on a hatpin."

Usually Justina would have laughed at that, but she found it too hard today and did not try for long. Hastily she sought an excuse for his visit. "He came to see Papa, but finding him out I suppose he thought it only polite to stay a while."

The captain squinted. "He brought flowers for your father?"

Justina cast her eyes over the crumpled bouquet. The way he'd thrust those flowers at her, they'd appeared to be more of an inconvenience to him than anything and she'd barely given them a thought—too seething with anger and eager to set him straight about his faults.

"I believe he came solely to see you, Jussy."

"Good Lord, no. Why would he?"

"Never can tell with a stuck-up fellow like that. Besides, I told you, the way he looked at you last night, Wainwright was thinking about having you bound up in ropes and brought to his couch—like one of those wicked Roman emperors!" He grinned slyly.

"Don't talk nonsense, Sherry."

"And he brought you flowers!" He chuckled. "Surely the oaf didn't propose marriage to you, Jussy?"

She was flustered, her nerves still on edge. "Certainly not." But the idea had quite suddenly forced itself into her mind as she took another look at those trampled flowers and thought of how he had paced before her. He had come all the way through the village just to apologize for his comments at the dance? That seemed most unlike him.

"I would wager he did mean to propose!" Sherry continued his teasing. "That was why he looked so very grim. I mean, even more grim than usual!"

Since she could not sit still and felt the need for something to do with her hands, Justina took a vase from the mantel and arranged the sad flowers in it. Once they had a little water they might perk up.

"He did not come to propose marriage," she said firmly, reassuring herself as much as her other guest. Gathering up all the spilled petals from the table, she wished they might somehow be stuck back onto the flowers.

"Whatever he came for, the man's a colossal bore, Jussy. Didn't speak a word to me."

Eager to change the subject, she grabbed the box of cigars he'd brought with him. "Show me these, then! I want to know what it's like."

"Of course you do! Mademoiselle Curious." He leaned forward and took the box from her hands. "Best open the window to let the smoke out, or your mama will have something else for which to blame me."

❧

Darius was through the gate before he realized he'd

left his hat and gloves behind in her parlor. His first thought was to keep walking and retrieve them at some other time, but then the image of Justina having a cozy tête-à-tête with the captain was enough to make him change his mind and go back. He would disturb them once more. Her father really ought to be told about this, he thought, incensed by the captain's sneaky visit and quite forgetting that he too had gone there to see her alone.

But as he approached the front door again, he heard their voices through the open parlor window.

"Are you telling me you haven't noticed his interest? He didn't take his eyes off you at the dance, and he plainly resented my interruption just now. The man was seething."

"Oh, do stop talking about him."

"I'm just warning you, that's all. Your romantic intentions to never marry for anything but love could soon meet an obstacle if he decides to have you. How could you overlook his fortune? Before you know what's what, your family will have you cornered into it. You'll be the unfortunate Mrs. Wainwright, destined for a life of painful duty as the wife of that dour monolith."

"You know me better than that. Stop teasing!"

"He's very rich, you know. Women are, when all is said and done, mercenary creatures. Even those who profess to love one man can change their mind when more practical concerns make themselves felt. I should know."

"For pity's sake, stop!" she exclaimed, her voice high with frustration. "*If* I ever marry, it will be to a man who knows how to love and does not think it nonsense to feel with his heart. To a man who will sweep me off my feet, not bowl me over with his fat-headed pomposity."

Darius stared at the path under his feet.

Now came the final assault, which she delivered with gusto, like a character in a bad stage melodrama. "I had not known Wainwright a month before I knew he was the last man in the world I could ever be prevailed upon to marry."

Well, that was clear enough.

There was so much he had still wanted to say to her, yet he could not get the words out now, even if she suddenly appeared at the window. It had taken Darius all night and all morning to ready himself for this and now his courage and his confidence were depleted.

✺

"Oh, he left his hat and gloves," she exclaimed, taking them up from the chair where he'd dropped them.

"I'm sure he'll send someone back for them. Leave them there."

But Justina was suddenly overwhelmed with two fears: one, that he would come back for them himself; two, that he would never come back.

She ran to the window to see how far he'd gone, expecting, by now, that he would be out of sight. But she was in time to observe him trip over the cat as he opened their gate. He righted himself and strode away down the lane, coattails billowing behind him like the ceremonial robes of a demon king.

Apparently he had come there on foot that day, which seemed odd; she'd never seen or heard of him strolling anywhere for pleasure.

Alarmed, she realized he might well have heard their conversation, or some of it at least, through the open window.

She ought to be glad. Better he know the futility of asking her to marry him. If he should ever have such a thought in his head. If.

The lane was very quiet now. The cat sat on the gatepost, cleaning his whiskers, and Wainwright marched round the bend, until he was out of sight.

"What are you looking at out there?" the captain demanded. "You must come here and tell me all the things that have happened in my absence. I can't trust my sister to tell me anything juicy these days."

Justina stepped away from the window and chewed her fingernail.

Now she had something more to hide; this she could not write in her diary either. And why not?

When it was merely her own sin and confession, that was one thing; when it involved the humiliation of someone else, that was entirely different.

❧

Darius found Miles in the orchard, tirelessly attempting to teach Sir Mortimer to fetch thrown sticks.

"It's not a dog, Forester," he commented brusquely as he stormed by.

"I know, but he's very intelligent."

He jerked to a halt and turned back. "The creature might be bright as a button, amusing and trainable, but I doubt he wants to be. He's remarkably stubborn, ungrateful, and sly." He spat out his words, still fuming. "Intelligence is not always used as it should and in the wrong hands, left to ramble freely with no good cause, it can be utterly and completely wasted."

"Poor Sir Morty!" Miles chuckled. "Your papa is cross with you today. What have you done to him now?"

The pig raised his head and grunted happily, then trotted over to sniff at his reluctant master's boots. Darius had taken the longer route back to Midwitch from the village and gathered quite a bit of mud in the process. Much to Sir Mortimer's excitement.

"Where have you been?" Miles asked.

"On a fool's errand," he snapped.

Gazing quizzically at those filthy boots, his friend exclaimed, "Apparently it *is* possible to get lost in only three lanes, eh?"

Darius spun around and marched into the house.

Inside the shadowy hall he stopped again, suddenly not sure what to do next or where to go. All in the house was quiet but for the steady clunk of the long case clock behind him. It was always quiet like this when *she* was not there. Too quiet. He'd never thought such a thing was possible until now. Head bent, he thoughtfully perused his filthy boots, as a ray of sunlight reached fingertips through the open door and cast his toes in a stark beam no less reproachful and withering than the regard of Miss Justina Penny herself.

"Oh, heavens above! I thought for one dreadful minute the ghost of old Master Hawke had come back again, young sir!" The housekeeper appeared at the other end of the hall, her big face very white, drained of its usual ruddiness. "You looked like him, standing there by the door! Just as he was years ago."

"Yes…well…as you see," he struggled for a breath,

"it is only me." Alone, he might have added. Quite alone.

She gave a sharp nod, wiping her hands on her apron. "You'll be ready for a spot of luncheon then, young sir?"

He looked down at his gloveless, empty hands. They looked so large and clumsy. And his ears felt cold. *What on earth did you think you were doing, Handles?*

"Sir?"

"Er…yes. Thank you, Mrs. Birch."

Recovered from her earlier shock, she laughed. "Fancy you frightening me like that! Turning into Phineas Hawke before my very eyes! Just like him all over again. Ah, looks like the sun is coming out after all. Good thing, too! All this damp plays havoc with my ol' bones."

When the clock chimed twelve, it seemed today to bear a mocking lilt and he wanted to reach in and stop the pendulum with his fist.

Twenty-three

Nothing much has happened.

The cat was sick in my slippers.

It has been so damp that Rooke's warped privy door stuck fast with him inside it, which caused some tepid excitement for half a day.

Lucy wore rouge yesterday, although she flatly denied it to me. No one's cheeks are that rosy unless they have been slapped with a haddock.

The Priory Players will commence with rehearsals soon. Despite being accused recently of enjoying drama, I find myself strangely unexcited to be acting again and the characters do not flow from my pen as they usually do.

Captain S came to tea and Mama was insufferably rude to him, as always. The poor man has no luck with the mothers in this village, yet he seems to take delight in his reputation and does nothing to improve it. I fear Mama is right when she says he chases wicked women because he thinks it is what he should be doing*.

I have not spoken to Mr. W since his strange visit.

I saw him yesterday, however, teaching Lucy's little brothers to ride his horse in the fallow field by Dockley's Barn. He was a *strict teacher, as might be expected, but the boys listened to him as they seldom do to me or anyone and most curiously seemed to enjoy the lesson.*

I suppose he may as well make himself useful while he remains here.

He did not come back for his hat and gloves, yet it has been almost a full week since he left them. Mama says it is a sign of his great wealth that he does not even miss a hat. She is convinced he left them here so he might have an excuse to return when Cathy is at home.

I do not like seeing his hat and gloves on our hall table every day when I come down to breakfast. It always makes me think—just for one terrible moment—that he must be here to visit, until I remember he is unlikely ever to come again. And thus I must, every day, relive the circumstances under which he left them there.

I am certain I was right to speak as I did. But I have discovered that the more often I am forced to remember an incident, the more chance there is I might find something to regret.

*I can hardly believe I wrote the words "Mama" and "right" in the same sentence. Alas.

                                        J.P. September 28th, 1815 A.D.

"Mr. Wainwright is really not the ogre you try to paint him," Cathy argued gently. Propped up in bed with two extra pillows and surrounded by blankets and quilts, she looked quite small and lost. "I cannot imagine why you took against that man so virulently from the start," she snuffled, before blowing her nose soundly.

Justina had been reading aloud to her from the foot of the bed, where she lay in an ungainly sprawl. Now she snapped the book shut. "I daresay he's been on his best behavior when you go there, but you have only taken my place a few times. Besides, you always want to think the best of everybody." And it was necessary now for Justina to only have proof of the worst when it came to Wainwright. Necessary for her peace of mind after all the things she'd said to him.

"Miles Forester assures me that Mr. Wainwright is a good man," her sister continued. "A little stern, perhaps, and solemn, which sometimes makes him appear too proud, but he is an honest, true friend with many excellent qualities."

"Goodness, Cathy, has the dratted man employed you to improve his reputation?"

Her sister frowned. "Why would he do that? I'm sure he does not care for anyone's approbation, and he certainly does not need ours."

"Yet he seems to have yours, sister, even when he has done so little to attain it."

Cathy carefully folded back the top edge of the bedcover and smoothed it over with both hands. "You are always saying how no one should care how *you* look, Jussy. That it does not matter how you dress or your lack of ladylike manners, because people should not judge you by it. They should care about your mind and your intelligence, not your looks and whether or not you spoon your soup from the right side of the bowl! Yet the appearance of Mr. Wainwright and his manners have offended you, it seems, from the first day. You have not given his character the same chance you expect others to give you. Is that not unfair?"

Justina reopened the book and became absorbed again, flipping through the pages to glance at the end and decide whether it was worth continuing.

"Mr. Wainwright has had many responsibilities thrust upon him since he was very young," Cathy added. "He has managed the entire family and a successful business since his father died. He has raised his brother's child as if she is his own. It may be true that he is a somber gentleman, but he has his reasons for it. Just as you have yours for deliberately driving our mama to distraction and putting off any man who shows the merest interest in you."

"Miles Forester is obliged to fib since he is Mr. Wainwright's friend and guest. He must owe the man a large debt of gratitude. It would seem the only explanation for the way he has worked so hard over the past week to lighten Wainwright's grim countenance with a halo." She paused, glancing suspiciously at her sister. "And you have been talking to Mr. Forester a great deal, Cathy. I ought to ask that young man his intentions."

"Oh, Jussy, Miles Forester is quite the most delightful gentleman I've ever met."

"He's certainly handsome. But as Mr. Darcy would say, *he smiles too much*."

Cathy chuckled. "There is something amiss with smiling?"

"In abundance, sister," she replied grandly, "there is less value."

"So Miles Forester smiles too much, and yet Mr. Wainwright does not smile enough to please you?"

Snapping the book shut for the second time, Justina leapt off the bed. "Do hurry up and get well, sister. It worked out so much better for you to go to Midwitch with Lucy. Better for everyone. Mama was delighted that you agreed to go in my place, and Mr. Wainwright must have been relieved to have your sweet-natured face for company instead of mine. Now I am stuck with the odorous task again."

Cathy wilted further into her extravagant nest of pillows. "I shall try to improve, Jussy, as fast as I can. And you are, of course, the best nurse, so I have no doubt your special broth will see me back to good health in no time."

"I hope so, sister! After the battle I endured with Clara, who kept trying to take my pot off the fire every time my back was turned, that broth had better put you back on your feet tomorrow."

Cathy laughed gently. "Poor Jussy! Believe me, I do wish I could go again to Midwitch in your place. I found Mr. Wainwright pleasant company."

"Oh, now I know you really must be ill!"

"He is not all noise and bluster like some gentlemen we know, Jussy. I think he is a man who could always be relied upon to speak the truth, even if it does him no favors."

She groaned. "Indeed. When it comes to expressing his opinions he is honest to a fault."

"I'm sure any woman who wins his regard would be fortunate indeed."

She stared at her sister. "What woman would win his regard? I'm sure he finds something to criticize about every girl who crosses his line of sight." Turning away, she caught her image in the mirror and quickly averted her gaze rather than look at that guilty countenance.

"I'm sure some lady will one day," Cathy replied. "And I hope *this time* she is deserving of his affections."

Justina pressed her lips tight and rearranged the little jars of balm and perfumed water on the dresser.

After a pause her sister continued softly, "Mr. Forester told me something…oh, but I should not repeat it."

"Told you what?"

"No, it was told in confidence—"

"Sister!" Justina swung around again, flourishing a hairbrush as if she might stab someone. "You had better tell me now or I shall imagine all manner of horrors."

Finally Cathy explained, "Mr. Wainwright was in love once before, years ago. But the lady was seduced away from him by another. She broke his heart. He has never recovered from it."

A mixture of feelings quickly took hold. First she felt an unexpected rush of compassion for Wainwright. Then came suspicion, for this story had come from his very good friend who had already shown himself eager to flatter.

Wainwright in love? It seemed as strange as the idea of Phineas Hawke ever giving his heart, and yet she had those letters he'd written to prove it.

"Do be gentle with poor Mr. Wainwright, Jussy. I am sorry you must resume the visits with Lucy, but while I am ill there is naught else for it. Diana claims it would be improper for her, as a woman engaged, and Rebecca is too busy with her brother these days."

Thus, with no one else to take her place, she returned to her duty that day, joining her friend on the walk to Midwitch Manor.

"Mr. Wainwright says there is not much left to be done," Lucy told her as they arrived at the tall wrought iron gates. "Our task will soon be complete and the house in a fit state to be sold or leased. He says Catherine is a much more efficient worker than you, Jussy, and less distracted. I heard him talk to Mr. Forester of his plans to return to London. Such a pity! I had hoped he would stay until the New Year at least."

Justina tripped over a tussock of grass, but recovered swiftly. Of course, she'd always known he meant to go back to his life in London once the house was ready for sale, but it was still a sudden shock to find the moment almost upon them. Wainwright had turned everything and everyone on their heads. At least, it felt as if he had.

"I was just becoming accustomed to him being here," Lucy muttered. "I do not know what we shall do with Sir Mortimer when the house is sold."

"We'll just have to find a new home for him." Aware of a stone that had crept through a hole in her boot and now rubbed painfully under her big toe, Justina leaned against the fancy swirls and forbidding bars of the gates and rapidly attacked her laces. "I daresay your wonderful Mr. Wainwright has not given a thought to Sir Mortimer. He would not trouble himself with it." Why would he? He had not even come back for his hat and gloves and now he was leaving. Planning to leave without another word to her.

And why would Wainwright have anything to say to you, hussy?

She tipped her boot upside down and shook it until the offending stone fell to the grass. It was much smaller than she'd expected. Funny how something no bigger than a pea could become lodged where it caused a person so much pain that she felt a tear in her eye.

Lucy lifted the latch without pulling the bell cord that hung beside it. "He never locks his gate now," she said.

"How lax of Mr. Wainwright. Is he not afraid of being visited by uncouth villagers at all hours?" Having banged her boot hard against the wall, expending some necessary energy on an item that could not object, Justina replaced it on her foot and followed Lucy through the orchard to visit Sir Mortimer Grubbins in his new sty. The pig greeted them with a merry twitch of his curled tail.

"He looks remarkably clean," Justina exclaimed.

"Yes. I do believe Mr. Wainwright has him bathed regularly."

She huffed. "Why am I surprised?"

Inside the house, Mrs. Birch was washing the hall tiles on her hands and knees. "What are you two doing here? He's gone out with his friend and won't be back till late. He said no one was coming today. Have you girls nothing else to do but chase after these gentlemen?"

"Well, really! He sent no message to us," Justina protested. "My sister is indisposed and told me to come in her place. I have plenty of other things to do rather than waste my time here, I can assure you."

The housekeeper was more troubled, at that moment, by the mud they'd brought in on their boots than anything else. "Look out, dozy clodhoppers! I just scrubbed this floor once and my knees are all in. And don't get that look in your eye, Miss Justina Penny! The master of the house may not be in, but that's no reason for you to go off exploring where you're not wanted."

Justina made a swift decision. Grabbing Lucy's sleeve, she tugged the girl into Wainwright's study, shouting over her shoulder that they would wait until the man returned. "He can tell me to my face that our work is done. I won't have it said that I did not complete my task."

"He won't want you in there while he's not home, saucy madam."

"Mrs. Birch, I smell something burning. I suggest you tend to your own work and let us do ours."

She shut the door firmly and after a moment heard the housekeeper waddling off back to the kitchen with her buckets clanging. "I'll let him sort you out," the woman complained loudly. "I warned him it was trouble letting you over the threshold in the first place. But, oh no, he thought he could handle you. Ha! Let him try then."

Lucy walked to the fire to warm her hands. "Perhaps we should not stay, Jussy. I don't want to make Mr. Wainwright angry."

"Heaven forbid he be forced to express an emotion! That man is utterly inconsiderate. I daresay he thought we had nothing else to do but traipse all the way here only to be sent away again."

Justina examined his desk which was now in neat order and polished to a good shine. The day was so grim an Argand lamp had already been lit. It cast a glow across his empty blotter and the neatly arranged seals. With Lucy looking on anxiously, she pulled out his leather chair and sat in it. Then she leaned back, propping her booted heels on the desk. "If he wasn't going to be here and he didn't want us roaming his corridors unattended, he should have told us not to come today."

She thought of what Cathy had told her about Wainwright's broken heart. Still, she did not know if she could believe that story. Her sister might, but then Cathy was gullible in her own sweet way.

Now, after tossing them all up in the air like a handful of jackstraws, he was leaving. Just like that.

Looking around the study she saw only one pile of papers left to go through. The room was clean, tidy, devoid of anything else to search. She sat up and began opening the drawers of his desk. Each one was in perfect order, carefully laid out. "I'm not certain you ought to sit in his chair," Lucy ventured cautiously.

But she rather liked sitting there. No sign remained of old Phineas, and the place was now very much Wainwright. She felt naughty sitting in his chair, without his knowledge.

Rain had begun to tickle the windows. It made her restless. The house was so quiet, greedily holding its dark secrets. There was, of course, still the matter of Nellie Pickles' disappearance, as well as many other curiosities probably hidden away in those Tudor-paneled walls.

She got up. "You wait here, Lucy."

"Where are you going?"

Justina took the Argand lamp from the desk. "To look around."

"But Mrs. Birch said—"

"You stay here where it's warm and make plenty of noise. That way she won't suspect a thing."

Lucy pouted. "Why can't I go with you? I might like to explore too!"

"And what happens if you see a ghost, Lucy Bridges?"

Her eyes widened. "You said there are none here."

"If there are any, they will be elsewhere in this house, won't they? Where people seldom roam. Dark, sinister, silent corners."

The other girl paled slightly under her excessive rouge.

"Besides, what if *he* comes back suddenly?" Justina

added. "I'll need you to warn me, shan't I? And you can keep him distracted."

"Yes…yes. I suppose you are right. I'll wait here."

"Sing something so that Mrs. Birch thinks we're both in here." Taking the oil lamp, she left his study and went exploring.

Behind her, as she closed the study door, she heard Lucy cough and then begin to sing. "*Soldier, soldier, won't you marry me, with your musket, fife, and drum? Oh, no, sweet maid, I cannot marry thee, for I have no hat to put on.*"

In Manderson, Darius had visited the solicitor, the bank, the tailor, the cobbler, and finally, his tasks complete, he allowed Miles to drag him into a rowdy tavern. There was no rush to get back. No one at the house to expect him.

"You did relay the message to Miss Penny as I asked, did you not, Forester?"

His friend smiled. "Of course."

Something about that smile seemed slightly off. Miles was never a good liar. "You told her that no one was needed at Midwitch today? You did not forget?"

"Yes, of course," Miles repeated amiably. "I urged her to stay home and tend her cold."

Darius examined his friend's countenance until it disappeared in a tankard of cider.

"I must say," Miles added, smacking his lips, "I'm quite accustomed already to this simple life in the country."

"Because life is generally so very complicated for you," Darius muttered drily.

"Pity you plan to sell the house. I'd like to have a peaceful place to come and stay away from Town."

"You could always buy Midwitch, Forester."

But he knew his friend didn't want the responsibility of his own house yet. Miles spent his time traveling between friends, making the most of their hospitality. He never made himself unwelcome, was always charming and helpful, never stayed too long. It was a wayfarer's lifestyle that kept things simple and easy for Miles, but must surely be exhausting after so many years of dashing about. Darius preferred to plant roots. He liked to know he could find things again once he put them down.

"If you kept Midwitch," said Miles, "I could visit you every winter, before the Season starts, and every summer when the odors of Town become too rife for my delicate nostrils."

"So you'd be here for half the year."

"If you insist! I know how you cannot do without my company, Wainwright."

Darius sipped his cider and found it surprisingly pleasant. Slowly he was acquiring a taste and a tolerance for the strength of the local brew, but perhaps it was inevitable since Miles insisted on drinking a great deal of it. "What has given you this passion for the country all of a sudden?"

Miles put on his innocent face. "Can't a man appreciate the beauties of nature?"

"Which one? Miss Catherine Penny or Miss Rebecca Sherringham? I believe Miss Lucy is too young for you. Too young for anyone yet."

"Why? She is only a year younger than Miss Justina and I do not think you would say *she* is not old enough," Miles replied slyly. "I notice you do not offer *her* name as a possible love interest for me, Wainwright."

Darius cleared his throat. "I merely had not thought of her."

"Oh, of course not."

"She would not suit you, in any case."

"Why not?" Miles studied his face so intently that Darius felt it necessary to turn away and signal for more cider. "Perhaps I might like her best of all, Wainwright."

His stomach tightened. Anxiety and frustration had twisted his insides into a heavy knot, and each time he remembered his abandoned attempt at a proposal that knot hurt with greater intensity.

Miles Forester would never understand how it felt to keep thoughts and words and longings inside until they stabbed at one's innards like a thousand little knives.

At that moment they were joined by Captain Sherringham, who seemed to have the irritating habit of turning up to interrupt his conversations. Having spied them across the tavern, he now came over with his big, stupid grin to begin to greet Miles. Of course, Darius thought churlishly, Forester had quickly made friends in the village, knew minute, trivial details about everyone, and was well liked already.

"I don't suppose you've given Captain Sherringham much of a chance since he monopolized your fresh little daisy at the harvest dance," Miles had said to him only a few days before. "But he is a merry fellow. I like him."

"You like everybody," had been his terse reply.

Now there was no escaping further acquaintance. It was the one drawback to friendship with Miles. The man was so easygoing he befriended anyone, and then Darius inevitably found himself forced into company with those he would rather not know better.

Before too long, the captain had invited them both to a night of cards at the Sherringhams' house, and Miles accepted eagerly. For them both.

"We have nothing else to do, Wainwright," he exclaimed. "It will be tremendous fun."

Fun, like *nonsense*, thought Darius, meant different things to different people.

He could only hope he might contract some terrible disease before Thursday evening.

As he rode back to the village with Miles, Darius remarked to his friend that he had never been dragged against his will to so many social functions as he had been since he came to Hawcombe Prior.

"It's doing you a world of good then, this country life," Miles replied with a laugh.

Darius looked away.

How could this place do him any good? He'd made a fool of himself with that young woman and yet still he felt a pang of wistfulness. It was surely unmanly and just as humiliating as a return to boyhood stammering. But he couldn't help wishing he might turn back his clocks and begin again with her.

Twenty-four

She quickly found her way to his bedchamber. There were only two rooms on the upper floor that appeared lived in, the furniture not shrouded in dust covers. Miles Forester's room was easily identified by the casual mess of clothes and books strewn about. Wainwright's room, on the other hand, was neat as a pin, just as recognizable as a mirror of his character.

Justina shivered in wicked anticipation. This was his bed. His washstand. There was a waistcoat folded and laid upon a chair, and she ran her fingers across the silk. He was not very adventurous with his garments and wore mostly dark colors, even in his waistcoats. It seemed sad to her.

If she was his wife she would sew him a few brighter things to wear.

What a strange thought that was, she mused, shaking her head.

Wainwright had his waistcoats properly and expensively tailored. What would he possibly want with one of her poorly sewn, badly fitted creations?

The room was dimly lit by slate gray lines that fell

through the windows, the drizzle of autumn rain leaving mottled shadows around the walls. It was an eerie light, for it made movement where there should be none. The gentle patter of rain might be mistaken for other foot-steps, and the lilting drift of wind occasionally tugging on corners of the house, finding its way in through slender cracks and old window frames, made unearthly whispers.

She was grateful for the oil lamp as that soft glow trav-eled with her across the creaking floor boards, and also for the low murmur of Lucy singing in the room below. "....Oh, no, sweet maid, I cannot marry thee, for I have no boots to put on."

This, it seemed, was the only song she could come up with so she repeated it, over and over. Mrs. Birch was very probably about to yell at her to stop her noise. But Lucy sang on.

A bird flew at the window, startling her, making her heart leap. She stood in the center of the room and listened. Her own heartbeat briefly obscured Lucy's song, thumping out a rhythm harder than that soldier's drum.

Now, where to search for his secrets? No doubt he had some. Just like Phineas Hawke.

She set the oil lamp on his dresser and found, to her surprise, the old bonnet with the wax cherries that she'd left behind in his orchard weeks ago. He had set it over Hawke's wooden wig stand and from there he must be able to see it every night when he prepared for bed. How odd. Justina had expected it thrown out by now or sent back to her with a terse note.

But there it was. Pride of place on his dresser, her frayed ribbons neatly tied under the faceless wooden egg that once held old Hawke's moth-eaten white wigs. She imagined Wainwright, in his solemn way, tying those ribbons in a careful bow. So fastidious, so tidy.

Funny how they'd both left hats behind and neither come back for them.

"Soldier, soldier, won't you marry me…"

Justina moved to his bed. It was an old four-poster, so high off the floor that a set of wooden steps were required to climb in. Unless, of course, one was accustomed to flying leaps. She very much doubted Wainwright was a leaper. Probably just as well, as he seemed a trifle accident prone.

She slid her hands under his pillow and found her little lavender sachet. So he kept it. Still.

Running her palm over his pillow she imagined a kiss of warmth, as if he'd not long risen from it. Only hours ago his great length had laid in that bed, sprawled across it. She suffered the sudden fluttering of Maiden's Palsy when she thought of his strong thighs and the hard, broad slabs of muscle across his chest. Had she never seen him without clothes, she would have no idea of the brute barbarian form beneath his cultivated, gentlemanly surface. Since their encounter in Bath, she'd caught herself looking at other men and wondering what they kept under their garments. Most, she was quite sure, looked nothing like Darius Wainwright.

Returning to his dresser, she slowly opened each drawer to investigate. In the back of her mind she heard her sister's reprimands, but why should she not look? Her relationship with Wainwright was hardly one of the normal variety, not that she could explain it to pure, innocent Cathy.

A sudden gust of wind blew hard at the window,

and she felt it reaching through the walls to move the fringe of her shawl. At least she hoped that was the wind finding a way inside, and not the ghost of Nellie Pickles trying to get her attention. The house groaned softly and the boards under her feet creaked. Somewhere in the distance she thought she heard rusted metal clang.

She paused, straining to hear.

If anyone came, Lucy would warn her with a hasty shout up the stairs. Had she stopped singing? Had she fallen asleep?

But no, surely that was her coughing downstairs, and then the singing resumed. "*Soldier, soldier, won't you marry me, with your musket, fife, and drum?*"

Justina had reached the bottom drawer of the dresser and this necessitated kneeling in order to investigate fully, but if one meant to do a job, it should be done well.

It was stiff to open, the wood warped by age and damp air. After only traveling an inch, it stuck. No amount of tugging and jostling helped ease the drawer further open, but she could just squeeze her hand inside. Linens. Old and forgotten, stale odor wafting up to her nose. The new master of the house had not bothered to wrestle this drawer open when he met with resistance. Why would he? He did not mean to stay long, had no need to use all the drawers, and was, apparently, not cursed with an inquisitive nature.

But there, almost immediately, her fingers found a stiff corner of folded paper tucked under the forgotten bed linens.

Another gust of wind blew against the house and the rain began to pelt down hard against those trembling windows. Even the flame of the oil lamp, supposedly sheltered by its glass chimney, fluttered and dodged about. The sound of the thrusting, thrashing rain obscured Lucy's song.

Justina wriggled her fingers further inside the drawer, desperate to recover whatever had been hidden there. Perhaps she had found more of Phineas Hawke's lost letters to his secret lady love. An entire stack of them. The excitement was almost more than she could bear.

Cursing softly, she struggled to stretch her fingers inside the cramped space.

And then, across the room, the bedchamber door slammed shut.

❧

When Darius found Lucy Bridges alone he commanded her to continue singing. He knew where Justina was without winkling a confession from her accomplice, for another set of footsteps could be heard creaking about in his bedchamber directly above the study. Meddling menace. Of course, she would never resist the chance to go spying the moment he turned his back.

And as for Miles...

"I did tell Miss Penny," he insisted. "She must somehow have misunderstood and sent her sister."

Darius suspected there was a certain amount of deliberate misunderstanding involved, but there was no time for that now. He had a trespasser to apprehend.

He quickly sent Miles upstairs to shut her in. The inquisitive woman would have only one exit, and Darius would be waiting.

❧

Oh Lord, now she heard heavy footsteps advancing along the corridor. A loud, hearty whistle echoed Lucy's song. She ran to the door but it was stuck fast. Just like the dresser drawer it would not heed her desperate tugging. The handle turned stiffly but there was no click. Had it locked itself somehow?

Her heart skipped uncertainly.

Had the ghost of Nellie Pickles locked her in?

Was the spirit of Phineas Hawke playing tricks on her, getting his vengeance for her years of trespassing?

A male voice bellowed through the house. "I'll get it, Darius! Is it in your bedchamber?"

The echo seemed directionless, could have come from anywhere. But she was about to be discovered there and what excuse could she make? It would be humiliating in the extreme.

She spun in circles, considering her choices.

Justina made a dash for the best hiding space.

"Under the bed, you say Wainwright? Shall I look there?"

She swore heartily, changing direction and heading for the window—the only way out. Fortunately there was trellis work, a great deal of ivy, and she was no stranger to climbing. If she fell to her death, so be it, she thought grimly.

Serve her right for being such a fool.

Knowing her luck, the window would be stuck too.

But no, it opened, sliding upward when she pushed it with all her strength.

With the bundle of found letters clutched under her shawl, she cautiously made her way out, over the window ledge, and onto the handy trellis.

The ivy was wet and slippery and she had not

descended far when there was a loud crack. Justina abruptly descended another five inches and the toes of her boots now tapped the glass panes of the window below. From the shocked exclamation that floated up to her she knew she'd been seen.

Twenty-five

FORTUNATELY THE RAIN HAD SLOWED TO A FINE drizzle. At that moment he did not particularly care what the weather did in any case. It might have snowed and he would have still enjoyed her performance. Not to mention her comeuppance.

Darius set a chair in the grass, flipped out the tails of his coat and sat.

Today, it was her turn to be mortified.

She dangled in midair, her skirt hooked up on the trellis, a pair of stockings and drawers on full display. "Tell me, madam, have we met before?" he called up to her. "You look familiar, in an odd way." He pretended to think hard, rubbing his chin.

"For pity's sake," she hissed, her voice muffled by the ivy. "Help me down, you fool."

"Hmmm. Let me consider it. Perhaps, for once, you ought to be polite to me, and respectful. For once. Or else you can hang there until Easter."

"Suit yourself, then! I can make my own way down."

"Shall you swing from my chandelier as an encore?" he asked politely, greatly enjoying the show.

She resumed her escape without his aid, accompanied by the slow, torturous sound of ripping. If she was not careful, she would soon fall the remaining distance and land on his head.

Miss Lucy Bridges was watching from the window, hands clasped in anxiety, but apparently not so concerned that she would brave the rain to come outside.

"We do have doors you know, Miss Penny," Darius shouted. "Several of them. That is the customary method of exit, even here in the country, I believe."

But in all the excitement he had not heard carriage wheels approach, and just a few moments later a tall, angular figure came around the corner, followed by a second, shorter and rounder lady in a very large bonnet.

"Darius?" the tall one demanded. "What are you doing out here in the blessed rain?"

Damn! His family never could leave him in peace for very long.

He stood hastily. "Mary."

"Since you decided to be so dreadfully rude and stay in the country, I thought I'd better—"

His stepsister must have caught sight of the slender, stocking-clad legs making their way down his ivy and a hand flew to her lips. The woman standing with her turned to a cooked shade of lobster under her enormous hat.

Fortunately, Miles trotted into view soon after, carrying a ladder and with Lucy Bridges trotting after him. As always, Miles was smiling, not in the least troubled by events. When he saw Mary he greeted her as if there was nothing odd occurring in their view.

Darius took the ladder from him and set it against the

house. The half-undressed young woman was still several feet from the ground and seemed to be searching for a new foothold, while the trellis bent away from the wall and wet leaves of ivy shook and shuddered ominously.

"Stay there," he shouted up to her. "I'm coming to get you."

"No!" she shrieked. "I can manage perfectly well without you."

He began to climb the ladder with no further ado, before she took it into her head to jump and break a leg.

"I suppose it would be the height of stupidity to ask what you're doing up there?" he muttered as he climbed the rungs toward her. "Did you find anything worth stealing?"

Her cheek flat to the wall, one gloveless hand clinging to the ivy, she exclaimed, "I can make my own way down, Wainwright."

Ignoring that, he reached over, meaning to guide her hands to the ladder. She struggled against him, of course, endangering his balance, so he was obliged to grab hold of the nearest item—which just happened to be her drawers.

"The trellis won't hold you up forever, woman!" he muttered under his breath. "Step onto the ladder. Just this once, do as I say. It shouldn't hurt too much, as long as you don't make a habit of it. And I doubt there's any danger of that, do you?"

At last she stepped from the trellis to his ladder and then they were eye to eye, she with her foot two rungs above his. Darius felt his heart sputtering away like a candle struggling in a fierce draft.

"Fine day, Miss Penny, is it not?" he managed.

She blinked slowly; her eyes showed confusion, her lips slightly parted so that a little ghostly mist escaped into the frigid air. "No. It's a horrid, horrid day."

"I've had worse," he said softly. "Recently." He couldn't help himself, wanted her to know how she'd wounded him. She thought him without feeling, which was partly his fault. He would not make the same mistake again.

"Are you sure this ladder will hold us both?"

"Best start down, to be on the safe side," he muttered. He still had hold of her drawers, but she seemed not to notice and stared intently at his mouth instead.

Darius wondered why she wasn't moving. She stayed there beside him on that narrow ladder, her mouth only inches from his, as if she deliberately tormented him. His wrist was on her hip, his knuckles resting against the soft curve of her bottom, the silky flesh all too evident through her rain-dampened linen drawers. He cleared his throat. "Shall we proceed, madam?"

◆

Proceed? In that moment she had no idea what he meant. Proceed with what?

She could smell the spiciness of his shaving soap and a faint whisper of cider. Beneath it all was the scent of a man. It stirred something inside her; like a tiny drop falling into a rain barrel, it left rings echoing through her mind and her heart.

Justina could not resist running a hand over the front of his chest, pretending to seek a steadying hold.

"Oops."

Her fingers had ripped a button right off his waistcoat.

He didn't seem to have much luck with his waistcoats, poor man.

Her gaze followed the button all the way to the grass below and then she said, "We can hardly stay here like this forever, I suppose." She decided to be very polite and formal now, as if somehow that would cancel out the awfulness of appearing on his trellis, exiting his bedchamber, and exposing her drawers to the elements.

They began their slow and careful descent back to earth.

Miles Forester was chatting amiably with the two ladies watching. "What a surprise to see you here, Lady Waltham! I'm sure Darius will be thrilled to have your company."

The tall woman with a long, horse-like face was staring hard at Justina without the minutest attempt to conceal her curiosity. "It looks as if he has company already," she snapped.

"But one can never have too much! The more the merrier, I always say," Miles exclaimed.

Justina felt the eyes of the two women sternly inspecting her dishabille. "Well, really!" came one shocked gasp. "Have revolutionaries come to Buckinghamshire already?"

"Did you see how her drawers are patched, your ladyship, with very clumsy stitches?"

"That she wears drawers at all, Augusta, is most distasteful and the sign of a fast woman. I do not agree with drawers."

"Oh, I am quite of the same opinion, your ladyship. Quite."

The two women discussed her openly, as if she was an exhibit in a circus tent and too stupid to understand.

Justina muttered under her breath, "I rather think

those two fine ladies ought to be glad I *am* wearing drawers, or they might have had quite a sight, far more offensive to their sensibilities than some patched linen."

Since Darius was the only one who could possibly hear her, she expected her sentence to go unacknowledged, but to her surprise he replied gravely, "Quite so, Miss Justina. An eyeful for them, perhaps, and a perfect handful for me."

She looked up at him in amazement.

"Uh"—he turned red—"by handful I meant you are one. Not that your....in my…"

"Please say nothing more, Mr. Wainwright." As he became hotter, so did she. All hope of collecting some composure, she knew, would soon be lost if they didn't both pull themselves together.

Mortified, Justina meant to dash off the moment her feet touched the grass. Certainly, she couldn't imagine he wanted her to meet his grand friends. But Darius caught her by the arm and held her tightly. His eyes were focused on the new arrivals and when he spoke again, it came from the corner of his tight lips. "Do stay and be introduced properly."

"Why? I don't care to—"

"This is Miss Justina Penny." He talked loudly over her complaints and presented her to the other women, not even giving her time to adjust her torn skirt over her undergarments. "The local doctor's daughter. Miss Justina, this is my stepsister, Lady Moore, Viscountess Waltham."

She was astonished that he thought it necessary to introduce her and had fully expected Wainwright to pretend he didn't know her at all, especially in the presence of his noble family.

Lucy was also introduced, but the new arrivals were far more interested in Justina's curious appearance.

"It would seem you are an excellent climber, Miss Penny," exclaimed the fashionably attired, well-groomed horse.

"Only as a last resort," she muttered. "When one is locked in a bedchamber, one must save oneself somehow."

Lady Waltham reared up and showed her gums in a high-pitched neigh. "*Locked* in a *bedchamber*?"

"His. I was locked in." In her agitated state and with the familiar eagerness to find excuses, she spurted this news out before she realized how it might sound.

"Miss Justina Penny," he clarified steadily, "likes to explore and pry into a man's things when he is out and not expected to return." He kept his hand around her arm, holding her hard to his side. "She is also the mistress of exaggeration. She was not locked in at all."

"Indeed I was! The handle would not turn. And I was not prying. I was doing the job you asked of me. It was your idea to have me here. I would rather not have come at all." Oh dear. She bit her tongue. So much for polite and cordial.

He reminded her coolly, "You owed me the favor, Miss Penny. I help you with Sir Mortimer and you help me. That was our arrangement. And you've been avoiding your duty these past few days."

"I had other things to do."

"What more important things could you have to do than come here to me?"

His stepsister's face seemed to lengthen even further, and her gaze sharpened on his fingers until he finally released Justina's arm. "Favors?" Lady Waltham sputtered. "Arrangements?"

Sir Mortimer Grubbins could suddenly be heard grunting contentedly in the distance as he scratched his back on the fence of his sty, making it creak and bang in a slow rhythm. There suddenly seemed to be something very naughty about that sound and the happy grunting only made it worse.

"You have torn your gown," the other woman exclaimed abruptly from beneath the brim of a bonnet that was almost as large as the rest of her.

"This is my companion, Miss Augusta Milford," the horse whinnied, gesturing at her friend with a limp hand. "I'm sure you must remember her, Darius."

He looked blankly at both ladies.

Justina was amused to find that his treatment of all women was much the same. Only she had been singled out for a different sort of notice, she thought with a little pinch of appreciation for that fact.

"We'd better go in, Darius," his stepsister exclaimed. "It is raining, although you appear not to care. It seems you have too much else upon your mind." Not waiting for an invitation from her host, she trotted her friend back around the corner of the house and proceeded to bellow at the coachman, warning dire punishment if he damaged her luggage. From the heaving, banging, and muttering going on, there must be a great deal of it to be managed.

"Your guests plan to stay a while," Justina remarked. "Does Lady Waltham not know you are leaving?"

"Not yet," he replied.

She squinted up at him, raindrops spitting on her face.

"She does not know yet, or you are not leaving yet?" Immediately annoyed with herself for asking and making it seem as if she cared, she added in haste, "If you mean to stay longer, you ought to get that bedchamber door handle fixed, sir. Or you might get shut in one day too. The trellis won't hold your weight as it did mine."

"If I became stuck, I could always have the door taken off its hinges."

"Oh. I suppose so."

"Because I wouldn't have been in there illicitly—prying through someone else's belongings—and need have no fear of discovery, therefore no need to climb through the window like a thief."

She backed away, folding her arms tightly over her shawl, under which she hid that bundle of letters.

"I suggest you wait for an invitation next time," he added, a new, decidedly wicked gleam lighting his gaze. Miles was laughing softly, even though he had turned away, pretending not to listen.

She sensed that Wainwright was trying to make her flustered again. It was odd to see him in this mood. It was almost flirtatious.

"Did you just suggest, sir, in front of your friend, that I might await an invitation into your bedchamber?"

At last there was a smile. A very shocking, full smile. "No, Miss Justina. I suggested you would never wait for one." He bowed his head toward her. "Neither would I expect you to. I shall be prepared, next time, for the assault."

Her mind spun faster and clumsier than a wooden spoon in heavy-handed Clara's fist.

Rebecca Sherringham's suggestion was right, she

thought, he *was* devastating when he smiled. She was tempted to smile back.

His gaze slipped downward to where she folded her arms over her bosom, and then slowly it drifted back up again to her face.

Was that a wistful look in his eye? Did he have any idea what he did to her with that rarest of smiles? A playful Wainwright was a very dangerous thing. She'd sensed it from the first hint of a twinkle. But he looked that way at *her*, and no one else as far as she could tell.

He raised a hand to his hatless, rain-dampened head and ran his fingers through the dark hair. He'd allowed it to grow out a little more since arriving in the village, she noted now. It was beginning to show that curl she'd always suspected was there.

"Did you find anything of interest today, Miss Penny?"

"Any...anything of interest?" She squeezed her arms even tighter across her knitted shawl. "No. Why?"

"Because if you did, it belongs to me, remember?"

"Of course," she muttered, quickly looking away.

"We've all been invited to join the Sherringhams for an evening of entertainment," Miles Forester blurted, like a boy suddenly bored with the adults' conversation. "I do hope we'll see you there on Thursday next, ladies. And your sister, Miss Penny. She will attend, I hope."

She nodded. "I expect so. Rebecca is a good friend of ours."

"So is the captain, I understand."

"Yes."

Justina thought she heard Wainwright exhale a low huff of disdain. One of his specialties.

"Well, good-bye. I see you won't need us here

again, so we'll take our leave. Come, Lucy." She grabbed her friend's hand and headed for the gate, not waiting to be reprimanded further for her antics that day. One of *her* specialties.

As they walked back to the village Lucy's dour mood soon became evident enough to break through Justina's daydreams.

"What's the matter with you?" she demanded, noting Lucy's heavy footsteps splashing through puddles with unusual disregard for the state of her petticoat.

"Oh, *nothing*! What do I matter?"

"Lucy Bridges, explain yourself."

The other girl stomped onward. "I don't exist when you're there. He only has eyes for you."

"Who? What?"

"You know very well who. And you don't even want him. It's such a dreadful waste."

Had it been so obvious? She didn't know what to think of it all. The shredded chrysanthemums, the pacing, the odd visit. And now the smile.

"Everyone has secrets except me," Lucy protested. "If I wasn't here none of you would even…"

They had suddenly spied Captain Sherringham climbing a stile some distance ahead. Justina slowed down at once, not wanting to meet him or be seen. Her head and heart were too full just then, and she was in no mood for him that afternoon; he would look for her to be breezy and joking as usual, but she simply could not. When she held Lucy's arm to keep her from running after him the girl complained again.

"What now? You *are* in an odd mood, Jussy."

"Me? Not nearly as odd as you."

As they waited behind a tree, they saw the captain was not alone. He turned back and offered his hand to help someone else over the stile behind him.

Diana.

They watched the two people converse. The captain raised Diana's hand to his lips, but she snatched it back and shouted something. The wind whipped her words away down the lane and Justina could not identify them, but she saw the anger on both their faces. Diana raised her skirt out of the mud and swept by him. The captain caught the edge of her mantle and tugged her back. Justina held her breath, expecting the couple to kiss. But they stood thus for a long time, their lips close but unmoving. Finally, Diana pulled her mantle out of his grip and ran off, leaving him to walk slowly after her, his head bent, his usually sunny demeanor thoroughly vanquished.

"I cannot think why the captain is so fascinated with Diana Makepiece," said Lucy suddenly. "She has never shown him the slightest affection."

"Perhaps that's exactly why."

"Well, the sooner she is married and gone to Manderson the better for them both. He can stop thinking of her. Nathaniel needs someone to cheer him up. He has had a dreadful fit of the blue devils lately."

But Justina was not looking forward to any one of their little group leaving the village. And it was a group that included more now than it once did. As for Captain Sherringham, she rather thought he was capable of cheering himself up. He wasn't the sort to be down for long.

"It's all so very frustrating," Lucy moaned.

"What is?"

"These men pining after women who don't want them."

"I'm sure no one pines for me."

Lucy shot her a frown. "I, for one, am quite sick of being overlooked."

But Justina was no longer listening to her friend, for she was too busy thinking of Wainwright's hands on her drawers and then of a certain unexpected smile.

Twenty-six

"WHAT A CURIOUS CREATURE, SO...UNKEMPT AND surly," Mary remarked later that afternoon when Miles raised the subject of Miss Justina Penny's unusual exit once again. "I cannot think any situation was such an emergency that she should react in that fashion, scaling the wall like a circus acrobat."

"I thought her exertions had put a very pretty bloom in her *cheeks*," Miles replied, deliberately lingering over the last word, just to tease Darius and horrify the ladies. He got away with it, of course, because a man with his charm could never offend. Not even in Mary's case.

"Miles Forester, you are a rascal of the worst order. I'm sure you are the reason for that creature being here. They flock to you like bees to lavender."

"Indeed, no, Lady Waltham. She is entirely your stepbrother's responsibility. Unlikely as it may seem. He is her favorite."

Darius said nothing. His hands tightened into fists on his knees. When Miles was in the mood to tease and torment it was often wisest to ignore it. Not to feed the beast.

Miss Augusta Milford exclaimed that she thought Justina a very odd name and was it, by chance, foreign? "Of course, one hesitates to make assumptions of that nature, but I should not be at all surprised to find she has foreign blood."

"It would explain her wild behavior," Mary replied with a sneer, "and her appallingly continental manners." She paused, examining the ruffles of taffeta at her wrist. "I shall say only this, if she is foreign, be very wary of trying her temper. They scratch and spit like feral cats. She reminded me very much of an insolent, slovenly chambermaid I once had the misfortune to encounter in Bournemouth."

"Bournemouth?" Darius scratched his head slowly. "That is hardly the continent, Mary."

"No. That is my point. One does not expect such surly behavior from domestic servants in this country. Nor from country doctors' daughters who show their drawers in public."

With a sigh he stared at the fire.

"I shall certainly keep my jewelry locked away while I am here," she added crossly, "if strange young women take to climbing walls as a matter of course."

"She is not a jewel thief, Mary."

"But what *was* she doing in your bedchamber? I cannot think what to make of that! What have you been up to with that girl?"

Rather than answer his stepsister, Darius got up and swiftly left the drawing room. He went directly upstairs, taking the steps three at a time, to find out for himself what she'd done in there. For it suddenly occurred to him that she might have found the rest of those letters, the last remaining pieces of a game he'd given up.

❦

By nightfall everyone in the village knew that Midwitch Manor had welcomed more guests. Justina—practicing her newfound discretion—said nothing to anybody, but Lucy could not help herself.

The equine Lady Waltham and her stout friend were seen at church the following day, seated in Wainwright's pew, looking down on the general populace, talking only to the gentlemen of Midwitch and sparing the rector a few moments of their condescending notice.

On Monday the two ladies graced Hawcombe Prior's main street to visit the haberdasher. Where they supposedly found nothing good enough to buy. That was sufficient cause for the majority of the Book Club Belles to decide they ought to be snubbed.

Within eight and forty hours, even worse news had reached the Penny household. Martha Mawby reported that Miss Augusta Milford followed Mr. Wainwright about his house like a concerned cow hovering over a young calf. According to Martha, Miss Milford liked to advise the gentleman on everything from his dress to his choice of food at breakfast. She had even, so Martha grumbled, snatched one of his waistcoats away to sew a loose button on for the gentleman herself.

It must be concluded that Miss Milford was serious indeed, for seizing anything out of Martha's ham-hock fists was no task to be undertaken lightly.

"This is a terrible development," their mother cried, dashing into their bedchamber again while they sat together, drying their washed hair by the fire. "That woman has come to steal him away! It cannot be borne.

I'm sure I shan't say a 'good morn' to her again when I see her in our lane."

Cathy was calm in the face of their mother's distress. "Mr. Wainwright was never really mine, Mama. I do not believe he has any interest in me. We must be civil to the ladies."

"Of course he was in love with you! Why else would our invitation to dine be the only one in the village he accepted?"

"But Mama, you must recall, he did not dance with me at the harvest ball. His only partner then was Jussy. Yet you do not assume he has an interest in *her*."

"*Jussy*?" their mother exclaimed, flinging her hands in the air. "Why on earth would he look twice at her?"

"I don't know, Mama," replied Cathy softly. "Should we ask Jussy?"

Justina glared at her sister. She'd begun to suspect that Cathy's cold was altogether too convenient in its coming and its going. There was also the matter of a certain message Darius Wainwright had claimed to send via his friend. A message that was either waylaid or ignored. "I don't know what you mean," she snapped. "I have done nothing. I resent the supposition that one silly dance means anything. I'm sure it is not my fault."

Their mother was equally adamant. "*You* are the one for him, Catherine, and he must be made to see it. I do not think you have made the effort you might. Now that plump, opinionated goose waddles into view and tries to take him away from you."

"Opinionated goose?"

She clasped her hands beneath her bosom. "I was outside beating the rugs this morning when Miss Augusta

Milford"—her head twitched with every syllable of that name—"passed by and thought herself called upon to tell me they were too worn to be saved and that beating them thus hard would wear the threads away entirely. Then she proceeded to point out the faded patches and suggested I did not turn my rugs enough to prevent the sunlight damaging the pattern! As if I have not managed my rugs for more years than she's worn a corset. And those rugs have sentimental value. My dear brother Justin brought them back from India! It is nothing to do with what one can and cannot afford." The border of her lace cap twitched madly. "Well, I gave her a very sharp look, I can tell you. And I beat those rugs twice as hard."

Justina laughed. "That showed her, Mama!"

"Indeed it did. Sticking her nose into my rugs."

"She was lucky you did not turn the beater on her. Next time you should."

"So I shall, Jussy! Wretched meddler. Stealing our Mr. Wainwright away!"

"Mama," Catherine gently intervened, "that lady is surely entitled to accompany her friend into the country without causing speculation about her motives. Perhaps she is simply the motherly type who concerns herself with the welfare of other people. There is nothing bad about that."

Justina was still laughing. "Miss Milford's concern, as far as I can see, is only for one particular person— herself—and anyone else can go hang themselves." While watching from their window that morning, she'd seen the lady skirting puddles in the lane yet making no effort to warn her noble companion of the same lurking danger. Justina had also witnessed Miss Milford sneak

back alone to the village shop, where she purchased the
last length of muslin in a pattern and color she had loudly
insulted as "garish and common" when dissuading Lady
Waltham from choosing it the day before.

"For pity's sake, sit closer to that fire," their mother
urged Cathy. "You are just recovered from a bad cold,
and we cannot have you laid low again now! Not with
that impertinent baggage sniffing about the place with
her *expert* opinions on all and sundry."

At the next meeting of the Book Club Belles, Rebecca
agreed that her impression of Miss Milford was of a
pushy, demanding, pretentious woman who, although
she followed Lady Waltham about like a lapdog, was by
no means wilting in her shadow, but sharing the light of
entitlement that shone upon that lady to boost her own
circumstances. "There is a slyness about her that I do
not like."

Diana had caught Lady Waltham sneering at her worn
boots in church and heard her whinny to her friend that
the services of a cobbler must not be easily found in the
area. That remark, and the subsequent snickering of both
ladies within her hearing, had almost reduced Diana to
tears. "I do not think Lady Waltham very stylish at all.
For a viscountess I would expect something quite different. Her companion certainly lacks refinement, which is
also a sign of the lady's bad judgment in friends."

And Lucy added that Miss Milford had very poor taste
in hats.

The Book Club Belles, therefore, were united in their
dislike of the newcomers. Only Cathy still held out some
hope for the two ladies, but she was never loud enough
to overcome the doubts voiced by the others.

ONCE UPON A KISS 293

Augusta Milford's forceful commandeering of Darius Wainwright and his waistcoat buttons was soon known and disapproved of throughout the village. She had a propensity, it seemed, to rub people the wrong way with curious faux pas in her speech, and she was indeed a meddler, poking her nose into anywhere she desired and not caring overmuch if others were affronted. Cathy insisted Miss Milford was merely unaware of the impression she gave. Justina was inclined to believe the lady intentionally rude.

But Justina had other things to do and little time to ponder the behavior of those newcomers. As the Book Society ladies read Mr. Darcy's long letter of explanation and confession to Elizabeth Bennet in *Pride and Prejudice*, Justina also had something enlightening to peruse—the last bundle of letters she'd found in the old dresser drawer in Wainwright's room.

The first, which she assumed to be the earliest, was tinged brown with age again, the ink faded.

My dearest angel,

From the first time we met, I was in your power. You have consumed me ever since. My waking moments are filled with thoughts of you and my dreams with visions of the same. I have not the courage to speak of my feelings and so I write them down.

In her hands, it seemed, she held more love letters of Phineas Hawke to his mystery lady. There were no addresses penned upon the fold so he must never have sent them. Curious. Poor man. Her heart opened to him more with every word she read. Every word he had not been able to say out loud to his sweetheart.

> *Forgive me my awkwardness. I am not a man familiar with the ways of soft words and courtship. I have been told, in fact, not to attempt it.*
>
> *Yet here I am, throwing my friend's warnings and my own doubts to the four winds, on a letter you may never read. At least, when you do, I will not be there to see your face or hear the derision in your laughter.*

But he gained confidence with his writing, for he found words to fill several more sheets of vellum over a passage of time.

Justina greedily guarded the pile of love letters, hiding them with the others she'd found earlier in her shawl inside a hatbox, taking them out to reread whenever she could be alone. She did not want to share her discovery with anybody.

Sometimes the letters were solemn, pensive. At other times they were lighthearted, self-effacing, even whimsical.

> *I saw you today*
> *it was but brief*
> *it served to give me*
> *some relief.*

How strange it was that the bent old miser Phineas Hawke, who once chased her from his blossoming trees with the threat of setting his dogs upon her, should be capable of writing these sweet words to his lady love.

If I had you, mine to please,
I would bring you pleasant ease.
Never would you lift a finger,
except to make the butterflies linger.

She thought of the butterflies from her father's collection and how she once purloined them for decoration in her hair.

How Wainwright had looked at her that night.

And so would you return to me
all the joy there is to be.
I do not smile so much, 'tis true.
How can I, when I have not you?

With a heavy sigh, she folded the letter and put it away with its companions in the hatbox. She really must stop thinking about Wainwright the Wrong, but everything seemed to lead her thoughts back to him these days, even these letters written by his great-uncle.

Nothing of any good could come from regret, she thought sadly. Soon he would leave and never return to their "mud rut" of a village. As her father had said, he was too grand for them.

Oh, but…that dreadful Milford woman.

Miss Augusta Milford, who could not spare a moment to warn a friend about a puddle, would never do for Darius Wainwright. He was accident prone and needed someone to point out things like puddles to him, or at least to fall in them herself first, to apprise him of the danger.

Sighing heavily, Justina rested her chin on one

upturned palm and watched raindrops slide down the window panes, racing one another. Sometimes they ran parallel for a while and then merged. Like lovers who could not stay apart.

> *I do not smile so much, 'tis true.*
> *How can I, when I have not you?*

Justina decided she must know more about the young Phineas. It became a very important mission to track down the woman to whom he'd written his letters and poetry. Although she remembered him as a mean-tempered, bitter old man, she supposed there must have been some reason why he got that way. People were not born thus. After all, one rarely saw a mean-tempered, bitter baby—unless someone had taken its teething ring away.

If she could uncover the truth of what happened to his love affair, perhaps she would know why he died alone and let his house fall into sad disrepair. It might be too late to help Phineas, but there was another who could benefit from a lesson about the past.

The next afternoon, her mother caught her leaving the house and wanted to know where she was off to.

"I am on a mission of discovery," she replied proudly. "I may be gone some time."

While she might have expected her mama to insist upon knowing her destination, or at least to ensure she was back for dinner, the only reply was a swift, "Well, for goodness' sake, use the boot-scraper before you come back in."

The ordinariness of her life was, at times, quite mortifying.

Ten minutes later, when Mrs. Dockley opened her door and found Justina standing there in the rain, she looked extremely cautious. Perhaps she wondered what new atrocity had now been committed against her property.

Justina quickly put the old dear at ease and explained it was purely a social visit. Even as she said it, she felt sorry that she had paid so few of those in the past to Mrs. Dockley. But at least she had brought treacle tarts, filched from the pantry while Clara was busy with her corns. Few things could ensure a better welcome in anybody's house or a warmer forgiveness for past sins.

She sat with the old lady for a while, enquiring into her health and the status of several relatives. Finally she angled the conversation around to Phineas Hawke and asked if he had ever courted anyone in the village.

"You have lived here longer than anyone, Mrs. Dockley. Surely you must remember."

At first the lady could not recall anything on the matter. It must have been many years since anyone showed an interest in old Hawke or gave thought to how he once was, so Justina supposed memories had become buried. But after another cup of tea and a treacle tart, glimmers of light began to break through the darkness and confusion.

"I believe there was an aristocratic young lady once. Very haughty, very superior. She came to Midwitch a few times and there were rumors of an engagement, but nothing ever came of it. I was a little girl then, no more than eleven or twelve, but I remember she had some lovely gowns and jewelry. We only saw her from a distance, of course, and when her carriage raced by it spattered us all with mud. Goodness, the dirt I used to get on my petticoats, Miss Jussy! Much like you do now."

Justina did not want to lose the purpose of their conversation, so she merely smiled and said, "I wonder why Mr. Hawke did not marry her, then."

After another bite of tart the old lady dug out more memory. "If I am not mistaken, the engagement fell through when the fancy miss discovered that Phineas was in love with a farmer's daughter from Hawcombe Mallow. His betrothed left in a huff and the village was all abuzz with it for days." She gazed into the distance. "Yes, he was supposed to marry that fine, very noble lady, but he was quite in love with the dear, sweet little thing who hadn't a penny to her name. But shining copper hair she had. Long waves of it. I remember that." She looked at the crumbs on her plate. "Of course, Phineas was a kinder, gentler young man in those days."

"Really?" It was hard to imagine, but she did have those oddly touching poems to consider.

"The young Phineas was quite different to how he became later after the hunting accident. In youth he was reserved. Even shy, some would call it, and not at all the dashing, rakish sort. I do not think he had much self-confidence. His elder sister was the one who made all the noise and ruled the roost."

"His sister?" Justina inched forward in her chair. "That would be Mr. Wainwright's grandmama."

"Yes, and as I remember it, she put an end to his romance with the girl from Hawcombe Mallow. She did not approve, thought a farmer's daughter too lowly. And Phineas, I suppose, did not think enough of himself to stand up for what he wanted. Until it was too late. By the time he sought to get his love back again, she'd gone off and married another. A soldier from the camp nearby, I believe. They moved many miles away. I doubt he ever saw her again." Mrs. Dockley sipped her tea. "Very sad really, when one considers how everything changed after that."

"Then his sister moved away too and married."

The old lady nodded slowly. "Phineas had quarreled with her bitterly, blamed her for the loss of his sweetheart. The siblings were estranged for the remainder of their lives. Then Phineas had the accident...well, it ended his life in many ways. Perhaps things would have been different had he been brave enough to defy his sister and marry where he wanted."

Justina agreed that it was very unfortunate and deeply sad. The story changed much about the way she thought of Phineas.

The front door bell interrupted her musings and the old lady flew into quite a tizzy.

"Well, goodness, two visitors today! I am lucky."

A few moments later Darius Wainwright appeared with a basket of apples and pears. He paled when he saw Justina sitting there and she was no less startled, but Mrs. Dockley expressed more delight.

"My dear Mr. Wainwright, how good of you to visit me again. As you see, I have a young friend with me today, Miss Justina Penny. Ah, but I believe you know each other, do you not? I saw you dancing at the harvest festival."

The gentleman recovered with a bow for both ladies and then explained that he had brought Mrs. Dockley the last of the fruit from his orchard. "I doubt there will be any more this year, and I thought you would make better use of it."

"Mr. Wainwright, that is too kind of you."

Justina realized she'd been staring and quickly looked down at her knees and then the fireplace.

"Do sit, sir," the old lady urged. "Coincidentally, Miss Penny and I were talking of your great-uncle Phineas Hawke."

"Oh?"

Justina raised her eyes sheepishly to his.

"Miss Penny wanted to know whether he ever had a sweetheart. She has been testing my memory."

"Ah." He hovered uncertainly and then backed toward the door. "Unfortunately I cannot stay. I merely wanted to bring you the fruit, madam. I have some other matters to attend. Please, excuse me." He bowed again, uttered a hasty "Good afternoon," and went out.

Justina's pulse would not settle. She glanced at the basket of fruit. "How very generous of Mr. Wainwright," she muttered.

"He is indeed. The young man often visits me, you know, and brings a basket for me." She hitched forward in her chair and winked. "I rather think he just likes an excuse to come here and talk. We have some lovely chats."

Justina almost burst out laughing. "Chats? I did not think Mr. Wainwright was very loquacious."

"I daresay he is not so shy with an old lady like me. And I rather like his quiet company. He lets me do most of the talking. As indeed you have done today too, my dear." Her squinting gaze drifted toward the door. "I wonder why he did not stay this afternoon. What a pity."

That Wainwright should take time out of his day to bring Mrs. Dockley fruit was very strange. That he should have called upon her regularly was extraordinary. How could she not have known this?

Even in the rain he had gone there. It was galling for Justina to discover she did not know everything that happened in Hawcombe Prior. Right under her nose.

Twenty-seven

WHEN SHE RETURNED HOME, JUSTINA STOOD IN THE hall and looked at the console table where his hat and gloves remained. No one dared touch them, it seemed. Her gaze wandered upward to the mirror above and she saw Cathy coming out of the parlor behind her.

"Mr. Forester called, Jussy, and you missed him."

"Well, he did not come to see me, did he?" Still slightly distracted by her thoughts, Justina looked at her sister, who was much improved after her cold. "I expect he came only to see the bloom back in your cheeks." She paused. "If Mr. Forester was here, why did he not take his friend's hat?"

"Oh. I forgot it was here." Cathy appeared similarly distracted, until her eyes sharpened in their reflection above the console table. "Jussy, you are soaked! Look at you! Did you fall in the pond?"

Standing beside her sister never did her many favors, but in her current state, there was no hope. Usually it didn't matter, for Justina was perfectly happy to remain in the background. Today it spurred her into action.

She went directly upstairs and came down a few

moments later, carrying an old, burgundy velvet gown that her aunt had given her last year. The material was slightly worn in places, but she'd heard that the pile of velvet could be raised again with the application of a warm iron and a wet cloth on the underside. As the most mature style of gown she possessed, it was seldom worn. She'd always felt it was wasted on her. It had been made for her aunt, a lady of elegance and fashion who never made a spectacle of herself. Justina always joked that the gown must have felt as if it were being punished when it was put into her custody. For a year it had lain in a drawer, which was the safest place for it. Now it was brought out into daylight again.

She set to work on it at once in the kitchen, and her mother, finding her there shortly after, wanted to know what on earth she was up to.

"Really, Mama, can a young lady not desire to be well-dressed when she goes out?"

Her mother looked askance.

"I have been waiting for a chance to wear this lovely gown, and I shall be warm in it tonight at the Sherringhams' card party."

Mrs. Penny shook her head. "I hope this is not all for that wretched captain."

"No, Mama. Of course not." As she reached for the handle of the iron to lift it from the range, her mother stopped her.

"Gracious, child! You'll burn your hand. Here...wrap this cloth around it. And be careful!"

Justina's mind had been too busy to think of it, but her mother acted quickly, muttering breathlessly about how she was surprised her youngest daughter hadn't maimed herself by now with the heedless way she carried on. She wound the cloth around the iron handle and stood by watching as Justina proceeded to work gently on the velvet.

"You know, my girl, that Captain Sherringham would do you no good at all. You and he are too much alike and there would never be a moment's content between you." For once her mother spoke with a gentler tone. "I know he's not all bad, and oh yes, I can see the charm in a red coat. I was betaken by a few of those fancies in my day too, before I met your father. But Captain Sherringham is not the right fellow for you, Justina. I don't want you thinking you'll be alone when your sister marries. No need to do anything desperate. Not yet, in any case. You've got *some* qualities a decent young man would appreciate."

"I know, Mama," she said, surprised.

"All is not lost. Yet. You've got quite a bloom about you these days."

"Thank you, Mama."

Her mother reached up and patted her cheek. "You have a natural, country prettiness that does not require gilding, that's for sure. You could give the Miss Augusta Milfords of this world—and their fancy viscountess companions—a run for their money, make no mistake! We'll get you a husband, Justina, my dear, by hook or by crook."

She was genuinely moved by her mother's attempt to lift her spirits and that determination to see her taken care of; however, little joy could be anticipated in the possible methods to which she might one day resort.

It was a rare moment of civil tranquility between the

two women and it lasted until Clara came in and had to
be chided for picking her nose.

Darius would usually anticipate a party, such as the one
planned at the Sherringhams' house, with nothing but
dread. However, since it meant seeing Justina again he
actually faced the event with some eagerness as the hour
drew near. It would be a chance to try again, set his
frown aside, and show his true self without hiding behind
the arrogance to which he'd always clung. Unfortunately,
his stepsister and her companion had decided they were
bored enough to join the party. Captain Sherringham
had met the ladies in the village and extended the invitation to include them.

Of course he did, thought Darius grimly. The more
women the better for a man like that. Exactly like Lucius.

Major Sherringham's house was one of the larger
cottages in the village, well furnished and brightly lit in
the evenings, which suggested he—unlike most of the
residents—had no need to budget candles. The major
was a jolly fellow with the look of a plum pudding due
to his rounded shape, and a rough, mottled skin colored
by long service abroad. His wife had apparently died
many years ago, according to Miles, who had a knack
for finding these things out. The major lacked both skill
and inclination to care for his children in a traditional
fatherly fashion, although he took them traveling with
him whenever possible, rather like old luggage to be
dragged and crashed along the cobbles after him. As
a result, Nathaniel and Rebecca had been raised by a
procession of nannies, tutors, and governesses. And each

other. They were attractive, vivacious, somewhat noisy, and clearly had never known much discipline. It seemed as if their father left his commanding manner behind in the barracks and on the battlefield. He had, so Miles said, retired to Hawcombe Prior several years ago out of fondness for his wife's memory, as it was where they first met.

"See?" Miles had laughed. "There *is* something romantic about this place."

At which Darius had rolled his eyes.

On the evening of the party, the major must have enjoyed several glasses of port before they arrived. He greeted Darius and Miles with a great, booming laugh, then made a genial fuss of the ladies, making certain they sat close enough to the fire to keep warm, offering them wine and sweetmeats, asking them how they liked Midwitch Manor, firing questions and bursts of laughter around the room. For the first quarter hour he was the cheerful, generous host. Then he fell asleep in a chair by the hearth and remained thus, snoring heartily, for the rest of the evening.

Despite the warmth of the room, there was a chill between the ladies. His stepsister's most annoying qualities were on display as she made no attempt to hide her disdain for her surroundings or her company. It was evident she had gone there that evening only out of curiosity and to keep watch over him. Somehow—and he was sure Miles had a hand in this—she had begun to suspect Justina Penny of being more to him than a mere acquaintance.

Earlier that evening she had snapped at Darius as they waited for Miss Milford to join them in the hall of his house. "I hope you know what you're doing. Unlike some women, I do understand that men must have their mistresses, but they are usually presentable, sophisticated, and cultured women. It is also far better if they are safely married in case anything…inconvenient might occur."

To which he'd replied, "Thank you for the advice, Mary. I will certainly keep it in mind." No explanation or clarification, he felt, was necessary, since his intimate affairs were none of her business.

He was even more reticent to set his stepsister straight when she added, "I shall say only this—while I believe a mistress is healthy exercise for a man, useful to keep him in docile spirits and out of his wife's bed as much as necessary, a deeply pious woman like Augusta would never allow it. I've told her she's a fool to expect or want fidelity in her husband. Once the act of procreation has achieved its purpose, there is no cause to want one's husband in one's bed. Yet Augusta insists on a faithful spouse. So it is as well for you to get all that business out of your blood now, if you must. Then you can dispose of the girl, when you have satisfied your prurient lusts, and settle down to marry a suitable woman—one who will not embarrass the family and who will take you despite your many foibles. I promise you, Darius, a fine, steady woman such as Augusta would never accept a husband who insisted on keeping his mistress even after the marriage."

"Your promise is duly noted," he replied.

"Good. Here she comes, so we will speak no more about it for now."

His stepsister's lack of moral standards had always been clear to Darius. Her side of the family would do anything for money except work and would turn a blind eye to any debauchery if it kept them in the manner to which they were accustomed. For all her self-important haughtiness she was, underneath that carefully polished and decorated veneer, a woman of fewer scruples than a grave robber.

Her "friends" were always carefully selected, first and foremost, for their sycophantic talents, then for looks and social connections. Intelligence was far down on her list of measures, if it figured at all. Augusta Milford appeared to fit perfectly with Mary's requirements, but Darius had a feeling Miss Milford was more wily than she first seemed; she was certainly not a spineless dullard. He had watched her only the night before take the precise number of potatoes at dinner, as dictated by Mary's own portion, but then slyly shovel several more onto her plate while his stepsister was distracted.

That evening as they entered the Sherringham drawing room, Miss Milford perched like a colorful parrot upon his stepsister's shoulder, nodding along with everything she said and interjecting a word or two when a glance from Mary permitted it. Darius sensed at once the tension between the ladies of the Book Society and the female guests from Midwitch. There was a very definite divide and conversation was subdued at first, leaving the captain and Miles Forester to do most of the talking.

"The Priory Players are planning to put on a play, Lady Waltham," the captain exclaimed. "I hope you will remain in Hawcombe Prior long enough to grace the audience with your presence."

"A play?" Mary's nostrils flared and finally there was a spark of genuine interest.

"It is only an amateur production and all in good

fun. I daresay, your ladyship, we might even have a part for you."

Darius sighed quietly and turned his gaze to his knees. There was nothing that would humiliate him more than to see his stepsister flounce about on a stage, but he had a feeling she would enjoy the attention.

"There are only a few parts for ladies," Justina muttered. "Even Rebecca has to play a man."

The captain shrugged. "Surely you can write in a few more female roles."

She looked startled, then peeved, her lips forming a tight pout.

Darius turned to her. "I did not know you were a playwright, Miss Justina."

"She's always scribbling stories," Lucy Bridges exclaimed.

"I see." And telling them, too, he thought.

Justina said nothing.

"Besides," added the annoying captain, "I doubt Diana will perform this year." His eyes darkened as he looked at the young woman seated on the couch beside her mother. "Now that she is engaged."

Miss Makepiece relaxed her lips long enough to reply that she had not thought about it yet.

"Of course Diana will act," said Justina. "She is the best actress we have and by far the most convincing romantic lead."

"But Mr. William Shaw might object," the captain replied. "He might not care to have his fiancée acting in a play. She must abide by the wishes of her green-grocer now."

"I do not think—"

"Well, that is her choice, of course," Sherringham

added. "That is the sacrifice she makes, and she does like to make those."

Darius observed the heightened color on Miss Makepiece's face and realized Captain Sherringham was deliberately tormenting her and possibly drunk, like his father.

"What do you think, Rector?" the captain slurred at round-faced Mr. Kenton, who must have been invited again to increase the male contingent. "Surely you would not think it proper for an engaged young lady to perform in a play on the stage?"

Mr. Kenton flapped his lips like a stranded pike. "Well, I—"

"The greengrocer's wealthy grandmama will certainly not approve of an actress in the family—even a very good one—and we must keep on that lady's favorable side. Anything for the money and respectability. Is that not so, Mrs. Makepiece?"

Diana's mother looked gray and held a hand to the cameo at her throat. No one seemed to know what to say or where to look. Even Miles, who usually had a cheery retort for any occasion, was at a loss for once.

Mary and her friend exchanged smug glances, which were not hidden from the other ladies.

The discomfort in the room was palpable.

Darius cleared his throat. "I'm sure Miss Makepiece knows her own mind and will do what is best for her." He looked at Diana and added evenly, "No man, in possession of his senses, would ever try to stop certain young ladies doing as they please. Invariably"—he shot a quick glance sideways at Justina—"I find such an attempt will result in him sorely wishing he never raised an objection. Some ladies will always get their own way, and in such cases it is often to the gentleman's advantage that she does."

"Quite so," said Miles jovially.

Mrs. Makepiece lowered her hand and when her gaze found Darius across the room the message in her eyes was clearly one of gratitude.

His stepsister muttered that his housekeeper must be mixing something odd in his tea. "I don't think I've ever heard you put so many words together at once," she added, frowning severely at him.

"I told Wainwright the country air has its advantages," Miles exclaimed.

Rebecca Sherringham leapt to her feet and suggested they all play cards.

The awkward moment had passed. It had won him no friendship with the captain, who now sulked into his cider, but Diana was smiling a little, and as for Justina... she stared at him as if he had two heads and at least one pair of horns.

Darius was satisfied with that for now. It was a beginning.

The group was quickly organized into two tables. Since none of the party from Midwitch knew the rules of the game chosen, they agreed to watch the first round and wait to join in. The first table, therefore, consisted of Justina and her sister, with Rebecca Sherringham and her brother. The second table held Diana Makepiece and her melancholy mother and Lucy Bridges and the rector.

Mr. Kenton was indeed fortunate to be one of an extinct breed in that village, thought Darius. He certainly took advantage of it, accepting every invite thrown his way and looking quite at home in his place as a stout, chirpy sparrow amid all the pretty doves.

Miles pulled up a chair between Lucy Bridges and the rector, who wanted his opinion on a new equipage he planned to purchase. Darius managed to move himself around the room slowly until he could take possession of a chair behind Justina, without anyone observing that it was not entirely by accident. At least, he hoped no one would notice.

Fortunately, she did not immediately find some excuse to leave his proximity, but sat composed and even answered his quiet inquiry into her health with steady politeness. Tonight she wore a simply cut, velvet gown in a rich, dark wine color that complimented her coloring. It had long, narrow sleeves with small puffs at the shoulders and a V-shaped décolleté with a high waist in the Empire style. He took it all in, paying more attention to a lady's gown than he had ever done before.

"Mr. Forester told us you have a niece in London," she said suddenly. "I wonder why you did not tell me of her. What is she like? How old is she? Perhaps she would have liked to perform with the Priory Players too."

"Sarah is fifteen. I think she is much too shy to act in a play." He hesitated. "She likes to paint."

"Is that why you once asked me whether I liked to do the same?"

"I suppose so," he muttered, running his palms up and down his thighs, his hands too restless to be still tonight.

She observed this, glancing downward. "It is a pity you did not bring your niece into the country. I would like to have met her."

These kind words, apparently uttered without sarcasm,

fell upon his aching heart like a replenishing summer rain shower. He almost found the courage to move his hand from his own thigh to hers.

The others at the table were laughing uproariously over some story the captain had begun to tell—complete with gestures and silly accents—so no one listened to the two of them.

"I hope your stepsister is enjoying her stay," she said, her voice so soft he had to lean closer to hear.

He glanced across at the second table, which was where Mary and Miss Milford had moved their chairs at Miles Forester's insistence. "She is no fonder of the country than I. Less so now."

Justina's head turned slightly, and he watched the edge of her dark eyelashes flicker. The mother-of-pearl earbobs she wore trembled as she chuckled. "I daresay she came to keep an eye on you. For her good friend."

"Hmm." He felt the near overwhelming urge to slide his finger between her earbob and her neck, to let his skin touch hers again. To stroke his fingertip down that gentle curve to her shoulder.

"She must have been surprised when you extended your stay in Hawcombe Prior."

"Hmm."

Suddenly she raised her hand and pressed her own fingers to the very spot he had in mind. It was as if she'd felt his thoughts caress her there.

"Darius!" his stepsister called out from the next table. "You must come here at once and help advise us on our cards. Now we are about to join in the game."

"You do not trust me to advise you, madam?" cried Miles.

"Indeed not, Mr. Forester! You are too mischievous and will deliberately lead us astray."

Darius caught the bend of Justina's lips as she smiled and then whispered, "Does your stepsister refer to herself in the first person plural, or does she mean for you to serve both her and her friend?"

"I neither know nor care."

"Goodness, that is rather cavalier of *you*, Mr. Wainwright." Her shock seemed genuine. Good. Let her be shocked.

"Did you think me the sort of man to dash about at the bidding of any woman? Did you, at any time, read that in my character?"

"But you just declared, before the entire room, that women know best. You should go where you are called."

A card slipped from her hand to her lap and while everyone else was preoccupied with the captain's story, Darius reached for it. His fingers brushed her thigh beneath the table, lingering over that soft velvet much longer than they should. There was no excuse for it and no apology. The need to touch her was too great and would not be denied.

"What I said was for the benefit of your friend."

She snatched the card from his fingers. "Oh, then you lied! And there," she chuckled teasingly, "I thought you said you never commit a sin and never did anything wicked."

"I did not say *all* ladies. I said *certain* ladies ought to get their own way."

"Does that include me?" she demanded with a funny little pout.

He licked his lips. "Depends what it is you might want."

At the next table his stepsister called out for him again, her voice more strident this time.

"Any moment now she will click her fingers at you," Justina remarked, her voice husky with lack of breath.

He feared that was all too possible, but then the woman beside him glanced across to the other table and called out merrily, "I'm afraid Mr. Wainwright is engaged in helping my sister and me, Lady Waltham. We need him here. I, in particular"—she turned her head to look at Darius—"am in need of his guidance. Am I not, sir?"

He answered immediately with no equivocation. "Yes."

Her eyes were smiling, but whether it was for him or simply because she had amused herself by winning a small victory over his stepsister, he couldn't know for sure. It was several moments before he could tear his gaze away from her, and then he saw that Mary and her friend were staring furiously at them both. Justina's playful manner—whether she was cognizant of what she did or not—had succeeded in solidifying their suspicions about his relationship with her.

He ought to move away and pay her less attention, before any wicked rumors were started. But then Captain Sherringham chided her crossly, "You don't pay attention to the game, Jussy."

And Darius decided to stay beside her.

Possibly the other man was angry because she had not listened to his foolish story. He was the sort to be discontented if he could not have the attention of every female in the room. *Jussy*, indeed, he thought resentfully.

"My mind wanders," said Justina, looking at the

cards in her hand again. "What shall I play next, Mr. Wainwright? You had better point so the others do not hear."

With no experience of the game they were playing, he had no advice to offer, but he did not care to admit that.

At the other table a quiet, orderly game took place; at this one all was noise and chaos, punctuated with groans and bursts of laughter. The object seemed to be that one should lie as efficiently as possible. Must be a country game, he thought dourly. Certainly it would appeal far more to those who were foxed or on the way to it. No doubt it was the captain's choosing.

"Perhaps you should whisper," Justina added, "so the others don't hear." Raising her fanned cards before her lips, she waited for his compliance.

Was she aware of his stepsister's eyes searing holes in them both from the other table? Or was it the captain she tried to irritate with this display?

Whatever her reasons, he would make the most of it. As she would say, "*When one is bound to be in trouble anyway, one may as well make the most of it.*"

So he leaned closer to her ear. Partially hidden behind her cards, he lost himself in her delicate perfume and closed his eyes.

He whispered.

Twenty-eight

AT FIRST SHE WASN'T SURE SHE HEARD HIM CORRECTLY. The warm brush of his breath against her cheek was enough to muddle her thoughts even before the words came out.

But the whispered syllables slipped inside her, wound their way through the labyrinth of her ideas and plans, and echoed until she could not mistake them for anything else.

"I know what happened to Nellie Pickles."

Another card slipped from her hand to her lap. As he reached for it again, she did the same and their fingers met on her knee. Heart pounding, she let him hold her fingers briefly beneath the table.

Rebecca prodded her arm. "Your turn again, Jussy. Do wake up!"

She lifted the fallen card and set it down, not even knowing what it was. The firm pressure of Wainwright's hand on her knee beneath the table suddenly moved slowly upward along her thigh.

She was hot, her pulse too rapid. Keening desire, more fierce than anything she'd ever known, held her in its thrall.

Only two more rounds of the table resulted in Rebecca claiming victory and disposing of all her cards.

"Mr. Wainwright does not appear to be *advising* you very skillfully," Rebecca muttered with a sly glance, as she gathered up her winnings. "Perhaps he is not a very accomplished liar. Unlike the rest of us."

"Hurry and deal the cards for another round," exclaimed her brother crossly. "I have no intention of letting you win every last farthing, Becky!" The captain was very sharp this evening, his temper on edge. Tonight it made him far less agreeable company.

Justina got up quickly. "I do not think I'll play again. I cannot seem to concentrate."

"You are red, Jussy."

"I am a little warm. Perhaps I need to move away from the fire."

Everyone looked puzzled. They were quite far away from the hearth and the snoring major. The other table was much closer to the heat.

"My gown," she explained haltingly. "The velvet..."

Wainwright got up with her. "Allow me to fetch you some apple cider, Miss Justina. That should help."

"Oh, bring some for me, Darius," his stepsister called out. "And for Augusta. You are quite overheated in this small, overcrowded room, are you not, Augusta?"

"I am indeed," the lady agreed, wilting dramatically in her chair and fanning herself with the cards.

Mr. Kenton scrambled out of his chair and exclaimed that he would get the cider for Miss Milford. The little man expressed such great concern for her that the lady could not protest and was obliged to accept his offer. Clearly frustrated, however, she kept her gleaming, unblinking eyes pinned to Darius and Justina as they moved toward the sideboard for refreshments.

The rector joined them there and held out two cups while Justina ladled the cider into them. As soon as he had rejoined his table, she handed another cup to Wainwright and he held it by the handle while she filled it.

"Please keep the cup steady, Mr. Wainwright." She finally laid her free hand over his to help hold the punch cup still, but it did not improve matters much. It seemed as if neither had a very steady hand.

Behind her the card players chattered and laughed. Miles Forester was very good at keeping Lady Waltham entertained, and the rector, despite being an awful jaw-me-dead, was managing to occupy Miss Milford. Cathy had not even looked up to see where Wainwright and her sister went and she was laughing again, deeply involved in the game. Justina was surprised that Mr. Forester had not sat beside Cathy tonight, but somehow the distance they kept was rather more obvious than if they had been inseparable.

"So you must tell me now," Justina whispered, turning back to Wainwright. "Nellie Pickles. What happened to her? She was murdered, was she not? How did you find out? Have you discovered her bones in the orchard? Perhaps Sir Mortimer dug them up? He does have a very good nose and likes to dig."

"Miss Penny, you have a most disconcerting habit of firing questions like musket shot."

"But I am eager to know her fate."

He looked at her hand on his. "I'm not certain I should tell you."

"Oh! Is it so terribly gruesome? Worry not. I have a strong tolerance for lurid details."

"You've overfilled the cup."

Alas, he was right. She had splashed cider on his cuff. Anguished, she dropped the ladle back into the punch bowl. "Hold it steady and I'll take a sip."

He raised the cup to her lips, and she drank carefully. It was her first drink of the evening, and she immediately realized it was very strong. "Good Lord!" She wrinkled her nose. Trust Nate! Of course, he'd added something to the innocuous apple cider. No wonder he was drinking so much of it.

"What is the matter?"

She shook her head. "Nothing." Once he had safely set the cup down, she gripped his sleeve. "Now tell me about Nellie Pickles, I insist!"

Darius squinted down at her, half-smiling. "You really want to know? Are you certain? I would not want to bore you," he sighed, "as is my habit."

She scowled as hard as she could. "You had better tell me, Wainwright, or else!"

But suddenly Captain Sherringham appeared beside them, empty cup ready to be refilled. "What are you two whispering about?" he exclaimed loudly. Swaying against Justina, he laughed. "You soon changed your tune, Jussy. I thought you said no one likes the fellow… that he is merely a stupid cockatrice…now here you are all dewy-eyed…whispering in his ear. Traitors. The lot of you. Betrayers, heartless wenches." He leaned over and thrust his cup directly into the punch bowl, not waiting for a ladle.

Justina saw that Darius was about to speak, but she

beat him to it, unable to bear her old friend making a fool of himself this way. "I think you've had enough of this concoction. It is hot in here, and the drink has gone to your head."

"Oh, Lord save us! Not you too. I've had my fill of humorless, lecturing females."

"This is nonsense, Sherry. Do not act in this foolish way. Trying to hurt Diana will hardly make her feel affection for you, will it?"

"What do you know of anything? You're a girl who takes nothing seriously. Get out of my way. I need a drink."

"I suggest you apologize to Miss Justina at once, Captain Sherringham." Wainwright seemed ready to explode. He'd gone white, which made his eyes even darker, coal-black with fury.

Nate leaned on the sideboard and turned his head to slur at the other man. "You pompous fool, I suppose you're pleased with yourself. I can see what you've been up to with Jussy. She's an innocent maid, a girl. I will not stand by and see her corrupted by the likes of you."

Justina was astonished to see and hear the captain becoming gallant on her behalf. Although completely unnecessary, it was rather touching.

On the other hand, an angry Darius, drawn to full height, was a terrifying prospect to behold. "I beg your pardon?"

Justina quickly grabbed her old friend's arms to pull him back. But the captain shook her off and in so doing, accidentally pushed her so that she fell against the punch bowl, sending it—and her—crashing to the floor.

Before her knees had hit the carpet, she saw Darius

swing a fist. It contacted hard with the captain's jaw. A return punch was thrown, but Sherry was already off balance and the excess of cider didn't help.

The room did not explode in chaos as might be expected. Perhaps the sight was so shocking that no one knew how to react immediately, or else they thought it was a scene rehearsed from one of Justina's plays.

Only when the captain suddenly cast up his accounts, all over the rug, did the onlookers emerge from their apparent trance. Lady Waltham cried out so loudly in her morbid enjoyment of the horror that the major finally awoke.

❧

The Midwitch folk prepared to climb into Mary's barouche for the ride back to the manor.

"Well, that was certainly riveting entertainment," she remarked snidely as she stepped up. "Better than the opera!"

Miss Milford had a handkerchief, of which she'd licked one corner, and she kept trying to press it to Wainwright's bloody lip, while he, equally determined, kept his head high to avoid her reach. "Really, Miss Milford, I am quite all right. It was barely a knick." The captain had been too drunk to properly aim his solitary punch and then he'd tripped over Justina's foot and tumbled to his knees, which brought a quick resolution to the argument. Darius was more concerned about Justina, but she seemed to be recovered and, with Mr. Kenton's help, was putting on her coat to walk home with her sister and the other two ladies.

Miss Rebecca Sherringham was profusely apologetic

for her brother's behavior, and Darius assured her it was nothing.

"We have all made mistakes in the heat of passion," he told her. "I have no doubt the captain will wake tomorrow with a heavy head and a great deal of remorse."

"You are very understanding, Mr. Wainwright."

"You sound surprised."

The young lady merely arched an eyebrow and hurried off to join the others.

"Do get in, Darius. It's bitter cold," his stepsister called out from the interior of the carriage.

He looked at Miles. "Perhaps we should give up our seats for Mrs. Makepiece and her daughter. We could escort the other ladies safely home. There is not room for everyone in the carriage."

Miles looked a little put out at first, but bore the idea bravely once it was pointed out that he could walk the eldest Miss Penny to her door and take advantage of the starry, chill evening.

"Don't be a fool," his stepsister argued, sticking her head out again. "I'm sure those women have not far to go."

But Darius moved swiftly away and a few moments later he had persuaded the Makepiece ladies to take the warm ride home. Captain Sherringham had offered to take them, but he was in no fit state, of course, and the major's gout would not allow him to try. Mr. Kenton had already started off with little Lucy in his gig, since the tavern and church were near neighbors, facing one another across the village green. That left the Penny sisters.

"We're quite capable of walking home alone," the eldest assured them demurely. "It really is not far, sir."

Darius insisted quietly. Miles held out his arm for Miss Penny, and she accepted with a charming blush.

❧

Justina could not quite ascertain Wainwright's purpose in managing all this, and part of her wanted to think he had devious motives. Perhaps he merely intended to lecture her again. However, he had displayed chivalry that evening, saving her friend from torment and reacting swiftly in retaliation when *she* was pushed. These were all the actions of a hero, rather than the villain she'd once decided he ought to be. But this plot was continually changing and surprising her as no fiction ever had.

He offered his arm. "Miss Justina, I'm sure the very idea of my company for a quarter of an hour disgusts you, but will you permit me to walk you home?"

What else could she do? Her sister and Mr. Forester were already at the end of the street and would soon be out of sight.

"Thank you, Mr. Wainwright." She looped her arm under his. "And I never said the word disgust."

"Really? I thought you did. It *felt* as if you did."

"Does your lip hurt?" she asked, changing the subject.

"It was merely a graze." He raised a hand toward her and while she waited, holding her breath, he pulled up the collar of her coat. "You have no scarf."

She exhaled a little cloud of mist. "It doesn't matter." After the card party drama she was quite glad of the cool air now.

"I hope your gown wasn't spoiled tonight."

"Surprisingly, it escaped the cider and Captain Sherringham's...expulsions."

"Good. I would demand the captain make recompense if there is any damage."

"But there is none," she assured him.

His eyes met hers and searched for something. "You're sure? He has not...hurt you?"

Now she began to suspect he was thinking of what else the captain might have spoiled. "Mr. Wainwright, rest assured I am unharmed."

With her collar adjusted to his satisfaction they moved on. "I am glad your gown survived the event." He hesitated, slowing his pace. "You look...well in it."

"I do?"

He cleared his throat. "Yes. I like the gown. Very much."

Justina turned her head away to hide her smile, not wanting to discourage him now that he'd actually found something pleasant to say.

"I thought, perhaps, you wore it for Captain Sherringham."

"Then you *and* my mama were wrong." She turned her smile into a wry one and let him see it.

The end of his nose and the tips of his ears were starting to turn red with cold, but she supposed it wouldn't be very ladylike to point it out. Rather endearing, though. Made her want to warm them for him.

"Will you tell me now about Nellie?"

"If you tell me, madam, why you were looking for Captain Sherringham's bed last year."

She swallowed. Oh, that. "It was a silly fancy I had."

"*Silly fancy?*"

"I know, I know! It was rash, reckless, childish, and thoughtless."

"Better choices of adjective, certainly. There are others."

"I don't care to hear them. I made a mistake."

"His idea, no doubt."

"No!" She stopped and looked up at him, slipping her arm from his. "It was entirely my idea. He never knew a thing about it." With a deep sigh, she added morosely, "If he did he probably would have laughed."

His eyes were suspicious, but not angry with her as she'd expected.

"If I tell you," she cried, "you had better tell me all about Nellie!"

He nodded gravely. "Of course. Proceed, madam."

She gathered her courage, twisting her gloved hands together. "I wanted to find out what *it* was like."

"It?"

"Between a man and a woman. Don't look at me that way! You know very well what I mean."

His breath formed frosty clouds around his mouth and his eyes were dark. She could not read his expression this time, so she rushed ahead. No going back now that she was this far in.

"I thought Nate was the best man to show me. And before you think me a complete and utter hussy, let me assure you—I imagined myself in love. Yes, I know you will laugh at that."

He did not. He was very still, just watching her lips.

"But my mother was so certain I could never find a husband—"

"You thought to prove her wrong."

"I didn't want to be paraded about and bartered over like a side of bacon at the market. If I could choose for myself, and quickly, then I wouldn't have to be compared anymore to Cathy." She paused and bit her lip. "I don't suppose you know what it is like to be the lesser of two siblings. As much as I love my sister and quite agree that she is far worthier of anyone's affections…it can get very wearing at times."

He tilted his head, contemplating her words gravely, it seemed. "Yes," was all he said.

Justina forged ahead. "I had known Nathaniel Sherringham for a long time—five years at least—"

"Oh, a very long time indeed."

"Hush, sir, and kindly allow me to finish! I thought that if I *must* have a husband…" Brittle in the cold air, her words shattered, falling away to dust.

"I see."

She gasped, frustrated by his apparent inability to show emotion. "Don't start I *seeing* me again!"

He licked his lips and a mist curled out between them as he exhaled. "You have a most troublesome curiosity, Miss Justina."

"So I am often told."

After another pause he held out his arm again, she took it, and they walked on. He seemed deep in thought so she did not disturb the quiet, but gazed up at the star-sprinkled sky and wondered why she had told him all that. She didn't have to. Not really. She could have made something up and not cared whether he believed her or not. Yet she'd told him what she'd never confessed to another living soul. Not even to Sir Mortimer Grubbins.

Well, his opinion of her could not fall much further anyway, she mused glumly. It was a wonder he still gave her his arm to hold, considering she was such a dreadful little slattern.

Eventually, unable to maintain this silence which only

she seemed to find unbearably tense, she blurted, "Are you going to marry Miss Milford?"

"*Miss Milford?*"

"I hear the lady thinks she has some sort of claim upon you, but I can't imagine she'd make you a very good wife." Then she shook her head and laughed lightly. "Of course, it is none of my business. You must do what you think best."

Justina felt his gaze on her again. "Thank you, madam, I shall."

She tried to keep from scowling, but her face was so cold just then she couldn't feel it properly to know what it did.

"Miss Penny, you're stomping your feet like a cart horse."

"Because my toes are numb," she snapped.

He looked down at her feet. Fully expecting him to make some remark about her worn boots, she was surprised when he remained silent. His gaze trailed upward and over her straining coat buttons, before he hastily took it away again and set it firmly on the horizon.

A few moments later they were at the gate and there was no time to say anything more. As she and Cathy watched the two gentlemen walk away again, she suddenly realized he still had not told her anything about Nellie Pickles. He had wormed a confession out of her about Captain Sherringham and then cleverly evaded his side of the bargain.

Again he cheated her, just like that kiss in his study. *Never fulfill your side of a business transaction while negotiations are still underway. Wait until the ink is dry.*

Damn the man! He was impossible. But she discovered

a new, begrudging respect for his skills. No wonder he was so successful in business and had gained the reputation—according to Miles Forester—for being thoroughly ruthless.

"Mr. Wainwright was very attentive to you this evening, Jussy," said Cathy, as the two girls entered the house.

Her reply was a nonchalant "Was he? I did not notice."

"Oh, I'm sure no one else did either. Your secret is quite safe."

In the process of untying her bonnet, she paused and stared at her sister. Cathy held her lips together as best she could, but her shrewd eyes shimmered with all that went unsaid.

Justina began to understand then what it was like for women such as Diana and her sister, who kept their worries to themselves and struggled alone, putting on a brave face for the world. Managing their own challenges without making a lot of noise and trouble for others. Her fingers toyed with the ribbons on her bonnet as it swung at her side and she followed Cathy up the stairs to bed.

> How funny it is that my sister and the people of Hawcombe Prior should feel protective of W already. As if, despite his superior comportment and evident faults, he now belongs here and to them, and no one has a right to steal him away. Since the arrival of his stepsister and her friend, W is no longer the stranger in our midst.
>
> Sometimes that is how it works in a village like ours.
>
> Even Diana's mother, who seldom has anything good to say of young men, says he is a "fine

gentleman." If not for the dreary greengrocer, one might think she now has her sights set on W too for her daughter! Is the poor man safe from no one?

Diana has boldly decided she should take the lead in our play after all, whatever her fiancé has to say about it. I am glad, for Cathy is always too shy to take the romantic lead, and Rebecca, aside from having no ability to learn her lines, cannot play a wronged maiden without laughing. And Lucy refuses to play any part that is poorly dressed and does not demand the wearing of perfect ringlets.

W still has not returned for the hat and gloves he once left here and although Papa promised to take them to Midwitch, he keeps forgetting. There they sit upon our hall table gathering dust.

I suppose I should remind Papa.

Mama, however, continues to hope W will return for them. Apparently I inherited my optimism from her.

J. P. October 6th, 1815 A.D.

Twenty-nine

DARIUS WAS IN HIS STUDY VERY EARLY ONE MORNING, a few days after the party, when he heard fingers tapping on his window. He turned in surprise and saw Justina there in her wilted bonnet. She looked rather pale and worried. Putting his pen down, he walked to the window and jerked it stiffly open.

"Miss Justina! What have I told you about doors? I thought we had the matter settled that you would use appropriate exits and entrances from now on."

"Yes. Yes. This is no time for jests, sir. Has Lucy been here? Have you seen her?"

He frowned. "No. She has not been here since the last time you both came."

"Oh." Her shoulders sank.

"Won't you come in? My stepsister and Miss Milford are not yet up, but I—"

"Thank you, sir, but no. I didn't want to wake your other guests or apprise them of the situation." Her gloved hands twisted together and she looked away into the orchard. "I had hoped she came here to see Sir Mortimer."

"I'm afraid not. Miss Lucy Bridges seems to have lost interest in her pet of late."

"Yes," she murmured. "It's a good thing you take such good care of him."

"I'm becoming…quite fond of the creature."

She looked at him again, blinking. "Yes."

"Are you sure you won't come in?"

"Quite. Thank you. Good day, sir."

She dashed off again, leaving him alone at the window. He closed it slowly and stood very still for a few moments, wondering.

"Well?" Catherine and Rebecca had waited outside the gates, one hopeful, the other impatient and anxious.

Justina shook her head. "No. She is not here."

Immediately Rebecca clutched her face and groaned. "I know what's happened. We all do. Now it is confirmed. We've looked everywhere."

"Do not despair, Becky. There must be some explanation."

"For my brother being gone in his new curricle and Lucy disappearing on the same day? I think we all know what the explanation is but none dare say it!"

At that moment Diana came running up, her bonnet clinging on only by the ribbons around her throat. "Mrs. Dockley said she saw Captain Sherringham's curricle go by very early this morning."

"That's it then," exclaimed Rebecca, crumpling by the wall. "My brother has finally ruined us all. He is thoughtless, indiscreet, selfish! Oh, this will surely kill our papa. And poor Mr. and Mrs. Bridges! Their only daughter! Oh, I cannot face them. I cannot."

"It is not your fault, Becky!" Justina assured her. "You are innocent in all this."

But she shook her head violently. "I knew something was building in him and I—"

"No. I will not believe it," Diana exclaimed firmly. "I know he has his faults, but he would never do this."

They all looked at her in surprise.

"He can be a most frustrating man, and he has made mistakes," she added, "as we all do from time to time. But he is not so very bad as he likes to pretend."

"I wish I had your faith in my brother."

Diana, however, was determined. "Nathaniel is our friend, just as dear Lucy is, and we must not turn our backs upon either of them. Whatever has happened, I am sure they meant no ill by it."

Cathy solemnly agreed, although her pale blue eyes were dampened by tears.

The rusty whine of the gate hinges behind them abruptly heralded the appearance of Mr. Wainwright. All the ladies immediately fell silent and looked at the ground.

"I suggest someone tell me what's going on," he said firmly. "Unless the Book Club Belles have taken to holding meetings outside my gate."

Justina's mind was racing. She looked at her friends and knew none of them would dare tell him. It would have to be her.

"It's Lucy. She's run off. With Captain Sherringham. It is just like Lydia and Wickham."

"Like who?"

Cathy intervened gently that they only "thought" this was what had happened. "We should not accuse anyone without proof, Jussy."

Wainwright sighed. "I see."

"Oh, why did you tell *him*?" Rebecca snapped angrily. "The fewer people who know, the better!"

Justina took a breath to calm herself and said, "I know we can trust Mr. Wainwright. He will be discreet."

She felt his eyes upon her, warm and appreciative. "I can assure you all that this will go no further," he promised.

Rebecca covered her face with her hands, and Cathy consoled her as best she could.

"Please tell me what is known already," he added. "I should like to be of some assistance, if I may."

Justina's gratitude almost bubbled into tears. It would have been difficult for any of the ladies to chase after the missing couple without assistance. For one thing, none of them had transportation and would have to borrow or hire it, which meant letting more people in on their unhappy secret. Mr. and Mrs. Bridges were so far the only villagers who knew of Lucy's sudden disappearance, and they were in great distress after discovering her empty bed that morning and a note bidding them a somewhat dramatic "Adieu." But they did not yet know about Captain Sherringham's departure at the same time. Only the Book Club Belles knew of both, and they had the fate of Lydia Bennet at the hands of George Wickham in *Pride and Prejudice* fresh on their minds.

"Oh, why did they run off?" Cathy had muttered sadly. "If they wanted to marry, there was no need for this. I cannot imagine Mr. Bridges would raise any objection if his daughter is in love. As for the major, he has long wanted his son to settle down in marriage, and Lucy is a sweet girl."

But Justina very much doubted marriage was on the

captain's mind. He was angry with Diana and wanted her jealous. Lucy was a pretty, naïve young girl with romantic inclinations. She had proclaimed to Justina, only a few days prior, that the captain needed "*someone to cheer him up.*" Nathaniel must have taken advantage of the situation.

"This entire village already distrusts Nate," Rebecca exclaimed, "and I am forever seeking to improve his reputation, to save him from his own worst demons. This is how he repays me. Causes a dreadful scandal that will never be lived down."

Once again Diana defended the missing pair. "I am quite sure they can be found and the entire incident explained. Nathaniel would never do anything to harm Lucy, or any of us."

"Do we know their means of travel?" Darius asked steadily. "Do we know their direction?"

He was so calm and collected, Justina thought. When he might easily have gone back inside and closed his gate, he volunteered his assistance and soon became the leader of a recovery mission.

The beat of her heart was thrown off-kilter when she looked up at him and felt his quiet confidence take control.

"I'll commandeer my stepsister's barouche—since my own vehicle remains mysteriously crippled—and bring the couple home."

"One of us ought to go with you," said Justina.

"No. You must all remain here. I'll deal with this."

When she caught the gleam in his eye, she had a sneaking suspicion he was rather enjoying playing the gallant rescuer. "Don't do anything foolish," she warned.

Stepping up into his carriage, he turned to look at her and smiled. "That's why I'm not taking you with me."

"Very amusing, Mr. Wainwright!"

Her heart and mind felt very full. She knew he was doing this for all of them—for Lucy, her parents, her friends. But he did it most of all to please her. A month ago he would not have involved himself in their troubles.

Suddenly she made a decision and, before he could shut the door, she'd leapt up into the carriage with him.

"You're not going anywhere without me!"

Somewhere behind her she heard her sister gasp. Wainwright looked as if he might insist she stay.

"She's *my* friend. And I wouldn't want you to punch Captain Sherringham again."

"What makes you think you can stop me?"

"I'm a lady, and you're a gentleman."

He smirked. "Are you sure about that?"

"About which?"

"Either."

Feeling rather warm, she leaned out to wave to her sister, shouting, "Tell Mama I am gone away on another mission and I might be gone some time. And yes, I shall use the boot-scraper upon my return." Her good-byes complete, she rapped on the carriage roof with her knuckles, the horses tugged them forward, and she fell back in her seat at the sudden jolt.

"I doubt your parents would approve," he muttered.

"If my friend is about to be ruined, I must save her."

His eyes narrowed. "I remember a time when you had a similar plan to discard your own virtue, Miss Justina Penny. Also at the hands of Captain Sherringham. Are you envious of Lucy perhaps?"

"Don't talk nonsense. I'm wiser now. About a great many things! And don't you dare say *I see*."

"I wouldn't dream of it."

The carriage rattled speedily along the lane. Darius had instructed the coachman to head for Manderson, as it seemed likely the couple would stop there first for provisions they might need on their journey.

"I have never been to Manderson alone with a man before," Justina exclaimed breathlessly as she bounced about on the seat.

"You realize, of course, that this will cause rumors, Miss Penny."

"Well"—she hung onto the little leather strap by the window—"I recently read in a book that it is the only reason we live—to make sport for our neighbors and laugh at them in our turn."

He smiled at that. "You have no objection to it then? To what people could say of *us* being alone in a carriage? An unwed young lady and a bachelor?"

"Goodness, how could they possibly suspect *us* of wicked motives?"

"Quite true."

But his presence seemed to fill the carriage, just as the man himself filled her mind.

She stared at him. "It's not as if anything might happen between us, is it?"

"You have decreed it so."

With those five words he put the reins completely into her hands. No one had ever given Justina such a responsibility and that, combined with the jostling pace of the carriage, quite took the breath out of her lungs.

❧

Her lips looked very full today and rosy. Several curls had

tumbled to her shoulders, escaping her bonnet. Those
two deep pools of blue watched him thoughtfully across
the carriage, taking his measure, it seemed, inch by inch.

"You must think me a rather stupid oaf, Miss Penny."

Her brows arched high. "Indeed not. Why would I?"

"For the clumsiness of my visit to your father's house
recently, when I failed even to deliver flowers in one
piece, let alone properly explain my purpose there."

A little color rose over her cheeks. "Perhaps we
have both not been entirely adroit in our dealings,
Mr. Wainwright."

He drummed his fingers on his knees and then spread
them wide, making a concerted effort to still their fidgeting. "Perhaps."

"Shall we put that behind us then?" She hitched
forward on the edge of her seat.

"I…I think we might."

"I am glad." She dazzled him with a bright smile and
then launched forward to sit beside him. "Now we can
be friends," she said.

"You had better return to your seat, Miss Penny."

"But I like this one," she replied. "I am much safer
wedged in beside you, and here I have more to hold on to."

He groaned. "Are you looking for mischief? Another
of your games? Think very carefully before you continue
in this vein."

"Oh, I have thought, sir. I have given our predicament much consideration."

"What is it you want from me, Justina?"

She reached up and with one small finger traced his
brows, first one and then the other. "I have decided I
want you to frown less, Mr. Wainwright."

His heart was beating too fast. He had never acted this way with a woman and never had one be playful with him. "And then?"

"Smile more."

"And then?"

"We'll see."

He had to laugh at that. "Are you setting me a test, Justina?"

"Yes." Now she ran her finger over his lips. "You may set one for me, if you like."

Her finger ventured over his mouth again and this time he caught it gently between his teeth. Those satiny, oceanic pools widened as he gave her a finger a little suck and tasted her skin. Soft, chalky lavender. Having her this close was causing discomfort of an ungentlemanly nature. He let her finger slip from his lips.

"I want you to call me Darius, when we are alone."

She nodded. "And?"

He wasn't sure how much more he could ask for, but she was teaching him to be bolder. "I want you to kiss me at least once a day."

"Mr—Darius," she gasped. "You ask a lot of a maidenly, properly raised young woman. I merely asked you to smile."

"But as you know, smiling is very hard for me. So once a day," he repeated firmly, "I should be rewarded with a kiss. At least once a day. In fact, madam, I should receive a kiss in payment for every smile."

To his amusement, she could not long keep her lips in a stern pout. "You drive a hard bargain, Mr...Darius."

He'd never liked the sound of his name much, but on her lips he did. Slowly he grinned. "I did warn you about bargaining with me. Several times now." Before she could speak again, he held her chin in his palm and lifted it. "Kiss me."

She did. It was gentle and sweet, her lips melting like butter against his mouth. He quickly decided he needed more and stole another three kisses before she slipped back to her seat across the carriage.

"Any more questions, Justina? You usually have many all at once." Darius would have been disappointed if she stopped asking.

She cleared her throat. "I have plenty, but I'm saving them for the proper occasion."

Although he had no idea what she meant, he looked forward to it.

Now she sat demurely, feigning innocence, with her knees together and her gaze fixed upon the window, but her coat was unbuttoned and he could see her bosom rising and falling rapidly. She must have been in haste to go out that day, looking for her friend, not sparing a moment to fasten the clasps and save herself from a chill. Someone really ought to look after this woman.

Suddenly she began shrugging out of her coat. "Now I'm too hot," she muttered, glancing briefly his way. The mischievous glimmer in her eyes was evident.

After a moment he swung himself across to sit beside her. When the carriage bounced violently at the same time and she lost contact with the seat, he caught her, setting her down in his lap.

"I cannot think this very proper, sir," she exclaimed, slipping her arms around his neck.

"I'm quite sure it is not." He spread his fingers around

her waist, holding her tight. "But I won't tell a soul, if you won't."

Her eyes shone brilliantly. Darius felt himself pulled in, surrounded by her warmth and laughter, embraced by it.

The urgency of desire streaked through him, left him short of breath. Needing to adjust her teasing, restless weight on his lap, his hand swept down to the curve of her bottom. But rather than ease her to a less troublesome position, he found himself too tempted by that handful, and much too distracted as she leaned in to kiss him on the lips again.

He groaned, let the kiss deepen while his hand squeezed her firm bottom. Her bonnet slipped back, the very lackadaisical knot slithering undone of its own accord due to the rough rhythm of their ride and the carelessness of the woman who had tied it. Darius felt the hat falling and did nothing to prevent it. Neither did she.

Lust was close to consuming him in that moment, with her body pressed to his, the alluring curves suddenly his to play with. Although he knew he took too great a liberty with the lady, he could not help himself. They were all alone, and whenever that happened he didn't seem to be able to behave himself. His fingers splayed over her bottom, traced gently upward to the small of her back, and then followed the sensual bend and sway of her spine, all the way up to her neck. There his fingers aided the escape of more tumbling brown curls, before sliding down again to the enticing swell of her breast.

Meanwhile she moved her hand under the high collar of his greatcoat and touched his cheek. "Your lap is rather uncomfortable, Darius," she whispered.

"Hmm." He let his thumb stray across the tiny peak that pressed against the front of her gown. It swelled further, igniting another flame of wanton need. Feeling possessive, he placed his hand over the full curve. Whenever he closed his eyes he could picture her as she was in Bath, when she leapt, naked but for silk stockings and garters, onto his bed.

"It's getting bumpier by the second."

"Hmm?"

"Your lap, Darius." Justina's hand now began a slow course back down his body, but he apprehended it before she reached her goal. That would be dangerous territory even for this intrepid and very lovely explorer.

She pecked at his chin with little kisses, her teeth gently nibbling at the rough skin. "You have not shaved today," she observed with a heated whisper. "I have never seen you so…imperfect."

There had not been time to shave since she interrupted him so early that day. Now he was glad of it, however, for her tone was suggestive of approval.

"Are you blushing, Darius Wainwright?" She chuckled.

"No." He tried to be stern. "You're making me hot."

"Shall I get off your lap then?"

Before she could slip away he grabbed her even tighter. And that, combined with the somewhat savage nip he gave to the side of her neck shortly after, was answer enough.

"I wish we might have gone the long way to Manderson," she gasped on a halting breath.

But Darius thought it was a very good thing for her that their journey could not last too long. He was extremely ravenous for once and had come out before breakfast. And she was quite possibly the most delicious morsel he'd ever tasted.

☙

It did not take long to find Captain Sherringham and Lucy in Manderson, because they made no attempt to hide.

"Good Lord!" the captain exclaimed when confronted outside the blacksmith. "I merely gave Miss Bridges a ride when I saw her along the side of the road in the small hours. She flatly refused to go home, so I thought it best to bring her where she wanted to go until she realized she'd made a mistake. Then I could take her safely back. Poor little thing. I do believe she's been feeling somewhat ignored, and I perfectly understand how that is."

"Nonsense," Justina exclaimed. "She is not in the least ignored and neither are you."

"In any case, she seemed very glad to have company, and I could hardly leave her unguarded to wander about the town, could I?"

It seemed as if the Book Club Belles had jumped to conclusions.

Lucy reluctantly admitted that she had planned to run away for some excitement of her own at last, but Captain Sherringham had been trying to talk her into going home again. It would not have taken him long to persuade her, as it turned out. She had brought all her savings with her on this journey, but since half was now spent on a new fur tippet already, her adventure was bound to be cut ruthlessly short.

The captain confessed to Justina that he had been on his way to Newmarket when he encountered Lucy on her ill-advised flight astride her father's mule.

"I've suffered some losses lately," he confessed dourly. "I hoped to recoup some coin at the races." Then he glared at Justina. "Surely you did not think me capable of eloping with Lucy Bridges? I hope you, at least, believed in me."

She had to be honest. "Apart from my sister, who would never say a bad word about anyone, I'm afraid only Diana defended you wholeheartedly."

This seemed to bring him some cheer. His shoulders went back, and he took a breath. "Diana? Really?"

Darius spoke up. "Miss Makepiece, it seems, holds you in high regard despite the way you have treated her."

Nathaniel looked away, his jaw grinding. Justina placed a hand on his arm. "We'll take Lucy back to Hawcombe Prior. Will you come?"

"No," he muttered. "I have things to do." Then he shook his head. "Before I bury myself forever in debt, I must find a way to pull myself out of it."

"By gambling more money on the horse races? Surely there are other ways?"

"You don't understand, Jussy."

"You're always saying that! But I am not a child anymore, Sherry."

He finally looked at her again. His eyes were sadder than she'd ever seen them, but they were determined too. "I want to be worthy of her," he said simply.

Justina knew, of course, that he did not refer to Lucy, who was now showing her new fur tippet to a hugely disinterested Mr. Wainwright.

"When will you come back home?" she asked the captain.

He took a breath. "When Diana can no longer say no to me."

"But she is marrying another."

Briefly he covered his eyes with one hand. "I do not believe she will. I know her. She can't marry without love, whatever duty she thinks she owes her mama. I will wait for her."

She did not know what to say. The captain was a broken man today, but perhaps this was what he needed in order to rebuild himself. Sometimes one had to fall to the lowest point before improvement could be made.

Oblivious to the panic she'd caused, Lucy wanted to stay longer and finish her shopping, but Darius insisted they return immediately to calm her anxious parents and friends. Justina agreed.

"One fur tippet does not seem much to show for my adventure," Lucy complained.

"You should be thankful that is all you have to show for it," Justina replied swiftly, pushing her friend up into the carriage while Darius secured the mule's reins to the back of the barouche.

The journey home was much less interesting since she and Darius had to keep their separate seats a very proper distance apart. Lucy was no longer shy in his company and chattered away almost without pause, but Justina did not feel the urge to talk in any case. How odd it was, she mused, that Lucy—once so timid in Wainwright's presence—should now make all the noise, while *she* had nothing to say to the gentleman. Nothing for the ears of other folk, that is.

And how ironic it was that the couple who caused a stir of concern that morning were perfectly innocent, whereas the couple of whom nothing could be suspected were, in fact, perfectly wicked.

⤨

When they arrived back in the village, Lucy responded with airy surprise to the concern of her friends. "I did not think any of you would notice I was gone." There was no apology for having upset them all and made them imagine terrible things, but then she had always been a self-absorbed young lady, thought Justina.

"Fancy assuming I had eloped with Captain Sherringham." Lucy chortled. "As if I am foolish enough to do that!"

Justina explained to Rebecca that her brother was attempting to get his life somewhat in order.

"I shall believe that when I see it," Rebecca replied.

Diana quietly asked where he had gone and Justina, feigning ignorance of all the facts, would only say, "He plans to return one day. When the time is right."

"I wish him every good fortune." Diana turned away, her head bowed. It was several minutes before she was recovered enough to show her face again, and even longer before she could speak.

As for Lucy's parents, they were so relieved to have her back again and in one piece, that she was not to be punished. Instead, she was pampered like a returned princess for several days. Anyone might think she'd sailed to China, not ridden halfway to Manderson on a mule, been transported the rest of the way in a curricle with Captain Sherringham, stayed for a few hours, bought a fur tippet, and come right home. At last she had the attention she'd always sought. It seemed likely she would talk of the event as "the time I ran away" until something more dramatic occurred to her. Which might well be never.

Justina could not even be annoyed with the girl, for the ride to Manderson had given her relationship with Darius a new level of intrigue and intimacy. They might never have had the chance to be alone again without fear of interruption. In that barouche he had, in fact, been her prisoner and utterly at her mercy. Hopefully she had persuaded him to stay a little longer.

❧

He kept his promise of smiling more and she, in turn, kept hers of calling him Darius in private. As well as granting him kisses at every sly opportunity.

The thrill of their secret bargain was such that she almost burst at the seams with it. Her friends had all noticed that Darius Wainwright was seen out and about in the village much more than usual, but no one could guess why. Or rather, Justina did not think anyone could. She imagined she hid it rather well, exhibiting her new and improved discretion.

But one day at the haberdashers, when Justina was admiring a new patterned taffeta with the ladies of the Book Society, Darius and his stepsister came in, and it soon became apparent that at least one of her friends had noticed the deepening attraction between the two acknowledged opposites.

"Oh look, Jussy," the cunning redhead, Rebecca Sherringham, whispered, "there is your special friend."

"I cannot think of whom you speak, Becky," Justina replied.

"Of course you can. I'm sure he only came in here to catch sight of you."

"What are you talking about?"

"I expect he's hoping for a chance to kiss you again while he thinks no one is watching."

Alarmed, she glanced over at her sister and the other young ladies, but they were all absorbed in admiring a length of plaid now and comparing it to the other pattern. Justina grabbed her friend by the sleeve and hauled her across the shop to look at a display of buttons. "When did you see us?" There was little point in denying it. Her main concern now was containing the damage.

"Let me see!" Becky put a finger to her lips and rolled her sparkling gold-sprigged eyes. "Yesterday in the lane by the oak tree. This morning behind the Pig in a Poke—"

"I hope you haven't told anyone else."

Becky laughed. "Of all the people to fall for Mr. Wainwright, I suppose it just had to be you. Poor thing! Although I don't know which of you to pity most."

"Hush." She quickly turned the button display, pretending to study it with great interest. "I have not—" Oh, no, he was coming toward them, his long stride echoing across the wooden boards.

"Good afternoon, Miss Justina, Miss Sherringham."

They both greeted him, Justina mumbling and Becky being very loud and cheery. "You're out shopping, Mr. Wainwright?" she said brightly.

"My stepsister is shopping. I am merely her escort."

Justina knew he was looking at her, but she couldn't

raise her own gaze from the buttons, still recovering from Becky's sudden accusation.

"I must thank you, Mr. Wainwright, for acting so swiftly the other day and going after Lucy and my thoughtless brother before rumors could spread. It was most kind of you to help us. I don't know what we can ever do to repay you. Do you, Jussy?"

Darius fidgeted. In the corner of her eye, Justina could see his gloved fingers twitching at his coat cuffs and then hanging at his sides awkwardly. He was uncomfortable with gratitude, it seemed, or perhaps it was merely Becky's boldness that made him shy. Justina swayed to one side quite casually and let her hand brush his little finger.

"It was my pleasure to help, Miss Sherringham." His hand moved against hers more firmly, hidden by the pleats of her coat. Just from that touch her heart sped and she felt a smile pulling persistently on her lips.

His forefinger swept up and tickled her wrist. She swallowed a giggle, and Becky looked at her oddly.

Across the shop Lady Waltham began to bellow like a cow overdue for milking.

"Excuse me, ladies." He gave a smart bow and walked quickly away.

Immediately Becky closed in. "You had better tell me what's been going on, Justina Penny," she whispered in a menacing fashion, one brow arched high and determined.

But Justina replied, "I could not possibly."

And then her friend surprised her. "If you tell me your secret, I shall tell you one of mine."

From the guilty paling under Becky's freckles it

was plain she had something burning to be let out, and the possibility of learning a juicy secret was more than Justina could resist. The two women moved behind a mannequin.

"Well? How far has it gone, Jussy? Must I take out my father's flintlock? He has acquired a new one, you know, very smart, with a flick bayonet. I am quite impatient for an excuse to use it."

"It is just a few kisses. That is all." She shook her head. "He bribed me into it. Why? Who have *you* kissed?" Since Wainwright had taught her an important lesson about bargaining, she would say nothing more until she'd heard her friend's story.

"I have kissed no one," Becky whispered, "but there was a man once…" She looked down at her hands and adjusted her gloves. "My brother owed him a debt."

Justina stared. "Go on."

"It was five years ago, and before we came here. We were encamped at Brighton. My brother was going to give the man our mama's music box to pay the debt, but I refused to part with it. That music box is all we have left of her."

"Of course."

"So the man…well, he agreed to excuse my brother's debt on one condition."

Justina covered her mouth with her hand. "You never did!"

"Oh no, not *that*." Becky chuckled. "He simply made me promise to owe him a kiss. The next time we met. You see, I was only seventeen and he said I was too young for him to kiss. But he forgave Nate's entire debt to him just on that promise. Don't you think that's odd?" She looked away across the shop, her eyes growing misty. "He was an eccentric fellow and I never saw him again. Sometimes I imagine he will come back to claim his kiss." Her shoulders shook in a little shiver that seemed more excited than fearful. "I don't suppose he will now. But seeing you with Mr. Wainwright made me think of it again, after so long."

Justina wasn't sure she believed the story. Becky might have made it up, just to have something to share in return. "What was his name, then?"

The other young woman raised a hand to tidy her hair, glancing around nervously. "I only heard him called by one name, which was even odder. Everyone called him Lucky. That's the only name my brother ever knew him by. He was perfectly horrid."

"Then you should be glad he hasn't found you again," said Justina solemnly. "It is very hard to be bribed into kisses." She turned her head and caught Wainwright watching her warmly. "As you say, it is perfectly horrid."

Becky agreed. "I don't suppose Elizabeth or Jane Bennet would ever be blackmailed into kisses."

"True," Justina replied, sighing wistfully as she watched his smile and realized that was now yet another kiss she owed him. "But they are fictional. It's much more difficult to live in the real world. As they would discover, if they had our problems."

Thirty

"RAINING, AGAIN! OH, THIS DISMAL PLACE." MARY glared out at the stream of water currently gushing against the rattling dining room windows.

"I think you'll find it rains just as much in Town as it does in the country," Darius replied croakily, flipping open a napkin.

"Why then does it feel so much worse? And colder, too. I'm quite certain it is never this cold and windy in Town." She turned away from the grim view and took her seat at the breakfast table. "I shall say only this—the villagers here are incompetent, rude, and unobliging. There is no fashion here, no style, no conversation to be had that is worthwhile. I cannot think why you have remained here this long, Darius. What can be your excuse? I see nothing but a bunch of forward young ladies who will do anything for your attention."

"I believe you just answered your own question, Mary." He sneezed into his napkin and she eyed him sternly.

"What was that, Darius?"

Rather than answer, he screwed up his face and readied the napkin again.

"I hope you have not caught a cold, Darius. How could you?"

"I agree. The acquisition of this cold was a wretched decision. What was I thinking?"

"Now look at you! I have never seen you ill, Darius. Never! First of all you dash off with my carriage and not a word to anyone about where you're going. And before you're even shaved. Then you come back sneezing all over us."

Augusta Milford grabbed the coffee pot and she poured it first for him. "You must drink lots of warm fluids, Mr. Wainwright." The next thing he knew she was trying to cut up his sausages for him.

He quickly took the knife from her hand. "Thank you, Miss Milford, but I always eat them whole."

She drew back.

Darius picked up his fork, speared a plump sausage and raised it thus to his lips, taking a large bite of one end.

The woman sat abruptly. "Well, goodness!"

"Don't pay any mind to him, Augusta. A sick man is always best ignored and left to get over it. He will be grumpy and tedious, like a teething babe. It is his fault entirely, and I have no sympathy."

In fact he wasn't very hungry at all, but the last thing he wanted was Augusta Milford fussing over him.

"We really ought to make plans for travel," Mary continued. "I have already left my darling little ones far longer than I should, just to bring you back to civilization."

"I wish you had not bothered."

"But someone had to fetch you."

"I certainly can't travel now," he muttered. "Not with this cold."

"I hope you didn't catch it from one of *those* women. Wasn't one of them sick not too long ago? Ugh." She shivered dramatically. "I shall say only this—the country is the most appallingly dirty place, so very unhealthy. Too many people crammed into little rooms, all breathing the same fetid air. These country folk have no sense of hygiene. I shudder to think of touching any of them."

He put down his sausage. "And vice versa, I'm sure."

"What was that?" she demanded shrilly.

He sniffed. "I know plenty of people in Town with whom I would never want to shake hands."

To his relief the front door bell clanged.

"Well, who on earth could that be?" Mary exclaimed. "Who would come out in such weather?"

A few moments later Mrs. Birch brought two drenched visitors to the dining room. Miss Sherringham and Justina.

Didn't she even possess an umbrella? he mused. The wayward Miss Penny looked bedraggled as a cat left out all night in a rainstorm. She stood there, making a puddle on his carpet, probably leaving a stain.

And he thought how lovely she was. Belatedly he remembered his manners, stood, and bowed from the waist.

A sneeze shot out of him.

"Bless you!" the new arrivals chorused.

Miss Sherringham gave him a wide smile. "Jussy has agreed to write parts for you all if you would like to join the Priory Players. I do hope your impression of us was not tainted already by what happened at the card party, Lady Waltham. We would be honored to have you take part. I'm sure it will be the highlight of the play."

Miss Sherringham, he concluded, was a canny young woman to have read Mary's vanity already and known exactly how to appeal to it. Very soon his stepsister was persuaded there might not be so much hurry for her to return to her "darling little ones" after all. Not when she could lend her talents to the Priory Players.

"Will Dockley's barn be a fit place to rehearse in all this rain?" Darius asked, trying to hold back another sneeze.

"We did not yet collect enough donations to get the roof fixed, but we have some old sail cloth to cover the worst of the holes. Besides, we've managed well enough in the past." Rebecca Sherringham's eyes were rich, treacle brown, surveying him with a knowing shine. "Will you join us too, Mr. Wainwright? We can always make use of handsome gentlemen in the cast."

"Good Lord, no!" exclaimed Mary. "Darius would never set foot on a stage."

He gave in to another sneeze that almost knocked him back into his chair. Justina immediately suggested she fetch her father.

"'Tis only a cold," he mumbled.

"But a bad cold can always develop into much worse," she replied, hurrying across the room to grip his jacket sleeve between her thumb and forefinger in what had already become a familiar way to him. "Let's get you to bed, Mr. Wainwright."

He went meekly, with only a token drag of heel, his stepsister's frown carving her irritation into his back.

৯৯

Darius would not hear of her going for her father on foot and insisted she take his stepsister's barouche. Justina saw Lady Waltham's infuriated glances, but the matter was settled quickly. Despite his quiet ways, Darius Wainwright usually got what he wanted, so she found.

Within a half hour she returned to Midwitch with her father and found the master of the house in his bedchamber. Of course it would be improper for the other ladies to enter, but they hovered at his door, feigning concern. Justina felt that if his stepsister was truly anxious, she would have sent him to bed already that morning and called for the doctor. As for Miss Milford, her concern, as usual, was about herself and her place in the pecking order.

"I must be the one to sit with him, for I have known him longest, and Lady Waltham's health is too fragile to be endangered with the task of nurse."

Justina's father merely smiled as he donned his "doctoring" wig—an item he avoided unless it was absolutely necessary, for he said it made him itch. "My daughter has attended many a bedside with me, madam. I'm sure she can be trusted to manage the gentleman. Unless he thinks otherwise."

There was no complaint uttered from inside the room, so her father shut the door on both the other ladies, leaving them out in the hall with Miles Forester, who quickly urged them away with the promise of entertainment and, most importantly, a warm fire in the drawing room.

Keen to prove herself capable, Justina stood at the patient's bedside with her father, ready to wipe the sick man's brow with a cool cloth. Not that it was nearly as hot as she expected.

"I blame myself, Mr. Wainwright," she said solemnly. "You should not have walked us home after the party in that bitter cold last week."

He looked up at her from his pillow. "But *you* are quite well."

"I am of strong country stock, sir."

"You mean a dandified Town gent like me is too delicate for your weather?"

"It would seem so, wouldn't it?"

He coughed feebly. "Then, since it's your fault, you must stay and nurse me, until I am fit and well. You must not leave my side or I fear my decline will be rapid. Perhaps even"—he paused for another cough—"fatal."

Justina glanced nervously at her father, but Dr. Penny was humming softly as he examined the patient. She threw Darius a warning look.

He gave a frail sigh. "Otherwise, Miss Milford might get her way."

Hmm. Perhaps she ought to stay and look after him. Wouldn't want Miss Milford to have her way with him.

Her father was in agreement. "You stay here, Jussy, and see him through the worst of it." Although it was merely a cold, he exaggerated the situation to such an extent that even Wainwright looked alarmed. "That fire must be built up at once," her father exclaimed, "and you, Jussy, must make him some of your good broth and a compress for his head. I'm sure Mrs. Birch has some goose grease for his chest. I shall leave you powders for a mustard bath. Make sure he rests. Keep him warm to chase out the fever." He itched under his wig with one finger, knocking it to one side so she had to straighten it for him again. "I cannot stay, but I'm sure your mama can spare you at home. If Mr. Wainwright has no objection. You should be where you are needed, Jussy."

Once again the patient uttered no protest to this idea.

Glad to be given a responsibility and a chance to prove herself, she nodded firmly. "I shall then, Papa. If you think it's best. Just until he sleeps."

Her father smiled at the man in the bed. "I leave you then in the capable hands of my daughter."

                                        ✐

The rain continued all day and the light was dim in his chamber, so she brought two lanterns upstairs for his bedside. As she moved around his bed, administering a compress for his sore head, preparing a steaming bowl of aromatic water to clear his nose, and feeding him beef broth, she was very serious for once, efficient and firm. No nonsense. He pondered his good fortune in having such a devoted nurse.

Mary would not want the duty. When anyone was sick she stayed as far away as possible—even from her own children, leaving them to the care of the nanny or nurse-maid. Miss Milford was successfully kept at bay by the fear of contagion. For a woman whose main enjoyment came from sticking her nose into the business of others, being kept off her feet and confined to bed would be torture. Although she came knocking at the door for progress reports throughout the day, he sensed her motive was not truly to see if he improved, but to ensure he really *was* sick.

As if he might possibly make up a fib to delay leaving Hawcombe Prior.

Really!

Bearing in mind that Miss Milford's first sight of Justina had been of her drawers, he thought with some amusement that the lady probably also wanted to ensure his nurse kept all her clothes on.

"Does Dr. Penny always provide his patients with dedicated caretakers?" he asked Justina, as she prepared to take his supper tray downstairs. "Even for a cold?"

"Only when the patient is very important and very rich," she replied with an arch look over her shoulder.

"His fee will be great then, I fear."

"Of course. We must take advantage of you while we have you, Mr. Wainwright."

When she left the room, Miles came in to see how he felt and to report on Sir Mortimer's training, which had become a battle of wits between the complacent, pampered beast and the complacent, pampered gentleman.

"How is your nurse?" he asked with a wily grin.

"Quite exceptional and very strict."

"You sly wretch."

"I cannot think what you mean, Forester."

"Oh, of course not."

"Please send her back up to me." He coughed. "I'm sure my fever has increased."

Miles left the chamber, laughing.

She was on her way up to the patient, carrying a jug of water, when she encountered Lady Waltham on the small half-landing at the turn of the stairs. Lost in her thoughts, Justina did not see the other woman until they almost collided in the dim light. The wall paneling was heavy and dark, with dying daylight barely strong enough to creep through the narrow window above them. There, shrouded in shadow, Lady Waltham cast a frightening figure. She might have been one of those suits of armor come to life and made its way down from the long gallery. Her large, ungainly form blocked the second flight of stairs.

"Excuse me, Lady Waltham."

For a long moment she did not speak, and seemed in no haste to move, either. Finally she opened her hard mouth and snapped out, "I know what you are, Miss Penny."

Justina squinted. The jug in her arms was becoming heavy. "Oh?"

"And I know that men will have their playthings. It is a necessary evil to which ladies such as myself and Miss Milford must turn a blind eye. But I hope you know that this is a temporary diversion for him. He would never marry the likes of you."

What could one say to that? In fact, many retorts came to her mind, but she decided to let none of them out.

"He will marry Miss Milford. Or if not her, another lady of similar breeding, class, and fortune. A lady I need not be ashamed to invite to my parties and balls. You, my dear girl, are merely a last minute rebellion for my stepbrother. Oh, I can see the attraction for you. No doubt he has spent money on you and your family. I have heard from Miles Forester all about my step-brother's plans to put a new roof on that broken-down barn where you and your friends entertain yourselves for lack of anything else to do. His attention must have done much for you. But it will not last. Such things never do."

She swallowed. Her hands had slipped, but she managed to keep hold of the jug.

Lady Waltham's eyes looked dry and hot as they bore down upon her. "You do not deny it then? That you are his mistress? That you have schemed and seduced your way into his bed while no one was here to watch over him?"

Suddenly she wanted to laugh, but curbed it. Shoulders back, head high, she replied, "I do not believe it is any business of yours what I am to Mr. Wainwright. If I am his mistress, you have declared me to be a necessary evil, so what is your purpose in asking me? Or do you want details?"

The other woman shook like a kettle about to blow its lid.

"*Excuse me*, Lady Waltham." This time she nudged her way by and continued up to the second floor of the house. As she turned the corner, she encountered a startled looking Miss Milford who, she had no doubt from her expression, had heard the entire conversation.

Since there was nothing to say that would not get her further into trouble, she nodded to the lady and walked onward with her jug of water.

Thirty-one

"THERE YOU ARE!" HE EXCLAIMED. "WHAT TOOK you so long? I sent Miles to fetch you half an hour ago at least."

"Oh, hush. You're not dying." She put the jug down on his dresser.

"Your father made it sound as if I was."

"I told you, he said all that so he could be justified in charging you a heavy fee." She came to the side of the bed. "We're after your money, of course."

Fists pushed into the mattress, he eased himself higher against the pillows and let the bedcover fall to his hips. If she had noted his nakedness, she made no comment on it, but he never could bear to sleep in clothes of any kind and had only worn a respectable nightshirt in the presence of her father.

"Did you tell your stepsister about our unfortunate meeting in Bath, by any chance?" she demanded, the words leaping out suddenly.

"No. Why on earth would I tell her?"

Walking around his bed, she ran her fingers over his coverlet and then gripped an oak post. "Lady Waltham thinks I'm your mistress. Where would she get an idea like that?"

A quick laugh bubbled out of him. "Perhaps it has something to do with finding you climbing out of my bedchamber that day." Then he made his face solemn again. "She did warn me that I'll have to give you up before I marry Miss Augusta Milford."

Her lips parted, her eyes widened.

"Apparently Miss Milford would never allow me to keep you. Or Sir Mortimer Grubbins." It was a struggle now to keep a straight face, but fortunately he'd had years of practice. "I'll have to find someone to take you both off my hands."

His nurse was watching him thoughtfully, her eyes smoky. "I see you have removed the flannel nightshirt," she said. "You're hardly likely to sweat the fever out of your body if you sleep in the nude."

"But I can't stand to have myself all twisted up in a nightshirt. You know that. You've seen me in bed before."

A light flush passed over her face, but she was trying very hard to be all business. It was quite charming. "Yes, I remember," she admitted finally.

Darius stared up at her lips. "Is it not time you kissed me today, Miss Justina Penny? I have not had one for at least four and twenty hours. You do not abide by our agreement."

"But you have a cold!"

"I'm sure your kiss will help me improve."

She shot him a dubious look. "Are you really sick?"

"Of course! Would I lie? For what purpose?"

"To gain my sympathy."

Capturing her hand, he held it firm, wrapped in

his long fingers. "Don't you want to know about Nellie Pickles?"

She opened her mouth and then snapped it shut quickly. She nodded, her eyes shining.

"Then come sit here." He tugged lightly on her hand until she sat on the edge of his bed, by his pillow.

"Very well, where is she? What became of her? Tell me, Darius!"

He held her captured hand to his chest. "Show me your stockings first. I was musing this morning on how much I have missed seeing them lately."

She gasped. "If you say things like that, 'tis no wonder your stepsister thinks of me as she does."

"Well, you have shown them to me several times. Unbidden. What can be the harm in it today?" The more he teased her, the easier it became and the more he enjoyed it.

"There is nothing special about my stockings today."

"I'll be the judge of that, madam."

"They are plain linen, not silk."

"Show me."

After another pause, which he suspected was more for effect than it was a sign of her modesty, Justina wriggled her skirt to her knee and lifted her nearest leg to the bed. "There! See? Now, Nellie—"

"Higher. I want to see the garter."

Her eyes gleamed down at him as he watched her from his pillow, and that was almost as arousing as the sight of her slender, shapely leg. "What for?"

"Are they pink silk?" he demanded.

"No."

"Damn and blast. Oh well, show me in any case. I suppose I must make do."

She was apparently about to comply, when she stopped. "Wait just a minute, Darius Wainwright. You taught me a lesson before. About bargaining."

"I did?" He lifted her fingers to his mouth and kissed them.

"Yes. *To never fulfill my side of a business transaction while negotiations are still underway*. So you must tell me something before I proceed."

Darius was pleased to hear that she'd listened to him for once. Ridiculously pleased. "Then I shall tell you... that Nellie is not dead. She is alive and well."

Justina stared hard, studying his expression. "Oh."

"You sound disappointed."

She shrugged finally. "Of course not. So where is she? Why did she leave?"

He ran his lips over her knuckles again, drinking in the sweet taste of her skin. "Garters first."

Exhaling a quick, unconvincing gasp of annoyance, his nurse slid her skirt and chemise higher until her white ribbon garter was exposed just below her drawers. Darius turned onto his side. Still holding her fingers to his lips, he lifted his other hand and placed it boldly on her knee.

"Continue," she gasped out. "Your turn."

He licked between her fingers and let his hand stray upward, moving smoothly along her thigh to her garter. Good God, he did not know if he could restrain himself today. Even weakened by a bad cold, he felt inspired to misbehave with this woman. She was a terrible influence upon him, he mused happily.

"Nellie left to be married."

"Married? I don't believe—"

His fingers had found the bow tying her garter and

began pulling on the knot. It was very tight and with one hand it was virtually impossible to untie.

"She wouldn't. Who would marry Nellie?"

"Garter. Off." He was thinking about using his teeth if need be.

With a groan, she replied, "I need my hand back to untie it." So he reluctantly released her fingers and she tackled the ribbon while he watched. She drew her knee up and her skirts fell back to her hips as she chattered, "I do not recall poor Nellie having any suitors."

As soon as her garter was untied, he put his hand on the linen stocking and rolled it down. Leaning closer he kissed her knee, then her bared thigh.

"Darius." Her voice was low, husky. "What are you doing?"

"Teaching you more about negotiations. And sweating off my cold at the same time." He ran his tongue across her thigh, while his hands continued rolling the stocking all the way down over her calf to her ankle. "Nellie married the gardener who used to work here. They moved to Beaconsfield together. That's why she left. Come closer." He reached around her hips and slid her further onto the bed.

"The gardener!" she exclaimed. "Really? Georgie Cropper? I would never have believed it! I am truly amazed."

"Hmmm." He moved his hand. "Good." He liked amazing her and intended to do it often.

~∽~

His long fingers slipped between her thighs and she felt his hot palm over her linen drawers, holding her. She was on his bed, one stocking off, her skirt up around her waist. Her heart was thumping so fast and so hard, she thought the people in the rooms below must have felt it vibrating the staid wall paneling.

Justina leaned back into his large, plump pillow and let him explore with his hand. She was damp there; she felt it. The delicious heaviness of want had mounted as soon as he laid fingers on her leg and now, as he caressed her so intimately, even with her drawers in the way, the sensations grew quickly beyond her control.

"They have three children already," he whispered, moving her drawers aside to kiss her inner thigh. "It seems they didn't waste much time."

"Gracious!" she gasped out, parting her legs wider, not knowing what he did, but liking it very much.

His mouth moved upward again now, following the path of his hand and those strong, flexing fingers. His lips kissed her drawers, right on the wet spot where she ached the most, at the apex of her thighs. With only that thin barrier of material between his flesh and hers, he licked slowly, deliberately, until she lost all capability of speech. Her heel pressed into his mattress, she raised her lower body, arching impatiently and thrusting. He held her wrists down on either side of her body and proceeded to tend her with his careful tongue until she hissed and squealed, losing her breath and any last shreds of her dignity. She wanted to remove her drawers completely and was considering suggesting it, when he stopped and rolled away onto his back.

"You won't leave the room a maid, if this continues."

"Then you should not have started," she pointed out, breathing hard, waiting for the trembling to cease.

Justina glanced over at the man lying supine beside

her on the rumpled bed and saw his arousal lifting the sheet that had fallen over his hips as he rolled away from her. Of course, as he'd pointed out, she already knew he slept as nature intended. But he had been wearing a nightshirt when her father was there. At that time he had acted the part of the innocent and oh-so-proper gentleman, who would never dream of bribing a lady into removing her stockings.

He was indeed a cunning menace, and very sweet upon the eye in his current state of naked vulnerability.

These, she thought, must be the "*activities of a mutual enjoyment*" he'd once mentioned to her.

Justina decided it was her turn to play.

He had his forearm across his eyes when he first felt her hand on his manhood. He froze, held his breath.

He should stop her.

But he did not.

Her hand rubbed slowly up and down the twitching length of his erection as it lifted the bed sheet and grew further still.

"That's enough, Justina," he groaned, still hiding his eyes. "Stop now."

"Do you really want me to?" she whispered. "When you're already bound to be in trouble…"

How could he answer? Inside his head the voice of conscience roared at him to stop her and send her out of his room. But his body objected strongly to the notion of pushing her away, and his heart, which she had wounded before with her tongue, still clung pitifully to hope.

Now, copying what he had done to her, she lowered

her head and gently kissed the arching sheet, directly over the bulging crest of his manhood.

"Oh, it's warm," she said.

He took his arm away from his eyes. "Yes."

She kissed a little further down. "And very hard," she added.

His fingers clawed at the sheet beneath him, gathering the material in tight bunches.

"It looks painful."

He laughed hoarsely. "Is your arousal painful?"

She considered this, her head on one side while she ran her fingers up and down his arching length through the sheet. "Only when it's left untended."

He turned his head on the pillow to look at her. "Then it is so for me, too."

Justina slipped the sheet off him so suddenly, with no warning, he hadn't even the time to cover himself.

And then after an amazed gasp, her mouth descended once more.

He couldn't breathe. His throat was on fire. Dear God, or the devil—or whomever was responsible for this—what was she doing to him?

Apparently she was an adept pupil. Having experienced the way his mouth brought her pleasure, she now returned the favor, licking and then gently sucking. Cautious at first, she was soon much bolder, caught up, it seemed, in the naughtiness of the act.

Darius reached down and held her soft curls, letting them run through his fingers and alternately twisting them around his hands.

He croaked out her name, hips raised off the bed, his entire body coated in sweat.

She was surprised to find she liked the taste of him. Although, really, why it should startle her she couldn't say. She'd enjoyed his kisses and the taste of his tongue, so why should his body be any less pleasing?

As he lay sprawled naked across the sheet, apparently speechless, she climbed off the bed, adjusted her garments, replaced her stocking, and then said good night. She kissed his brow and tucked him in, like a good nurse.

Like the very best of nurses, she thought proudly and rather wickedly.

"I'll be back tomorrow. Get plenty of rest."

"Justina."

"Yes?" She paused.

He just looked at her, his eyes dazed. Finally he said, "Come tomorrow. Early."

"I'll be here sometime after breakfast and my daily chores."

"When?" he demanded.

"I just told you. Don't you listen?"

"It had better be before noon."

She ought to remove all the blasted clocks from his room, she mused. "I'll try."

His eyes narrowed.

"I'll try," she repeated. Lord, he was a sulker.

It was more proof of why a man only got in the way. He wanted her when and where it suited him, and she had other things to do with her day.

But the anticipation of her next visit to Darius Wainwright's bedchamber was enough to make her perspire on that chilly October day. She might have other things to do, but she'd rush through them as fast as she could to be back there with him. No need to let him know that, though, was there?

That evening, lying in bed beside her innocent, sleeping sister, she read more of Phineas Hawke's letters to his mystery lady. She was in that sort of mood, she supposed. Writing in her diary was out of the question, for what could she say about her time spent at Midwitch that day? So instead, she sat quietly and enjoyed her other secret treasure.

> *I have watched the way you lick your lips and it reminds me of the taste, intoxicating, sublime. When will I have that pleasure again?*
>
> *At night I cannot sleep. My head is filled with thoughts of you and schemes to place you at my side, where you do not desire to be, it seems.*
>
> *Like a bird you fly about, sometimes venturing close to see if I have crumbs for you. At other times you keep a nervous distance, fearing I might try to trap you.*
>
> *If I did, my love, it would never be to keep you in a cage. You would fly freely if you were mine. As long as I knew you sang for me alone.*

She had worked her way from the aged sheets to the newer letters, and these seemed far sadder than the earlier ones.

> *Once you asked me what I did for pleasure.*
> *Well, this is it, I give you treasure.*

Beside her in the bed, Cathy turned over, murmuring softly in her dreams. Justina stared at the words on the paper and after a moment she began to read all the letters again from the beginning, this time with newly opened eyes.

❧

He woke from a nap later when Miles came in.

"The ladies have retired to bed, so you have my company, old chap."

"How lucky for me."

Miles pulled up a chair to sit at his bedside. "Mary is most unhappy about your nurse. I think I have heard the phrase *I shall only say* at least twenty times this evening."

"I'm sorry you are left to listen to it."

His friend laughed. "Don't fret about me. I am adept at turning a deaf ear, as you know, and I am delighted to see you falling in love again. I had begun to think it would never happen."

Darius looked at his friend's open and merry face. There was no point trying to deny what had happened to him. Miles had seen his fascination with Justina almost immediately. Of course, these things were easy for his charming friend. He was not afraid to let himself love unguardedly.

Suddenly Miles, who had been fidgeting in the chair, said, "I wanted to ask you what you thought of Miss Catherine Penny."

He replied carefully, "She appears to be a very pleasant young lady. Very demure." He added wryly, "Quite a departure for you."

"Yes." Miles got up and began to pace around the bed. "I think so too."

This was nothing new for Miles Forester. He always enjoyed the company of a pretty face. But Darius perceived his friend to be considerably more restless than usual.

"I think I might be in love with her." Miles stood at the foot of the bed and had a very determined look on his face for once. "I might ask her…to marry me."

Darius stared. "I see."

"I suppose you will tell me I'm being impulsive and a fool, and a lot of other things, no doubt. That I have not known her long enough. That I cannot possibly be in love so quickly. That she is not the sort of girl I should marry. That her father is only a country doctor and she has very little dowry. Go on, you may as well say all those things."

There was a pause. "Do you *want* me to dissuade you from it, Forester?"

"I suppose you will try." Miles squared his shoulders. "I am prepared. Continue…do your worst, Wainwright. Tell me of all the disadvantages."

Slowly Darius shook his head. "I cannot think of any."

"But the things I just said—"

"Are meaningless. If you *are* in love, the only foolish thing to do would be to walk away from her."

"But you always say love is messy and uncouth and an excuse for people to misbehave."

"It is all that and more. Unfortunately there is no stopping it from setting root and flourishing. Strong men can be rendered powerless by it. If you are in love with Miss Catherine Penny, then marry her. Presuming she accepts you, of course. She might just be silly and addled enough to do so."

The other man's shoulders sagged. He looked forlorn. "Damn it all, Wainwright! I thought that you of all people would talk me out of it."

Finally, he allowed his lips to bend in a smile. "Try my stepsister. I'm sure she will oblige you. If that's what you want."

Miles looked sideways. "Why the devil are you being so bloody genial tonight?"

"I really couldn't say, Forester. Perhaps I'm feeling better."

"Your nurse must work miracles."

"Oh, yes." He grinned. He couldn't help himself.

Thirty-two

BREAKFAST PASSED AS IT ALWAYS DID. SOME THINGS, she reflected, never did change. Her family sat around that table and shared all their usual chatter. Dr. Penny was absorbed in a pamphlet advertising an exhibition of Egyptian artifacts and only listening with one ear to his wife's dissertation on the price of good lace and how the quality was not what it used to be. She had, it seemed, become involved in a squabble over a card of lace at the haberdasher's and insults were thrown. Now she retold the entire story, including every detail, from the time she placed her hand on the door of the shop, until the time she swept out again. Through all this, Catherine mused aloud on the tragedy of a dead hedgehog she'd seen in the lane—expressing hope that it had not left babies behind, waiting to be fed. Meanwhile, Clara slopped in and out with jugs and plates, banging each one down as if it had offended her and protesting that someone had been nibbling at the cheese again. And it wasn't a mouse.

Justina sipped her hot chocolate and watched her family, imagining what they would all say and do if she told them of her plans for that day. Perhaps they would merely ignore her, as usual, and assume it was another of her stories.

Dr. Penny finally put down his pamphlet and asked his wife what on earth she was talking about, prompting her to gasp impatiently and then begin her story all over again. Fortunately for her, she hadn't yet got all the bitterness out of her spleen and she was willing to waste more breath in the hopes of finally achieving a satisfying reaction of outrage from her husband. Catherine continued to worry about the deceased hedgehog and a possible nest of orphaned babies. Sometimes Justina wondered how her sister got through the day with so many tragedies—real and imagined—to fret over.

But for all their faults they were her family and she was lucky to have them. They must tolerate her eccentricities just as she put up with theirs, and despite their occasional quarrels, in the face of an enemy they were united, loyal. That was love.

"You're quiet today, Jussy," her father said eventually. "Thinking about your patient, perhaps?"

"Yes, Papa." She got up and pushed back her chair. "I had better go to Midwitch early and see how he is."

"Indeed, my dear! I'm sure you won't be easy until you know how he fares. We don't want to lose our wealthiest client. Not before he pays his bill, in any case."

She hurried out to get her coat, blood racing through her veins.

When she arrived at Midwitch, she entered through the kitchen, hoping to avoid his female guests, but as she passed along the dark hallway, she heard their voices in the drawing room.

"I am shocked the affair is so openly tolerated, and even the father seems complicit."

"Do not concern yourself, Augusta. He will be made to give her up."

"Well, I do not know that I would want a man who is forced to like me, my lady."

"All men have to be forced. They never know what they need, what is good for them."

"Oh, but…I do not feel I am so desperate. I'm sure I will have other chances. I would much rather marry a gentleman for whom I could truly be of service."

"Really, Augusta, you are being most ungrateful! What has come over you? Don't tell me the country air has ruined you too?"

Smiling to herself, Justina continued up the stairs.

༄

"You took your time," he exclaimed when she came in.

"I told you, I would come when I could."

"And I told you before, I do not know what else of more import you would have to do than come here to me."

She closed the door and he saw her bolt it. He thus decided quickly to forgive her for keeping him waiting. Her coat soon discarded, along with her crumpled bonnet, she came to his bed and proceeded to test his forehead, look at his tongue, examine his eyes, and check his pulse. Darius sat meekly and waited for her judgment.

"You seem much improved today, but you should not go out in this weather until you are fully recovered."

"Thank you, nurse. I shall heed your advice."

She rolled her eyes.

He laughed softly. "How long can you stay with me?"

She pondered his face for a moment. "For as long as you feel inclined to entertain me."

"Good. Because you are needed here, and as your father said, you should be where you are most needed."

Justina sat on the edge of his bed. She seemed solemn today. He hoped he had not frightened her yesterday. She licked her lips and said, "It was you who wrote those letters, was it not?"

"Letters?"

"The letters I found in your great-uncle's papers and in the dresser that day." She raised her hand to his cheek and caressed it gently with her small fingers, then that same hand lowered to his chest and she pressed it there, over his heart. "You wrote them to me."

His pulse slowed. *Breathe*, he told himself. "I began the letters before I made the monumentally humiliating mistake of trying to propose marriage."

She looked down at her hand on his chest. "It was not a mistake as far as intentions go. It merely lacked in the execution. In fact, so poorly did it lack finesse that I had no idea that's what you came to do that morning."

"How could you not have known?"

"You thrust some abused flowers at me and told me I read too much romance. Goodness, how could I not have known your purpose there?" she exclaimed drily.

"I found I could not say the words aloud." He expected her to ask why, to make scornful fun of him for the inability to express his feelings.

But she nodded. "I don't suppose anyone has ever encouraged you."

She continually surprised him, but he no longer felt that

to be a bad thing. "I wrote those letters because I wanted you to find that treasure which so intrigued you," he said.

Her eyes shone warmly. "It is the sweetest thing anyone has ever done for me. And romantic too."

"*Romantic?* What a dreadful thought."

She chuckled, leaned over, and kissed him on the lips. "I believe you really are just a romantic old fool, beneath your stern and proud exterior."

Darius returned her kiss, sweeping his hand up to hold the back of her head, to tangle his fingers again in those silky curls. He was overbrimming with need for her.

Fortunately she felt the same, it seemed.

Two minutes later she had removed her walking boots and wriggled under the covers with him, muddy petticoats and all. "I have some more questions for you, Darius Wainwright."

"Good Lord, then I'd better answer them."

Her gown, chemise, corset, and drawers were cast aside after some inelegant tugging and impatient cursing from both parties. And then with most barriers removed they could explore to their hearts' content.

How happy she was that it was him and not Captain Sherringham to whom she would give her maidenhead. "It was a lucky mistake I made when I leapt upon you," she whispered.

"I should have taken the opportunity you so brazenly presented at the time," he muttered, nuzzling the side of her neck. "Had you not landed on me in the dead of night as if shot from a trebuchet, I might have had more wits about me."

"But then we would never have had the chance to despise one another, before we fell in love."

He raised his head. "Is that a necessity, then?"

"Of course. Any good romance worth its salt must have a hero and heroine at odds in the beginning."

"I see." He bent his head again and ran his tongue over her proud nipple. And then, when he sucked gently upon it, she moaned softly, completely forgetting the path of her thoughts, or that there had even been any ill feelings between them.

"You do know how to do it, I presume?"

Again he looked up. "I...believe so."

"You know where everything goes and such?"

He blew gently on her dampened nipple. "I can give an educated guess."

She sighed. "I'm sure! My sister assures me men know everything."

Darius chuckled, shifted forward, and kissed her on the mouth. "True."

"Of course, men have more opportunity to learn." She writhed, feeling his hardened manhood against her thigh.

"Are you going to chatter continually throughout?" He nibbled gently on her earlobe.

"Am I supposed to be completely silent?"

"I would never ask the impossible," he muttered wryly, licking his way down her neck.

"Were your other lovers quiet?"

He stilled, lifted his head again and looked at her. "There was only one."

She bit her lip. "Only one?"

"Only one with whom I thought myself in love. She left me for another."

This must be the woman Cathy had told her about. Justina decided swiftly that she didn't want to know any more about it. In his eyes there was a lingering shadow cast by the pain of a bad memory, and she was sorry she ever raised the subject.

"Long ago," he muttered, wrapping one of her curls around his finger. "I wasn't much more than a boy. Only nineteen."

The age she was now. Justina steadily regarded his face. "But it cured you of seeking out love again, I suppose."

He smiled. "Oh, it was not love. I know that now. My pride was wounded more than my heart. When I overheard you once talk of wanting love, I remembered how I was once your age—when I thought I knew all about love and how it felt." Darius paused, his finger still wrapped in her curl. "But there was more to my story. More than misplaced calf-love."

"Tell me," she urged.

For once he did not sink again behind the wall of reserve. "It was my brother with whom she ran off. Lucius took her with him to India. I never saw either of them again."

Shocked, she was silent for a moment.

"In truth, you are the first woman I really wanted to kiss since then. You reawakened something inside me that I thought was long gone."

Overcome with love, she could only nod a little and murmur a gentle "I'm glad."

His large hands were incredibly tender with her. Far more so than they had been the first time they kissed, and she sensed he made an effort to restrain his strength. As for his mouth—he did remarkable things with it.

Justina began to think she would never again be capable of watching him eat without the yearning of a distinctly *un*maidenly palsy making itself felt in her belly and lower. Indeed, throughout her whole body.

"You wore your pink silk garters," he observed, his voice deepened further still with desire as he made his way down to her thighs.

"Of course. You were so disappointed yesterday, I had to make it up to you today."

He kissed each ribbon, but did not untie them.

Her garters and stockings—some of the most expensive articles of clothing she'd ever purchased with her allowance—were left in place as he parted her legs, slid forward slowly, and penetrated her at last.

There was no one in existence then but the two of them. The outside world had vanished in a mist, and she gave herself to him with a soaring, unbound happiness. She did not know how long they might have together or what would happen the next day. But of one thing she was sure: She loved him and she would never regret what they shared.

Her soft, satin warmth enclosed him tightly. For several moments he could barely breathe, such was the sheer driving force of his need. He shook with it, holding back the wild desire coursing through him, knowing he must be gentle.

But the woman beneath him arched her body and clamped her silken thighs around his flanks, urging him on, apparently fearless. As he should have known she would be. Her fingernails raked at his back and stroked his hair. He could not deny her the ravaging she wanted, and so he tore off his gentlemanly bonds and let the wild, hidden side of Darius Wainwright take over.

As the bed creaked and groaned, she gasped his name and it sounded like a prayer.

❧

Never in her wildest fantasies discussed with Lucy Bridges had she thought it would be like this. There was a moment of pain, soon passed. Then the blissful waves, one rippling atop the other. She did not want them to stop. Ever. But at the same time, as they grew higher and higher, the sensation was so exquisite she was overcome, helpless to stop herself from drowning. Merrily she submitted to her demise at his hands.

She opened her eyes as the sea subsided slowly, and she watched this beautiful man meet his own summit. He moaned deeply, gazing down at her with hunger and desire, the heat of his black eyes melting her body until she seemed to be a part of him, her softness merged with his strength.

He stilled, let his head fall back, and then he drove himself into her fiercely, wildly. She cried out and so did he.

His weight tipped forward so that he lay over her and as his mouth covered hers in a deep, wanton kiss, she felt his seed spilling into her. He had claimed her. Justina knew she would never feel this way for any other man and nothing would ever be quite the same again. She was not merely a woman now. She was his woman.

The thought of that should have quelled the passionate feelings dancing and spinning through her body like heedless children. But it did not.

Because she loved him.

Love, she realized now, was the real treasure that had been lost in that house and was now found.

They spent the afternoon in bed. No one in the house knew she was there, and when Miles came knocking at the door, Darius pretended to be sleeping.

He liked lying with her in his arms. Of course he enjoyed the lovemaking too, and discovering all the many places he could touch her and reduce her to hapless giggles. But merely holding her tight and feeling her breath against his chest produced a heavenly feeling of contentment.

Now they must talk of marriage again, but he'd made such a mess of it before that he hesitated to find the right words this time. He did not want to spoil this tranquility between them. She was his now; there was no rush, he assured himself, to speak of weddings and formalities. Later.

"Come at three o'clock tomorrow," he said.

"I have the Book Society meeting tomorrow and rehearsals for the play. I'll come as soon as I can."

"At three o'clock."

She wriggled in the circle of his bare arms and looked up at him. "As soon as I can."

"It seems contrariness is a matter of principle for you, woman. Do you ever do as you're told?"

"Do *you*?"

Darius realized glumly that he may never win an argument with her. Then she kissed his chin and her hands reached down between them to that part of him that had briefly rested. He groaned. "I suppose I must learn to manage with your quarrelsome nature."

Her lips found his nipple, while her hands cupped his sac, stroking and lightly squeezing. "What a funny thing it is," she muttered, running her hand up his shaft as it came awake again. "I remember the first time I saw it. I was not sure if it was a deformity, or whether all men had one. I could not imagine where they managed to keep such a large appendage hidden away in their breeches. I did not know then, of course, that a man's penis changes so remarkably when in repose."

He laughed huskily, not certain how to answer, or whether she even expected a reply. Although she was very bold with her words and in the way she studied his body, it was nothing less than he should have expected. She was a uniquely impertinent young woman, and he'd been aware of that from their first encounter. "You did not appear very traumatized by the sight of it at the time," he muttered gruffly.

"But I was! I thought of nothing else for months afterward. I was quite resolved no man would ever come near me again with that thing."

She licked his chest and slowly made a course downward with her tongue.

"I see you changed your mind about that," he said, bemused.

"Only when you kissed me. We awakened each other."

Darius gave himself up to her again, powerless to resist. If he died of exhaustion, at least he'd die a happy man.

Thirty-three

THE BOOK CLUB BELLES HAD REACHED THE END OF *Pride and Prejudice*. Down to their last chapters, they sat in Diana's parlor and listened in avid silence as Cathy finished the reading.

> *Elizabeth's spirits soon rising to playfulness again, she wanted Mr. Darcy to account for his having ever fallen in love with her. "How could you begin?" said she. "I can comprehend your going on charmingly, when you had once made a beginning; but what could set you off in the first place?"*
>
> *"I cannot fix on the hour, or the spot, or the look, or the words, which laid the foundation. It is too long ago. I was in the middle before I knew that I had begun."*

It is true, thought Justina, that is how it happens. Love comes unexpectedly and it spreads and flourishes like a climbing rose around a heart, before one knows it has even been planted there.

He had not said he loved her, but in those letters he

had written it in many different ways. If he never said it aloud to her, she reasoned, what did it matter? Perhaps that would have to be enough.

❧

"I shall say only this," Mary squealed in his ear, "when Mama hears what you are up to here with that common doctor's daughter she will fall into a fit of hysterics and faint away. I doubt even smelling salts will revive her. Miles Forester has told me all. I scarcely could believe it, until I saw that girl sneaking out of this house yesterday at dusk."

Darius shrugged his shoulders into a greatcoat and pulled on his riding gloves.

"Only the day before that she had the audacity to look me straight in the eye when I confronted her. She would not deny being your mistress. She cares not for what is right, proper, and decent. That girl has no shame. None!"

He paused. "I see."

"But I promised Augusta that you will indeed dispose of any lingering affairs and pay proper court to her. She has come all this way and now she is to be humiliated in this fashion by your continuing refusal to give that wretched girl up."

"She is not a girl, Mary. She is a woman. And her name is Justina."

"As for the others—those wayward young misses with whom she cavorts about the place—not one of them shows me the deference I am due. The redhead is positively feral."

"Miss Sherringham? Yes, I would be wary of getting

on her bad side, Mary. I understand she's a mean shot with a flintlock pistol." He picked up his hat and tucked his riding crop under one arm. "I have business in Manderson." With that he walked out of the house.

The lane was littered now with the first fall of dead leaves. In a twisty breeze, they spun about her skirt as she and Cathy walked to Dockley's Barn for a rehearsal. Cathy was always content with a small part in the annual play, far too shy for more than a few lines, but a keen, inventive, and resourceful seamstress when it came to the costumes, so usually the sisters would have much to chatter about. Today, however, they were both quiet, lost in their own thoughts.

As they neared the barn and heard the noise of hammering, they looked at each other and then quickened their steps. Rounding the last curve of copper-trimmed chestnut trees, there they saw Dockley's old barn with two men hard at work on a new slate roof.

Rebecca and Diana were already there.

"We know who we have to thank for this," said Rebecca. "The men will not say who sent them, but it is not hard to make out."

Justina kept silent on what she knew—what she'd heard from Lady Waltham's angry lips. Later, when the Midwitch guests arrived in the barouche, Justina instantly asked how Mr. Wainwright was improving.

"Oh, he has gone to Manderson," Miles Forester replied with a cheery smile.

"Gone out?" she cried. "But he is recovering from a bad cold. He should not be out in this weather!"

Lady Waltham haughtily replied, "I daresay he is in haste to get the business of that house sorted, so he can come to Dorset with us for Christmas. He said he was going to see his solicitor and there were papers to sign. Oh," she stopped and blinked, "I see you did not know."

She turned away at once to hide her expression, but from then on her mind was on Darius leaving.

The moment she could slip away from the rehearsal, she ran all the way to Midwitch to see for herself. He had told her to be there by three o'clock. Was that because he planned to be gone until then and did not want her to know he'd been out? Perhaps he meant to play the sick man again later and make the most of her nursing.

The gate was unlocked, as it always was now. She ran down the carriage drive, around the side of the house, and in through the kitchen door again. Mrs. Birch was scrubbing the table and looked up with a scowl. "What do you want, Trouble?"

"I'm here to see Mr. Wainwright. I'm surprised at you, letting him go out in his state! A cold like that can quickly become much worse, and I told—"

"Miss Penny, is that you?" he bellowed. "Do come in."

He was standing in the flagged passage just outside the kitchen, removing his greatcoat and hat. Evidently he had not long been home. Justina marched up to him. "You were supposed to be resting in bed. You won't get better if you don't heed the doctor's orders."

"But I *am* better." He turned to her and smiled. "Your nursing cured me, Miss Penny."

Darius certainly looked healthy. Practically bursting with vitality. She began to suspect he *had* tricked her this entire time.

"Mrs. Birch, perhaps you would bring us some tea," he called out. "We'll take it in the study, if you please."

Behind her she could hear the housekeeper muttering about "Bossy little madams who come and go as they please, unguarded."

Darius shouted again, "Quite right, Mrs. Birch. It's time someone took her in hand." He winked at Justina and then turned away. She followed him into the study, where a warm fire was lit already. He carried, she noticed, three large boxes, which he set down on his tidy desk.

"You went to Manderson to see your solicitor about the house," she blurted. "Lady Waltham told me."

"I did."

She was appalled. He was leaving then; it was true. After everything that had happened, he would go away and never come back. Consumed by sadness and heartache that now seized her in a violent grip, she felt like a daisy with all her petals being ripped off, one by one—*he loves me, he loves me not, he loves me, he loves me not...*

As little girls, she and Cathy used to chant those words amid the daisies and buttercups of the meadow, scattering white petals to the summer breeze, teasing one another about their imagined fancies. But then it was meaningless, a game. Now the agony of doubt was unbearable. If he was leaving, as he always planned, then she was no more than a passing fancy.

Oh, if this was what it meant to be a real woman and in love, they could all jolly well keep it, she thought churlishly.

What a state she must look! She had run all the way there down two muddy lanes and climbed a stile. Her bonnet was half off, clinging around her neck by damp ribbons, and her hair very probably sticking out in all directions. When he looked at her in that searching, bewildered way she wanted the floor to open up beneath her, like a stage trapdoor.

"I bought you something for being such a good nurse," he said. "I hope you don't mind." He handed her the first box. "I know my stepsister had words with you and that you did not back down as she expected. She was quite outraged this morning. Mary wants us to leave Buckinghamshire at once, before you take me for every farthing, but I fear it's too late for that."

In the box, there was a warm fleece scarf, and when he handed her the second box it contained a coat. The third box held new boots.

Justina had not known such finery could be found in Manderson. She would certainly be the talk of Hawcombe Prior in those garments. Gifts from a gentleman. The gossip would have reached every cottage before she had walked all the way home in those new boots.

"Is this…is this your way of saying good-bye to your mistress, Mr. Wainwright?"

His eyebrows jerked upward. "*Good-bye*? Have I done it all wrong again?" He cursed. "This proposal business will be the death of me."

The carpet seemed to be moving under her feet, but somehow she remained upright and found words to encourage him. "Just start at the beginning."

For a moment he studied her in silence, then he nodded. "Very well." He moved closer, his head bowed, hands behind his back. "Justina, I know I am not the most genial of fellows. I trust very few. I avoid exposing myself to new places and people, because I am uncomfortable where I am not familiar."

"No!" she scoffed, nerves making themselves heard in sarcasm. "Really?"

He sighed. "Will you let me finish this time, madam?"

"It depends. Will it take long?"

"Shall I demand that you return my gifts?"

"These things are intended to buy my silence, I suppose?"

"Yes, please. Now, may I continue?" Darius took the new boots out of her hands—which required some tugging as she clung to them ferociously—and set them on the carpet. Then he held her fingers very gently. "The point I attempt to make, Justina, is that I have faults and these led me to make mistakes, sometimes to say the wrong thing."

"Yes. We all make mistakes and some of us have more experience of that than others, so we handle it with greater aplomb."

He looked at her, waiting.

"Go on then," she managed, her voice little more than a tight squeak.

"Of all the people I ever met, you puzzle me, irritate me, frustrate me the most."

"And coming to Hawcombe Prior was the worst mistake you ever made?"

"No. The worst mistake I ever made has become the best thing I ever did. To fall in love with you." He smoothly went down on one knee. "It's the worst because it changes everything I thought I knew. It has altered my dreams, my routine, my appetite, my desires. It has made me a vulnerable, impatient, jealous fool."

She was dizzy suddenly. It was hard to believe this

man knelt before her and spoke as he did, with his heart in his hands, outstretched.

"And yet it has also made me brave, Justina. *You* have made me brave."

She took a breath at last. "Say the part about falling in love again."

He gripped her fingers now so tightly she could hardly feel them. "I've fallen in love with you, Miss Justina Penny. Deeply and irrevocably. From the first moment you leapt naked upon me, I was a lost man."

"Nonsense. You thought I was a hussy."

His face solemn, but his eyes shining with amusement, he replied, "And I was right. But I fell in love with you in spite of it."

"Oh very well, do get up now, before Mrs. Birch comes in and thinks I knocked you down with the coal scuttle." She was sure his knee must be hurting.

But he stayed in his gallant pose and said, "I've decided to keep Midwitch and live here for two thirds of the year. I might get used to the country, after all."

"Sir Mortimer will be very glad."

"Marry me, Justina."

She closed her eyes and listened to the everyday, ordinary sounds. The crackling of the fire in the hearth, the steady click of one of his precious clocks, rain falling softly on the window, almost like a lullaby today, her heart beating hard and fast.

Lastly, Mrs. Birch hobbling along the passage, the tea tray rattling in her large hands.

Yes, her life was quite mundane and unexceptional, and few astonishing things ever happened in it. Not a poisoned chalice, headless ghost, or secret heiress in sight. But he made the day magical so that even the commonplace felt special.

"Jussy?" he urged.

She laughed. It burst out of her in a gust of breath. "Yes. Of course I'll marry you! Such a fuss about naught! What on earth did you think I'd say?"

"I know not, woman. You were taking so damned long about it."

"I was savoring the drama, because I want always to remember this moment."

He swept her into his arms and promised her that he would never let her forget it.

❧

They shared tea by the fire, like any other respectable, newly engaged couple. Later he wrapped her up in her warm new coat and scarf and sent her home.

"I'll come in the morning to see your father."

She pouted at being sent away, but he was adamant.

"From now on, until the wedding night, we'll do this properly, Justina." But he did call her back for a lengthy kiss, before he said good-bye and walked her to the gate.

His mind felt like a bird soaring amid the clouds, and Darius realized then that for the first time in his life he knew true gladness.

In the space of little more than a month he'd acquired a pig he never wanted, a house he didn't think he needed, and a wife he could never have imagined. He'd never been happier.

❧

Such a strange few weeks we have had. The

weathercock on Dockley's barn was right, after all. The Book Club Belles have indeed changed direction lately, and where we shall all end up, I have no idea. This is one plot that has me completely nonplussed.

Cathy told me last night that she has accepted a proposal from Mr. Forester! Our mama is beside herself with joy. All is merry in our house for once, and even Clara was hugged this morning, much to her horror and indignation. Yesterday was indeed a very odd day for a Friday and a 13th.

I have not yet shared my news.

I wanted Cathy to have her moment of celebration without my interruption and nothing should dilute her happiness, or the gladness of our parents. But even more than that—somehow I do not feel I can entrust it to be true until he comes, as he said he would, to see my father.

Last night I woke and thought I had imagined everything. I was convinced that I'd fallen asleep reading a horrid, stupid novel and that none of this truly happened.

But then I came down this morning and there were his hat and gloves again, proof that he does exist and is not a figment of my imagination. Oh, I blame this entirely on reading romances, and I shall not pick up another. I must have suffered a knock upon the head. Or he did. He might yet regain his wits.

No, he will not come. I have resolved myself to it.

How gray the sky is today. So many leaves are blowing about in the lane that I cannot

Justina dropped her pen and leaped up for a better view through the window.

Darius Wainwright strode down the lane with a letter in his hand. As he neared their gate he encountered a puddle and rather than walk around it, as one might expect of a very proper gentleman, he jumped, clearing it easily. She saw him smile as he opened the gate.

Knocking her chair over in haste, she ran from the bedchamber, flew down the stairs, across the hall, and flung open the front door while he was still reaching for the bell cord.

"You came."

He looked startled, then his features relaxed in a broad, wretchedly handsome smile. "Of course."

Standing aside, she gestured for him to enter, glancing nervously over her shoulder, not wanting her mother to know he was there until he had spoken with her father and all was settled. Although she did not expect anyone to raise an objection at the prospect of being rid of her at last, she still could not quite allow herself to believe it was all happening. Not to her.

"Did you come for your hat and gloves?" she asked in some belated attempt to be demure.

"No." He laughed. "I came for my mistress."

Oh, gracious, she sincerely hoped her mama was nowhere nearby to hear that.

"This arrived for you," he said, handing her the letter. "I passed the haberdasher just as the post arrived, and he had this in his bag today. It must be important, as I've seen you waiting impatiently for the mail before, so I thought I'd better bring it here directly."

She opened it while he waited. One quick scan of the letter was not enough to absorb what she read. Two more perusals made it certain.

Her manuscript had been accepted for publication.

With all these things falling around her like the autumn leaves in their lane, she could not think what to do first. After turning and stepping in every direction, she suddenly came up against Wainwright's chest again and he held her arms.

"What is it, Justina? You've gone white as the ghost of Nellie Pickles."

She looked up at him gravely. "You may not wish to marry me now."

"Whyever not? What have you done now, woman?"

When she handed him the letter he read it quickly. She watched him, wringing her hands together. Surely he would not want a wife who wrote books. What gentleman would?

Finally, he folded the letter and gave it back to her. His eyes were warm as he cupped his hands around her face and kissed her. "This is wonderful news, Justina. Why on earth would I *not* want to marry you now?"

"You don't mind?"

"Good Lord, no! You have an incredible imagination, and it should be put to use."

She flung her arms around his neck, knowing then that she loved him deeply and need have no more fears about the future.

He chuckled gently. "Just don't ever write about me in your books."

"Don't worry about that," she assured him. "Someone already has."

Epilogue

HIS NIECE, SARAH, BOUNCED ON HER HAY BALE, applauding wildly as the players took their final bow. Darius had never seen her quite so animated and excitable, but she had evidently enjoyed the play. Her face was shining with merriment, and she had laughed throughout— even at parts that were not supposed to be humorous.

It was gratifying to hear her say, "Uncle Darius, I'm so glad you sent for me. I'd much rather spend Christmas here with you and Aunt Jussy than in Dorset or London."

He was cognizant now of not always having concerned himself with her entertainment. His first priorities had been fixed elsewhere, but his niece was almost sixteen and would soon be out in Society. He did not want her to be shy and withdrawn as he had been, afraid to laugh or to love. She was lucky to have an aunt like Justina, who would encourage the girl out of her shell. The two were good friends already.

Too furious with Darius for marrying a bride of his own choosing, his stepsister had dashed off to Dorset, not remaining to fulfill her role in the play. Much to everyone's astonishment, Miss Milford stayed behind and took over the lady's part. She had, it seemed, taken an unexpected liking to the village of Hawcombe Prior and found herself useful in managing the life of Mr. Kenton.

Miles had taken Miss Catherine Penny to meet his family in London and their wedding would take place in the spring. Darius and Justina had not felt it necessary to wait that long. Just as well, considering his young wife's condition. She had been content with a very brief engagement and a hasty, small wedding, for he didn't want her changing her mind before he got her to the altar.

His wife rushed over now to find out what he thought of her play.

"My darling," he smiled at her, "what was there not to love? Scenery falling on the actors' heads—particularly on Augusta Milford's. Improvised lines substituted for those forgotten, and Miss Sherringham speaking not only her own part, but that of the other actor in her scene too. It was a triumph."

"Next year, you must play a part, Mr. Critic!"

"Only if I get to kiss a pretty girl named Justina."

She pursed her lips. "It's a serious play, Wainwright, not a Parisian music hall burlesque."

So he had to make do with kissing his wife there and then, much to the shock of the good residents of Hawcombe Prior.

"Now, Sarah, tonight I shall introduce you to the Book Club Belles," she said, taking his niece's hand. "They are all anxious to meet you." Thus she whisked the timid girl away to where Rebecca, Lucy, and Diana waited.

The old Darius might not have approved of his niece reading romances with the wayward ladies of the Book Society. Mrs. Birch, he thought with a smile, certainly wouldn't.

Better get back to Midwitch and make certain Sir Morty had a few extra bales of straw tonight. Wouldn't want the dear old fellow to catch cold.

As Darius turned away, carefully avoiding eye contact with Farmer Rooke, who was still intent on securing a standing bacon order for Midwitch, he glanced toward the open door of the barn and saw it was snowing outside. The merry Yuletide scene was complete. Justina would be pleased.

But a tall figure stood framed against the dark sky—a man in military uniform under a tattered greatcoat. He wore no hat and snow gathered on his dark hair. At his booted feet rested a large leather sack. His face was sun-browned, his eyes startling, capturing a strange, intense heat. A thick trimming of snow covered his wide shoulders like an ermine cape, so he must have been out in the snow for a while.

He looked at Darius and his weatherworn, deeply tanned face eased into a broad grin. "Hello, Handles! Yuletide felicitations to you."

It was Lucius "Lucky" Wainwright, back from the dead.

In his sty, warm and comfortable, Sir Mortimer Grubbins had dug himself a snug hole in the thick straw. Here he settled down for a nap as night fell and the snow came with it. For a moment he kept his bright eyes open and fixed upon his newfound treasure, the pearl and ruby locket he'd dug up out of the orchard and brought here to his cozy nest. But eventually sleep overtook the beast, and he closed his eyes, slumbering contentedly.

Acknowledgments

Thanks so much to Aubrey, Danielle, Cat, Rachel, and all the folks at Sourcebooks for everything they do. Thanks also to my friends, family, and readers for their support.

About the Author

Jayne Fresina sprouted up in England, the youngest in a family of four daughters. Entertained by her father's colorful tales of growing up in the countryside, and surrounded by opinionated sisters—all with far more exciting lives than hers—she's always had inspiration for her beleaguered heroes and unstoppable heroines. Visit www.jaynefresina.com.

Sinfully Ever After

The Book Club Belles Society
by Jayne Fresina

To Rebecca Sherringham, all men are open books—read quickly and forgotten. Perhaps she's just too practical for love. The last thing she needs is another bore around—especially one that's supposed to be dead.

Captain Lucius "Luke" Wainwright turns up a decade after disappearing without a trace. He's on a mission to claim his birthright and he's not going away again until he gets it. But Becky and the ladies of the village Book Club Belles Society won't let this rogue get away with his sins. He'll soon find that certain young ladies are accustomed to dealing with villains.

Praise for *The Most Improper Miss Sophie Valentine*:

"A unique historical romance…pleasingly edgy." —*Booklist*

"A true charmer of a read." —*RT Book Reviews*, 4 Stars and KISS nominee (favorite historical heroes of the month)

For more Jayne Fresina, visit:

www.sourcebooks.com

Desperately Seeking Suzanna
by Elizabeth Michels

— ❧ —

Her Cinderella Moment

Sue Green just wanted one night to be the pretty one. But a few glasses of champagne and one wild disguise later, she's in some serious trouble. Who knew the devastatingly handsome face of Lord Holden Ellis would get in the way of her foot? And how exactly did all that high-kick dancing start in the first place? At least she blamed it all on her new persona—*Suzanna*—so Society's most eligible bachelor will never find out the truth.

All Holden wants is the truth. Who was that vixen who seduced him so thoroughly, then disappeared? The only one who seems to have any answers about Suzanna is Miss Sue Green. She's promised to help him find his mystery woman, but she's not being all that helpful. And the more time Holden spends with Sue—witty, pretty, and disarmingly honest—the more he realizes he may have found exactly what he's been looking for all along…

— ❧ —

The Trouble with Harry

by Katie MacAlister

New York Times Bestselling Author

———— ❧ ————

You think you've got troubles?

As a spy for the Crown, Lord Harry Rosse faced clever and dangerous adversaries—but it's his five offspring who seem likely to send him to Bedlam. At his wits' end, he's advertised for a wife and found one, but perhaps he should have been a bit more forthcoming on certain points…

Wait till you meet Harry and Plum…

Frederica Pelham, affectionately known as Plum, spent years avoiding the scandals of her past, and is desperate for quiet security and a chance to make a family. What she finds is a titled husband and five little devils who seem bent on their own destruction, not to mention hers. And while all kinds of secrets are catching up with them, Plum knows the real trouble with Harry…is that he's stolen her heart.

———— ❧ ————

Praise for Katie MacAlister

"MacAlister's combination of adventure, thrills, passion, and humor make her a superstar. Unstoppable fun!" —*RT Book Reviews*

For more Katie MacAlister, visit:

www.sourcebooks.com

To Charm a Naughty Countess
by Theresa Romain

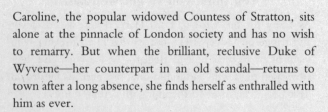

Caroline, the popular widowed Countess of Stratton, sits alone at the pinnacle of London society and has no wish to remarry. But when the brilliant, reclusive Duke of Wyverne—her counterpart in an old scandal—returns to town after a long absence, she finds herself as enthralled with him as ever.

Michael must save his family fortunes by wedding an heiress, but Caroline has vowed never again to sell herself in marriage. She offers him an affair, hoping to master her long-lasting fascination with him—but he remains steadfast, as always, in his dedication to purpose and his dukedom.

The only way she can keep him near is to help him find the wealthy bride he requires. As she guides him through society, Caroline realizes that she's lost her heart again. But if she pursues the only man she's ever loved, she'll lose the life she's built and on which she has pinned her sense of worth. And if Michael—who has everything to lose—ever hopes to win her hand, he must open his long-shuttered heart.

For more Theresa Romain, visit:

www.sourcebooks.com

Meet the Earl at Midnight

Midnight Meetings
by Gina Conkle

~❧~

The Phantom of London. Enigma Earl. The Greenwich Recluse.

Half of his face, shadowed by gold and brown whiskers, showed male perfection, but the other half, a bizarre pattern of scar lines and puckered flesh. Truly, staring at his face was akin to seeing a painting of two men, split down the middle. Lydia recoiled as much from the hot anger flashing in his eyes as from astonishment.

He's a mysterious recluse

Lord Greenwich is notoriously elusive. His tendency to hide his face in public and refusal to appear in London Society have even earned him some choice monikers, including "the Phantom of London." Is he disfigured? Mad? Hiding something? With a reputation like that, no woman wants to get near the dark earl. And no one is more surprised than Miss Lydia Montgomery when she is betrothed to him to save her family from penury. But if Lydia wants a chance at happiness, she'll have to set aside her fear and discover the man hiding behind the beastly reputation…

~❧~

For more Gina Conkle, visit:

www.sourcebooks.com